For Jennifer

ACKNOWLEDGEMENTS

. . . . .

My thanks to the following beta readers for their generous donation of time and their insightful comments: Rephah Berg, Jennifer Brinkman, Barbara Gordon, Sarah Jaernecke, Katie MacKay, Robert Oliver, and Monica Smith. Thanks also to Marg Gilks, for correcting my commas and helping me improve my writing.

RYMELLAN 1

SARAH ETTRITCH

DISOBEDIENCE MEANS DEATH

NORN PUBLISHING

TORONTO, CANADA

Library and Archives Canada Cataloguing in Publication

Ettritch, Sarah, 1963–
Rymellan 1 : disobedience means death / Sarah Ettritch.

ISBN 978-0-9813320-1-7

I. Title.

PS8609.T77R95 2010   C813'.6   C2010-900140-0

Editing by Marg Gilks
Interior design by Fiona Raven
Cover design by Boulevard Photografica/Patty G. Henderson and
Fiona Raven

v1

Published by Norn Publishing
www.NornPublishing.com

CONTENTS

.....

THE DANCE

. . . . .

MO GLANCED AT THE TIME ON her comm station and resisted the urge to drum her fingers against her desk. Class should have ended five minutes ago. If she didn't get out soon, Les would give up on her and walk home by herself.

Instructor Daly lowered his pointer. "Pull up assignment two on your monitors, please."

Everyone groaned.

"Be quiet," Daly snapped. "You've only been out of the Indoctrination Academy a week and you're already behaving like spoiled children."

Mo wished she could shoot laser beams from her eyes and vaporize him. Why had she taken History, anyway? Fighter pilots didn't need History. If she'd taken Advanced Law instead, she and Les would be in the same class. Advanced Law, though—ugh. Not right after the Indoctrination Academy. She wanted to be with Les, but she had her limits.

Daly started walking around the classroom, checking monitors. Uh-oh. Mo hit the key that would bring up the assignment and scanned the screen. A five hundred-word essay on the only Preeminent Ruler ever executed. How exciting. She flipped through the history text on her desk, trying to look as if she was already thinking about what she'd write.

Daly wandered by her. "Due Friday. No excuses."

Friday! That was only two days away. As soon as she got home, she'd have to start working on the essay, get a couple of hours in before heading to the lake. She and Les had been talking about the lake for weeks;

it would be their first night out in two years. No way was she skipping it for a stupid essay.

"Monitors off," Daly said. "Dismissed."

Mo flicked off her monitor, shoved the history text into her knapsack, and hustled into the corridor.

"Oh, Mo," someone called. "Wait a second."

She stopped and turned to see Patty and Evelyn walking toward her. Odd—usually they barely acknowledged her existence. She lowered her knapsack to the floor and waited.

"Are you going to the dance on Friday?" Patty asked.

Flaming Argamon, Patty wasn't going to ask her to the dance, was she? "I'm going with Les."

Patty and Evelyn exchanged glances. "Don't you think it's time you stopped being so clingy with Lesley?" Evelyn said.

"Give someone else a chance," Patty added.

Evelyn leaned forward, hands on hips. "It's not like you're Chosens. Stop acting like you are."

Out of the corner of her eye, Mo saw a third person hovering nearby, probably enjoying the show.

"I've tried to be polite, Mo," Patty said. "But this is getting ridiculous. I'd like to take Lesley to the dance. I could have gone ahead and just asked her, but I figured I'd be nice and let you know first. And I'm sure you, being mature, will stand aside, right?"

"You know, Darren and I have been going together for a while, but we see other people," Evelyn said. "We're not Chosens. We don't pretend we are."

"It's pathetic," Patty said under her breath, but loud enough for Mo to hear.

Mo's cheeks burned. "Les has never said anything about wanting to see other people."

Patty's face softened. "Oh, Mo. Lesley's too kind to tell you."

"She doesn't want to hurt you," Evelyn said, patting Mo's arm.

"You poor thing," Patty cooed. "I know this is difficult to hear. But everyone can see she wants a change."

"Really?" Mo squeaked.

"Um, yes," Evelyn said. "Have you had your eyes checked lately?"

   DISOBEDIENCE MEANS DEATH

Mo didn't want to believe them, but it was hard not to when she had her own doubts about Les's feelings for her.

Patty crossed her arms. "Give her some space if you don't believe us. Tell her you won't be going to the dance. You'll see how quickly she goes with someone else."

"I—I don't know."

"Are you afraid of what you'll find out?" Evelyn asked.

"No."

"Yeah, sure."

The silent observer finally spoke. "She knows what she'll find out. That's why she won't do it."

Mo recognized the voice. Julia, always wanting to be in with the popular crowd. It figured that she'd side with these two airheads. "That's not true," Mo retorted.

"Then don't be so immature," Patty said, her mouth set. "Tell her you're not going to the dance."

But she and Les liked to dance, and they'd had few opportunities to do so at the Indoctrination Academy. They were looking forward to Friday night.

Evelyn sighed and looked at Patty. "I told you not to bother talking to her."

Patty nodded. "Look, Mo, I'm asking Lesley to the dance, whether you like it or not. I'm sure she'll leap at the chance to go out with someone else for a change, instead of having little Mo following her around all the time. If you really do care about her, stop thinking about yourself. Think of her. Let her out of her cage." She motioned to Evelyn. "Come on, Ev. Let's go."

"Nice talking to you, shorty." Evelyn patted Mo's head as she walked past. Julia snickered and ambled after them.

Mo slung her knapsack over her shoulder and headed for the Learning Academy's west exit. It was a longer route to Les, but she didn't want to bump into Patty and company again. She tried to shrug off the unpleasant conversation—or rather, confrontation. Patty was obviously interested in dating Les, so nothing she said could be trusted. Of course Patty would say Les wanted a change. Of course she'd imply that dating one person exclusively was immature, even wrong. And it was no surprise that Evelyn had backed her up. If Evelyn was same-oriented, she'd probably be dating Patty, not helping her steal other people's girlfriends.

Pushing the exit door open, Mo shielded her eyes until they'd adjusted to the sun. She set off for her and Les's usual meeting spot, her mind still turning over the confrontation with Patty. Patty would have to find someone else to take to the dance. Let her ask Les—she'd only be humiliated. Mo was sure Les would say no. Les wouldn't turn her back on their plans for the evening, would she?

Mo rounded a curve in the path and smiled. There was Les, sitting against a tree with her nose in a book. She stopped walking. Who was she trying to fool? Yes, she and Les had been dating for a while, but things had changed. Maybe when they'd started seeing each other, Les had been content with her plain best friend. But now . . . Les had blossomed. She was the prettiest girl at the Learning Academy. No, probably the prettiest girl in the entire sector. She was tall, and slim, and smart, and confident. Mo swallowed. She, on the other hand, had grown—what? A whole two inches in the past three years? She looked down at her chest. In some ways, not much at all. And pretty wasn't a word anyone would use to describe her. She wasn't ugly, but she certainly wasn't anything special. And smart? Well, she wasn't stupid, but she learned more through experience than she did from reading books.

Lately, she'd wondered if Les remained with her out of habit. After all, they'd known each other forever, lived next door to each other. Maybe Patty was right. Maybe Les was being kind. She could be biding her time, hoping circumstances would eventually force a breakup. They'd leave the Learning Academy in less than a year. Unless Les found the courage to stand up to her parents, she'd be off to college, not the Military Academy. Maybe that was why Les hadn't pushed for them to see other people. In a year she'd be free, and without having to hurt anyone.

Or maybe Les was still in the relationship because she wanted to be? Mo desperately wanted to believe that, but how could she know for sure? Everyone else seemed to think Les felt trapped and wanted their relationship to end, or at least wanted the freedom to take out other girls. Mo bit her lip. Was she totally oblivious to signals Les was giving off, signals that were clear to everyone else? Was she only seeing what

  DISOBEDIENCE MEANS DEATH

she wanted to see? How could she know? *If you really do care about her, stop thinking about yourself. Tell her you're not going to the dance. You'll see how quickly she goes with someone else . . . She knows what she'll find out. That's why she won't do it.*

No, she *would* do it. Not attending a dance together wouldn't kill them, not if their relationship still existed because they both cared. She was mature—she could handle Les going on a date with someone else. It wasn't as if they'd be spending the rest of their lives together— eventually the Chosen Council would end their relationship for them anyway. And if Les enjoyed herself at the dance and wanted to date others more often, Mo would rather know. Better to know the truth, even if it hurt, right? She squared her shoulders and resumed walking.

Les looked up from her book and smiled. Mo's heart thumped. It always did when Les beamed at her, but this time apprehension and dread were helping it along.

"I was starting to wonder where you were." Les tucked a bookmark into the book, carefully slid it into her satchel, and stood. "It'll be beautiful at the lake later. Might be a bit chilly when the sun sets, though." She brushed off her pants. "We should take a blanket."

Mo took a deep breath. "Actually, Les, I can't go."

Les stopped brushing and stared at her.

"I have to start an essay. It's due Friday."

"We're not leaving for a few hours. You can start it before we go."

"I know, but—"

"I've got homework, too. If we're pressed for time, we'll leave right after the sun's gone down. Mo, we've been talking about the lake ever since we left the Indoctrination Academy. You can spare an hour, can't you?"

Mo almost gave in. Lying next to Les at the lake watching the sun go down was right up there on her *Things I Love to Do* list, and it had been two years. But tonight it wouldn't be the same, not after Patty and Evelyn. Now she'd wonder if Les was really enjoying herself, or wishing she was somewhere else—or with someone else. "Well, you see, the thing is, I think maybe we see a little too much of each other. We're not Chosens. I mean, I like being with you, but we shouldn't be too attached to each other, you know?"

"But we *are* attached to each other." Les reached for her.

Mo stepped back. Her resolve would crumble if Les touched her.

Les stiffened and lowered her arms. "What's wrong, Mo? Did I do something wrong, say something?"

"No. As I said, I like being with you, but we're not Chosens. It would probably be better if our relationship was a little more casual."

"Our notifications are at least seven years away," Les said. "And we might be Solitaries. I hope not, but we might be."

"We can't count on being Solitaries. At least one of us probably isn't."

Les cocked her head to one side, puzzled. "Why are you suddenly concerned about it? You've never said anything before. Is it because you want to be with someone else?"

"No!"

"Then what?"

"Les, will you stop being so immature? We're not Chosens. If you— if we want to take other people to the dance on Friday, we should be able to."

Les gaped at her. "The dance? You won't go to the dance with me, either?"

"I'm not sure I'm going. So if you want to take someone else, go ahead."

"Will *you* be taking someone else?"

Not likely. Girls flirted with Les, not her. To think she'd thought for a split second that Patty was going to ask her . . . Not that she would have said yes. If she wasn't going with Les, she didn't want to go with anyone. Argamon! Was she doing the right thing, telling Les to take someone else? *If you really do care about her, you'll think of her instead of yourself. Tell her you're not going to the dance. You'll see how quickly she goes with someone else.* Right. One dance wouldn't kill them, remember? "I don't know. Like I said, I'm not sure I'm going."

"You won't go with me?"

"No."

Les stared into the distance, her lips trembling. Mo looked up at her, surprised and dismayed. Les looked like she might cry. Les hardly ever cried. The last time Mo remembered her crying was when they were

 DISOBEDIENCE MEANS DEATH

eleven, when Les had fallen off her bike and ripped her knee open. "We can still see each other," she added quickly, wishing she could take back every word she'd said in the last five minutes. "But maybe we shouldn't be so clingy with each other."

"Clingy," Les echoed flatly. "I have to go." She picked up her satchel and marched away.

Mo wanted to run after her and say, "Les, I'm sorry. I want to go to the lake with you, I want to go to the dance with you, I want to be with you more than anything!" But that would only make her look stupid. Okay, she *was* stupid, for listening to Patty and Evelyn, unless Les bounced back and danced Friday night away with someone else. Once Les calmed down and realized she was free to go with anyone, she'd probably jump at the chance to go with Patty. Everyone would see Les and Patty together and figure Les was available. Same-oriented girls at the academy would buzz around her, competing for her attention. Les would be on her comm unit constantly, fielding invitations. She'd quickly forget she'd ever been in a relationship. "Mo who?" she'd say, laughing with her new friends.

A sick feeling formed in the pit of Mo's stomach. She blinked back tears. If this was what mature felt like, she'd stick with immature from now on.

LESLEY RAISED AN egg sandwich to her lips, sighed, and put it back into her lunchbox. Egg sandwiches were her favourite—usually, she'd devour them and wish there were more. But usually Mo was here, too. She'd sat down at the picnic table hoping Mo would show up—a vain hope, as it turned out. She glanced at the empty place next to her and rubbed her eyes. Mo's sudden change of heart mystified her.

She'd spent the previous evening going over what had happened yesterday, replaying the day from when she'd walked with Mo to the academy to when they'd had that horrible conversation. She must have said something, done something, to upset Mo, but she couldn't figure out what it was.

Yesterday, at this very spot, they'd talked about the lake and agreed that they were looking forward to it. Mo hadn't known about the essay at the time—that is, if she'd even been assigned an essay. But even if she'd been telling the truth about her assignment, one hour at the lake wouldn't have made much difference.

And then there was the dance. On their way to the academy, they'd laughed as they'd done a couple of practice whirls on the path. "I wonder if everyone will be as rusty as we are," Mo had said, grinning. Why would she suddenly decide she didn't want to go to the dance? Well, she'd said she probably wouldn't go. She'd also made it clear that if she did go, she'd go alone or with someone else.

Lesley sighed again. Despite analyzing and re-analyzing every word they'd said yesterday, she honestly didn't think she'd said anything terrible. But she must have hurt Mo. Why else would Mo suddenly decide that she wanted their relationship to be more casual? Lesley had considered the possibility that someone else had caught Mo's eye, but that didn't make sense. Mo wasn't fickle, one of the reasons Lesley cared for her. She wouldn't toss aside a three-year relationship because someone looked cute one afternoon. If things between them had cooled over time or they'd grown less content with each other, maybe Lesley could see Mo wanting to date others. But their relationship had seemed as strong as ever, and Mo wasn't the type to bottle up a list of grievances and pretend everything was all right. So why, then? What had happened?

A shadow fell across the picnic table. Lesley's breath quickened, but her shoulders sagged when she looked behind her.

"Mind if I join you?" Patty said.

"Go ahead," Lesley replied, hoping the disappointment she felt wasn't evident in her voice.

"No Mo today?" Patty asked as she lowered herself into Mo's spot.

"She's, uh, eating inside today. She's working on an essay. Didn't want any distractions. Including me."

"Oh."

Lesley picked at an imaginary thread on her sleeve.

"Nice day," Patty said.

"Yes."

"I hope the weather holds for tomorrow. Walking to the dance in the rain wouldn't be much fun."

"No."

"Though the train station isn't that far away. It's only a couple of minutes' walk to the academy. Less if you run," Patty added with a smile.

"True."

"But I'm not sure I'd want to risk tripping and falling into a puddle."

Lesley searched for something to say that would consist of more than one word. "You probably wouldn't trip," was all she could manage. Why did she always have to be polite? She should have told Patty to sit somewhere else.

"Are you going to the dance?" Patty asked in a higher than usual voice.

"I don't know." Mo could still change her mind.

"Do you have a date for the dance?"

Lesley hesitated. She wanted to say yes, but Mo might not change her mind—or worse, go with someone else. Saying she had a date and then not showing up for the dance would start everyone gossiping. She'd already fibbed to Patty once. Twice would be asking for trouble. "No." She briefly met Patty's eyes, then looked away.

"Do you want to go with me?" Patty asked, her voice shrill.

Lesley focused on her lunchbox. The conversation had suddenly turned awkward. Maybe she should have lied. "It's nice of you to ask, but . . . well, I wasn't completely honest before. I won't be going to the dance." She forced herself to look at Patty. "With anyone."

Patty frowned. "If you're worried about Mo, don't be. I talked to her. She doesn't mind if we go together."

"You talked to Mo?" Now her own voice sounded shrill. "When?"

"I don't know. Yesterday, I think. Does it really matter? The point—"

"It matters to me. Did you talk to her in the morning or the afternoon?"

"After History class, I think."

History? That was Mo's last class of the day. "What did you say?"

"I said, 'Mo, do you mind if I ask Lesley to the dance?' She said, 'No, go ahead.'"

Lesley looked at her for a moment, expecting more. "That's it?"

Patty let out an exasperated sigh. "Yes."

"You must have said more than that."

"This is worse than being interrogated by the flaming military! She said she doesn't mind if we go to the dance together. That's all that matters."

Lesley snapped her lunchbox shut, struggling to control her temper. The last person she'd go to the dance with was a meddling, insensitive girl like Patty. "Well, we won't be going to the dance together. I'm sure you're a very nice girl," she said through clenched teeth, "but if I go to the dance, it'll be with Mo."

Patty's face fell, but she shrugged. "It was just a thought. We can go another time."

"No, I don't think so."

"You're as bad as she is," Patty shrieked. She jabbed a finger at Lesley. "You and Mo, acting like you're Chosens. What will you do next, show up at the Reproductive Technology Centre and tell them you want to have a baby? You're both crazy. Grow up! Stop clinging to each other!"

"You said the same thing to Mo, didn't you?"

"What if I did? It's pathetic, watching the two of you pretend you're Joined."

"Though I guess if it was me and you rather than me and Mo, that would be okay."

Patty stared at her, open-mouthed. Then she found her tongue. "Don't flatter yourself! Going to the dance with you would have been a bit of fun, nothing more." She stood and cupped Lesley's chin in her right hand. "Because you're such a pretty thing, aren't you, Lesley?" she cooed. "And a bit of fun is all pretty things are good for." Smirking, she ran her finger along Lesley's cheek, then dropped her hand and walked away.

Lesley grimaced. Next time she went to the bathroom, she'd give her face a good wash. If she wanted to be snotty, she could go to the office and report a violation of Article 442, but the resulting stink would outweigh the benefits, and the accusation would be difficult to support. It would be her word against Patty's. She glanced around the immediate area. Nobody else had witnessed—

A familiar figure caught her eye: Mo, standing outside the nearest entrance to the academy. Lesley grabbed her lunchbox and scrambled to get her long legs out from under the picnic table. "Mo!" she called.

    DISOBEDIENCE MEANS DEATH

Mo wheeled and pulled open the academy door.

"Mo!" Lesley shouted, wincing when the corner of the table jabbed into her thigh in her haste to get around it. "Wait! I want to talk to you."

Mo disappeared into the academy. Lesley ran to the entrance and yanked the door open. Mo was already at the other end of the corridor.

"Mo!" She ran after her, almost barreling into a passing student. "Excuse me," she murmured, her eyes on Mo.

"Lesley Thompson!" a woman's voice cracked behind her.

She inwardly groaned and turned around.

Instructor Carter strode toward her. "I must have missed the announcement that running is now acceptable within the academy."

"I'm sorry."

"As you should be. What's your next class?"

"Literature of the Law."

"Which I believe is that way." Carter pointed in the direction opposite the one Mo had taken. "You can use the remaining ten minutes of your lunch period to review your notes from yesterday's class. Now go."

"I'll have to go to the common room first to pick up my notes."

Carter glared at her. "Lesley, you're testing my patience."

"I'm just asking permission to go to the common room before I go to the classroom."

Carter rolled her eyes. "Do I have to spell everything out? Go to the common room, pick up your notes, then go to your Literature of the Law classroom, which, I'll point out, is right next to the common room. Sit at a desk, open your notebook, and review your notes from yesterday's class. Breathing, swallowing, and blinking are permitted. Clear?"

Lesley nodded.

Carter pointed down the corridor again. "Then go. Now!"

Since lunch period wasn't over, the common room was empty when Lesley entered. She slid her lunchbox into an empty slot and bent down to open her satchel, stored on a shelf near the floor. Mo's knapsack sat next to it. Perhaps she should scribble a quick note, suggest that they meet in their usual spot at the end of the day to talk things out? No, Mo might not find the note until it was too late. More importantly, handling someone's personal items without permission would be a violation of

Article 366. That had never stopped them from slipping notes into each other's bags before, since they had each other's permission, but with the mood Mo was in, Lesley didn't want to risk it. She pulled her notes from her satchel and left.

Lesley took her usual spot in the front row of the empty classroom and opened her notebook, but all she could think about was Mo. They needed to talk, but when? They had a class together later, but they'd had a class together that morning and Mo had treated her like a stranger, nodding curtly to her as she sat down and collecting her things without a word when class finished. Lesley would likely receive the same treatment, or worse, later. Maybe the academy wasn't the best place to have the conversation, anyway. Carter may have done them a favour.

She could beep Mo later, after supper. No, that wouldn't work. Thursdays were *discuss an article* night, which meant supper wouldn't really be over until about nine, and then she'd have to do her homework. Normally she wouldn't mind; she enjoyed listening to her parents expound on the finer points of a selected article, especially one for which they'd successfully advocated an amendment. Having two advocates to consult when doing her Advanced Law homework didn't hurt, either. But tonight she'd find it hard to concentrate. She'd have to try, though. She wouldn't want to upset Mama.

There was no way around it. Talking to Mo would have to wait. She'd go over to Mo's tomorrow night; after all, neither of them would be going to the dance. If Mo refused to see her, she'd keep trying until Mo gave in.

Lesley had to understand why Mo had changed the rules of their relationship based on one conversation with Patty. There had to be something she didn't know, something that had made Mo receptive to Patty's poison, and she was determined to find out what it was before it destroyed their relationship. She rubbed her forehead. *If it hasn't already.*

MO THREW HERSELF onto her bed and tried to clear her mind, but it was no use—the same terrible images monopolized her consciousness. Les and Patty at the picnic table; Patty reaching out and caressing Les's face; Les staring up at Patty, entranced. And, had she imagined it, or had Patty's fingers lingered on Les's face as they'd said good-bye? Mo rolled onto her back and buried her face in her hands. Before her spot at the table had even been cold, Les had moved in another girl, and not just any girl—Patty. Okay, she'd figured Les would find someone else, because that was what Les wanted. But within twenty-four hours? That was all their relationship had been worth? Twenty-four flaming hours? Well, good riddance! Les could have Patty. Mo hoped they'd be very happy together.

They were probably together right now, walking arm in arm to the dance, laughing at each other's witty comments and at little Mo and her stupidity. And soon they'd be swinging around the dance floor, Patty sticking her perky breasts under Les's nose and putting her hands where she had no business putting them. So yeah, good riddance. She was better off without Les. She should celebrate; she could do all sorts of things, now that Les wasn't holding her back. Like ask others out.

So why did she feel so lousy? Why didn't she feel like doing anything? Why couldn't she get Les out of her mind? Mo squeezed her eyes shut. Because she flaming-well cared about Les, that was why. And now she'd ruined it. Sure, Les eventually would have tired of her and found another girlfriend, but they could have stayed together until that happened.

No, she was kidding herself. Patty had said Les was only staying around out of kindness, and sure enough, at the first opportunity, Les had started getting cozy with someone else. And who could blame her? Out of the blue, her girlfriend of three years had practically dumped her. Why wouldn't she move on? But would she have moved on at all if they hadn't had that conversation on Wednesday? Mo squeezed her eyes shut again. Argamon, she was so confused!

Someone tapped at the bedroom door. Mo rolled over so she was facing away from it and shouted, "Come in."

The door opened. "Are you okay?" Mama asked.

"I'm fine," Mo muttered.

"Are you sure? You didn't touch your dessert. And it's not like you to shut yourself in your room. Should I beep a physician?"

"I'm okay."

Silence, then, "Aren't you going to a dance tonight? Shouldn't you be getting ready?"

Mo's chin quivered. She'd have to explain why Les wouldn't be coming around anymore. *Les and I have decided to cool things for a bit*, she imagined herself saying, but only for an instant. She trusted Mama; she didn't like lying to her, and she didn't much like lying to herself. "Mama, I think I've done something stupid."

The door clicked shut. "You haven't committed a violation, because I would have been notified by now."

"It's nothing like that."

"You want to tell me about it?"

"Yeah."

The mattress sank as Mama sat down. A moment later her fingers brushed Mo's arm. "What did you do?"

"I told Les I didn't want to go to the dance with her. But I did want to go to the dance with her." It sounded even more stupid when she said it out loud.

"Oh." Mama paused. "Why did you tell her you didn't want to go if you really did?"

"We're not Chosens." That wasn't the only reason. It wasn't even the main reason. But it was the least embarrassing reason.

"I don't understand," Mama said.

"We shouldn't act like Chosens when we aren't."

"How have you been acting like Chosens?"

Did she have to explain everything? "We've been together for a while. And we only see each other."

"Oh, Mo." Mama rubbed Mo's arm. "So you're dating, and you only want to date each other right now. You're seventeen. If you were twenty-four I'd be concerned, but seventeen?" She squeezed Mo's shoulder and leaned over to touch her cheek to Mo's. "Don't worry about it. You're young. Enjoy yourself. Beep Lesley and tell her you'll go to the dance after all."

"I can't."

"Why not?"

"Because she's going with someone else." Mo's face crumpled as reality hit. "She . . . another girlfriend . . . I saw them," she said between sobs.

Mama straightened and rubbed Mo's back. "What do you mean? She has another girlfriend already?"

Mo nodded, sniffling into her hands.

"When did you tell her you didn't want to go to the dance?"

"Wednesday."

"And on Friday she has a new girlfriend? That doesn't sound like Lesley."

The mattress squeaked and lifted slightly. Mo heard a drawer slide open. Mama swam into view and handed her a handkerchief. She sat down where Mo could see her this time.

Mo wiped her eyes and dabbed at her cheeks. "She's pretty, Mama. It wouldn't be hard for her to find another girlfriend."

"She's pretty, but she's not insensitive, or spiteful. Are you sure she's seeing someone else?"

Mo's hand clenched around the handkerchief. "I saw them together. Yesterday. Having lunch."

"Yesterday? That's even worse." Mama shook her head. "No, I just can't see it. Have you talked to her about it?"

"No."

"Well, you should." Mama reached out and touched Mo's cheek. "If you don't want to beep her tonight, go see her tomorrow. Talk to her."

And apologize for not talking to her in the first place. It would be uncomfortable, but she owed Les that much. Though she'd want to crawl away and die if it turned out Les was seeing Patty, because she couldn't get Les out of her mind and wanted to be with her all the time. She cared about Les so much—perhaps too much. They weren't Chosens. Their relationship couldn't last. Someday, they would have to part. And that terrified her. She couldn't imagine life without Les. At all.

Her eyes welled up again. "Mama?"

"What?"

"If I ask you a question, will you promise not to get mad at me?"

"I won't get mad at you."

"Can you fall in love with someone who isn't your Chosen?"

Mama's forehead creased. "We're talking about Lesley, I presume?"

Mo nodded. Feeling exposed, she hid behind the handkerchief as she blew her nose.

Mama tapped Mo's nose. "See? Your Mama's brilliant."

Mo smiled through her tears. "Well, can you?"

"Of course you can. Why would I get mad at you for asking that? Level Four and Five students ask me that all the time."

"Really?" Mo would never dream of asking an indoctrinator such a personal question. She inwardly snorted. What was she doing right now? Though this indoctrinator was her mama first, an indoctrinator second. Maybe that was why it felt so personal.

"I'll tell you what I tell them," Mama said. "The Chosen Council doesn't find your only match, it finds your best match. So yes, you can fall in love with someone who isn't your Chosen." She wagged a warning finger. "But it should only happen before you're Joined. Never after. Anyone who falls in love with someone who isn't their Chosen after they're Joined is weak in the Way. And we know what happens to those weak in the Way."

"I know. I just wondered if it's possible at all."

"Most Rymellans date before their notifications, just like you're doing. So don't worry about it. Enjoy your time with Lesley. You're a long way from twenty-five," Mama said, brushing a stray hair off her face.

The Chosen ring on Mama's third finger caught the light. The names *Anderson* and *Middleton* were engraved on it. Mo hoped the names *Middleton* and *Thompson* would be engraved on hers. It wasn't outside the realm of possibility. "Mama, I know I keep saying Les isn't my Chosen, but she could be, couldn't she?"

Mama's face darkened. "No. You don't want to start down that path, young lady. You have to trust the Chosen Council."

"I do."

"But you feel so strongly for Lesley, she must be your Chosen. That's what you're thinking, isn't it?"

Mo didn't answer.

"That's a mistake. Remember, the Chosen Council considers all the same-oriented girls around your age when it chooses your mate. It has the entire planet to choose from, not just those who live in our sector. And the girl it chooses won't only be the best girl for you, but for everyone, because you'll be sure to have children strong in the Way."

"I know, Mama." But there was still a minuscule chance it could be Les. She'd try not to hope it was Les, but it could be Les.

"When the Chosen Council summons you, you have to accept your

Chosen." Mama playfully nudged Mo's arm. "And that's a lot easier when you don't have someone else in mind."

"I might be a Solitary." After all, two of her three older siblings were.

"That's true, and it won't be long before we find out if you are. But you're young, Mo. If it turns out you have a Chosen, you won't be summoned for at least seven years. So don't worry about your feelings for Lesley right now. A lot can happen in seven years. Beep her tomorrow, okay?"

Mo nodded. She dreaded talking to Les. Not only would she feel like a complete idiot, she wasn't sure Les cared anymore. But she'd beep her. She'd apologize, at least. And if she had to watch Les and Patty making lovey-dovey eyes at each other at the academy, that would be her punishment for listening to an airhead like Patty in the first place.

Mama leaned over and hugged Mo, then stood. "I saved your pudding for you. Why don't you come downstairs?"

"I'll come down in a few minutes." Mo rolled onto her back. "Thanks for saving it."

Mama smiled. She left, closing the door behind her.

Mo turned onto her side again and sighed. She hadn't planned to fall in love with Les. During her Level Three at the Indoctrination Academy, when the indoctrinators had first started teaching the Chosen Tradition, she'd vowed not to fall in love with anyone but her Chosen, since there didn't seem much point. But then she'd gone ahead and fallen for Les during their Level Four. Stupid, stupid, stupid! And why Les? They'd grown up together, knew everything about each other. You'd think they would have been sick of each other. Why couldn't they have stayed friends? Then she wouldn't care about Patty, and she wouldn't care whether Les turned out to be her Chosen.

If she had a Chosen.

In ten months, she'd find out if the Chosen Council had found a match. Les would find out in five. Mo swallowed. If it turned out Les was a Solitary but she wasn't, or vice versa, they'd know for sure they were doomed. She snorted. They were already doomed—she'd seen to that. She was lying here worrying that Les wouldn't be her Chosen, and Les was probably hoping with everything she had that she wasn't!

Someone knocked on the door and opened it. Mama again. "You have a visitor."

"Who?"

"Lesley."

"She's here?" Mo sprang off the bed, her heart pounding. "Do I look okay?"

Mama studied her. "Go give your face a little wash," she said quietly, placing her hand on Mo's back and steering her into the hallway. "Then come down."

In the bathroom, Mo splashed water on her face and looked in the mirror. Who was she kidding? No amount of water would make her presentable. She looked like she'd just awakened with a bad head cold. Returning to her bedroom, she grabbed her comb from the dresser and raked it through her hair. Why was Les here? Had she stopped by on her way to the dance to gloat? Was Patty with her? Mo's hand stopped in mid-stroke. No, Mama would have mentioned that, prepared her. She tossed the comb back onto the dresser, braced herself, and headed downstairs. Maybe Les had decided not to go to the dance. Maybe she was here to talk.

Her heart fell when she reached the bottom of the stairs and caught a glimpse of Les sitting in the living room. Les was dressed for the dance, in the navy blue outfit that set off her blond hair and matched the blue eyes Mo loved staring into. And here she was—Mo looked down at herself—in an old shirt, the pants she'd worn when she painted her bike last week, threadbare socks, and her breath whistling through one stuffed-up nostril. Patty, watch out!

She hesitated outside the living room, wanting a few more seconds of believing their relationship still existed before Les opened her mouth and crushed the illusion. Then she forced herself forward.

Les looked up. Mo wanted to go to her, hug her, but an unfamiliar awkwardness hung between them. She sat at the other end of the sofa from Les and crossed her legs, trying to look relaxed. "I see you're on your way to the dance," she said, not as evenly as she would have liked. Petty questions ran through her mind: *Did you forget who you're going with? Did you come here out of habit?* But she was smart for a change. "Why are you here?" she asked. "I mean, I'm glad you dropped in. I

   DISOBEDIENCE MEANS DEATH

want to talk to you. About what happened. But I was going to do it tomorrow."

In response, Les made a show of rolling her eyes to the left. She tipped her head that way, too. Mo looked across the room. Nathan sat perched on the edge of one of the chairs, watching them. She'd been so focused on Les, she hadn't noticed him. "Nathan, go play or something."

"I don't feel like it." He swung his legs. They hit the base of the chair with a thump. He did it again. *Thump.*

"Don't you have homework?" Mo asked.

"Nope."

"Why don't you go find Andrew?"

"I don't feel like it." *Thump.*

If he didn't stop swinging his flaming legs, Mo would tear them out of their sockets. "Stop with the legs, all right? Go find Andrew. We want to be alone."

"I don't feel like it." *Thump.*

"I know why he doesn't want to leave," a voice piped up from the doorway. Andrew entered and plunked himself down on one of the other chairs.

Oh, great. "Why doesn't—"

"He wants to see you kiss." Andrew squeezed his eyes shut, puckered his lips, and smacked them loudly.

Nathan giggled, then mimicked Andrew.

"Mama!" Mo shouted. "Get these two out of here. Mama!"

Mama rushed into the living room. "What's all the—" She put her hands on her hips. "All right, that's enough. Go upstairs and play."

The smacking noises stopped. "We don't want to," Nathan said.

"Well, you can't stay in here, so if you don't want to go upstairs, you can help me cut the flowers I brought in earlier. Unless you've changed your mind about going upstairs."

"Upstairs," Andrew said, looking at Nathan. They tore from the room. Mama winked at Mo and followed them out.

Les chuckled. "I bet you wish they were back at the Indoctrination Academy."

Mo met Les's eyes and managed a weak smile. For a moment, she felt the comfortable connection that usually existed between them. But only for a moment. Les was all dressed up to go out without her. Les would dance and laugh and who knew what else, while she sat at home alone. Not that she could blame Les, who was only doing exactly what she'd told her to do. And looked so cute while doing it. "You look nice."

"Thanks," Les said, her cheeks colouring slightly.

"Is it Patty . . . that you're taking to the dance?"

"No."

Mo was momentarily speechless. Did Les have a new girl every five minutes? No, it must be Patty. She must have heard Les wrong. "But you were having lunch together."

"No, we weren't."

"I saw you! And you looked pretty cozy."

Les's face tightened. "First of all, we didn't have lunch together. I ate alone. She showed up later. And as far as what you think you saw, did you see me doing anything?"

Mo replayed her memory. Les sitting at the picnic table. Patty reaching out and touching Les's cheek, then leaving. "Well, no," she admitted.

"I think she noticed you watching."

"Oh." Come to think of it, Patty had glanced in her direction. Mo hadn't thought anything of it at the time; she'd been so shocked at seeing Patty in her place that she hadn't been thinking at all. She'd stood paralyzed, her mind blank, until Les called her name.

"She did ask me to the dance," Les said. "But I said no. And I know she talked to you about it. She didn't tell me exactly what she said, but I gather it was something about us acting like Chosens when we aren't."

Blood rushed to Mo's face. She wanted to blurt "I hope we are," but she bit her tongue. "I'm sorry. They ambushed me after class. I didn't know what to say. I didn't agree with her, but she said she was going to ask you to the dance whether I agreed or not."

"But then you not only told me that you didn't want to go to the dance, but that you couldn't go to the lake. You made it sound as if you didn't even want to date."

"I was trying to do the right thing." Mo felt her chin trembling. "They made it sound like we were doing something wrong. And I thought . . ."

"Thought what?" Les said, an edge to her voice.

    DISOBEDIENCE MEANS DEATH

Mo couldn't—she couldn't tell Les that inside, deep inside, she was afraid she'd eventually be cast aside for someone prettier, someone taller, someone curvier, someone who looked stunning on Les's arm. How Les turned heads and she didn't. How she pretended not to notice the coy looks girls shot Les in the corridors. How invisible she felt when girls flirted with Les. About the gnawing doubt that grew every time Les smiled at another girl, stopped to talk to someone pretty, paid another girl a compliment.

"Thought what, Mo?" Les repeated.

Les looked concerned, but she was also dressed for the dance, the dance they weren't attending together. "It doesn't matter what I thought," Mo said.

"You can't mean that. It doesn't matter? Our relationship doesn't matter?"

"Les, I made a mistake, okay? I wish I could take back everything I said about the dance, about us, about everything. But it's too late."

Les's brow furrowed. "Why is it too late?"

"Well, maybe it isn't. I don't know. I guess it'll depend on whether you'll still want to talk tomorrow."

"Why can't we talk now?"

Mo swallowed. "Because you have a date waiting for you." Her chin started to tremble again. She looked at her lap.

"Mo, I'm hoping to go to the dance with you," Les said softly. "I don't want to go to the dance with anyone else. I never did."

"Really?" Mo lifted her head to study Les's face.

"Do you think I'd stop here first if I was going with someone else? You think I'm that mean?"

Mo sighed. "No. That's why I asked why you were here. Because I couldn't understand why you'd stop in."

"On the way to somewhere else?" Les frowned. "I guess I should have made my intent clear right away, but it never crossed my mind that you'd think I was going with someone else."

"I'm sorry." Mo tried to rally—Les wanted to go to the dance with her! But it was hard to feel elated when she felt like an idiot.

"It's okay. I should have said." Les stretched her arm across the back of the sofa and leaned forward slightly. "You want to meet me halfway?"

More than anything. Mo grasped Les's hand. They smiled, slid toward each other, and embraced. Mo buried her face in Les's shoulder and held her as tightly as she could. If it was up to her, she'd never let go, not until the Chosen Council forced her to.

"I want things to be right between us," Les murmured.

"Me too."

Les drew back. "But there's something you're not telling me. All of a sudden, you seem to expect the worst from me."

Not all of a sudden. Mo tried to pull Les close again, hoping she'd drop the subject, but Les wasn't having it.

"Is it something I've said or done? I've tried to figure it out, but I can't think of anything. I don't understand why you were so willing to listen to Patty. Or why you thought I'd move on to someone else so quickly." Les looked away. "It hurts . . . that you think I could do that."

"I don't. I mean, not really. I mean . . ." Mo trailed off. She'd have to tell Les. It wouldn't be fair to let Les think she'd done something wrong, nor did she want to lie to her. Maybe things would be easier if Les knew. Or maybe she'd completely embarrass herself and Les would have a change of heart about reconciling. But at least she'd have told the truth and admitted what nagged at her deep down, instead of hiding behind Patty and everyone else like her. After the mess she'd made of things, she owed Les that much. "It's not you. You haven't done anything wrong."

Les met Mo's eyes. "No?"

"No." Mo reached for Les, feeling awkward and shy. It would be easier if Les wasn't looking at her. She relaxed ever so slightly when Les didn't protest and she felt the warmth of Les's cheek against hers, but only for a second. She stared over Les's shoulder at a point on the paneling in the hallway. "Patty did say we act like Chosens, when we aren't."

"I figured. We're not doing anything wrong, you know. Our Chosen Papers are a long way off."

"I know. But that's not all she said." Mo hesitated. Once it was out, she couldn't take it back. "She said that you want to date others, but you're too kind to tell me. That I should give you some freedom, let you out of your cage."

Les shook with laughter. "Yes, Patty's an expert on what I want."

     DISOBEDIENCE MEANS DEATH

"It's not funny!"

Les started to pull back, but Mo held onto her. Fortunately, Les seemed to understand; she rested her chin on Mo's shoulder and took one of Mo's hands. "You believed her," she said, her voice tinged with surprise. "I don't understand. I'm not even friends with Patty. She hardly knows me. Why would you believe anything she says about me?"

Fleeing the room crossed Mo's mind, but it was too late for second thoughts. "Because sometimes I think the same things myself. About you wanting to date others."

Silence. Uncomfortable silence.

Mo quickly filled it. "I should have talked to you. But Patty . . . I don't know—I guess all my doubts came out and I panicked."

No response.

"You're mad at me."

"No," Les said, so softly that Mo wouldn't have heard her if Les had been farther away.

"You're awfully quiet."

"I'm thinking. Look, none of what Patty said is true. None of it." Les paused. "I couldn't care less about Patty and her lies. But these doubts— you said I haven't said or done anything wrong, but I must have done something to make you feel the way you do."

"You haven't done anything."

"Then I don't understand!" Les's hold on Mo's hand tightened.

"We're different."

Les chuckled. "I know that."

"Physically."

Les sighed. "Mo, you're not telling me anything I don't already know. What does this have to do with anything?"

"You're tall and slim. And you have a nice figure. Everyone thinks you're pretty." Mo felt Les's smile against her cheek.

"Stop trying to distract me," Les said. "Now, come on. Tell me what's bothering you."

Mo pulled back in frustration. Why was Les being so dense? She gripped Les's arms and looked right into her eyes. "Les, you're pretty and I'm not. You're tall, I'm not. You have a chest. The girls like you. They flirt with you all the time. You can date anyone you want. How long before you decide you want someone who looks better on your arm than I do? I mean, when we first got together, sure, you were already taller and more graceful than me, but not to the extent that you are now. A lot has changed in three years. You're beautiful. And I . . ." Mo let go of Les's arms and dropped her hands to her lap. "I'm nothing special."

"That's what this is about?" Les hugged Mo, planted a kiss on her cheek, and hugged her again.

Mo didn't protest. She threw her arms around Les's neck and buried her face in Les's shoulder, feeling vulnerable, and silly, and apprehensive.

"I want to be with *you*," Les said, giving Mo a squeeze.

"Yeah," Mo replied, "this is when you'll tell me I have a great personality."

"Well, you do! And as far as I'm concerned, you're the best-looking girl at the academy."

Mo snorted.

"You're the only girl I've ever wanted to kiss. And touch."

"With everyone after you, how long will that last? Someone flirts with you almost every day."

"They're not interested in me the way you are."

"Yes, they are. They'd all love to be with you. They'd take my place in a second."

"I don't think so. I doubt they want what we have."

"They flirt with you right under my nose!"

Les exhaled sharply. "I wish they didn't. And they're wasting their time." She drew back and took Mo's face in her hands. "I don't know what to say. I had no idea, no idea at all. Probably because, to me, you are, and always have been, the cutest girl I've ever seen. I like the way you fit under my arm. I like kissing the top of your head. And I like your body just the way it is. If you had big breasts, you'd look funny. You'd probably fall on your face a lot."

Mo couldn't help but smile.

"I like that smile, too," Les said, pinching Mo's cheek.

They sat grinning at each other, but then Les grew serious. "You know, assuming you know what I want because you think I'm pretty is kind of ironic." She pointed at herself. "I'm the one who was rejected because of looks, not you."

     DISOBEDIENCE MEANS DEATH

"I suppose that's true," Mo said, despite thinking that the parallel was a little shaky. She'd rejected Les because she was trying to protect herself. Les wouldn't be doing that if one of the flirty airheads managed to catch and hold her attention.

"You could try trusting me," Les said.

"I do."

"Then talk to me next time, okay? I hope there isn't a next time, but if there is, talk to me. This whole thing could have been avoided if you'd just talked to me."

"I know."

"Don't assume you know what I want."

"I won't." But a sense of futility mocked her. She couldn't talk to Les every time she felt insecure, or they'd never talk about anything else.

Les took one of Mo's hands, kissed it, and curled her fingers around Mo's. "So, you coming to the dance with me?"

"I don't know if I should."

Les's face fell.

"No, no! It's not that I don't want to go with you," Mo quickly said. "It's just that I'm not really in the mood. And no matter what you say, I look terrible right now. Don't try to deny it."

"Well, I want to spend some time with you. Do you want to do something else?"

"Sure."

"You owe me a visit to the lake," Les said, wiggling her eyebrows.

The lake sounded wonderful. "I'll change."

"What you're wearing is fine. I definitely have to change, though. So come on." Les stood and pulled Mo up from the sofa.

"Mama!" Mo called when they stepped into the hall.

Mama walked down the hallway from the kitchen, three flowers in her left hand and pruning shears in her right. "What?"

"We're going out. To sit by the lake."

"You're not going in those clothes, are you, Lesley?" Mama asked.

"I'm changing first."

"Good. Say hello to your parents."

"I will."

"Mo, take your cloak. It might get chilly. And have a good time."

"We will, Mama," Mo said. "And thank you," she added softly, reaching for her cloak.

Mama's mouth turned up at the corners. She retraced her steps down the hallway.

As soon as Mo and Les stepped outside, Les put her arm around Mo's shoulders and kissed the top of her head. "See? You fit perfectly."

Mo slipped her arm around Les's waist and squeezed her. If every moment was like this, she'd never doubt, never wonder, never question Les's feelings. Maybe Mama was right. Maybe she shouldn't worry so much about what might happen. Even if she and Les stayed loyal to each other, the Chosen Council would eventually break them up. So what was the point of worrying about how Les saw other girls, or about what other girls might do? The Chosen Council would ultimately decide who would be the most important girl in Les's life, not Les, not her, and not other girls.

Yes, Mama was right. Mo leaned into Les and squeezed her again. She had no future with Les, so the best thing she could do was enjoy the time they did have together—at least until the next time a girl flirted with Les.

THE MILITARY ACADEMY

. . . . .

LESLEY LOOKED AT HER LAP AND stifled a yawn. The warmth of the dining room, fed by the afternoon sun streaming in through the windows, was lulling her to sleep. The topic of conversation didn't help, either. She shifted in her chair, trying to rouse herself. The worst thing she could do was doze off.

"Are you listening?" Mama asked.

Lesley lifted her head, hoping her eyes conveyed interest she didn't feel. "Yes."

Papa slid a sheet of paper across the table toward her. "It's a lot of information to absorb."

Feeling another yawn coming on, Lesley picked up the paper and shielded her face with it as she read *Entrance Examination Dates for the Advocacy Training Program.* She scanned the list of colleges and dates in despair.

Mama yanked the paper from Lesley's hand and laid it on the table. "The ones in Sectors C4 and D2 are the closest," she said, pointing them out on the sheet with her pencil.

"But all the colleges are good," Papa said. "All of them teach the same curriculum."

"You went to the one in H2, right?" Lesley asked.

Papa nodded. "And your mama attended the one in A7."

"I did. An excellent college," Mama said. "But Papa's right, they're all decent." She paused. "It would be nice if you could still live at home during your studies, but you have to think ahead." She tapped another name on the sheet. "Advocate Cooper teaches there."

"A brilliant advocate," Papa murmured.

"You'll want him to supervise your final year," Mama said.

Lesley hoped there wouldn't be a final year, but played along. "Everyone will want him."

"True, but assuming you keep your marks up, which you will, your name will give you an extra edge. The Thompsons have had at least one advocate in every generation. The archives are filled with cases handled by our family, and we're not finished yet," Mama said, indicating herself and Papa.

Papa smiled. "And now you and your brother will carry on the tradition."

Yes, well, Jason would jump off a cliff if Mama told him to, and shout about what a wonderful idea it was on the way down. Lesley crossed her legs. "Karen won't be an advocate."

"No, but we knew early on that your sister's interests lay elsewhere. She'll make a fine physician." Mama patted Lesley's hand. "And you'll make a fine advocate. I wasn't surprised when you sent us the list of courses you'd chosen for your final year at the Learning Academy."

"Neither was I," Papa said. "You love the Law. You love the Way. Qualities every advocate needs."

Lesley wanted to scream. "Every Rymellan serves the Way, no matter what they're doing."

Mama nodded. "Of course they do. But advocates serve the Way more directly than most others." She looked down at the pile of papers in front of her, material she'd had delivered to her office and brought home with her that day. "Material you should have already requested," she'd said to Lesley with a frown at the beginning of the conversation.

"Advocates aren't the only ones who directly serve the Way." Lesley paused to swallow before forcing out her next words. "Maybe I should look into other vocations, too."

Mama's head came up. "Like what?"

"Indoctrinators serve the Way," Lesley said, starting with a vocation she had no interest in pursuing.

"That's true."

"Overseers."

"Overseers are all former advocates or admirals," Papa said.

Exactly. "That's another one. The military."

"The military?" Mama snorted. "The military isn't for thinkers. It's for those who need to be told what to do. Here." She picked up the papers and held them out to Lesley. "The areas the advocacy exam will cover, along with a suggested study list. You should go to the Trading Centre as soon as you can and pick up the books. The exam is only two months away. You have a lot to cover."

"Admirals who become overseers must be thinkers," Lesley said as she accepted the papers.

"Admirals who became overseers should have been advocates," Papa said. Mama turned to him and laughed. He laughed along with her.

Lesley's shoulders sagged. What was the use? "I'll go to the Trading Centre right now. If we're done."

"Isn't this exciting?" Mama exclaimed. "You're about to take your first step toward becoming an advocate."

Lesley could hardly contain herself. She forced a smile. "I'll probably stop in at Mo's on the way home."

"Supper's at six. And you'll have to buckle down now, Lesley, not spend all your free time with Mo. Keeping up with your Learning Academy classes and preparing for the advocacy exam won't be easy."

Mama didn't know the half of it. "Mo has to study, too."

"I doubt the Military Academy entrance examination will be as demanding as the one you'll be taking."

Lesley felt her face tighten. "May I go now?"

Mama motioned toward the dining room entrance. "Yes, go."

"We'll see you later," Papa said.

"Wait!" Mama pointed at the sheet listing the examination dates. "Don't forget that one."

Lesley snatched it from the table, went up to her room, and slipped the pile of sheets into her satchel. Outside, she strapped the satchel onto her bike's rear rack. Her comm unit beeped. As soon as she hit the connect button, Mo said, "Where are you?"

"I'm just leaving, but I have to go to the Trading Centre first."

"Well, hurry up. If we don't get through at least two sections, we'll fall behind."

"I'll ride as fast as I can." She pressed the disconnect button and mounted her bike.

LESLEY CLIMBED THE stairs to the second floor of the Middleton home and peered through the open door at Mo, who lay on her stomach on her bedroom floor, open books and several diagrams scattered in front of her.

Mo looked up. "You finally made it. What was so important that you had to go to the Trading Centre right away?"

Lesley opened her satchel and handed Mo the study sheets.

"I thought you were going to tell them," Mo said after glancing at the top sheet. She handed them back to Lesley.

"I tried. But they have their hearts set on me becoming an advocate." She put her satchel down and sat on the floor next to Mo, resting her back against the side of the bed. "I'm thinking maybe I'll have to do it."

"What?" Mo pushed herself up from the floor and sat cross-legged, facing Lesley. She rested her hand on Lesley's arm. "You can't do that. It's not what you want."

Lesley covered Mo's hand with her own. "I'll get used to it."

"Get used to it? You think you'll get used to it? Because this is what your life will be like." Mo picked up one of the books lying on the floor and adopted a stern expression as she held it away from her. "Yes, Overseer, I am here today to request an amendment to Article 721. The article states that a maximum of three Rymellans may view announcements on the same public monitor at the same time. I am here to request that the word 'three' be amended to 'two.' I have prepared this four hundred-page case that supports my proposed amendment, which I will now read to you, explaining every word in detail."

Lesley chuckled. "It's not that bad."

"Just about." Mo set the book back on the floor. "And why should you get used to something you don't want to do? Why not do something you like?"

"If I don't become an advocate, they'll be disappointed. Terribly disappointed."

"So? Les, this is the rest of your life we're talking about. You have to think of yourself. They'll get over it."

"But they're right. I do love the Law. And the Way."

"Who doesn't? But we're not all advocates. Look me in the eye and tell me you want to be an advocate."

Lesley looked directly at her. "I can't."

"That settles it, then."

"It's not that simple."

"Yes, it is," Mo replied. "Look, all you've talked about the past few months is the Military Academy. You were so excited after those cadets visited the Indoctrination Academy. I mean, you got *me* interested. I didn't know what I wanted to do. The military crossed my mind, but I wasn't interested in Interior. I forgot about Defence. Then we went on that tour of Installation 22, tried out the simulator, got to sit in an actual fighter. I was hooked! And I never would have signed up for that tour if it hadn't been for you."

Lesley smiled at the excitement in Mo's eyes. "That *was* fun, wasn't it?"

"Yes! And you were as excited about it as I was. What did we say afterward? Oh, I know—we'll be able to serve the Way, hands-on, without being stuck in an office all day."

"But then I left the Indoctrination Academy and found out my parents will hate me unless I become an advocate. So now what do I do?"

"You write the entrance exam for the Military Academy. They won't hate you. They might be mad at you, but they won't hate you."

Lesley grimaced. "I don't know."

"You don't even have to tell them unless you pass the exam. The exam is only the first phase, remember?" Mo squeezed Lesley's hand. "So write the exam. Keep your options open." She looked at the satchel. "Where are those sheets again?"

Lesley flipped open her satchel and pulled them out.

"Those entrance exams are held year-round, right?"

She nodded.

"When did you say you'd take it?"

"I agreed to take this one." Lesley pointed to the listing for the college in Sector C4. "Two months away."

Mo was silent for a moment, then said, "Okay, so you can take both exams. You'll have five weeks to study for the advocacy exam after you've written the one for the Military Academy."

"Mo, that's a lot of work."

"I know. But you can probably pull it off, if you have to. So this is what you do: we'll get our exam results around two weeks after taking the exam. If you pass, you tell your parents and postpone the advocacy exam for a few months. If things work out and you're accepted into the Military Academy, you can postpone it permanently."

Lesley doubted it would that easy. Her parents wouldn't forget about advocacy just because she'd passed the entrance exam. They'd be disappointed, perhaps angry. "I don't know."

"If you pass, you'll have to tell them. The next phase is the three-day evaluation. How will you explain being away for three days?"

She wouldn't be able to, and wouldn't have to if she declined the evaluation and gave up on pursuing the military. As Mo had said, the exam was only the first phase.

"And don't forget, the Military Academy exam isn't held year-round. So if you don't write it and then decide you want to, you'll have to wait an entire year. You'll end up a year behind me, and we wouldn't want that, would we?" Mo looped her hands around Lesley's neck. They touched foreheads. "So what do you say? You going to throw away all the hard work you've already done, or take the exam?"

Lesley took Mo's face in her hands and kissed her. What would she do without her? "I'll take the exam. But I don't know what I'll do if I pass."

"That's fine. One step at a time." Mo grinned and pulled away. "So let's get back to studying, before we get caught up in doing other things."

Lesley let go of Mo's hand, got down on her hands and knees, and reached under the bed to drag out a knapsack.

"Did you start section seven?" Mo asked.

"Barely. I'm on page three," Lesley said, opening the knapsack and lifting out all her study material for the Military Academy entrance exam.

     DISOBEDIENCE MEANS DEATH

MO PACED OUTSIDE the examination room, her agitation growing every second. Where was Les? The exam would start in ten minutes, and there was no sign of her. Les better not have changed her mind. Not showing up would sink her military career before it even started. If she missed the exam she'd registered for, she'd get a zero, and she probably wouldn't be permitted to register for it again.

Without thinking, Mo reached for her comm unit, but its holder was empty. As required, she'd surrendered it, along with her knapsack and cloak, when she'd signed in at the reception desk. "We'll provide everything you need," the clerk had said. Yeah? Well, right now, she needed her flaming girlfriend to show up. Last night, Les had said she'd be here. What could have happened since then?

Mo stopped pacing. Maybe Les had been in an accident. She could be lying in the infirmary! Or maybe she'd lost her nerve. Mo peered into the examination room. The clock at the front read 9:52. Eight minutes. Wait— She listened to rapid footsteps, the sound drifting from a nearby corridor. Someone was coming, someone in a hurry. And whoever it was would turn the corner and come into view just . . . about . . . now.

"Where have you been?" Mo snapped when Les reached her.

Les took a few seconds to catch her breath. "Mama wanted to talk about plans for the Festival of the Way. I couldn't say, 'Sorry, I have to go, I have to take the Military Academy entrance exam.'" She glanced over her shoulder.

"Maybe you should have."

Les glanced over her shoulder again.

"Will you stop doing that? They won't pop up out of nowhere."

"I'm not used to lying to them, okay?" Les replied. "If it were you, you'd be jumpy, too."

"Karen's covering for you," Mo reminded her.

"I know, but what if they decide to visit her?"

"Les, if they wanted to visit her, they would have turned it into a family outing when you told them you were planning to see her. But Karen invited you because she wants to show her little sister around the college. She wants to introduce you to everyone, spend some time with you because she's only seen you once since the Indoctrination Academy."

"She wants no such thing! It's not even happening!"

"They think it's happening. That's all that counts."

A pained expression crossed Les's face. She rubbed her forehead. Mo reached up and touched her cheek. "It was either that, or tell them about the exam. You didn't want to tell them, so—"

"I know. I just don't feel good about lying to them, that's all."

"At least one member of your family understands what you're doing. Karen thinks it's great that you're taking the exam."

"She won't think it's so great when Mama figures out she was in on the whole thing," Les said.

"Your mama won't have to figure it out. If you pass, you'll have to tell them. About everything."

"I'll worry about that if I pass."

"You are going to try to pass, right?" Mo said, her temples pulsing. "You're not going to throw the exam?"

Les shook her head. "I'd never throw an exam. But I have to take this one step at a time."

"Well, if we don't get a move on, you won't have to tell them at all. Come on." Mo grabbed Les's sleeve and tugged her toward the exam room.

Few empty seats remained, all near the back of the room. Les would hate that. "Over here," Mo said, pointing to two desks in the same column. "You take the one in front." At least then, Les wouldn't be right at the back.

Mo settled herself into her chair and adjusted the positions of the monitor and keyboard until she felt comfortable. Ignoring the pencil and several pieces of scratch paper on the desk for now, she read the orange letters on the screen: *MILITARY ACADEMY ENTRANCE EXAMI-NATION*. Where she was, and why, suddenly became real. She better not blow this. Unlike some people—she glanced at Les's back—she wasn't a natural study. But she wanted this badly. If the military accepted her, she could serve the Way, really serve the Way, without sitting in an office shuffling paper. If she failed, she didn't know what she'd do.

She had to pass. She would pass. Argamon knew she'd studied enough. And here she was, sitting in a military outpost in C2, taking what she hoped would be the first step to her future career. Okay, it wasn't military headquarters, but it was one of the larger outposts, not one of those single-room jobs.

Someone plunked himself down at the desk to her left. Good, they hadn't been the last ones to arrive. She stared at Les. Was Les as excited to be here as she was, or too busy worrying about her parents?

The door shut behind her. The proctor, who'd been sitting at the front of the room when Mo had first stuck her head in to see if Les was there, stood. A woman, presumably the person who'd closed the door, bustled to the front and stood next to him.

"Welcome to the Military Academy Entrance Examination," the proctor said. "This is the examination location for residents of Sectors C1 through C3, inclusive. Is anyone here not a resident of Sectors C1 through C3?"

Nobody raised a hand.

"Good. The examination will run from ten to noon. You will then have a one-hour break for lunch. The second part of the examination will start at one o'clock sharp and run until three. During the examination, there will be no talking. No leaving the room without permission. If you need to leave the room, raise your hand." He raised his hand in demonstration. "Wait for me or Sub-lieutenant Kent to come to you. When you've finished the examination, turn off your monitor and sit quietly. Any questions?"

Silence.

"At exactly ten, your keyboards will unlock and your monitors will display the first page of the exam. Good luck." He focused on the clock.

Mo glanced around the room, counting heads to keep her mind occupied. Around thirty people, but this wasn't the only exam room. She recognized only one other person from C3. He'd graduated from the Learning Academy the previous year. What had happened in the meantime? Les was sitting as stiff as a board, facing straight ahead. Was she—

"Begin!" the proctor's voice rang out.

LESLEY FINISHED READING a page of the study material for the advocacy exam and imagined herself ripping it to shreds. That was the second time she'd read it, but she still hadn't absorbed anything. Studying for the Military Academy entrance exam, keeping up with her classes at the Learning Academy, and cramming for the advocacy exam had proven too much for her.

No, that wasn't true. She rested her head on her desk, using her arms as a cushion. The truth was that the study material bored her. Yes, she loved the Way; yes, she loved the Law, but that didn't mean she wanted to spend her life arguing over the wording of articles, or preparing cases that requested minor amendments to them. She wanted to serve the Way by protecting it against threats. The military was the best place to do that.

Her comm station beeped twice in rapid succession, announcing the arrival of a dispatch. Lesley flicked on the monitor, requested the list of new dispatches, and gulped. *Military Academy Entrance Examination Results*. Her mind raced. What if she'd passed? What if she'd failed? Because she loved her parents and wanted them to be proud of her, part of her wanted to read *We are sorry to inform you*. But in her heart, she hoped to read *We are pleased to inform you*, despite the problems that would cause. Finally telling her parents about her dream to serve the Way in the military would be a relief. Hiding part of her life from them, going along with their plans for her future when she'd rather do something else, was too much of a strain.

She glanced at her closed bedroom door. *Stop dithering*. Mama could burst in at any moment and see the dispatch list on the screen. Quickly hiding it wouldn't work. Lesley knew she'd look guilty. She swallowed and opened the dispatch.

Her shoulders slumped as she let out the breath she hadn't realized she'd been holding. She'd passed. She'd passed! But the next phase was the three-day evaluation.

The dispatch provided two prepared replies—one that confirmed her intent to proceed to the next phase and one that essentially said she'd changed her mind and wished to be removed from the evaluation process. Without giving herself time to think, she sent the confirmation dispatch and snapped off her monitor. There, it was done. She couldn't back out—not that she wanted to.

Now came the hard part. But first she wanted to share her excitement at passing, the excitement that had clawed its way to the surface

 DISOBEDIENCE MEANS DEATH

despite the dread she felt, before telling her parents subdued it. She snatched her comm unit from the desk and opened the bedroom door. Silence greeted her. Mama must still be in the study. Good.

She hurried downstairs and slipped out the front door. Her bike tempted her—she could see Mo, rather than beep her. But she'd only be further avoiding a conversation she'd already delayed too long. Plus she hadn't heard from Mo, which probably meant Mo hadn't received her results. She'd stick to her original plan.

It could also mean that Mo had failed, Lesley realized as she walked down the path leading to the entrance to the estate. That wasn't likely. Mo had studied hard, really applied herself, and had seemed optimistic after the exam.

Lesley stopped as soon as the path curved and hid the house from view. She felt a bit silly—it didn't matter if anyone saw her. She wasn't doing anything wrong; all she was doing was beeping Mo. Well, beeping Mo about her exam results, the exam her parents didn't even know she'd written because she'd lied to them about seeing Karen and had deliberately misled them into thinking she wanted to be an advocate, that was all.

She punched Mo's code into her comm unit and smiled when she heard Mo's voice. "Mo, it's me. My exam results came. I passed."

Mo whooped, but then went quiet. "I haven't received anything," she finally said.

"They probably haven't reached your name yet. You'll get the dispatch soon."

"Maybe they're notifying passes first. Maybe I failed."

"I doubt it. Remember when we talked after the exam? We answered almost every question along the same lines. So if I passed, I'm sure you passed."

"I hope so." Mo paused. "You'll have to tell them now."

Lesley sighed. "I know. Mama's home. I thought I'd tell her right after we disconnect, before Papa arrives. Then it won't be two against one."

"Too bad it's not the other way around and your papa was home."

"I know."

"Do you want me to come over?"

"No. That could make things worse. They might think you—"

"A dispatch just arrived. Just a sec." Silence, then Mo screamed, "I passed! Les, I passed!"

Lesley grinned. "Mo, that's great."

"Did you confirm?"

"Yes."

Mo screamed again. "I just did, too. We're going to the Military Academy. We're going to the flaming Military Academy!"

"What's all the commotion?" Lesley heard Susan say.

"I passed the entrance exam, Mama." Mo's voice was fainter than before; she must have turned away from her comm station.

"That's wonderful! We have to celebrate. Michael! Michael, come here," Susan shouted. "Mo passed her exam."

"Les, beep me after you've—"

Her papa's voice drowned out the rest of her sentence. "I knew you'd pass," he said. "Come on, we'll all go out for supper."

"Yeah, okay, okay," Mo said. "Oh, Les passed, too."

"Lesley?" Susan said. "I thought she was studying for the advocacy exam."

"She is. She, um, hasn't decided exactly what she wants to do yet. But she's glad she passed."

"She should be. I'll beep Adelaide. We can all go out together."

"No!" Mo shouted. "She hasn't told them. That she passed. Her papa isn't home yet."

"I was planning to tell them over supper," Lesley said, her hand clenched around her comm unit. What was Mo thinking?

"You could tell them as soon as your papa gets home," Susan suggested.

"Mama, let her do it the way she wants to," Mo said. "I'm starved. I want to go now."

"Well, if you want to."

"I do."

"Okay. If that's what you want."

"I'll round up the boys," Michael said.

"Beep me later," Mo said to Lesley, then whispered, "Beep me sooner if you need to. Good luck." She terminated the connection.

Lesley slid her comm unit into its holder and started walking back to the house. Somehow, she doubted her parents would react the way Mo's had. They definitely would not be going out for a celebratory supper. Perhaps she should beep Karen, ask her if she could visit within the next few days and hold off on telling her parents until then? No. Not only would that be unfair to Karen, but Susan was Mama's closest friend. It couldn't wait. Mo had forced the issue by telling her parents. Lesley couldn't blame her—Mo knew her too well.

She paused on the doorstep, then entered the house. Beyond the open study door, Mama sat at her desk, head down, scribbling on a notepad. Mama hated using a comm station to make notes. She only used a station when she was ready to write the case she'd present to the overseer. Lesley hesitated outside the door. How many times had she run to the study when she'd scraped her knee, had an argument with Karen or Jason, or needed help with her homework? The study, the familiar sight of her parents' heads bent over their desks, was usually comforting, reassuring. But not today.

"Mama?" she said, tapping at the door.

"What do you want?" Mama asked, without looking up.

"I want to talk to you about something."

"If it's about the exam, I don't have time to help you right now." Mama stopped writing, flipped over the paper, and continued to write on the other side. "Ask your papa when he gets home."

"I don't need help," Lesley said, stepping into the room and standing directly in front of Mama's desk.

"Well, what is it, then?"

She might as well get to the point. "I wrote the entrance exam for the Military Academy."

Mama stopped writing and looked up. "What?"

"I wrote the entrance exam for the Military Academy."

"When? I don't rem—" Mama's eyes narrowed. "The exam was the same day you were with Karen. You told us you'd decided on that day because Mo would be tied up most of the day at the exam."

"I'm sorry."

"You're sorry." Mama stared at her.

"I tried to tell you. But you wouldn't listen, neither of you. You—"

"Don't you dare blame your papa and me!" Mama shouted, making Lesley jump. "You lied to us."

"I—I know. Because I knew you'd be disappointed. But it's what I want to do, Mama. I don't want to be an advocate. I want to serve in the military."

"Why? You're bright. You could do anything. Why waste yourself on the military?"

"What's wrong with the military? It serves the Way. It defends the Way."

"Of course it does. But it's for those who don't have any initiative. Who don't want to think. Who can't serve the Way in a more . . . stimulating capacity." To Lesley's surprise, Mama smiled and leaned forward, clasping her hands on top of the desk. "Don't stand there looking petrified. Sit down. So you want to serve in the military. Fine. Let's talk about it."

Lesley lowered herself into the chair next to Mama's desk. She sat stiffly, uneasy about Mama's sudden mood change.

"Now, I want you to listen to me," Mama said. "You're young. I can see how the idea of walking around in an orange cloak seems exciting to you. Perhaps you think wearing an orange cloak gives you power. It doesn't. Everyone in an orange cloak is doing exactly what they're told to do. They never think. They don't have to. They're always told. Thompsons are thinkers. We're leaders. We aren't followers. The military is for followers. You won't like it. You'll be bored."

Well, she'd definitely be bored if she became an advocate. "I might be bored," she allowed.

"No, you *will* be bored. Once the novelty wears off, you'll regret not entering the advocacy program. You'll also regret all the time you wasted. You don't want to graduate from college when you're thirty. Listen to me. I don't want you to ruin your life."

"Mo's parents don't think she's ruining her life."

Mama rolled her eyes and leaned back in her chair. "Now, you know I love the Middletons. They're dear, dear friends, especially Susan. But they're not . . . ambitious. They're happy sewing clothes and cutting people's hair. Having Mo at the Military Academy will be a step up for them."

Lesley took a deep breath and slowly exhaled. "Susan's an indoctrinator."

"Yes, well, I said the Middletons, but all of them except Susan have Anderson blood. From what I know, the Andersons aren't exactly driven. The Middletons have a bit more initiative. Michael Joined into that estate."

"I know, but—"

"And yes, she's an indoctrinator. But she ended up with a master tailor. The Chosen Council selected an advocate for me. That should tell you something."

"Michael's planning to run for the government."

"Michael's been planning to run for the government for years," Mama said, dismissing the notion with a wave of her hand. "He'll still be planning to run for the government when you're fifty. As I said, I love the Middletons. They're good neighbours. But I want more for my children than Susan does. Susan wants everyone to be happy. That's all well and good, but I want more. I want you to live up to your potential. You won't do that in the military."

"Mama, I won't be happy being an advocate."

"You don't know that. You should give it a chance."

"Why shouldn't I give the military a chance?"

"Are you listening?" Mama leaned forward, jabbing her finger against her desk for emphasis. "Because the military won't challenge you. There are better ways for someone like you to serve the Way. Leave the military to those with fewer options." She sighed and sat back. "Now, I'm not pleased that you lied to us, and I'll certainly have a talk with your papa about it, including Karen's role. But at least you finally told the truth. Susan said that if Mo passes, she'll have to undergo another phase, some evaluation step. Just decline that step. I've seen you studying for the advocacy exam. You have been studying, right, not just pretending?"

"Yes, but—"

"Good. Continue with your studies. Once you start the advocacy program, you'll forget all about the military."

Lesley shook her head. "It's too late."

"What do you mean, it's too late?"

"I passed the entrance exam."

Mama shrugged. "So you passed. Just decline the next step."

Lesley stared at her.

"What?" Mama's face fell. "Oh, you haven't. Oh, Lesley! Why didn't you talk to us first?"

"Because I knew you'd react badly."

"Well, that's one thing you got right." Mama pursed her lips. "But you haven't been accepted into the Military Academy yet. What's the next step? When is it? What do you have to do? I vaguely remember Susan talking about it, but I wasn't paying attention. I didn't think I had to."

"It's a three-day evaluation at the Military Academy in C6. At the end, you find out if you'll be admitted to the academy."

"Ah, so there's still time, then. When do you have to go?"

"In three weeks."

"And you'll write the advocacy exam in two," Mama said, brightening. "It would be perfectly reasonable to decline your acceptance into the Military Academy because you've decided to pursue advocacy instead. You can say that you couldn't make up your mind and so you decided to write both exams, but since then, you've settled on advocacy. Make it sound good. Tell them it was close, that the military would have been a worthy career and it was a difficult choice."

Lesley couldn't believe her ears. "But it's not true! If I'm accepted, I'm not turning it down, Mama. I can't."

"Of course you can."

"No, I can't. I don't even want to write the advocacy exam. I'm tired. I've been studying non-stop for exams for weeks now, and trying to keep up with my homework at the same time. And now I have to prepare for the evaluation. I can't do everything."

"You have to write the advocacy exam," Mama said, her voice firm.

"Why? There's no point. Even if I pass, I won't enter the advocacy program. I don't want to. What's so bad about the military? The military protects and defends the Way. Can't you say even one positive thing about it?"

"It's not the military per se, Lesley. It's *you* being in the military that I don't like." The clock on the wall behind Mama chimed. Mama waited until it had finished announcing six o'clock before continuing. "But Interior does uphold the Law and the Tradition. That means you'll have to keep up with every amendment. And I guess having a solid grasp of how the Way is applied in practical terms could serve an advocate well. Given that, you won't be too far behind when you finally admit you're bored and switch to the advocacy program. If you're not stubborn and proud, you'll only waste a few months before you get back on track."

Lesley gripped the arms of her chair.

Mama stared at her. "What? You asked me to say something positive. I'm trying!"

"I know. It's just that . . . I'm not planning to join Interior. I'm hoping to join Defence."

"Defence?" Mama's mouth tightened. "Wait a minute. What exactly are you hoping to do in Defence?"

Lesley braced herself for the inevitable explosion. "Be a fighter pilot."

Mama shot out of her chair and leaned over the desk, her eyes ablaze. "You stupid girl! Don't you have any sense at all? You're throwing your life away because of Mo. Mo isn't your Chosen. The relationship won't last. It can't. Following her to the Military Academy is pointless."

"I'm not following her. I want to be a fighter pilot. I'm the one who got Mo interested, not the other way around."

"Sure you are."

"I am!"

"Mo's been talking about being a fighter pilot for months. You've been talking about it for thirty seconds. But you know what? Maybe you're right. Maybe you'd be better off being a fighter pilot. Advocates think." Mama tapped her temples. "They're capable of rational thought. You obviously aren't."

"I'm not stupid."

"Throwing your life away because of Mo? I'd call that stupid. Because that's what you're doing. You just can't see it."

"I told you, it's not because of Mo."

"You can't be sure of that, Lesley."

Yes, she could. Mo hadn't given a second's thought to the military or flying until Lesley had persuaded her to sign up for the tour at the military installation.

"But nothing I say will change your mind. Common sense can't compete with teenage hormones. So go ahead." Mama thrust out her hands. "Throw your life away. Go into the military. It's probably for the best. Your papa and I would have loved another advocate in the family, but I'm starting to see that you would have disappointed us. At least we'll have Karen and Jason to talk about when people ask. At least that's something. Now get upstairs and do your homework."

"Mama—"

"Go!"

Lesley rose from the chair and turned toward the door.

"Oh, and forget about seeing Mo later," Mama said.

She tensed.

"I haven't forgotten that you lied to us, and when I tell your papa, he'll have something to say about it, too. I don't think you'll be seeing Mo outside of class for a while."

"I wasn't planning to see Mo later anyway," Lesley said without turning to face Mama. "She's out celebrating her exam results with her family."

"Well, isn't that nice. I'll tell you what. When you do something worth celebrating, we'll go out, too. But that hasn't happened yet. Now go!"

Lesley left the room and headed for the stairs, fighting tears. The conversation had gone much worse than she'd expected. She'd not only disappointed Mama, *she* was a disappointment. She'd failed to live up to the Thompson name and to her parents' expectations. Was it worth it? Should she do what Mama had suggested—take the advocacy exam and decline the invitation to enroll in the Military Academy if she passed the evaluation?

She reached her room and snapped on her station monitor to reread the military's dispatch. Had it mentioned a procedure for backing out of the evaluation after accidentally confirming? She didn't think so, but she sat at her desk and reread the dispatch anyway.

Once again, excitement managed to burst through her despair. She didn't want to back out; she wanted to serve in the military. Not following through would only lead to a regret she'd carry with her for the rest of her life. Every time she saw an orange cloak, she'd cringe, reminded of her lack of courage. It came down to being a failure to her parents or a failure to herself. The former would be easier to live with. Selfish, but true.

Her bedroom was at the front of the house. She heard the faint thump of the front door closing, then muffled voices. Mama's rose and fell, while Papa's remained calm—when Papa had a chance to speak. The voices stopped. Papa was climbing the stairs, his heavy footsteps growing louder. A sharp knock at the door, then Papa swung it open and stepped into the room without waiting for an invitation.

He closed the door behind him and stood with his arms crossed. "So, you're determined to enter the military. I'm a little confused. You seem to enjoy our weekly discussions. You can be quite animated when defending your point of view."

"I do enjoy them." Lesley said. "They're one of my favourite times of the week."

"So what's wrong with advocacy?"

"Nothing."

"Then why the military?"

"I want to protect the Way. Defend it."

"Advocates protect the Way, with the help of the overseers. We ensure that every amendment preserves its spirit," he said, tapping his fingers against his arms.

"I understand that, and I know it's important. But it's not how I want to protect it. I want to protect it from threats. Concrete threats, not theoretical ones."

"I see. And you've thought about this?"

"I have, Papa, a lot."

"Then why haven't you mentioned it before? Why did you lie to us?"

He was trying hard to hide his disappointment, but she could hear it in his voice. "I tried to tell you. But every time I mentioned the military, you dismissed it."

"Perhaps if you'd tried 'I'd like to join the military,' we wouldn't have."

"You still would have tried to talk me out of it."

Papa was silent for a moment, then said, "Probably."

"That's why I had to write the exam without telling you. If I'd told you, you would have been upset and I wouldn't have written the exam.

Same with moving to the evaluation phase. If I'd told you before confirming, I might have ended up backing out. But I don't want to back out, Papa. It's what I want."

"Are you sure it's what you want and not what Mo wants? Because your mama's right. If you're doing this because of Mo, you're being foolish."

"It's what I want. One of the reasons Mo and I like each other is because we tend to be interested in the same things. Why can't anyone understand that? You and Mama are both advocates."

"Me and your mama are Chosens," he said sharply. "And we were both advocates when we met. You and Mo can't last. You know that. So make sure it's what you want, Lesley. Because in a few years, you won't want to be working with Mo. If she's the only attraction, you're making a huge mistake."

"It's what I want."

"Why Defence and not Interior?" Papa asked. "At least in Interior you'd be directly applying the Law and Tradition."

Lesley knew he wanted a logical answer, one that would help him understand the connection between her love of the Law and her choice of Defence. But there wasn't one. How could she explain the visceral reaction she'd had when she'd sat in a fighter's pilot seat and knew she wanted to learn how to fly? How could she make him understand her fascination when the guest speaker had provided a brief and simplistic overview of combat tactics, and the excitement she'd felt at the thought of belonging to a group of Rymellans working as a team to protect the Way, dependent on each other for their very lives? Would he understand if she told him that preserving the spirit of the Way was pointless if nobody was there to ensure that a species didn't take it away through hostile action, or would he think she was saying that advocates weren't important? Yes, Interior also protected the Way, by ensuring that Rymellans themselves didn't threaten it, but she wouldn't learn how to fly a fighter in Interior.

"It's hard for me to explain why, Papa," she said. "I wish I could tell you something that obviously connects studying the Law and Tradition with Defence, but I can't. I do love studying the Way, and maybe someday I'll end up in Interior. But right now, Defence appeals to me more."

"And you're sure that's not because of Mo?"

   DISOBEDIENCE MEANS DEATH

"Yes."

He looked as if he were going to question her response, but said instead, "What about the advocacy exam? Your mama says you don't want to write it."

"I have to start preparing for my evaluation at the Military Academy. And I have to keep up with my homework. My Learning Academy record has to be good, no matter what I decide to do. I don't have time to study for the advocacy exam and to keep up with everything else." Plus, the study material was putting her to sleep, but it was probably best not to mention that.

"Well, you're right." He dropped his arms. "If you've decided that serving in the military is what you want to do, then you have to give it your all."

"Does that mean you approve?" she asked, surprise making her voice sound higher than usual.

"I don't seem to have much choice. I'm disappointed, but it's your decision. If you're making a mistake, you'll face the consequences. And isn't that the Way? Responsibility, accountability?"

She nodded. "Mama's sure I'm making a mistake." Mama thought she was a failure.

"Your mama wants what's best for you. Maybe that'll turn out to be the military. We'll see. I'm willing to suspend my judgment and see what happens." Papa frowned. "But I won't excuse your dishonesty, or Karen's. No article of the Law dictates that you have to tell your parents the truth, but several dictate that you must always tell the military the truth. I think it would be appropriate for you to study one of them. Tomorrow, I'll bring home a few cases pertaining to Article 882. After you've read them, you can discuss them with me and your mama." He held up his hand. "And before you tell me you already have a lot to do, since you won't be leaving the house for a few weeks, except to go to the Learning Academy, you should be able to squeeze it in."

"A few weeks?" Lesley exclaimed.

"At least until you've undergone your evaluation at the Military Academy. You said you need to prepare. Well, now you'll have lots of time to do so."

Lesley swallowed. "Can friends visit?"

"No, Mo can't visit. You can see her at school. And no, you can't beep her, either."

"She might beep me."

"Send her a dispatch explaining the rules, all right? Or would you rather I send it?"

She hid her face behind her hands. "No, no, I'll send it."

"Good. Do it now, and then come down for supper." Without another word, he left the room.

MO POINTED TOWARD the window in the train station waiting area. "Here she comes."

Mama shielded her eyes and looked out. "She's alone."

"Of course she's alone," Papa muttered. "Adelaide and Alan didn't want to lower themselves by coming to see her off."

"Oh, hush," Mama said. "Though you're probably right."

"I know I'm right. I can't believe the fuss they kicked up. You'd think they'd be pleased, but no—joining the military isn't good enough for their precious children."

"They want what's best for Lesley, that's all."

"What's wrong with the military?"

"Nothing. But they were hoping—"

"Will you two please stop?" Mo said. "Les doesn't need to hear this." And Mo was sick of it, too. That was all they'd talked about for the past three weeks, ever since Adelaide had marched into the living room unannounced and insisted that Mo must have persuaded Lesley to give up on advocacy. Relations between the two families had never been as tense as they'd been since then, though Mama and Adelaide were showing signs of putting the rift behind them.

"Please don't say anything," Mo said to her parents as Les passed through the station entrance. Then she smiled at Les. "You made it. Train leaves in ten minutes."

Les didn't return Mo's smile, but her face softened. She nodded a greeting toward Mo's mama and papa.

"Your parents not with you?" Mama said.

Mo wanted to groan. *Flaming parents!* They ordered her around and expected her to do everything they said, but ask them to do one simple thing . . .

"No." Les studied her shoulder and started to tighten one of her knapsack's straps.

"I think we should go down to the platform," Mo said before her parents could say anything else stupid.

Les looked up. "I still have to pay." She pulled out her comm unit and wandered over to a nearby trade station.

"I'll carry your bag," Papa said to Mo, lifting it off the floor.

"No, I'll take it. Please don't come down to the platform with us," Mo said.

Mama pinched Mo's cheeks. "Will we embarrass you?" Papa dropped Mo's bag back to the floor.

She pulled Mama's hands away. "Stop it."

Mama grinned and enveloped Mo in a hug. "Good luck." She pulled away and held Mo at arm's length. "Next time I see you, I'll be congratulating you."

"I hope so."

"We will be," Papa said, putting his arm around Mo's shoulders and squeezing her. He kissed her forehead. "See you in a few days. You can beep us, you know."

"I know."

"Bye, Lesley," Mama called. "Good luck." Les looked over her shoulder and waved. Papa waved in return. "It's a shame," Mama said as she and Papa walked away.

"I bet they're hoping she fails," Papa said.

Mo willed them to walk faster and keep their voices down. She jumped when Les tapped her shoulder and said, "Ready to go?"

"Yeah." Mo wanted to hug her, but Les seemed distant and preoccupied. Maybe she'd relax once they were on the train, putting distance between themselves and her parents.

"Is that your bag?" Les asked, pointing. In response, Mo hefted her bag from the floor and struggled to get her arms through its straps. "It's almost as big as you," Les said. "We're going for three days, not three weeks."

"Well, you never know what might happen. I want to be prepared." Mo grunted as the left strap finally slipped over her shoulder. "The last thing I want to do is fail the evaluation because my clothes are wet or dirty." Les opened her mouth, but then closed it. "Anyway, let's go." Mo walked toward the steps that led down to the platform. The bag weighed a ton, but she was determined not to let it slow her down.

"Do you want me to carry it?" Les asked from behind her.

"No, I don't," Mo said, though she hung onto the railing and moved carefully down the stairs. If she lost her balance, she'd be at the mercy of wherever the bag wanted to take her.

The train pulled into the station shortly after they reached the platform. They boarded, stowed their bags, and settled into two empty seats near the rear of the car. "Finally we get to spend some time together," Mo said, snuggling against Les. "I'm sick of snatching a minute here and there."

Les stiffened. "We're not going on holiday."

Mo's stomach sank. Hadn't Les missed her at all? "I know that. But this is the first time in three weeks that we've even talked to each other outside the Learning Academy. It wouldn't have been so bad if you'd carried on using our bags to exchange notes. Or walked with me to and from the academy."

"They were clear that I wasn't to walk with you. And as far as the bags go, I was worried they might check my bag when I got home. I didn't want to risk it. They're upset enough as it is."

"I know it's been rough," Mo said, rubbing Les's arm. "And I know I'm being selfish. It's just that I missed you. A lot." She held her breath. *Please say you missed me, Les. Please!*

Les grabbed Mo's hand and held it still. Mo tensed, half expecting Les to pull her arm away, but she relaxed when Les's fingers curled around hers. "I'm sorry," Les said. "I missed you, too. And I should be happy to be with you and excited that we're going to the Military Academy. But I can't be. Not when I know my parents wish I wasn't doing it. I don't mean seeing you," she said, giving Mo a quick smile. "I mean going through with the evaluation."

"Are you sure? They're not thrilled with me right now."

"They're getting over that. I stole a peek at the seating plan for the

  DISOBEDIENCE MEANS DEATH

Festival of the Way supper. Mama's seating us next to each other. She wouldn't do that if she was still mad at you. It's me they're mad at."

"You're not doing anything wrong."

"I know that up here," Les said, touching her forehead with her free hand, "but it's hard to feel good about it."

A number of responses ran through Mo's mind. *You're doing what's right for you. They'll come around. You'd only hate them if you put your dreams aside for theirs.* But nothing she said would matter. "It would be dumb to change your mind now, on the way to the evaluation," she said, opting to focus on the pragmatic.

"Oh, I don't want to," Les said. "I wish I could get excited about it, that's all."

The announcement system crackled to life. "The train will depart in one minute. Please clear the doors."

Mo eyed the monitor fitted into the back of the seat directly in front of hers, but decided not to read the latest announcements or military bulletins. The train ride could be the last chance to relax for the next three days. As soon as the doors closed, she leaned her head against Les's arm. The train started to move. Station lights whipped by, then it looked as if night had abruptly fallen. Mo closed her eyes. There wouldn't be much to see for the next hour or so except tunnel walls and train stations, and all the stations looked the same.

She lifted her head when Les nudged her arm. "What?"

"We're almost there."

"Already!" She must have dozed off. "Sorry, it took me a while to fall asleep last night. Excitement, I guess." And nerves.

Les waved away Mo's apology. "I didn't feel like talking anyway."

The train pulled into the station. "Military Academy, Sector C6," the announcement system reported.

When they stepped onto the platform, Mo looked in dismay at the flight of stairs leading to the station's waiting area. There must be four times as many steps as there were in the station they'd left. Suddenly the weight was removed from her back. She turned around.

Les shrugged into Mo's bag and held out her own. "Here."

"You don't have to," Mo said, trying not to look too eager to accept Les's bag.

"I know."

Mo slipped Les's bag onto her back. "Thanks."

As they ascended the stairs, Mo's excitement grew at the sight of military personnel heading down to the platform in their orange cloaks. That could be her in a few months! Well, no; cadets didn't have orange cloaks, they had light blue ones, but still.

A *Registration for Evaluation* sign in the waiting area pointed them to one of the many station exits. They crossed a courtyard and entered a three-storey brick building where four lines had formed in the lobby before a rectangular table. The hum of conversation filled the air. From what Mo could see, four of the military behind the table registered the arrivals, while a fifth answered questions from those who had already received their registration packet. The lines were moving quickly, with no clear winner, so she and Les joined the nearest one.

Mo glanced around, wondering if she'd recognize anyone. A girl in the next line seemed to be staring at her. No, at Les. Mo bristled when the girl raised an appraising eyebrow. Oh, great. They'd been here five flaming minutes and already someone was eyeing Les up and down. She glared at the airhead and slipped her hand into Les's. Les stared toward the front of the line, oblivious.

"Comm unit," a man barked.

"Oh, sure," Mo said, bewildered. They'd already reached the table. She let go of Les's hand, quickly slipped her comm unit from its holder, and handed it to him.

He slid a thin black rod down the comm unit's side and looked at the monitor in front of him. "All right, Middleton. You're in Barracks 22, Bed 6. You'll find three jumpsuits folded at the end of the bed. Wear a jumpsuit to all your sessions and appointments."

Now that Mo was at the table, she could see the boxes of envelopes on another table against the back wall. He spun his chair around, rolled forward, and leafed through a box. "Here we are." He rolled back and handed the envelope to her. "All the information you need is in there, including a map of the academy and the rules that apply to the evaluation. Read the rules carefully. Any violation of the rules will result in the automatic failure of your evaluation. Understood?"

"Yes."

     DISOBEDIENCE MEANS DEATH

"Good. Proceed to your barracks." He looked past her. "Comm unit," he barked.

Mo moved aside and decided to wait for Les in the courtyard. Outside, she slipped the information from the envelope and found the itinerary. Nothing until supper, then a two-hour orientation session. *This is as much your opportunity to evaluate us as it is ours to evaluate you,* the preamble to the itinerary stated. Yeah, sure. Somehow she doubted the military would be crushed if it failed her evaluation and she decided not to join after all.

She read the next day's schedule—06:00: *morning alarm.* 06:15: *breakfast*—and her eyes bulged. *What's 06:00? Six o'clock in the morning?* They better not expect her to be coherent.

A shadow fell across the papers. "What barracks are you in?" Les asked.

"Twenty-two."

"I'm in nineteen."

"Too bad."

"Maybe it's better that way."

"Maybe. Did you see what time we have to be up? Six o'clock!"

Les grinned. "Did you think you were going to lie around all day?"

"Well, no. But six o'clock?"

"You'll cope." Les patted Mo's arm. "Come on. Let's find our barracks and get changed."

"Don't forget to give me my bag," Mo said.

"Believe me, I won't." Les shot out in front of Mo, then turned around and spread her arms. "Can you believe it? We're at the Military Academy!"

Mo smiled, pleased to see Les excited, so excited that Mo could hardly keep up with her as they went in search of their beds for the next three nights.

LESLEY LEFT THE classroom and sat in a nearby lounge area, grateful for the breather. The day had been a whirlwind, a rush to get from one session or appointment to another. She'd undergone a rigorous medical examination, written an essay about why she wanted to join the military, spent two hours in conversation with a counsellor, which she guessed had actually been a psychological evaluation, and had just finished writing an exam. A surprise exam, one the lecturer had sprung on them immediately after his talk about past military campaigns. It hadn't been difficult, but it would separate those who'd prepared for the evaluation from those who hadn't. Not all the answers had been covered during the lecture.

She glanced at the classroom door. Mo was still inside, and she must be exhausted—she'd arrived on time for breakfast, but with her eyes barely open. Given the pace since then, she probably felt dead on her feet, and the day wasn't over yet. Supper was next on the agenda. After that, a workshop. The itinerary offered no details beyond the workshop title: Group Dynamics. Forcing everyone to work together at the end of a long, busy day was almost cruel, but they were all there to be evaluated, after all. Fortunately the workshop would end at nine, and nothing was scheduled afterward. Lesley knew what she'd do—go straight to the barracks and get into bed. Tomorrow's agenda was as packed as today's.

The classroom door opened. She hoped to see Mo, but a short, slender young man with cropped brown hair stepped into the corridor. He caught her eye and walked toward her. "Taking a short break before heading to the mess hall?" he asked.

"I'm waiting for someone."

"Oh, right, your friend. With the black hair. You always sit together."

She was surprised someone had noticed.

"I'm David. David Bryson."

"Lesley Thompson."

He sat in the chair closest to hers. "I've hardly had time to breathe all day."

"I know what you mean," she said, trying to look past him without being obvious.

"At least we finish up at nine."

"Yes."

"I'll need to wind down before trying to sleep," he said, leaning forward. "I was thinking of walking around the academy grounds. Maybe you'd like to go for a quiet stroll, just me and you? I'm sure your friend can find something else to do."

     DISOBEDIENCE MEANS DEATH

She stifled an angry retort. "I'm same-oriented."

He flushed and drew back. "I'm sorry. I didn't—I mean, I should have—I guess you and your friend, you're, um . . ."

Lesley nodded.

"I'm usually not this dense or rude—honest!—but I'm operating on four hours of sleep."

"Only four?"

"I don't sleep well in strange beds. Look, I really am sorry. I should have realized."

"You couldn't have known we were more than close friends," she said, feeling some sympathy for him. He seemed genuinely contrite.

"Maybe not, but I could have asked before making a fool of myself."

"I guess it's safe to assume you're diff-oriented."

David chuckled.

The classroom door opened again. Mo, this time. Lesley waved; Mo immediately came over, shaking her head. "That was completely unfair, giving an exam like that. I hope I didn't write anything stupid. Oh, hi," she said, noticing David.

"Mo, this is David Bryson," Lesley said. "David, Mo Middleton."

They nodded to each other. "Mo must be short for something," David said.

"Ramona. But nobody ever calls me that."

Lesley inwardly smiled. If the stories were true, she was responsible for Mo's nickname. *When you started talking, you couldn't pronounce Ramona. You called her Mo. And that's what everyone else started calling her, too. For some reason, it stuck,* Mama had said, an explanation Mo's parents had corroborated.

David stood. "Well, I'd better get something to eat. We seem to be in the same group, so I guess I'll see you at the workshop later. Nice meeting both of you."

"If you're going to the mess hall, we might as well go together," Lesley said. He seemed pleasant enough, and it wasn't as if she and Mo would have had a quiet, romantic supper in the crowded, noisy mess hall. Everyone sat at long tables, with very little elbow room and zero privacy. On top of that, getting to know some of the other candidates was probably a good idea. Perhaps the military was evaluating everyone's behaviour between sessions, too. She and Mo wouldn't want to appear unsociable.

"Yeah, why not?" Mo said. "If we're all accepted, we could end up seeing a lot of each other." She paused. "I hope I did okay on the exam. I wasn't sure about question six."

David nodded. "That was a tricky one."

"What did you both put?" Mo asked.

They compared answers on their way to the mess hall and while they pushed their trays along the rail, adding dishes to them. By the time they sat down at a table occupied by other Rymellans in jumpsuits, Mo seemed more confident that she'd passed the exam. "Most of my answers match yours," she said. "And I'm pretty good at, um, making it sound like I know more about something than I do."

Lesley opened her mouth to tease Mo, but Mo forestalled her with a quick, "And no comment from you."

David grinned. "So where are you from?" he asked as he spread butter on a bread roll. "I'm from B8."

"C3," Lesley said.

His eyebrows drew together. "C3? What are you doing here?"

Lesley's jaw clenched. Not him, too. "What do you mean?"

"Well, you're probably both from old families with connections. You could do anything."

"What's wrong with the military?" Mo asked. She bit into a vegetable pie and made a face. "Military food," she muttered, as if offering an answer to her question.

"Nothing. I'm just surprised it's your first choice."

"Isn't it your first choice?" Lesley said. "There's nothing stopping you from doing anything else."

"I guess not. But I'm still surprised about you two. I haven't met many military from C3."

"You know a lot of military?" Lesley asked.

David took his time chewing a mouthful of food before replying. "My papa's a lieutenant commander." He smiled sheepishly.

Lesley snorted. "You're better connected than we are." She picked up her knife and fork and glanced at the large clock over the entrance to the hall. They had to be at the workshop in twenty-five minutes and she hadn't touched her food. Mo could do the talking from now on.

"I don't know any military," Mo said. "I mean, I know a few faces and names, the ones that patrol the estate, mainly, but that's it. Is your papa in Defence or Interior?"

"Defence."

"We want to join Defence. And we want to try for the fighter pilot program."

His eyes widened. "Me too! I want to be a fighter pilot, too. I always knew I wanted to join the military, but I wasn't sure which division. My papa said it was up to me. Then I toured an installation when I was at the Indoctrination Academy, and that's when I knew."

"The same thing happened to us," Mo said, awe in her voice.

David looked at Lesley. "You'll be tall for a pilot."

"Really?"

"Papa tells me they're usually short."

"I'll fit right in, then," Mo said, grinning. "This is great! It's great talking to someone who wants the same thing we do."

Lesley, her mouth full, nodded. It was certainly more enjoyable than talking to her parents.

"But we better hurry up and finish supper," Mo added. "It'll take us ten minutes to walk to the workshop."

They put their conversation on hold and focused on eating. David finished first. He leaned back in his chair and pulled his itinerary from a pocket in the leg of his jumpsuit. "Did you see we have a session with a commander tomorrow?" he asked, unfolding and smoothing the itinerary and then pointing at a line on the second page. "But there's no description of what the session's about."

Mo shrugged. "Probably executions."

"SINGLE FILE," THE commander shouted. "Everyone move in and form a circle around the clearing. Face the clearing, please."

Lesley followed the Rymellan in front of her and stopped when he stopped. She turned toward the dirt clearing. Mo had been right. The commander had arrived at the classroom and ordered them to line up and follow him to this execution site. She glanced at Mo, now standing on her left. David, next to Mo, looked at her and raised his eyebrows.

"Face me," the commander shouted as the tail end of the line filed into the site.

Lesley surveyed the clearing. There weren't enough aspiring recruits to fully ring the site. A military stood in the gap, near a metal pole at the clearing's southernmost edge. The commander and another military remained at the centre of the clearing. If an actual execution were about to take place, military would ring the site, not potential cadets, and a criminal would be secured to the pole. Lesley had learned the details during her Level Four at the Indoctrination Academy.

The commander signaled for silence by raising his hand. The few Rymellans who'd been whispering immediately stopped. "I am Commander Morton." He turned to his left. "This is Lieutenant Commander Eckles, and near the pole is Lieutenant Danson. Before we begin, let's say the *Words Every Rymellan Knows*."

Lesley reached for Mo's hand and the hand of the Rymellan on her right. Morton and Eckles walked to Danson and held out their hands. When the circle was complete, Morton nodded. Everyone spoke the Words. "Disobedience means death. Death to those who commit a Chosen Violation. Death to those who disobey. Death to those who violate the Way. Death to those who violate the Way. Death to those who violate the Way!" They all let go of their neighbours' hands and applauded.

Another difference, Lesley thought. Before an execution, the circle would be incomplete. It would break at the criminal, the only time Rymellans said the Words without completing a circle. After the execution, those present would complete the circle and say the Words again.

Morton returned to the centre. "Now, as you can see, we're standing in an execution site. I thought I'd start our session on the Interior Division here, to remind everyone that Defence isn't the only military division that defends the Way.

"All Rymellans preserve the Way by observing its articles. The Way is the foundation of Rymellan society, and many of us dedicate our lives to its service, notably our overseers, advocates, indoctrinators, counsellors, the military, and, of course, the Chosen Council. We all support each other. We all want to follow the Way.

     DISOBEDIENCE MEANS DEATH

"It seems unbelievable that a Rymellan would fall from the Way, but some do. And when they do, they end up here." He pointed at the pole. "Death to those who disobey. The Interior Division ensures that no Rymellan will ever harm the Way. Because no Rymellan is more important than the Way."

A chorus of agreement rose from the group. Lesley nodded and added her "yes" to the many others.

"The gravest threat the Way has ever faced in recent history didn't come from another species. It didn't come from out there somewhere." Morton pointed above his head, then to the ground. "It originated right here, on Rymellan soil. Rymellans threatened the Way. And it happened just three years ago, an event known as . . . ?" He looked to the group to complete his sentence.

"The Adams Incident," the group said in unison.

"That's right. The Adams Incident. The worst case Interior—" A loud gasp drowned out his next word. He spun to his left.

Lesley leaned forward to see what was going on. Three Rymellans appeared agitated, furiously whispering to each other.

"What's the problem?" Morton shouted.

"He said something awful," said one of the three, pointing at the boy next to her. Lesley recognized him. He'd introduced himself to her and Mo on the first day of the evaluation, at the mess hall. Tom Elliott.

"I heard it, too," said the Rymellan to Elliott's left.

"Heard what? What did you say?" Morton asked.

"Nothing. I didn't mean anything," Elliot said, his face ashen.

Morton marched over to him. "What did you say?" he shouted into Elliott's face.

Everyone leaned forward for a better view. Lesley shifted position slightly, using her height to her advantage.

"I just—I said I wondered if the Adamses and the other two . . . I wondered if they were all secured to the pole together."

The girl shook her head. "That's not all he said. He also said that if they were, they probably enjoyed it."

More gasps.

"Silence!" Morton shouted.

"It was a joke. It was just a joke!" Elliott shrieked.

Morton reddened. "Two Chosens violate their Chosen bond, four Rymellans executed, the worst threat to the Way anyone can remember, and you're joking about it?"

"I'm sor—"

"I wasn't planning to offer a demonstration today, but now it looks like I will be." Morton straightened and motioned to Danson and Eckles. "Secure him to the pole."

"What?" Elliott drew back, his eyes widening.

Morton grabbed Elliott's arm and pulled him into the clearing.

"No, please. I'm sorry. I'm sorry!" Elliott wailed.

Danson and Eckles took over from Morton, each taking one of Elliott's arms. They started to haul him toward the pole, but he resisted, pulling back and digging his heels into the ground. "It was just a joke. Please. Please don't—" His voice choked off.

Behind them, Morton shoved him forward. "Move!"

Elliott's head snapped back; he lost his balance and hung limp between Danson and Eckles as they dragged him toward the pole, his toes leaving two parallel trails in the soil.

"I'll beep for a physician and load my stick," Morton said. "And you will all remain silent. Anyone who speaks will be next." He strode from the clearing.

Elliott sobbed as Danson and Eckles forced his back against the pole and secured him to it using metal restraints Eckles pulled from a box at the pole's base. "Please," he managed to say. "Please, don't do this to me." He dropped his head and wept.

A metallic ringing filled the air. Lesley didn't understand where it was coming from. Bells? No, but it had a rhythm to it. It— She swallowed. Elliott was shaking, causing the restraints to vibrate against the pole. She felt Mo's fingers brush hers and squeezed them, but didn't dare look at her.

Morton returned and lifted his stick in the air. "The physician is on his way," he announced.

Lesley looked at the stick in disbelief. He wasn't actually going to do it, was he?

"What's your name?" Morton shouted at Elliott. When the only reply

 DISOBEDIENCE MEANS DEATH

he received was a whimper, he grabbed Elliott's hair and yanked his head up. "I said, what's your name?"

"Tom. Elliott."

"Well, don't worry, Tom. Once I inject you, you'll be dead within seconds. You won't feel a thing."

Morton let Elliott's hair go. Elliott dropped his head. The metallic ringing intensified.

"What's your name?" Morton asked, pointing at the girl who'd gasped.

She looked at him uncertainly.

"You can speak if I speak to you," Morton said. "What's your name?"

"Rosemary Mathers," she said proudly, standing ramrod straight with her hands clasped behind her back.

"And yours?" Morton asked the boy who'd been on Elliott's left.

"James Gladstone."

"And, of course, you both agree that I should execute Elliott."

Mathers nodded enthusiastically. Gladstone seemed unsure, offering only a half-hearted nod.

Morton took a few steps back "Does anyone here think I'm wrong?" He slowly turned in a circle, surveying the group. "Does anyone think I shouldn't execute him?"

Lesley took a deep breath and forced her hand up. Mo inhaled sharply.

Morton rushed toward her. "You think I'm wrong?" he shouted, his face so close to hers that she could tell he'd had fish for lunch. "You thought his joke was funny?"

"No," Lesley said.

"I know what you're thinking. It was only a joke. Oh, boo-hoo-hoo," Morton said, raising his voice an octave. "Let him go, Commander. Let the poor thing go."

"No."

"You don't think those who violate the Way should be punished?"

Lesley resisted the urge to step back when spittle hit her cheek. "No, they should be."

"Well, then, why do you think I'm wrong? Are you a coward? Afraid to watch a criminal die?"

"No. Disobedience means death. Death to those who commit a Chosen Violation. Death to those who disobey. Death to those who violate the Way."

"Don't parrot the Words at me. Why shouldn't I execute him?"

"Perhaps you'd tell us what capital article covers distasteful jokes."

Morton cocked his head. "Perhaps Elliott has a record filled with strikes and this pushed him over the threshold."

Lesley shook her head. "I doubt he'd be here, being evaluated, if that were the case. And you didn't know his name. If he had that many strikes on his record, you would have known his name."

Morton stared at her a moment, then laughed. "What's *your* name?" he asked, stepping back.

"Lesley Thompson."

"Well, Lesley Thompson, you're right!" he roared. "Which is why my stick isn't loaded." He returned to the middle of the clearing.

Lesley wiped her cheek while his back was turned and hoped her legs would stop shaking.

"What's the matter with you?" he shouted at the group. "Were you all going to stand there and watch me do it? Listen to me. We all serve the Way, even executioners. The Way protects us." He pointed at Elliott. "The Way protects him. It ensures that no commander will ever execute him unless that commander can justify his execution under the Way. Any commander who abuses his or her position would end up at an execution site him- or herself. If any of you ever sees someone about to violate the Way, you must speak up, no matter who it is. Even if it's a commander."

Morton nodded at Danson and Eckles. They released Elliott from the restraints; he fell to his knees, trembling. "Still think the Adamses enjoyed it?" Morton said to him. "Now get up!"

He struggled to his feet.

"Look at me."

Elliott lifted a face streaked with tears.

"While joking about the Adams Incident isn't a capital offence, it's certainly enough to show that you're not right for the military," Morton said. "Lieutenant Danson, escort him to the barracks to pack his things. Then escort him to the train station."

"Yes, Commander." Danson grasped Elliott's arm and led him from the site.

"As for the rest of you, let's return to the classroom. In addition to discussing in more detail how Interior defends the Way, I think we'll also review the articles that dictate what to do if you suspect the Way is about to be violated. Lieutenant Commander Eckles, take up the lead."

As the line that ringed the clearing followed Eckles from the site, Lesley noticed that Mo moved stiffly. She understood why—every muscle in her body had been clenched, too.

MO TURNED A page of the book she wasn't really reading, then gave up and rested the book face-down on her lap. Another one for the insomnia pile next to her bed. It wasn't the book's fault. She couldn't concentrate, not when she was about to find out if she was in or not. What would she do if the military said no? Ever since she'd decided she wanted to be a fighter pilot, she hadn't considered for a second that the military could reject her application. But now, waiting for her name to be called, the possibility was frighteningly real. She had absolutely no idea what she'd do with her life if she'd failed.

One of the three doors on the opposite wall swung open and a grinning Rymellan bounded through the doorway. Well, it looked like he was in. In the thirty-five minutes she'd sat here, about half had come out looking like he did. The other half had tried to smile, or at least not cry, but a quick shake of the head to a waiting friend or the redness and strain around the eyes had betrayed them. Mo had told Les not to wait with her. "I don't want everyone to think I can't do anything by myself," she'd said, and now added another reason to the list: if she hadn't made it, she wanted to sneak off and have a little cry before she had to put on a brave face and pretend her life wasn't ruined.

A military stepped into the waiting area. "Nelson," she called. A boy stood. She ushered him into the office and shut the door.

Mo glanced around the room. Only seven left, including her. That would take care of the Ls to the Ps. Les's group, the Qs to the Ts, would be next. Les didn't have anything to worry about, not after her performance at the execution site. Morton had even spoken to her after the session, wanting to know if she planned to train for Interior or Defence. Nope, Les was in, and so was David. He'd already left the academy, anxious to return to his family to celebrate the good news.

"Good luck," he'd shouted as he'd waved to them and disappeared down the steps to the train platform. Then, ten minutes later, he'd beeped them and made them promise that they'd beep him once they knew. Well, she'd beep him if she was accepted; otherwise she'd send him a dispatch. It would be bad enough facing Les and her family without having to actually talk to him.

Another door swung open—the doom door. As far as she could tell, everyone who'd been called into that office had been rejected. Rosemary Mathers stepped out, her face grim. So, even Rosemary-flaming-Mathers had been taken down by the doom door. Good riddance. Elliott's joke had been in poor taste; it had probably been the stupidest, dumbest, most moronic thing he could have said, but it hadn't been a violation. Anyone else would have realized that everyone was tired, stressed, and uneasy and let it go, or at least talked to Elliott in private. But not Rosemary-flaming-Mathers.

Fortunately, the Defence session the previous evening had been nowhere near as tense as the Interior one. Mo had learned that cadets could only apply to the fighter pilot program after they'd completed their second year at the Military Academy. Apparently the curriculum for the Interior and Defence streams was pretty much the same during the first year of training. The second year was when the two streams significantly branched. "So if you change your mind about divisions, it's better to do it during your first year," the lieutenant commander had said. Cadets were only eligible to enter special programs like the fighter pilot program—those with a limited number of spaces and rigorous entry requirements—when they began their third year.

"But we won't wait until our second year to start planning for the fighter pilot program," Les had said afterwards. "We have to make sure we take the right courses, get involved in the right activities, from our very first day." Yeah, well, that was if they were both at the academy. Les talked as if they'd already been accepted. She had reason to be confident. Mo didn't.

  DISOBEDIENCE MEANS DEATH

She heard shuffling inside the doom door's office and picked up her book, hoping that shielding herself with it would mean she wouldn't have to pass through the doom doorway. But no such luck. "Middleton," bellowed the military who'd emerged from the office.

Mo stood and placed her book on her chair, trying not to look crestfallen. Only six people, maybe a couple less, would see her on her way out. That wouldn't be too humiliating. No, the humiliation would come later, when she told Les, and Mama and Papa. She forced herself to follow the military into the office.

"I'm Lieutenant Williams." He gestured toward the chair in front of her. "Sit."

She did so, crossing her legs in an effort to look relaxed. He flipped through a file on his desk, presumably hers, occasionally stopping when something on a page caught his interest. Maybe he enjoyed dragging it out and making the candidate squirm before delivering the bad news.

"It says here that you've expressed interest in the fighter pilot program," he said.

"Yes."

"You'll have to work very hard to get in. The number of applicants is always much greater than the number of spots. And more than half the students usually fail the program."

A glimmer of hope rose within her. "I'm not afraid of hard work."

"That's good. If you thought the Indoctrination Academy was demanding, you're in for a shock."

Her mounting excitement got the better of her. "Does that mean . . . ?"

He looked up from her file and managed a small smile. "Are you still interested in serving in the military, or has the evaluation changed your mind?"

"I'm still interested," she said, a little more eagerly than she would have liked.

"Well, then, welcome to the Military Academy, Cadet Middleton."

"Thank you," she said, grinning. Jumping up and down and whooping would have to wait. *Take that, doom door!*

"Within a week, you'll receive a dispatch with your report date, which will be two to three weeks after your final day at the Learning Academy. Congratulations, and good luck."

Being accepted was one of the best things that had happened to her, but he made it sound so routine. "Thank you," she said again, more subdued this time.

"Dismissed."

It took everything she had not to run for the door, hurl it open, and race to the barracks where Les waited. As it was, she was halfway across the courtyard before she realized that she'd left her book behind. Three hours and fifty minutes remained before the book would be considered abandoned, but she didn't want to take any chances. Not only would violating Article 302 not be a good start to her military career, but doing so at the Military Academy would be horribly embarrassing. She may as well have put a *Strike Me!* sign on her back. She rushed back to get the book and then walked as fast as she could to Barracks 19.

Les sat cross-legged on her bed, reading. Unfortunately, she wasn't alone. Two girls were busy packing their bags. Mo recognized one of them. If the girl's face hadn't lied earlier, she was also a new cadet. Les snapped her book shut and put it aside when she spotted Mo. Mo motioned for her to meet outside and stepped back into the midday sun. She wanted to share her news privately.

"So?" Les said, joining her.

"I'm in!" Mo launched herself into Les's arms. "I'm a cadet!"

Les's arms tightened and Mo felt her feet leave the ground. "That's great!" Les said.

Mo wanted to give Les a lingering kiss, only drawing back when she felt light-headed. But Les didn't like displaying overt affection in front of others, and she'd seemed even more sensitive about it here, at the academy. She'd stiffened up at the smallest peck on the lips. She'd even balked at holding hands in the mess hall. Mo hoped she'd loosen up a bit when they returned in a few months. After all, they'd be spending the next three years of their lives here. Other days, she would have told herself that they probably wouldn't be together in three years so it didn't matter, but today, everything seemed possible.

Her feet touched the ground. Les held her at arm's length and smiled. "I knew you'd get in. You had nothing to worry about." Her smile faded. "Now it's just me."

"Come on, you're in," Mo said. "I'm surprised Morton didn't tell

 DISOBEDIENCE MEANS DEATH

you you'd passed the evaluation yesterday. Oh, guess what? Rosemary Mathers didn't make it."

"I'm not surprised. I would have been surprised if you hadn't made it, though."

"But I did! And so will you."

"I'll feel better about me when I get the official word." She glanced at her comm unit. "I should probably head over there."

"I'll join you after I finish packing. And I want to beep Mama and Papa."

"They'll be so proud."

The wistfulness in Les's voice immediately tempered Mo's excitement. She squeezed Les's hand. "Yours will be, too."

"I doubt it," Les said. "Anyway, I'd better get going." She started to walk away, but turned back. "Mo?"

Mo stepped toward her. "What?"

"I'm glad you made it." Les paused. "Not just for you. For me, too. It wouldn't have been the same. I would have missed you—if I've made it, I mean." Her cheeks reddened. "Okay, now I really have to go."

Speechless, Mo watched Les walk away. Tears stung her eyes. She wanted to be a fighter pilot. If she had failed the evaluation, she would have been devastated and left wondering what to do with her life. But the terrible truth was that she wanted Les more. If the Chosen Council promised her that it would make Les her Chosen if she gave up her dream to become a fighter pilot, she'd do it in a heartbeat. And that was wrong, and something she could never, ever tell Les.

She willed herself to focus on the present, on today, a happy day! She'd just been accepted into the military. *And perhaps gained another three years with Les,* a little voice whispered.

LESLEY DID HER best to smile when the train pulled into Station C3-8. A long face wouldn't be fair to Mo. "We're home," she said a little too brightly.

Mo looked out the train window. "I don't believe it. My parents are on the platform. I hope they don't act too embarrassing."

"At least they're here," Lesley said, knowing hers wouldn't be, but searching for them anyway.

"You should have beeped them," Mo said.

"Why? They won't consider it good news."

"Well, they should."

The train stopped. They collected their bags and stepped onto the platform. As one, Mo's family rushed toward them. Mo dropped her bag. Susan pulled her into a hug, then drew back. "Do we need to salute?" she asked, smiling.

Mo groaned. "Mama, please."

"Congratulations," Michael said, putting his arm around Mo's shoulders and squeezing her.

"Look at me, I'm saluting at Mo." Nathan stood at attention, smartly saluting, his eyes crossed. Andrew started to laugh, then covered his mouth.

"Nathan, stop that now," Michael snapped. "You must never do anything that disrespects the military."

"Sorry," Nathan mumbled, dropping his hand.

"You don't have to salute. You're not in the military," Mo told him.

"And neither is she. Not quite," Lesley added.

"Yeah, that too." Mo caught Lesley's eye. They exchanged bemused smiles.

"But she will be." Susan embraced Mo again. "We're so proud of you."

"Can we go for supper now?" Andrew asked.

Michael picked up Mo's bag. "Sounds good to me."

"Matthew can't make it." Susan lowered her voice. "I think he has a date." She let go of Mo and looked at her. "But Neil and Mary will meet us at the eatery."

"They don't have to." Mo sounded as if she didn't care whether her two older siblings made it, but Lesley could tell she was pleased.

Susan's eyes widened. "They want to. They wouldn't miss it. A Middleton isn't accepted into the Military Academy every day." She turned to Lesley. "Neither is a Thompson. Congratulations are in order for you, too."

"Thank you," Lesley said, uncomfortable at suddenly gaining the spotlight.

"Where are your parents? I thought they'd be here."

Lesley looked away. "Oh, I haven't told them yet."

"But they must have known what time the train was arriving. And why didn't you beep them with the news?"

"I want to tell them in person."

"She wants to see the happiness in their eyes," Michael said.

"Papa!" Mo said, her voice strained.

Lesley pretended she hadn't heard him. "Well, I guess I should get going or they'll wonder where I am. Enjoy your supper."

"We'll go with you," Susan said. "It would be nice if we all went for supper together."

"No, that's okay," Lesley said quickly. "I don't know if—I mean, they might be busy. I don't know."

"Yeah, really Mama, it's probably not a good idea to just show up," Mo said. "And I'm starved. Aren't you starved?" She nudged Nathan, who obliged her with a nod. "Plus, Neil and Mary might be waiting."

"They won't have left yet. I said I'd beep them when we know for sure what time we'll be there. Now, come on." Susan's mouth pressed into a determined line and she led the way to the waiting area.

"I'm sorry," Mo whispered, falling into step next to Lesley. "I had no idea."

"Maybe it'll help," Lesley whispered back. "My parents won't react too badly while you're all there. By the time we're alone, they might have calmed down." But the knot in her stomach mocked her. It would have been depressing enough facing them by herself. Now she'd have an audience. Everyone would see how disappointed they were, how she'd let them down by passing the evaluation. And everything they said to slight her would slight Mo, too. This was a day of celebration for Mo, for the entire Middleton family. She'd hate it if Mama and Papa ruined it.

"So what sorts of tests did you do?" Michael shifted Mo's bag to his left shoulder. "Or is it a secret?"

Mo frowned. "They didn't say anything about it being secret, did they, Les?"

Lesley shook her head.

"Okay, well, we didn't have a moment's rest." Mo paused as they all filed through the exit. "Classes, workshops, tests—one thing after another."

Susan slowed her pace. "Did you have a physical?"

"Yeah, and a long talk with a counsellor."

"And they still wanted you?" Andrew quipped.

Mo swatted at him. He ducked and ran ahead to join Nathan, busy kicking stones off the path.

"Anyway, we didn't always know we would have a test. A couple of them were surprises." Mo launched into a detailed account of the evaluation period.

Lesley only half listened, her mind on her parents. Her apprehension deepened when the *Thompson Estate* sign loomed ahead. By the time the house came into view, her dread was almost making it difficult to breathe. If she hadn't seen Mo's bag on Michael's back, she would have sworn it was on hers, along with her own and every other recruit's.

"Settle, boys," Susan said as they approached the front door. "Actually, you know what? Why don't you stay out here and play? Don't go far."

"Can we borrow a couple of bikes?" Andrew asked.

"If you can find two that fit," Lesley said.

"I'm taking Jason's," Nathan announced. He sprinted to the bike rack near the front door, Andrew hot on his heels. A tug-of-war ensued over Jason's blue bike.

"His older bike is still there. The other blue one," Lesley said to them as she opened the front door. She dropped her bag to the floor inside. The hallway was empty and the house quiet. For a split second, her mood lightened. Maybe they were out. But then she heard footsteps in the study. Mama appeared, followed by Papa.

"So, you're home." Mama's face tightened. "And the Middletons are with you."

Lesley could see Mo out of the corner of her eye and sensed Susan and Michael behind her.

Papa stood behind Mama and put his hands on her shoulders. "Did you pass?"

"Yes."

Awkward silence. Well, what had she expected, that they'd rush to her and tell her how proud they were, as Mo's parents had done?

Susan stepped into view. "Isn't it wonderful? Both our daughters will serve the Way in the military."

Mama and Papa stared at her.

"We're on our way to supper to celebrate. Why don't you join us?"

"Oh, I don't know," Mama said. "I have an early case tomorrow."

"We won't be out late."

"We have fresh salmon in for tonight."

"Well, do you mind if Lesley comes with us?" Susan said with exasperation. "It would be nice if you both came too, but if you don't want to, at least let Lesley."

"She stood up to a commander," Mo said. "You should be proud of her. She—" Mo broke off when Susan glanced back and motioned for her to be quiet.

"Stood up to a commander?" Papa said. "I'd like to hear that story."

"We can all hear it over supper," Michael said.

Papa nodded. "Why not?"

Mama whirled to face him. "Alan, the salmon—"

"We can have it tomorrow." He moved forward and reached for Lesley. "Congratulations."

Lesley hugged him, surprised and grateful. "Thank you," she managed to say. Mama hovered on the periphery of her vision. Lesley let Papa go and turned to Mama, holding out her arms in anticipation.

Mama turned away. "If we're going, let's go." She whipped her cloak off its hook.

Susan and Michael met Lesley's eyes. She quickly looked away, shamed by their pity. Mama left the house without a backward glance.

"You okay?" Mo murmured.

She nodded, determined not to let her dismay show.

"I'm proud of you," Papa said, patting her arm as he walked past to catch up with Mama. Susan and Michael followed him out.

Lesley pasted a smile on her face, took Mo's hand, and walked outside to join everyone. One day, Mama would be proud of her. One day, Mama would look back and realize how important today had been. One day.

TURNING EIGHTEEN

.....

MO STARED AT HER REFLECTION IN the dresser mirror and sighed. No matter how she looked, she'd have to endure the sympathetic glances of others when they thought her attention was elsewhere. If she showed up a mess, they'd also whisper that she was too depressed to care for herself. She picked up her comb.

"Mo!" Papa bellowed.

"Coming." She shoved the comb into her back pocket and went downstairs to join her parents. As soon as they were on the train, she'd excuse herself, go to the bathroom, and touch up her hair. She might fall apart at midnight, but she was determined to arrive tidy and composed.

"Finally," Papa said, already in his cloak. "What were you doing up there? Trying on every outfit in your closet?"

No, procrastinating. Usually she looked forward to a party, but she couldn't muster up any excitement over this one. Les, eighteen. Mo wished she could celebrate the milestone with her, but the entire day was a reminder of where her relationship with Les was going—or rather, not going. She grabbed her new cloak from its hook and shrugged it on.

Mama studied her. "It looks lovely. You outdid yourself this time, Michael."

Papa beamed and started to fuss, adjusting the cloak's collar and pulling down the sleeves, much to Mo's annoyance. "I'll have a light blue one soon," she said, stepping around him and heading out the door.

Mama and Papa followed her. "I know that," Papa said. "But I want you to look smart when you arrive at the Military Academy."

Mo managed a small smile for him. "I certainly will, in this."

Mama quickened her pace. "If we hurry, we can catch the five o'clock train."

"We don't want to be late for the supper," Papa said. "The meals at the Dance Hall are always tasty."

Mo wouldn't know. She'd only been to the Dance Hall once, and that eighteenth party hadn't included a proper sit-down meal. Rymellans under eighteen weren't admitted to the Dance Hall—private functions like Les's party were an exception. Now that Les was eighteen, would she want to spend all her free time at the Dance Hall, dancing the night away with other eighteen-year-olds?

"Any Solitary Notification yet?" Papa asked.

Mo perked up, all thoughts of Les leaving her behind forgotten.

"Not when I spoke to Adelaide an hour ago," Mama said. "They usually arrive by seven, don't they? Only a few hours to go."

Papa shook his head. "It can happen right up until midnight. Ten to twelve—that's what time the Solitary Notification arrived at an eighteenth I attended."

"That's late," Mama said, frowning.

Papa sniffed. "A family of half-wits. Nice enough, but none of them had two brain cells to rub together. Up to that point, all the children had received Solitary Notifications. I think a member of the Chosen Council must have realized that one was about to slip through and breed, and rushed a Solitary Notification over."

Mo rolled her eyes. "Papa, that can't be true. That's not the way it happens."

Papa ignored her. "And at another eighteenth, the military delivered the Solitary Notification, not a courier. What happened was that someone spotted the Chosen Council's courier and alerted the family. They figured that if they could dodge the courier until midnight had passed, the Solitary Notification wouldn't be valid."

"Were they related to the family of half-wits?" Mo asked.

"Eventually the courier contacted the military. They finally caught up with everyone around eleven-thirty and had to coax the young man out of a tree to hand him the Notification."

Mo snorted. "First of all, they would have activated his comm unit beacon, so it wouldn't have taken them long to find him. Second, they wouldn't have coaxed him down. They would have shaken him out of the tree and dragged him to an execution site. Article CT43." In accordance with the article, Les had sent a dispatch to the Chosen Council that detailed her expected whereabouts on her eighteenth birthday. Mo had watched her do it. *Mine will be easy. We'll be at the Military Academy,* she remembered saying.

"I must admit, when I saw that CT43 had been added to the Tradition, I wondered if it was because of what happened at that eighteenth," Papa said.

"What?" Mo shrieked.

"Don't listen to him," Mama said with a grin. "That article was in the Tradition when I did my Level Four, and he's younger than I am."

Mo nodded. "It's probably been there for centuries."

Papa let out an exaggerated sigh. "It was a lot more fun telling you stories when you were younger."

"Yeah, I'm sure it was." Mo paused. "Anyway, what's wrong with being a Solitary? You aren't disappointed with Mary and Matthew, are you?"

"Of course not," Mama said firmly.

"But it can be disappointing for the Solitary," Papa said. "No children, for one thing."

Mama stared at him, wide-eyed. "Better no children than children weak in the Way! You don't have to have children to serve the Way. Look at the Preeminent Ruler. He's a Solitary."

"I agree. I was just saying it can be disappointing for them when they first find out."

"Were Mary and Matthew disappointed?" Mo asked.

"Why don't you ask them?" Mama said. "They'll be at the Dance Hall."

"I just might," Mo said, despite knowing she wouldn't. She wasn't close to either of them. Funnily enough, she felt more comfortable with Neil, even though he was the oldest. Mary had never wanted her little sister around when their breaks from the Indoctrination Academy coincided, and Mo didn't have much in common with Matthew. Plus,

    DISOBEDIENCE MEANS DEATH

he never laughed at her jokes. How could she be close to someone who never laughed at her jokes?

"And don't worry. We won't be disappointed if you turn out to be a Solitary. Chosen, Solitary, as long as you serve the Way, it doesn't matter," Mama told her.

It mattered to Mo. She wanted to be whatever Les turned out to be. If they were both Chosens, she could cling to the minuscule possibility that they were each other's. She shouldn't, but she would. If they were both Solitaries, they couldn't have daughters, but they could choose to stay with each other for the rest of their lives. Nobody could split them up, not even the Chosen Council.

But if one of them turned out to be a Solitary and the other a Chosen . . . Mo's throat tightened. That would be it. Their relationship would be over. Staying together would be torture, and pointless, and stupid. Every look, every touch would remind them that they had no future. They'd try to be friends, end up acquaintances that only saw each other in class and on exercises, and request assignments on different ships upon graduation. And that downward spiral could begin in as little as five months, on her eighteenth birthday.

LESLEY WIPED HER mouth with her napkin and stole a look at Mo, sitting on the other side of the table, four chairs down. Usually they sat next to each other when the Thompsons and Middletons dined together, but doing so tonight, the night she'd know for sure if she was a Chosen or a Solitary, would have raised eyebrows. Considering how many Thompson relatives were in attendance, Mama seating the Middletons at the head table indicated how close the two families were. She could have placed them at one of the many tables assigned to family friends and acquaintances.

Suddenly Mo caught Lesley's eye and smiled, or tried to—she looked more pained than anything. Lesley smiled in return and shifted her attention back to her dessert.

". . . be okay."

"What?" Lesley said, turning to her right.

"I said, she'll be okay." Karen sipped her water. "I remember Derek's party. When everyone was clapping and cheering at midnight, I felt like crying my eyes out. But by the time my eighteenth rolled around, I was over him. I haven't spoken to him for a couple of years. I don't even know what he's doing."

"I heard he's apprenticing with Bradley Walker."

"See? You know more than I do. So don't worry about Mo. She'll have mixed feelings about you being a Chosen. You might, too. But your Chosen Papers are still a long way off."

"I could be a Solitary." Though she hoped she wasn't. She wanted children, and she didn't want Mama to have yet another reason to be disappointed with her. Few Thompsons had received Solitary Notifications.

"I doubt it. Your Notification would have arrived by now. It's not as if the Chosen Council met this morning to decide."

"It's not official until midnight."

"Well, when it's official, don't try to comfort Mo with a bunch of empty promises."

"Karen, I'm not stupid."

"Maybe not, but when it comes to Mo, you're too sensitive. So remember me and Derek. She'll get over it. So will you. You'll have moved on by the time you're twenty-five."

"You went on to college and Derek didn't," Lesley said indignantly. "Mo and I will both be at the Military Academy. We'll see each other every day."

"You won't break up as soon as you leave the Learning Academy, but you will eventually. You'll have to. So no empty promises, okay?"

"I wasn't planning on making any. Like I said, I'm not stupid." Lesley narrowed her eyes. "Did Mama put you up to this?"

Karen chuckled. "No! I'm older than you. I've been to more eighteenth parties."

"You're only four years older. Wait, now you're only three."

"Three and a half."

"Oh. Well, then."

"There's a big difference between eighteen and twenty-one," Karen told her.

They jumped when Mama leaned in between them. "Are you two talking about anything I should know about?"

"No," Karen said.

"Are you sure?"

"Yes."

Mama arched an eyebrow. "You see, I never used to worry when the two of you had your heads together. I never thought anything of it. But then you lied to us about the Military Academy entrance exam. I can't be complacent anymore."

"We're talking about eighteenth birthday parties, that's all," Karen said, her voice strained.

"Is that what you're talking about, Lesley?"

"Yes, Mama, that's what we're talking about."

Mama gave Lesley a long, hard look. "I guess I'll have to trust you. Don't make me regret it." She straightened and patted them both on the shoulder, then went back to her place.

"She'll never forgive us," Karen mumbled. She turned back to her cake.

Mama's intrusion had killed the conversation, probably what she'd intended. Lesley lifted a forkful of cake to her mouth, then almost dropped it when someone—it sounded like Susan—shrieked with laughter. Was Mo laughing, too? Lesley wanted to check, but Karen would think she couldn't keep her eyes off Mo. Instead, she focused on her plate.

Yes, tonight was awkward, and yes, she'd have mixed feelings at midnight. But her Chosen Papers were years away. When they arrived, she'd meet the woman the Chosen Council had selected—her ideal match, the woman she was meant to be with. Wouldn't that mean she'd eventually have stronger feelings for her Chosen than she'd ever had for Mo? And wouldn't the same thing happen for Mo and Mo's Chosen, assuming she had one? After all, the Chosen Council knew what it was doing. One look around the room was ample proof, along with the rarity of Chosen Violations.

So sure, when the clock struck midnight and it was official, she'd think of Mo. And yes, okay, she'd want to go to her, hug her. Not to make empty promises, but to show Mo that she understood that, for them, it was the beginning of the end and hardly something to celebrate. But she wouldn't. It would hurt not to, but she couldn't. Even though it may

not feel like it, tonight *was* something to celebrate. She had a Chosen!
Someone the Chosen Council had selected for her. Someone she'd love
and have daughters with and grow old with. Someone who would not
only please her, but please the Way. And someone more suited to her
than Mo. Hard to believe, considering how deeply she felt for Mo, but
the Chosen Council had the entire planet to choose from and didn't
make mistakes.

It did not make mistakes.

MO LET GO of Les and applauded the band. The musicians bowed, set
down their instruments, and left the stage. Seeing Alan, Adelaide, and
Karen bound up the steps, Mo nudged Les's arm. "Les, you better go,"
she said as Adelaide scanned the crowd. "It's two minutes to midnight.
They're looking for you."

Les touched Mo's cheek, then turned away. Mo's stomach churned as
she watched Les make her way to her family. They'd only managed two
dances together. Les, the guest of honour, had dutifully danced with
everyone who'd asked—all Solitaries or those not Joined, of course.
Three times, Mo had been on her way to suggest they dance, only to see
someone else get to Les first.

She'd resigned herself to standing on the sidelines while Les danced
with others, but then Les had sought her out at about ten-thirty. "I don't
know if we'll have another chance to dance before midnight," she'd said.
Mo had assumed they wouldn't, so she'd been surprised when Les had
tapped her on the shoulder at seven minutes to midnight and extended
her hand. She didn't know whether to read anything into it. Had Les
wanted them to have the last dance before midnight? Had it been her
way of saying good-bye? Had she meant to signal that tonight wouldn't
change anything, at least in the near future? Or had it been happenstance,
in that she'd suddenly found herself without a dance partner?

"I guess it's time for the big moment," Mama said behind her. Mo
glanced over her shoulder. Papa and her older siblings were there, too.
"Adelaide must be pleased," Mama continued. "She was hoping—"

Applause drowned her out. Les had made it onto the stage. Mo started
to clap, not wanting to look surly. She could hardly believe it: Les up on
that stage, a Chosen. She'd grown up with the Chosen Tradition, been

surrounded by it from the moment she was born. But it had never felt
as real as it did tonight.

Alan raised his hand to quiet everyone and gazed at his comm unit,
waiting for the right moment to begin the countdown. If Les had been
a Solitary, they would have thanked everyone for coming and the dancing would have resumed. But she wasn't.

"Ten, nine, eight," Alan started. Everyone joined in, their voices
growing louder with each second. "Two, one . . ."

The room exploded into another round of applause. Mo joined in,
feeling insincere and self-conscious. Was everyone looking at her?
Because they all knew what it meant, and they knew she did, too. Well,
let them cluck their tongues in sympathy. She'd hold her head up and
show them how strong in the Way she was.

Suddenly Mama's arm was around her shoulders. Mo leaned into her,
grateful. It was a good thing Andrew and Nathan were at the Indoctrination Academy, or they'd probably be laughing at her right now.

Les embraced each of her parents and then hugged Karen. The four
Thompsons waited for the applause to die down. Then Adelaide stepped
up to the microphone. "So, you're a Chosen," she said to Les, smiling
broadly.

More applause. Mama's arm left Mo's shoulders. Mo didn't know
how much more she could take. She focused on Les, but couldn't tell if
Les was happy, embarrassed—what?

Adelaide moved aside; Les took her place. Mo inwardly cringed. Les
would do exactly what was expected of her. She'd beam at everyone and
babble on about how wonderful it was to be a Chosen and how much she
looked forward to receiving her Chosen Papers. Mo wanted to bury her
face in Mama's shoulder and cover her ears. But that would be cowardly.
She'd continue to hold her head high. Anyone who glanced her way would
see her looking directly at Les, not clinging to Mama for support.

"Yes, I'm a Chosen," Les began.

Mo felt for Mama's hand and hung onto it. A little covert support
wouldn't hurt.

"As the Song of Rymel says, 'We are Rymellan and always shall be.
We are one, Chosen and Solitary.'"

Okay, this was different.

"It wouldn't have mattered if I had turned out to be a Solitary. All that matters is that we serve the Way. And I have never had a greater appreciation of what it means to serve the Way than I do right now."

Much to her amazement, Mo agreed with everything Les was saying.

"As all Rymellans do, I trust the Chosen Council. I know the Chosen Council has selected the best woman for me, for my family, for all of us."

Mo tightened her grip on Mama's hand. *Here it comes.*

"And as all Rymellans do, I will embrace my Chosen, Join with her, and serve the Way." Les paused. "I won't hold up the dancing any longer," she said, to Mo's surprise. "Thank you very much for coming and celebrating my eighteenth with me. Let's say the *Words Every Rymellan Knows.*"

Still holding Mama's hand, Mo reached for Neil's. She was slightly bewildered; Les hadn't gone on and on about how wonderful her Chosen must be and how much she looked forward to meeting her. That suited Mo just fine, but what would others think about Les's atypical eighteenth speech?

Les, having formed a circle with her parents and Karen, waited until a few in the room had finished clearing their throats, then nodded. "Disobedience means death. Death to those who commit a Chosen Violation. Death to those who disobey. Death to those who violate the Way. Death to those who violate the Way. Death to those who violate the Way!" Everyone let go of their neighbours' hands and clapped.

The band was waiting to take the stage again. Les followed her family down the steps only to be swallowed in a crowd of well-wishers. Mo craned her neck to see her as the musicians settled into their places on the stage and picked up their instruments.

"We should dance," Papa said to Mama when the band immediately launched into the next piece.

"Will you be all right?" Mama asked Mo.

Mo nodded. "I'll get a drink or something." Mary and Matthew brushed by her, on their way to the dance floor, she presumed.

"I'll go with you," Neil said.

Apparently satisfied that Mo wouldn't dissolve into tears and that

Neil would take care of her if she did, Mama accepted Papa's arm. They disappeared into the crowd.

Neil eyed her sympathetically. "If it helps, I felt the same way at Catherine's eighteenth."

It didn't, but she loved him for saying it. "Whatever happened to her?" she asked as they manoeuvred toward one of the refreshment tables. "When I entered the Indoctrination Academy for my Level Three, you two were inseparable. By the time I left, it was as if she'd never existed."

"She was going to college and I wasn't. Since we'd be living sectors apart, we decided it was a good time to end our relationship."

"Just because you wouldn't be living on each other's doorstep? You really cared about each other."

"And had Chosens waiting for us. We could have made the effort to see each other, but why?" He patted Mo's shoulder. "You and Lesley will do the same thing. After the Military Academy, you'll go your separate ways. You'll see."

Mo didn't know what to say. To agree would be lying, but to disagree would be weak in the Way.

Lucy Benton planted herself in their path, forcing them to stop. "Neil, there you are. Do you want to dance?"

"Um . . ." He turned to Mo.

"Go ahead," Mo said, relieved. "I don't mind. I'll be fine."

"Well, let's go, then." Benton grabbed Neil's arm and pulled him toward the dance floor. Neil looked back at Mo and pulled a face.

Any other night, Mo would have laughed, but she stood stone-faced until she couldn't see them anymore and then continued on to the refreshment table. Several punch bowls and an assortment of dessert trays awaited her. She'd come for a drink, but now that she was here . . . She picked up a plate from the stack and added a chocolate cupcake to it.

"I'm surprised it ended so quickly," Mo overheard a man say as she slid a piece of lemon cake onto her plate.

"I wasn't surprised at all," a woman said. "I would have been more surprised if she'd stood up there and gushed. Lesley's not like other girls, you know."

"Oh, I know. Very serious, that one."

"Precisely. She's very strong in the Way, and it was the Way she wanted to talk about."

"That's true. I . . ." The voice faded.

Mo resisted the urge to glance over her shoulder. Whoever it was had already moved away. A platter of cookies caught her eye. One or two wouldn't hurt. She added four to her plate and decided she better find somewhere to sit before other goodies called out to her.

"Excuse me," she murmured to a man next to her, one of Les's great-uncles, she thought. Up ahead, two of her classmates watched the dance floor. Everyone knew Steven and Roberta had crushes on each other—maybe one of them would pluck up the courage to ask the other to dance before the party ended. Mo reversed direction and skirted around them. She'd only be in the way.

A couple of empty chairs stood at a nearby table. Mo nodded to the Johnsons, who lived several estates west of the Middleton and Thompson estates, and sat down.

Caroline Johnson's eyes widened. "Are you sure you'll be able to manage all that?"

"Do you want a cookie?" Mo asked, pushing her plate toward Caroline.

"At this hour? No, thank you."

"I'll have one," said Sandra, one of the Johnson daughters.

"Go ahead," Mo said.

Sandra smiled shyly and selected a cookie from the plate.

"What do you say?" Elaine Johnson asked.

"Thank you."

Elaine nodded. "Good. Now, after you've finished that, it's time to go."

The three daughters groaned in unison. Caroline and Elaine had five, but two were at the Indoctrination Academy.

"Can't we stay a bit longer?" Anna asked.

"No."

Anna looked at her other mama. Caroline shook her head. "We said we'd stay until midnight. So come on, time to go."

"We should say good-bye to Lesley," Anna said.

"We already did that." Caroline shifted her attention to Mo. "I hope you don't think we're running out on you. But I'd told them five more minutes just before you sat down."

"No, no, don't worry about it." Mo didn't need company to eat and feel sorry for herself.

"Well, good-bye, then. Say hello to your parents. Tell your mama I'll pop around next week with the seeds I promised her."

"I will."

After they'd gone, Mo shoved a forkful of cake into her mouth and looked around the hall to see how many people were still there. Okay, who was she kidding? Where was Les, that was what she wanted to know. Les wasn't near the stage. Perhaps back at the head table? Mo leaned to her left to see if she could catch a glimpse. Nope, Les wasn't there. Maybe on the dance floor? She couldn't see it through the crowd. She sliced off another mouthful of cake, lifted it to her mouth, and froze. There was Les, walking right toward her! She smiled and lowered her fork.

Les abruptly stopped, then stepped forward, then pivoted to her right and darted between two groups of Rymellans. Mo stared after her in disbelief. So that was the way it was going to be from now on, was it? If she had any sense, she'd break it off right now. After all, as of today, she was only the stand-in until the Chosen Council handed Les the real thing, the woman with whom Les would Join. So why bother?

Mo repeatedly jabbed her fork into the remaining cake, reducing it to a crushed mess. *Forget the cake.* She put the fork down and picked up a cookie. The problem, she thought as she took a bite, was that she'd already made the mistake of breaking up with Les when she hadn't really wanted to. They were still young; there would be plenty of time for them to break up later. For now, they were together—or at least she hoped they were.

And now she knew what she wanted to happen on her eighteenth. She wanted to be a Chosen. Desperately. It was her and Les's only chance. If she received a Solitary Notification, she would . . . their relationship . . . their relationship wouldn't survive past midnight. As much as she loved Les, she couldn't stay with her, knowing they were doomed. How could they ever laugh with each other again?

Nope, the only solace a Solitary Notification would offer was that she wouldn't be forced into a relationship with someone else. Because she didn't think she could love anyone other than Les. Not even her Chosen. And that meant she was weak in the Way.

Mo swallowed the last bit of cookie and stared at the two couples sitting a table over. She'd always taken for granted that Joined couples were happy and loved each other, but now she wondered if some Chosens were going through the motions, living in quiet despair while praising the Chosen Council for its wisdom. She shivered and grabbed another cookie from the plate. If any of the military on-duty at the party knew what she was thinking, they'd probably drag her back to the Indoctrination Academy for a refresher stay. Not only would that be horribly embarrassing, since she'd completed her Level Five within the past year, but she'd have to forget about the Military Academy.

She couldn't be the only Rymellan who'd felt this way, though—worried about her future, her Chosen Papers, her life; hopelessly in love with someone and unable to imagine being happy with anyone else. But given how few Chosen Violations were committed—only the Adams Incident in the past thirty years—the Chosen Tradition obviously worked. She had to be stronger, trust the Way, expect all her doubts to be swept away when her Chosen Papers arrived and she met her Chosen.

Mo shook her head. She was assuming she was a Chosen, and for the wrong reason.

"What are you talking to yourself about?"

Mo jumped, and twisted to look behind her.

"Sorry, I didn't mean to scare you." Les rounded the chair so Mo could see her without straining her neck. "And I'm sorry about before. I don't know why I did that." Les looked past Mo for a second, then refocused on her. "I don't know, it's awkward. I just want it to be over."

"Want what to be over?" Mo asked, her heart pounding.

"The party."

"Oh."

Les held out her hand. "Would you like to dance?"

"Yes. I would."

"Then let's dance."

Mo took Les's hand and did her best to smile at her. Some girl out there was the luckiest girl on the planet, and she didn't even know it.

Was it so wrong to want to be a Chosen so she could keep the tiniest shred of hope alive that the luckiest girl was her?

She squeezed Les's hand when they walked onto the dance floor and hugged her before they got into position and fell into step with the couples whirling around them. But despite being in Les's arms, she felt unsettled and scared. Her relationship with Les, her entire life, could be shattered on her eighteenth birthday. She wished she could know right now what the Chosen Council had decided for her, but she'd have to wait. The next five months were going to be the longest five months of her life.

Five Months Later

MO OPENED HER eyes to darkness and inwardly groaned—she'd woken up early, yet again. She thrust her arm out from under the blanket and groped around on the nightstand for her comm unit. Her fingertips brushed against it, but she couldn't quite grasp it. She slid closer to the edge of the bed and reached out . . . and it fell off the nightstand and thudded onto the floor. A pencil rolled off after it. Mo froze and listened. Kary's breathing was still rhythmic. Good; she hadn't woken. Kary always slept soundly, falling fast asleep moments after lights out and never waking until her comm unit sounded her morning alarm. Mo envied her.

She slipped out of bed and picked up her comm unit. Its illuminated display read 06:12. Great. Her first class was at 08:30. Shivering as goose bumps rose on her arms and back, she ducked back under the blanket and closed her eyes, hoping to grab another hour's sleep. But it was no use. Today was the day she'd dreaded and the day that couldn't have arrived fast enough. Today could turn out to be the worst day of her life. Today she'd find out if she was a Chosen. And today she'd have to do what she'd done on most days for the past month—operate on barely six hours of sleep.

Figuring she might as well get up, Mo slipped out of bed again. She scooped her sneakers from the mat near the door and grabbed her track suit from the back of a chair. In the bathroom, she pulled the suit on over her pyjamas. Nobody had noticed her odd attire so far—but then, not many jogged at the crack of dawn.

She left the room and crept down the corridor to the stairs that led to the first floor and the dormitory's exit. She'd expected to be assigned a bed in one of the barracks, a notion that had earned an incredulous look from the admitting lieutenant and the admonition, "The barracks? Those are temporary lodgings, for potential recruits or Defence members on leave or visiting students from other academies. They're not for you, Cadet!"

Sharing a room with Les would be ideal, and they'd discovered that they could request each other as roommates for their second year. But neither had pushed the other to fill out the form, even though the earlier they submitted the request, the greater the chance it would be fulfilled. Mo knew why they were stalling. If she received a Solitary Notification today, there wouldn't be any point in sharing a room. They might as well volunteer to be targets when the cadets practised shooting to wound with live weapons. It would be less painful.

As soon as she was outside, she broke into a jog, too keyed up to stretch. Jogging was okay. Flat-out running would earn her a strike. She'd wait until she reached the track before trying to outrun her fears.

"Cadet," barked a passing lieutenant, obviously in a hurry to get to her post.

"Morning, Lieutenant Dunnigan," Mo replied, then stopped and looked over her shoulder. Was that her? Was that Les's Chosen? Her hands balled into fists. Today would be stressful enough without playing the *Is that Les's Chosen?* game, a game she played much too often. And anyway, Dunnigan must be at least twenty-six or twenty-seven, too old to be Les's Chosen. At most, Les's Chosen would be twenty-three, maybe twenty-four, depending on when her birthday was. So Dunnigan couldn't possibly—

Mo sighed. She was doing it again. Some days she hardly thought about it; other days it constantly occupied her mind. Worse, the shadowy figure who would eventually take Les away from her lurked in the background whenever she and Les were together. Sometimes Mo felt as if she was in a relationship with two other people.

She resumed her jog, and picked up the pace the moment her sneakers hit the track. Her poor body was running on nervous energy. Something had to give, and soon. Her studies would suffer and her health would fail unless she calmed down. The only reason she'd wanted this day to arrive quickly was because it would settle the uncertainty around her and Les's relationship—permanently, if she was a Solitary; for at least seven years, if she was a Chosen. Ha! As if they'd still be together in seven years. A lot could happen between now and then, and for the millionth time, she told herself to worry only about today, not tomorrow. Hey, she was eighteen today. Eighteen! But who flaming cared if she lost Les?

LESLEY SHIFTED THE warm bag to her left hand and tapped on Mo's room door. She waited. Nothing. Mo probably had her comm unit set to wake her at 08:00, just enough time for her to quickly shower, dress, and make it to her first class, albeit on an empty stomach. Well, not this morning. Lesley knocked again, a little louder this time, and strained to hear movement within. A faint thump, then shuffling toward the door. It opened a crack.

"Oh, hi." Kary swung the door open and smothered a yawn.

"Did I wake you?"

"What time is it?" she murmured, her eyes barely open.

"Just after 07:00."

"Well, yeah, you did, but my alarm would have gone off in ten minutes anyway."

"Sorry."

Kary yawned again. "Doesn't matter." She sniffed. "Do I smell eggs and, um, hash browns?"

Lesley smiled. "I thought I'd surprise Mo with breakfast today."

"Oh." Kary glanced back into the room. "She's not back from her morning jog."

What morning jog? "I figured she'd be back by now," Lesley said, making the effort to speak evenly.

"I'm sure she'll be back soon." Kary stepped back from the door. "So come on in."

"Thanks." She walked into the room and took in the tangled bedclothes lying in a heap on Mo's empty bed. Since when had Mo jogged in the mornings, and why hadn't she mentioned it?

"She'll kick herself for missing breakfast in bed," Kary said, opening a drawer and rummaging through it.

"I brought breakfast for you, too. But I wasn't sure what you like." Lesley opened the bag and carefully lifted out a covered plate of eggs, hash browns, and toast. "If you don't want it, that's okay."

"Want it?" Kary dropped a pair of pants onto her bed and eagerly accepted the plate. "Of course I want it. Thanks. It was sweet of you to think of me."

Lesley handed her a knife and fork. "I have tziva, too. Do you want some?"

"Argamon, if I was same-oriented, Mo would have a problem," Kary said, grinning. "But no, thank you. I'm fine."

Lesley rolled the bag shut, set it on Mo's nightstand, and moved a pile of folded clothes from the nearby chair to the bed so she could sit down. Kary perched herself on the edge of her bed and balanced the plate on her lap. They stared at each other. "Go ahead and eat," Lesley said. "Mo could be a while."

"If you don't mind." Kary lifted the steamed cover from the plate and set it face-up next to her. She tucked in. "Everything set for the party tonight?" she asked around a mouthful of food.

Lesley nodded. "Try to be there by 19:45 at the latest."

"Does she suspect anything?"

"I don't think so." Lesley paused. "So she's been jogging for a while, hasn't she? When she first started, I didn't think she'd keep it up."

"Me either. I mean, you know how much Mo loves her sleep. Never thought I'd see her getting up every morning at dawn."

Neither did Lesley.

Kary gestured with her fork. "But she's having problems sleeping."

Lesley nodded.

"I tried to talk to her about it, but she brushed me off. I've wondered if her eighteenth has anything—"

The door opened. Mo walked in, red-faced, her hair plastered to her head. She gaped at Lesley. "What are you doing here?"

"I brought you breakfast," Lesley said, standing. "It's your—"

"Have you heard of a flaming comm unit?" Mo slammed the door shut. "You couldn't beep me to let me know you were coming over?

Maybe I don't want breakfast. Maybe you could show a little more consideration."

Lesley stared at her in shock.

"I think I'll hop in the shower," Kary said, flipping the cover back over her plate. "This'll still be warm when I'm finished." She gathered her clothes, glanced at Mo and Lesley, and hurried into the bathroom.

Mo threw up her arms. "Great. Now I can't get a towel." She snatched a shirt from the pile on her bed and wiped her face with it. "And I was hoping to shower as soon as I got back. Now I'll have to wait. Because *you* woke her up." She flung the shirt onto the bed.

Lesley bit back a retort and waited until she could hear the shower running before speaking. "I wanted to surprise you with breakfast. I didn't think you'd mind."

"I don't feel like breakfast," Mo mumbled.

"I have eggs and hash browns. And toast. I even threw in a couple of blueberry waffles."

"Blueberry waffles?" Mo said, her face softening. "You hate eating blueberry waffles in the morning."

"You don't."

Mo's shoulders slumped. "I'm sorry. I don't know what's wrong with me. I can't believe I yelled at you for bringing me breakfast. I just . . . I didn't expect you to be here."

"You didn't want me to know you've been getting up early." Lesley wanted to hug her, but didn't know if she'd receive a hug or a slap in the face in return. She lowered herself into the chair so she wouldn't tower over Mo. "Kary said you're having a problem sleeping."

"Kary's got a big mouth," Mo muttered.

"What's bothering—"

"You know, we should eat that breakfast before it gets cold." Mo stepped toward Lesley, hesitated, then held out her arms.

Lesley pulled Mo onto her lap and held her tight. She'd let Mo get away with diverting the conversation—for now.

Mo pulled back. "I shouldn't have done that. I'm all sweaty."

"If you hadn't done it, I would have, given that irresistible outfit you're wearing."

Mo looked down at herself. "I didn't want to wake Kary up. And nobody ever notices."

"I noticed," Lesley said, caressing Mo's cheek with her thumb. She'd also noticed that Mo had been quieter than usual lately, and the dark half-moons under Mo's eyes. But she hadn't thought anything of it. Everyone was tired—their busy schedules didn't allow much time for relaxation. When they weren't in class or participating in practical exercises, they were doing homework or getting to know the other cadets. Privacy and time alone were at a premium. Everyone looked a little ragged these days, but adjusting to the Military Academy apparently wasn't the only reason behind Mo's fatigue. Kary had mentioned Mo's eighteenth. Lesley knew eighteenth birthdays could be stressful, but why hadn't Mo talked about it? She wasn't the type to keep things bottled up.

"Let's eat," Mo said, breaking into Lesley's thoughts. "I definitely have to shower and change before going to class." She moved from Lesley's lap to her bed.

Lesley unrolled the top of the bag and lifted out one of the two remaining breakfasts. "Move your stuff so we can use the nightstand."

Mo slid the nightstand's top drawer open, scooped two pencils, several scribbled sheets of paper, and what looked like a half-eaten cookie into it, and pushed it shut. Lesley opened her mouth to make a crack, then closed it. *Not this morning.* She focused on emptying the bag, transforming the nightstand into a tiny table for two, although it was barely able to handle two breakfast plates, a jug of tziva and two mugs, and the cutlery and napkins. The two blueberry waffles ended up in Lesley's upturned plate cover, next to Mo on the bed. If they weren't careful, the tziva would end up on the bed, too. She lifted the cover from Mo's plate with a flourish and dropped it into the bag, now resting on the floor.

"Thank you," Mo said with a small smile.

"When will your parents be here?" Lesley asked when they were halfway through the eggs and hash browns. She hoped Mo would eat both waffles, but she'd force one down if she had to.

"I told them to come on the 16:20 train. I'll just have time to meet them and show them my room before my last class. They said they'd

   DISOBEDIENCE MEANS DEATH

walk around until supper." She gulped down some tziva. "I could have told them to arrive on the 17:50, but I didn't want to meet them and then rush them to the mess hall."

"And they'll probably want to present you with your gift in private."

"They'll have time for that after supper."

Lesley smiled to herself. They wouldn't, but Mo didn't know that. Mo picked up a waffle and bit into it. They lapsed into silence again.

"I hope I'm a Chosen," Mo suddenly said. "Mama and Papa said it doesn't matter one way or the other, but three Solitaries in a row would be a bit much." She paused. "Do you think it would be better for me to be a Chosen?"

The question took Lesley by surprise. "Of course I do."

"Why?" Mo asked, staring at her plate.

The bathroom door opened. Kary emerged, rubbing her wet hair with a towel. "All done," she announced. "And I think I'll finish my breakfast in the kitchen."

"You don't have to," Lesley said.

"I have to finish the assignment for my first class. I need to think."

"Kary, I'm sorry about before," Mo said. "I'm an idiot."

"Well, you certainly didn't react the way I would have reacted to breakfast in bed. But I wouldn't say you're an idiot. Insane, maybe?" She bent down and examined herself in the mirror standing on her nightstand, then straightened. "Anyway, you two sorted it out, I take it?"

They nodded.

"Good. Be back in a sec." Kary disappeared into the bathroom again and returned a minute later without the towel, her hair combed. "Happy eighteenth, Mo. Lunch?" She picked up her half-eaten breakfast.

Mo glanced at Lesley.

"I have my flute lesson, remember?" Lesley said.

"Right. Sure, Kary."

"See you around 12:30, then. Bye." Kary slung her knapsack over her shoulder and left.

"I'm glad she's not mad at me," Mo said. "She's a good roommate."

"Do you want the other waffle?" Lesley asked.

"Oh, no, you have it." Mo held it out to Lesley, who forced a smile and reached for it. "But if you don't want it, I'll have it."

"It *is* your birthday," Lesley said, snatching her hand back.

Mo grinned. "So you want me to be a Chosen?"

"Yes."

"Because?"

"You want children, don't you?"

"Yeah." She chewed a mouthful of waffle and stared at Lesley.

Lesley's heart sank. Perhaps Mo wanted her to say they could be each other's Chosen? They could be, but what were the chances? They'd be setting themselves up for a huge disappointment if they allowed themselves to believe they were Chosens. Not only that, they had to trust the Chosen Council. Whenever Lesley considered, even for an instant, what it would be like to spend the rest of her life with Mo, she reminded herself that the Chosen Council had already selected her best match. Her feelings for Mo were strong, so imagine how she'd feel about her Chosen? Well, she couldn't imagine it; she just knew it would be wonderful, beyond anything she'd ever felt before.

It would be best to stop any silly fantasies in their tracks. That was what Mo should be doing, and what Lesley was confident Mo would do. Once they—once Mo was well past her eighteenth, she'd forget about the Chosen Council for a while. And perhaps sleep a little better? Was that what it was all about? Then it was definitely best not to encourage any hopes Mo might be harbouring about them being Chosens. They weren't. Even though they lo—cared about each other.

"I want you to be happy," Lesley said. "I see you with a big family and a Chosen you love. I don't think you'd be happy being a Solitary."

"Is that what'll make you happy, Les? A big family and a Chosen you love?" Mo asked softly.

Lesley swallowed. "Yes."

Mo blinked rapidly and looked away.

"The Chosen Council knows what it's doing." Lesley reached out and squeezed Mo's fingers, then gently held onto them.

Mo pulled her hand away. She bit off another piece of waffle and slowly chewed it, but then dropped the waffle to her plate. "I think I've had enough. You want the rest?"

Lesley shook her head. Suddenly her breakfast wasn't sitting right. Eating blueberry waffle would be risky.

"I guess I should get into the shower."

"I can wait, if you want. We can walk to class together."

Mo stood. "No, that's okay. I'll feel rushed if I know you're waiting." She turned her back and started to sort through the pile of clothes on the bed.

Sensing that Mo didn't want to chat, Lesley gathered up the dirty dishes and napkins and returned them to the bag. She hesitated, then pressed herself against Mo's back and wrapped her arms around her. "See you in class?"

Mo nodded.

She kissed the top of Mo's head and searched for something reassuring to say. But there wasn't anything. Nothing Mo would want to hear, anyway. "Enjoy your shower." She forced herself to let Mo go, picked up the bag, and headed for the door.

"Les?"

She turned.

Mo met her eyes. "Thanks for breakfast." She shifted her attention back to the shirt she held, her face tight.

"Sure." Lesley stepped into the hallway and shut the door behind her. Halfway to the stairs, she stopped. Maybe she should go back, tell Mo she understood how difficult today was and how it would be nice if they did turn out to be— No! She wasn't weak in the Way. She trusted the Chosen Council, and so should Mo. Lesley squared her shoulders and continued walking.

MO SAT PARALYZED at the desk, one of her knapsack's straps in her hand. Fellow cadets rushed by, eager to leave the stuffy classroom. She should get moving, too—Mama and Papa's train would arrive in ten minutes. But a courier from the Chosen Council could be waiting for her in the corridor, waiting to hand her a Solitary Notification.

Her hand tightened around the strap. She willed herself to stand. That morning, it hadn't been so hard, not after Les had practically said she didn't care one way or another if they were Chosens. But as the day had worn on, Mo had forgiven her. What else could Les have said? That whole part of the conversation had been stupid. She should have known better than to put Les on the spot and expect her to thumb her nose at the Chosen Council. Too bad they hadn't had much of a chance to talk during their three classes together. Then again, what would they have said?

Mo slipped her arms through the knapsack's straps and fell into step behind another cadet. As she left the classroom, she walked as close to him as she could without risking a strike for harassment. For once she was glad she was short. A courier scanning for her could easily miss her. But what good would that do? She was acting like those supposed half-wits in Papa's story. She couldn't escape the Chosen Council's will. Nobody could, if they wanted to live.

She stopped. A Rymellan was coming toward her, a man she didn't recognize. He didn't look like an instructor, didn't have a knapsack or books, didn't seem familiar with the layout of the building. Her heart pounded. She couldn't breathe. Everything around her looked distorted, except the man—the man a few feet away from her, closing fast. She clawed at her throat to assure herself that it wasn't really collapsing and stared at him in horror.

He strode past, not even glancing at her.

She scurried away, not caring where she went. Somehow, she made it outside. She sucked in air until her senses returned to normal and her brain started to work again, the brain that had seized up the moment she'd spotted the stranger. Of course he hadn't been a Chosen Council courier. They wore gold cloaks—his had been green. Wait! She frantically scanned the crowded courtyard for gold cloaks, ready to duck back into the building if she saw one.

Her eyes welled up, making it impossible to see clearly. No, she wouldn't cry. Not here, in front of everyone. But Argamon, she was tired, and frustrated, and fed up with feeling scared all the time. Maybe it would be better if she did receive a Solitary Notification. If she was having such a hard time coping with today, how would she cope if she and Les were still together when they turned twenty-five, when their Chosen Papers could arrive at any time? Every day would be like today. Every flaming day!

"You all right, Mo?"

Mo turned toward the voice. Bruce, a member of her study group, peered at her. "You look lost."

 DISOBEDIENCE MEANS DEATH

"No, I was just wondering if I have time to drop off my bag before
I go meet my parents." She made a show of checking the time on her
comm unit. "But I don't think I do. I'll see you in class."

"Yeah, sure. See you in a bit." He strolled off.

Mo hustled to the train station and dashed down to the platform,
arriving as the train pulled in. The doors slid open. The number of dis-
embarking passengers in orange and light blue cloaks made it easy to
spot her parents. Despite her mood, she smiled and waved.

Mama waved enthusiastically and made a beeline for her. "Happy
birthday!" She held out her arms.

Mo clung to her, struggling to control herself. At least now she
wasn't alone. If a Solitary Notification arrived, she'd have Mama's
shoulder to cry on. And Papa's. He enveloped her in a hug as soon as
Mama let go of her.

"You look tired," Mama said, studying her.

"I was up early . . . preparing for class."

"Have you lost weight?"

Papa touched Mama's arm. "Stop fussing."

"We should head over to my room," Mo said, half because it was
true and half because she wanted to distract Mama. "I have a class in
twenty-five minutes."

"Lead the way," Papa said.

"You're dressed normally," Mama said as they climbed the stairs to
the waiting area.

"What do you mean?" Mo asked.

"You're not wearing a uniform. Or your cadet cloak."

"We only have to wear our cloaks when we leave the academy," Mo said.
"And we don't get uniforms until our second year, after we've chosen our
division." She figured they didn't want to waste time sewing uniforms
for first-year students, when thirty percent of cadets failed their first
year and were ejected from the academy. "To be honest, I feel like I'm
still at the Learning Academy, except I live here."

"That sounds more like the Indoctrination Academy," Papa said.

"Yeah, maybe." She spent most of her time sitting at a desk, as she
had at the Learning Academy, but the courses had a narrow focus, like
the Indoctrination Academy. She also had scheduled physical exercise

and practical sessions, like weapons training and combat manoeuvres. Okay, the Indoctrination Academy won.

They crossed the courtyard and came to a crossroads; Mo veered to the right. "I didn't expect the academy to be so big," Mama said.

"It's huge. I doubt I've seen all of it. But the dormitory isn't far." Mo walked faster—she didn't want to have to race off to class the moment they entered her room. "I'm on the second floor," she told them as she pulled open the dormitory's main door. A minute later, she ushered her parents into her current home with a sweep of her arm. "Here we are."

Mama glanced around the small room and placed her hands on her hips. "Are you sure this is your room? Look how neatly those clothes are folded. I didn't know you could fold clothes. Did you know she could fold clothes, Michael?"

"Mama!"

"I know your room had to be tidy at the Indoctrination Academy, and you're managing to keep it tidy here. Why can't you do that when you're at home?"

Because there weren't spot checks at home. An untidy room wouldn't lead to a black mark on her military record or a rod across her back. Mama and Papa would tut and nag and eventually ground her until she cleaned her room, but that was it.

Papa laid his hand on Mo's shoulder. "The important thing is that her room here is neat. We can talk about her room at home next time she's home. She's a big girl now, and a busy one. So let's get on with it."

Mama gave Papa a long look, then reached into her inner cloak pocket and pulled out an envelope. "This is from Papa and me. Happy eighteenth." She held out the envelope, her eyes bright. "I can't believe you're eighteen already."

Mo accepted the envelope and opened it. She had a good idea of what it would contain—a deposit into her trade account. No more allowances for her. She slid out a sheet of paper and unfolded it. Her eyes bulged. "Are you sure there isn't an extra zero on the end?"

Papa leaned over her shoulder and read the amount. "Positive," he said gruffly.

"I don't know what to say. This is very generous." Generous? She could never earn a credit in her life and still die with a healthy balance. "Thank you." Mo reached for them.

"There should be another sheet," Mama said. "Underneath?"

Mo took a closer look. There was. She flipped to the second paper and read it, then looked at her parents in confusion. "This is a land deed." Land was usually presented the day before meeting with the Chosen Council, and only to Principals. "But I may not be the Principal. I may even be a Solitary."

"We said being a Solitary didn't matter, and we meant it," Mama said. "We did the same with Neil, Mary, and Matthew on their eighteenths. We know it's not customary, but it's only a small piece of land, barely enough to build a house. If you turn out to be the Principal of your Joining, we'll give you more."

"We just wanted to make sure you know that you can always come home," Papa said.

Overcome, Mo launched herself into his arms. Her cheeks felt wet, but she didn't care. As long as she had Mama and Papa, maybe, just maybe, she'd get through the next few years and learn to cope with losing Les without losing herself. "I love you. Thank you so much," she managed to say.

Papa cleared his throat. Mo let go of him and reached for Mama. "And you, too, Mama."

"I love you, too," Mama murmured, hugging her.

Mo sighed and drew back. "I know what I'm going to do with some of these credits."

"What?"

She wiped her nose on her sleeve before replying. "Take aviacraft lessons."

"Aviacraft lessons?" Papa exclaimed. "Why would you want to do that?"

Mo gave him a withering look. "Because I want to be a fighter pilot. Les figures knowing how to fly an aviacraft could give us an edge when we apply for the pilot program."

Mama raised her eyebrows. "Lesley plans to take lessons too? Does Adelaide know?"

Probably not. "I don't know. I mean, we've only talked about it a couple of times. We were waiting until I'm old enough to get a licence before seriously looking into it."

"And until you had enough credits?" Papa said.

Mo flushed. "Well, yeah, that too." Along with waiting to see if they still had a relationship; the same reason they hadn't rushed to request the same room, though neither of them had ever said that out loud.

Mama frowned. "Adelaide's still holding out hope that Lesley will switch to advocacy."

"I doubt that'll happen." Les seemed content at the academy. She hadn't mentioned advocacy once.

Someone knocked at the door. Mo tensed. Blood pounded in her ears. Fortunately, her apprehension was short-lived—the door opened and Kary peered into the room. "It's just me. I hope I'm not interrupting anything."

"No, come in, come in," Mo said, resisting the urge to run over and hug her. "These are my parents, er, Michael and Susan." Calling them by their first names never felt right, and probably never would. "And this is Kary, my roommate."

Kary nodded at them; they nodded in return. "Mo mentions you a lot," Mama said.

"She talks a lot about you, too." Kary stepped into the room. "I wasn't sure I'd get the chance to meet you later. I knew Mo was planning to bring you here before her class, so—"

"Flaming Argamon!" Mo checked her comm unit. "I forgot about my class. I have to go. I'll meet you back here in an hour." But then she hesitated. Running out on her parents would be rude, especially given their generosity. Then again, Lieutenant Bailey would have a fit if she was even a minute late—he didn't suffer latecomers very well. "Sorry, but I have to go now." She looked around for her knapsack, realized it was still on her back, and headed for the door. Oh, but— "Wait! I have to sign you in. You need a pass to wander on your own." Her shoulders sagged. "I'll be late for class."

"We'll stay here until you get back," Mama said. "Don't worry about us."

Kary shook her head. "I'll sign you in."

"You sure?" Mo said, trying not to sound too eager.

    DISOBEDIENCE MEANS DEATH

"Positive. I'm done for the day. Now go, before Bailey pops a blood vessel." She shooed Mo out the door.

MO CAUGHT LES sneaking a look at her comm unit and quelled her irritation with difficulty. That was the third time. If Les was bored, she should excuse herself. Sitting with Mama and Papa wasn't the most exciting thing they could be doing, but it wouldn't kill Les to pretend she was interested.

"It's much quieter now." Mama sipped her tziva. "I could hardly hear myself think earlier."

"We could have eaten in my room," Mo said.

"Oh, no, we wanted the mess hall experience," Papa said. "And it gave us a chance to meet some of your friends."

All of whom had rushed off after wishing her a happy eighteenth. Not that she could blame them—they weren't obligated to socialize with her parents. Only Les, being her girlfriend, was stuck with that apparently excruciating task.

"So what should we do now?" Mama asked.

Les leaned forward. "Do you want to see the recreation centre?"

So Les *was* paying attention. The recreation centre wasn't a bad idea, but it was already almost 20:00. It would take at least an hour to show them around the centre, a network of connected buildings. They hadn't said how late they planned to stay. "If you have time," she told them. "It's pretty big."

"We're here until at least midnight."

"You don't have to stay until midnight," Mo said, though she hoped they would. She wanted to celebrate with them if she was a Chosen, and lean on them if she wasn't. If she hadn't been at the Military Academy, they would have thrown her a party. They'd offered, but she'd turned them down. Rules were rules—the military wouldn't grant her an overnight leave for something as frivolous as an eighteenth party. So her parents had come to the academy, and she grew more grateful to them by the minute. They were keeping her mind busy. She hadn't thought about Chosen Council couriers for at least an hour. Okay, now she'd ruined it, but still. If Mama and Papa weren't with her, she'd probably be in her room, hiding under a blanket with the light turned out.

"Nice try, but you're not getting rid of us that easily." Mama plunked her empty mug onto her tray. "Let's go see this recreation centre. We've been sitting here for over two hours. Time to stretch our legs."

Mo's anxiety level rose as soon as they stepped into the cool night air. She'd be easy to find out here, if anyone was looking. "No Solitary Notification yet," she felt compelled to say, then wished she hadn't.

Mama put her arm around Mo's shoulders and gave her a squeeze. "It's almost eight o'clock. I think we may have another Chosen in the family."

Mo wondered if Les, walking a few feet ahead of them, had heard.

"I thought you'd be a Chosen," Papa said.

"Why?" Mo asked.

He pursed his lips. "I don't know. I just had a feeling."

Her parents' certainty made her uneasy. Declaring she was a Chosen before midnight was tempting fate. "It's not midnight yet."

Papa nodded. "True."

Mo relaxed a bit when he said nothing more. "You see those buildings off to the right?" She pointed. "Those are the barracks. We stayed there when we were here for the evaluation." Mama and Papa squinted toward them. "And coming up is the infirmary." She continued to point out landmarks, determined to keep the conversation away from Chosens and Solitary Notifications.

"You were right. This *is* big," Mama said when they arrived at the recreation centre.

Les held the main building's door open. "Let's start with the meeting rooms on the second floor."

Mo opened her mouth to ask why they'd start on the second floor when there were all sorts of facilities on the first, but Les and her parents were already climbing the stairs. "I take my violin lessons here, in one of the other buildings," she said, but they ignored her. "And Les takes her flute lessons."

Nothing.

"We may as well show you one of the larger rooms first," Les said as they strode along the second floor corridor. She started to open a door, then stopped. "Mo, why don't you lead the way?"

Les was acting awfully strange tonight. "Sure," Mo said, not wanting to be difficult in front of Mama and Papa. She pushed open the door and flicked on the light.

"SURPRISE!"

Time seemed to stop. Mo stood confused, staring at the multitude of faces peering at her. David and Kary. Neil and Matthew and Mary! Bruce and others from her study group. And was that Adelaide and Alan standing in the corner? *Happy Eighteenth, Mo* the banner strung across the back wall proclaimed. A party? For her? "Wow!" When everyone clapped, she realized she'd said it out loud. "I had no idea."

"You didn't suspect anything?" Les said.

"No. Who arranged it?" One look at her parents provided the answer. They were grinning from ear to ear like a couple of children. "Thank you," she mouthed to them.

"We couldn't let you turn eighteen without a party," Mama said, to another round of applause.

"So let's have a party," David shouted. "Put the music back on."

Bruce, nearest the comm station, turned and hit a key. Up-tempo music filled the air. Everyone quickly grabbed a partner.

"Can I have the first dance?" Les asked.

Mo responded by holding out her hand. "You must have helped," she said once they were out of earshot of her parents.

"I cleared it with Richmond and booked the room. Oh, and helped with the invitations. That's it. They took care of the catering, the decorations, everything."

Now Mo noticed the refreshment tables against one wall and the streamers stretched across the ceiling. It was almost like being at the Dance Hall. Well, except the room was much smaller and supper hadn't been served, but who cared? This was her party, and the room was packed. She hadn't known she had so many friends at the academy.

"I can't believe you never let it slip," Mo said, reaching up and looping her arms around Les's neck. "I never would have guessed you were planning a party for me."

Les looked down at her. "I guess we all have our secrets." The next piece blared from the comm station. "I like this one." She spun Mo around. They fell into step with the music.

Mo silently thanked the station for saving her from what might have been an uncomfortable conversation and tried to concentrate on dancing. Tonight, it would be her turn to dance with everyone. Though that would leave Les available to dance with others, and there were probably a couple of women here who'd love to spin Les around the dance floor. Like Joanna, for example. Mo was convinced that Joanna had a raving crush on Les. The moment Les was without a dance partner, Joanna would move in, try to impress Les with her fancy moves and—

Tears prickled at Mo's eyelashes. What was she doing, tonight of all nights? Why worry about Joanna? What was the point? Les's Chosen would get her in the end. Who cared what happened until then? What did it flaming matter? *You're only the stand-in, remember?* Her feelings for Les . . . they didn't count, not to the Chosen Council. So let Joanna dance with Les. Some woman out there would eventually live with Les, sleep with Les, have daughters with Les, be everything to Les, so what would one dance matter?

She stopped dancing. Les looked at her, puzzled. Mo let go of her and drew back. "I should go properly thank my parents for arranging this."

"Now?" Les asked, her arm still around Mo's waist.

"Yeah." She turned and walked toward Mama and Papa. When Les's hand brushed hers, she grabbed it and held on. Les must be terribly confused. Mo knew she wasn't being fair to her, wanting her one second and rebuffing her the next. But her heart and mind were at constant war, and her behaviour reflected whichever was winning at the time. It would be easier for both her and Les if they agreed with each other. She needed to find the button that all other Rymellans apparently found—the one that would instantly turn off her feelings for Les and have her beaming brighter than the sun when the Chosen Council summoned her. If it summoned her—there were still a few hours to go until midnight.

Her parents, Adelaide and Alan, and her siblings stood in a corner, deep in conversation. It figured that all the old people over twenty would stick together.

"My parents are here," Les said with surprise. She must not have noticed them earlier.

"You didn't know they'd be here?" Mo asked.

Les shook her head.

 DISOBEDIENCE MEANS DEATH

Mama's brow furrowed when she saw them. "I thought you were dancing."

"I sort of felt bad, running off without really thanking you," Mo said. "I mean, you didn't have to do this, but you did, and it was a nice surprise."

"Aw," Mama said, squeezing Mo for the umpteenth time that day.

Mo looked at Neil, Mary, and Matthew. "And I can't believe you're all here." She nodded toward Adelaide and Alan. "And you."

"I didn't know you were coming," Les said to her parents.

"We wouldn't miss Mo's eighteenth," Adelaide said indignantly.

Les's hand tightened around Mo's. Mo glanced at her, just in time to see Les smooth her features and resume the mask of indifference she worked so hard to maintain around her parents. Les had invited them to visit her twice, and had received excuses in response. Mo wished they hadn't come.

"Well, maybe you'll come see my room." Les paused. "When you have a minute."

Alan nodded, but Adelaide appeared to mull over the request. "Since we're here, I suppose we should," she finally said. "But it'll have to be soon. Unfortunately, we can't stay until midnight. We both have early cases tomorrow."

"Why don't you go now?" Mama said.

Adelaide shrugged. "We might as well."

Mo squeezed Les's hand. What she really wanted to do was hug her and tell her how much she loved her and how proud she was that Les had stood up to her parents and followed her dream. But such an obvious display of affection in front of their parents would mortify Les. Plus, Mo had never told Les that she loved her, not explicitly. She couldn't commit to Les, promise her anything, or plan a future with her. "I love you" would sound desperate and hollow—Les may even think her weak in the Way. If Les ever said it, Mo would definitely say it back. But Les never had, maybe because she didn't feel the same way, or maybe because she knew it would only be a reminder of the future they probably wouldn't have. Why say something that would only hurt?

"Maybe we can try dancing again later?" Les said, turning to Mo.

"I'd like that." She pulled on Les's hand. Les bent forward. "I'm sorry about before," Mo said into Les's ear. "It's a weird day today, you know? I—"

"Hey, Lesley, you're not going to hog Mo all night, are you?" bellowed Carl, a fellow cadet. "There's a whole lineup of people waiting to dance with her. I'm first." Mo wanted to strangle him.

"Save me a dance," Les whispered, then straightened. "Perfect timing. I'm just about to take my parents over to the dormitory." She let go of Mo's hand and motioned for her parents to follow her.

"Happy eighteenth!" Carl offered Mo his arm.

Mo accepted it and smiled weakly, though her attention remained on Les, who was almost at the door. The room was filled with people, but the moment Les left, it felt empty.

LESLEY POPPED A cheese-topped cracker into her mouth and watched Mo and the rest of the Middletons gather at the front of the room. She'd deliberately chosen to stand in a dark corner. She wanted to be alone, and Mo would have to strain to see her. Only four minutes to midnight. She doubted a Chosen Council courier would suddenly race into the room and thrust a Solitary Notification into Mo's hands, so it was official. Mo was a Chosen.

Good. That was what Lesley wanted. It would be easier knowing that Mo had a special someone in her future—for Mo, too. Now it was crystal clear that their relationship, while important, was temporary. To pretend otherwise would not only be futile, but cruel. Actually, it had been crystal clear since Lesley's eighteenth, but Mo seemed to be clinging to the possibility that they could be each other's Chosen. Lesley had no intention of saying or doing anything to encourage that notion. She cared too much about Mo to help set her up for disappointment. Reiterating that they must trust the Chosen Council and reminding Mo that they'd come to love their Chosens, as all Rymellans did, would be the best thing she could do for her. Though it would be hard, perhaps even hurt.

Maybe they should stop seeing each other? No, that would be silly. Were they that weak in the Way that they'd have to remain single until their Chosen Papers arrived? Other Rymellans didn't shun relationships. She and Mo weren't the only couple in the room without a future. As

   DISOBEDIENCE MEANS DEATH

long as they were honest about where the relationship was going—
nowhere—they had no reason to distance themselves from each other,
especially when they were at the Military Academy and couldn't avoid
each other. If they were still together in a few years' time, they'd have
to cool things. Staying together now wouldn't do them any harm. Ideally, the relationship would naturally run its course long before they
turned twenty-five.

The music stopped. "Everyone count with us," Michael and Susan
shouted together, clearly enjoying themselves. "Ten, nine, eight—"

Mo was scanning the room. Lesley stepped forward and waved. She
didn't want Mo focused on her at midnight, but she didn't want Mo to
think she'd left, either. Mo caught Lesley's eye and quickly shifted her
attention to her parents. Lesley stepped back into the shadows.

"Three, two, one—" Everyone broke into applause. A few whistled. Mo
suddenly disappeared, crushed between her parents as they embraced
her.

Lesley couldn't help but smile. Mo's parents were so different from
hers. She hadn't received land on her eighteenth—Mama and Papa always
followed tradition to the letter. They'd only give her land if she turned
out to be the Principal of her Joining. She hoped she was, because she
couldn't imagine living anywhere but the Thompson estate.

Susan and Michael parted. Mo hugged her siblings and then stepped
forward. "Shh," someone said over the noise. The applause petered out.
Lesley shifted her weight to her left foot.

"I'm not one for speeches," Mo began with a smile—Lesley was too
far away to see if the smile reached Mo's eyes. "So I'll be brief. It looks
like I'm a Chosen. And I'm very happy about that." She shoved her hands
into her front pant pockets. "It'll be a while before I find out who my
Chosen is. Let's see . . . right now, she could be as old as twenty-three
or as young as thirteen. No matter—"

"Thirteen and already taller than you," someone shouted.

The room exploded into laughter. Mo laughed too, but Lesley couldn't
bring herself to join in, despite knowing the joke was only a bit of good-
natured ribbing. Mo seemed to have taken it in the spirit intended, but
as far as Lesley was concerned, whoever had said it should have kept
it to himself.

Mo waited for the laughter to die down before continuing. "Yeah, I guess I can say that whoever she is, she'll probably be taller than me." She glanced in Lesley's direction. "But what I was going to say is that no matter how old she is, I'm sure we'll get along very well. The Chosen Council has selected her for me, and me for her. I'm sure I'll be happy with her, and I hope she'll be happy with me."

She'd better be, Lesley thought.

"My family . . . and I . . . will look forward to meeting her." Mo smiled again. "I can't really think of anything else to say. Like I said, I'm not one for speeches. The party has to end at 00:30 and it would be nice to squeeze in a few more dances, so I'll stop there. Except to thank my parents for the party. And, of course, Lieutenant Commander Richmond, for allowing us to have it." She nodded at him and clapped; everyone followed her lead. "And now let's say the *Words Every Rymellan Knows*."

Lesley moved toward the centre of the room and joined the circle that hastily formed. "Disobedience means Death. Death to those who commit a Chosen Violation. Death to those who disobey. Death to those who violate the Way. Death to those who violate the Way. Death to those who violate the Way!"

Everyone smiled and clapped. Mo nodded. "Thank you all for coming."

Another round of thunderous applause, this time for Mo. Lesley enthusiastically clapped her hands, so proud of Mo, who'd looked so composed in front of everyone after what had probably been a tiring and stressful day. Whoever heard the name Ramona Middleton during her notification meeting with the Chosen Council would be very lucky indeed. Lesley certainly wouldn't be disappointed if Mo was her Chosen. Wouldn't it be funny if she cared so deeply for Mo *because* they were Chosens?

She stopped clapping and dropped her hands to her sides. What was she thinking? Mo was *not* her Chosen. She must never allow that thought to enter her mind again. That it had in the first place was worrisome. Her hands clenched. She was growing weak in the Way.

Had she already forgotten what she'd learned at the Indoctrination Academy? Nothing was more important than serving the Way and trusting the Chosen Council. Not her military career, not Mo, not

   DISOBEDIENCE MEANS DEATH

anything. Perhaps she should join the group that met twice a week to discuss the articles of the Chosen Tradition. Heather, the group's leader, had invited her to a meeting, but she'd declined. Reading the history of an article each week, along with commentaries by several advocates, would be a challenge to fit into her already busy schedule. Few first-year cadets belonged to the group for that reason. But now, she reconsidered. It would diminish the meagre amount of time she and Mo had to spend together when they weren't in class or studying, but the Way must come first. Tomorrow, she'd beep Heather and tell her she'd changed her mind.

She needed to put her relationship with Mo into perspective. They enjoyed each other's company. They trusted each other. And yes, they cared about each other. But they also had Chosens. Eventually Mo would look back on their relationship, see it for what it was, and realize how silly she'd been to think it would be difficult to leave behind. Lesley would do the same. She'd love and cherish her Chosen beyond anything she'd ever felt for Mo, and Mo's Chosen would share Mo's life in a way Lesley never had. And that was exactly as it should be.

Her fingers ached. She unfurled her hands and stared at the angry red indentations her fingernails had left in her palms.

MO WATCHED THE train pull out of the station, then left the platform. Even though she'd been up early and it was past 00:30, she felt wide awake. What a day! Was there any emotion she hadn't experienced? And to top it all off, despite spending the entire day hoping and wishing and silently bargaining with the Chosen Council, despair had tempered her relief when the clock had struck midnight and sealed her fate as a Chosen. A Solitary Notification would have ended it—the relationship, the agony, the idiotic fantasy she couldn't shake no matter how hard she tried. And oh, how she pitied her Chosen! Not only would the poor woman never live up to Les, she'd be stuck with someone who went through the motions while pining for someone else. *I hope she'll be happy with me.* Mo snorted. Yeah, sure. Good luck to her.

She was a coward, intending to remain with Les because a Solitary Notification hadn't arrived to force an end to their relationship. She should have the courage to end it now, tonight—to do what anyone with the tiniest amount of sense would do. After all, she wasn't a child. She was eighteen. An intense period of grief and adjustment would be better than clinging to a dying relationship. And what if they were still together when Les turned twenty-five? Every knock at the door, every sighting of a Chosen Council courier would send Mo into a panic. Not only that, if they couldn't break up now, how would they break up after they'd been together for eleven years? Unless their relationship eventually became a habit, a mutually agreed-upon, casual affair until one of them received her Chosen Papers, ending it would only become harder with time.

Splitting up now made sense. It was the right thing to do. It would be painful at first, but better in the long run. And she was a complete idiot, because despite everything she'd just told herself, she didn't want to do it. If she honestly believed that she and Les belonged together, why would she end their relationship?

There must be something wrong with her. She shouldn't feel like this, shouldn't hope for a particular Chosen. Other Rymellans didn't, or if they did, they hid it well. Had she hid it well, when she'd stood in front of everyone and talked about her Chosen, all the time thinking about Les?

"Argamon, Mo, what's with the grumpy face? You're eighteen! You're a Chosen!"

Mo jumped at David's voice. She hadn't seen him, even though he was directly in front of her. "I know. It's great," she said, forcing a smile. Nobody could ever know about the turmoil inside her. Nobody. Anything she said could be misinterpreted, twisted to sound like she wouldn't accept her Chosen. That wasn't true. She would—she'd just never love her, that was all.

David returned her smile by leaping into the air. He landed on both feet with a thud, a wide grin on his face.

"What are you so happy about?" Mo asked, grateful for the diversion. "You'd think it was *your* birthday."

"I asked Lynn out on a date and she said yes!"

"Lynn? Lynn Fielding?"

"Yes!"

What could he possibly see in her? Okay, Mo could think of one

     DISOBEDIENCE MEANS DEATH

attraction. Well, two. Was it just physical, then? "Wasn't it you who said that Lynn probably got into the academy because her uncle's a captain? You said she'd be more suited to working in the mess hall." He'd practically called her an airhead.

"Mo, we're going on a date, not Joining. Come on. She's a Chosen, I'm a Chosen. I want to have a little fun, pass the time until my Chosen Papers come. She won't be the only woman I date, believe me."

Was that what she and Les were doing? Passing the time?

"Will you help me decide where to take her?" David asked.

"You want to talk about that now?"

"No, tomorrow. It's almost 01:00, and you know what Richmond said. You're walking in the wrong direction."

"I want to say good night to Les. Is she still there?"

"Yeah, I think they've almost finished cleaning up. Anyway, I'm going. I'll see you tomorrow." He waggled his fingers at her. "Bye."

Mo jogged the rest of the way to the recreation centre, pulled open the door, and—oh! "All done?" she asked Les.

Les nodded. "Kary's still stacking chairs, but there's only a few left."

"We should go help."

"No, no, she said to go ahead. Richmond's given her until 01:15 to get back to the dormitory. And Ben's helping her."

"Ah. Best to leave them to it, then."

Les held out a rolled up piece of cloth. "Do you want it? It's the Happy Birthday banner."

No, she didn't. It would remind her of how stressful the day had been, not of how touched she'd felt because her parents and friends had cared enough to throw her a party. But she nodded and took the banner. In time, she might change her mind. If she didn't, she'd quietly dispose of it in a few months, when nobody would be offended.

"Let's go," Les said, motioning for Mo to move.

Mo stepped aside and held the door open until Les had walked past. "Thanks for cleaning up. I should have come back sooner," she said as they walked toward the dormitories.

"You were seeing your parents off. And it wouldn't have been very nice to make the guest of honour clean up after her own party."

"Well, thanks." Mo paused. "I'm sorry we didn't get a chance to dance again. Every time I started to look for you, someone grabbed me."

"That's okay. You probably wouldn't have found me anyway. Showing my parents my room took longer than I expected. And around fifteen minutes after we got back to the party, it was time to take them to the train station."

"How did that go . . . showing them your room?"

"Better than I thought it would. I think Mama was curious about it." Les shot Mo a bemused look. "She just didn't want to admit that she wanted to see it. The party gave her the perfect excuse."

"Did you mention the aviacraft lessons?"

"No. I didn't want to spoil things."

Would Les ever tell her parents? She didn't have to—the lessons were only a means to an end. They wouldn't be landing on the estates or flying anywhere near them, so her parents need never know. "Think they'll visit, now that they've been here?"

Les sighed. "I don't know. And I don't really care. It's up to them. I won't keep asking."

Mo was sure that Les did care, but didn't look at her. The whole conversation felt weird. Not awkward, not uncomfortable, just stilted. She felt as if she was making polite conversation with an acquaintance. They hadn't touched each other once, and they were walking with a respectable distance between them, as if they were already Joined to other women.

The dormitories loomed ahead. Mo reached out and lightly touched Les's sleeve, wanting to break through the barrier that had sprung up at midnight before saying good-bye. When Les didn't move away, Mo veered over and slipped her arm around Les's waist. Les stopped walking. Mo drew back and looked at Les uncertainly. She dropped the banner when Les's arms wrapped around her. The ground was dry, the banner could wait. Mo threw her arms around Les's neck and pressed her face against Les's shoulder. She squeezed her eyes shut. She wouldn't cry. She would not cry. Les's hold tightened; Mo could feel Les's heart beating. How could the Chosen Council force them apart? How? They belonged together.

Suddenly it all became clear. Mo opened her eyes, excitement coursing through her. The Chosen Council would give her Les! It had to. Nothing else would make sense. She wouldn't be content with anyone else—could never be happy without Les. So if she and Les weren't Chosens, then everything she believed in, everything she'd been taught, was a lie. And that wasn't possible. Everyone important to her, everyone she respected . . . they couldn't all be deluded.

She felt better than she had all day—no, than she had in weeks, months, even; ever since Les had turned eighteen. No more agonizing. No more worrying about meeting her Chosen. No more dreading a life without Les. She'd do what every other Rymellan did and trust the Chosen Council. She'd stay with Les, love Les, and look forward to receiving her Chosen Papers, her way of showing that inside, deep down inside, she truly believed that she and Les were Chosens, that it wasn't a pathetic, childish fantasy she clung to because she couldn't accept the inevitable.

"We have to go," Les murmured into Mo's ear. "Richmond was firm about everyone being in bed by 01:00, and it's probably that now. He might do a spot check."

Mo reluctantly pulled back. She smiled at Les and held her hand as they walked the remaining distance to the dormitories. For the first time in a long time, she felt optimistic about the future. *You're kidding yourself,* a little voice whispered. Well, maybe she was. Maybe her epiphany was her way of coping, a way to keep herself sane until she had no choice but to let Les go. Or maybe, just maybe, time would prove her right, and she and Les would stand next to each other in the Joining Chamber.

PRIORITIES

. . . . .

ESLEY BUTTONED HER CLOAK AND FOLLOWED Mo from the mess hall, leaving the cacophony of voices and clattering dishes behind. She slipped her arm around Mo and steered her toward the dormitories. "I'm glad we had supper together."

"Me too," Mo said, smiling up at her. "You're—I mean, we're so busy these days, we hardly ever sit down and talk. Not that the mess hall is the best place to talk, mind you."

Lesley inwardly cringed. That was precisely why she'd asked Mo to meet there. Her plan had worked—the topic of sharing a room hadn't come up—but would Mo broach the subject on the way back to their rooms? Usually Lesley enjoyed strolling with Mo on a clear, crisp evening, but not when she was worried about what Mo might say next.

"Oh, I forgot to tell you that I talked to Mama earlier today," Mo said. "Newton's retiring."

Lesley relaxed slightly. "Really? None of the mandatory bulletins mentioned it." Newton had been C3's commander for as long as she could remember.

"They haven't announced it yet. She found out through an indoctrinator whose Chosen works at B5 headquarters."

"I wonder who'll take his place."

"A Commander Finney, apparently."

Finney . . . The name sounded familiar, but Lesley couldn't place it. "Apart from the name at the bottom of C3 bulletins, I doubt we'll notice a difference. I think I saw Newton once, from a distance." She held up her right index finger for emphasis, even though Mo couldn't see it. "That's it."

"I don't think I ever saw him," Mo mumbled.

They lapsed into silence. Lesley felt relieved and disappointed when they reached her dormitory's entrance. She lifted her arm from Mo's shoulders and faced her.

"Can we go to your room for a few minutes?" Mo asked. "I want to talk to you about something."

She nodded, despite knowing what was coming. With luck, Jackie would be in the room, though she'd more likely be at the library. "I don't have much time," she said over her shoulder as they climbed the stairs to the third floor. "It's group tonight."

"That's at 20:00. It's 19:15."

"An advocate is speaking. I want to get there early so I can review my notes." Not true. She'd already gone over them twice, determined not to slip up in front of an advocate who specialized in the Chosen Tradition.

"We can't keep putting this off," Mo said when they reached Lesley's room.

Lesley opened the door. Unfortunately, no Jackie. "Putting what off?"

"You know what I'm talking about. The deadline for room requests is in two weeks."

She crossed to the satchel lying on her dresser and made a show of buckling its straps. Out of the corner of her eye she saw Mo hovering, waiting for a response. "Well, I can't talk about it now."

Mo let out an exasperated sigh and slapped her thighs. "When, then? Tell me when. Every time I bring it up, you suddenly have to rush off. I thought we'd have time tonight."

"We'll be home in two days. We can talk about it then." Lesley grasped the satchel's handle and started to lift it from the dresser.

"Most of our time at home will be taken up with the festival and visiting."

She stopped. Mo had a point. Maybe they *should* discuss it now. No, they couldn't. She hadn't made up her mind about what to do—Mo could talk her into something she'd quickly regret. And once they'd started, they'd probably want to talk for more than five minutes. She couldn't risk missing group. Choosing to miss group so they could discuss sharing a room would be choosing Mo over the Way. Not acceptable. "We'll make the time."

"You promise?"

"Yes." Lesley lifted her satchel and looked at Mo. "I really do have to go now." She reached for Mo's hand. Mo stared at her for a moment, then slipped her hand into Lesley's.

Without a word, they left the room and headed down the stairs to the lobby. Lesley searched for something to say. "I'm sorry I don't have more time."

"Are you?" Mo pulled the dormitory's main door open. "You better keep your promise."

"I will."

"We'll see."

They stepped outside and stared at each other, the air heavy between them. "What will you do for the rest of the night?" Lesley asked.

Mo shrugged. "Homework, I guess. And get in some practice for the concert."

Oh no, another uncomfortable subject. Now would be a good time to leave. "I'll see you tomorrow, then." She lowered her head to kiss Mo.

Mo barely brushed Lesley's lips. "Enjoy your meeting." She turned and walked away, her shoulders stiff.

Lesley watched her for a few seconds, then forced herself to start moving toward the recreation centre. Now she had a deadline—no more avoiding the question of whether to share a room. But every time she tried to make up her mind, she felt torn in two. Normally decisions didn't paralyze her, but this one involved the two most important things in her life: Mo and the Way.

She couldn't come up with an answer that would satisfy both. Sharing a room would make Mo happy, but living together—because that was what they'd be doing—would put their relationship on a more serious footing. Not a good idea, since they both had Chosens, but Mo probably wouldn't see it that way. Lesley dreaded the hurt she'd see in Mo's eyes when she finally stopped avoiding the issue and told her what she should have told her weeks ago.

Well, the indoctrinators had never said that following the Way would be easy. She'd love to share with Mo, but her priority had to be the Way, not what she and Mo personally desired. Anything less would be weak in the Way, and those weak in the Way were ejected from the Military Academy, or worse.

Her hand tightened around the satchel's handle. Perhaps Advocate Phillips's talk would give her the courage to tell Mo that she wouldn't share a room with her.

MO RIPPED OFF her cloak and threw it at its hook. She eyed the violin case propped up in the corner, but all she'd do was rage at Les on her way to the practice room, then smash her violin to pieces at the first sour note. Homework? No, she was too keyed up to concentrate.

She threw herself onto her bed, rolled onto her back, and interlaced her fingers behind her head. Her frustration had gotten the better of her. Despite knowing that pushing Les wasn't the right way to handle her, she'd gone ahead and done it anyway. It was that flaming deadline! If she had more time, she'd do what she normally did when she suspected something was tying Les up in knots: wait for Les to bring up whatever was bothering her.

Les preferred to solve problems on her own. She thought everyone would think her weak if she asked for advice or needed help to figure something out. It was okay for someone to ask *her* for advice, but she held herself to a tougher standard. When Les seemed troubled, Mo had learned not to push, not to probe, not to try to wheedle anything out of her. Eventually Les worked it out, or swallowed her pride and talked.

But this time, Mo's patience was wearing thin. If Les didn't agree to share a room by the deadline and then decided shortly afterward that sharing would be okay, they'd have to wait until their third year. Mo sighed. And she'd stupidly told Kary to go ahead and request another roommate, positive that Les would jump at the chance to share. So not only could she not end up with Les, she could end up with a roommate she didn't like.

Mo wanted to shake Les, but she also wanted to hug her. As frustrated as she was, she didn't like to see Les tense, nor the weariness and unhappiness she glimpsed on Les's face whenever Les let her guard down. If Mo knew for sure what was bothering her, maybe she'd work subtle advice into their conversations by talking about "a friend" with similar concerns. But she only had suspicions, and ever since Les had joined that Chosen Tradition study group, they'd had less time for serious conversation.

Flaming group! What did they do at those meetings anyway, examine every word in the Tradition with a magnifying glass? That advocate would probably drone on for two hours about an article that consisted of five words. If she'd been thinking, she would have joined the group months ago, around the time she'd turned eighteen and was having problems sleeping. One meeting would have instantly cured her insomnia. No, just preparing for a meeting would have had her snoring at her desk.

The door opened. Kary bounced into the room and dropped her knapsack onto the floor. "You look comfortable," she said with a grin. "Taking a break?"

"Not exactly," Mo mumbled.

Kary frowned. "What's wrong?"

Mo hesitated, but decided there was no harm in telling her. "Les still hasn't agreed to share a room."

"You asked her again?"

"Tried to."

"And she still won't talk about it?"

Mo shook her head.

Kary opened her mouth to say something, then closed it.

"What?" Mo asked apprehensively. Kary wasn't one to hold back.

"Well . . . have you considered that maybe she's trying to tell you something?" Still wearing her cloak, Kary perched herself on the edge of her bed and leaned toward Mo. "You have to admit, things have changed between you two. You don't see each other half as much as you used to."

"She has her group. And the guest speakers committee."

"She doesn't have to do both. Doing both pretty much eats up all her free time, leaving none to spend with you. It's as if she's avoiding you."

"I don't think she is," Mo said. She stopped there, unwilling to discuss her suspicions with Kary. Les was a private, guarded person. Mo wouldn't betray her. "Anyway, she's promised to talk about it when we're home for the festival."

"Do you think she will?"

Mo hoped so, but said, "I don't know. I've decided to leave it up to her to bring it up. If she doesn't, I'll let it go." Pressuring Les would get her nowhere and could damage their relationship—she had to remember that and restrain herself. She'd rather have Les and not share a room than not have her at all.

Kary reached out and patted Mo's arm. "Good for you. Enough chasing her about it. You have to have some self-respect."

She wished Kary hadn't brought up self-respect. First of all, her decision to stop trying had nothing to do with self-respect and everything to do with how best to get what she wanted. Second, Kary wouldn't think she had much self-respect when she told her that Les wouldn't attend the concert, something she hadn't mentioned because it would reflect badly on Les. But since she and Kary were already talking about her, now was as good a time as any. "That's why I'm not going to push her about the concert, either," she said as casually as she could.

Kary's brow furrowed. "The concert? What about the concert?"

Mo braced herself. "She's not going."

"What?" Kary shrieked, almost bolting off the bed. "What do you mean, she's not going?"

"It's the same night as group."

"Who flaming cares?" Kary said, her eyes ablaze. "She can skip group for one night."

"She doesn't want to."

Kary balled up her hands. "She—same night—the nerve!" She took a deep breath and slowly exhaled. "Let me talk to her."

Mo nearly gasped. "No, don't!"

"She should be there. Did you tell her they only selected four violinists out of everyone who takes lessons? They didn't ask her to play her flute."

Because Les didn't like playing in front of others. She'd rather be paraded naked around the Military Academy than get up on stage and perform. Okay, maybe not, but give Les the choice and it would be a close call. When the music instructors had started to organize the concert,

Les had made it clear that she wasn't interested. She'd only ever played her flute for her instructor and Mo.

"Stand up for yourself! Tell her you're more important than her flaming group," Kary said.

No, no, no! That would be the worst thing she could say, especially right now. She appreciated that Kary was trying to help, but Kary didn't know Les very well. "I'm not going to push her, Kary. If she doesn't want to go, she doesn't want to go." She cursed the quaver in her voice.

Kary's face softened. "Are you sure she's not trying to tell you something?" she asked gently.

Positive. Almost. They didn't spend as much time with each other as they used to, but when they were together, their relationship felt solid. She didn't have the impression that Les wanted out. Les seemed to be trying to figure out how their relationship fit into her life, now that they knew they had Chosens. Mo had thought she was the one who'd struggled with turning eighteen and that Les had breezed through the experience, but now she'd calmed down and Les seemed to be struggling. She was certain that Les did want the relationship, though, and also sure that pressuring her to put it first would have the opposite effect.

So she was doing her best to accept that Les wouldn't be at the concert. She hadn't pouted, cried, or stamped her feet and insisted that Les be there. "If you change your mind, let me know," was all she'd said. Then she'd gone ahead and submitted Les's name for one of her four allotted reserved seats, along with Mama's, Papa's, and Kary's. Probably a stupid thing to do, but Les could indeed change her mind. In the meantime, she'd practice, hope, and keep reminding herself not to be resentful, that Les's behaviour had more to do with Les than with her.

Her eyes welled up; she bit her lip. It still hurt, despite knowing that.

"I'm sorry, I didn't mean to upset you," Kary said.

Mo blinked back her tears. "No, it's not you." It was that woman she wanted to hug and shake. "But I think I've had enough of talking about Les."

"Then let's not talk about her." Kary stood and gazed sympathetically at Mo. "Listen, Ben and I are going to the track semis. It's the F8 academy against us. We're meeting in, oh . . ." she flipped up her comm unit and read the time ". . . twenty minutes. Want to come?"

How pathetic would that be, tagging along with Kary on a date?

"It's a beautiful night out there," Kary added.

Mo sat up. "Thanks, but I do need to practice." She wouldn't make a fool of herself on that stage, Les or no Les.

"We won't mind if you come."

"Maybe next time." She paused. "Did you request Ben as a room-mate?"

Kary chuckled. "Um, no. We talked about it, but it's too soon. So I don't know who I'll get. I wonder if I can cancel the request, if it turns out you and Lesley won't be sharing after all?"

"If you can, would you?"

"Hmm." Kary looked at the ceiling and rubbed her chin, then grinned. "Of course I would. But I hope Lesley comes around. I really do."

"Me too."

"We can talk more about Lesley later, if you want."

She probably wouldn't want to, but nodded.

"I better go. I want to stop at the mess hall to pick up a snack or two before heading to the field."

Mo managed a smile. "Have a good time."

After Kary had gone, she eyed the violin case again, then collected it and headed to the recreation centre. On the way, she forced herself to mentally review the two pieces that needed the most attention, to keep her mind off Les. But as she passed Building B, she couldn't help but think about Les sitting inside, and quickened her pace, wanting to be long gone before Les's meeting ended. If they bumped into each other, Les would think she'd planned it that way. She wasn't that desperate. Yet.

Lesley stretched her legs under the table and tried to concentrate on Advocate Phillips's closing comments. "I've had a wonderful time," he was saying. "Thank you for the lively and challenging discussion."

She half-heartedly joined in as the group clapped. When the applause petered out, Heather rose to say, "Thank you, Advocate Phillips. It was an honour to have such a distinguished advocate lead us tonight."

Phillips nodded in acknowledgment. "I hope you'll invite me back," he said with a smile. "There's more to the Tradition than Article CT65."

"We'd love to have you back," Heather said. The majority of those around the table nodded, including Lesley. Perhaps next time she'd be more in the mood. "I know we said the Words at the beginning of the meeting, but I think it would be fitting for us to say them again." Heather motioned for everyone to stand.

Lesley held hands with her neighbours. "Disobedience means death. Death to those who commit a Chosen Violation. Death to those who disobey. Death to those who violate the Way. Death to those who violate the Way. Death to those who violate the Way!" She clapped and forced a smile, then quietly sighed. Not even the Words could cheer her.

Several in the group gathered around Phillips, wanting to continue the discussion. Normally Lesley would be among them, but there was no point, when she couldn't focus. She tuned out their voices and the chatter going on around her and gathered her notes.

Nothing was turning out the way she'd expected. She'd regularly attended the Chosen Tradition study group, not missing a single meeting, and she sat on the committee that engaged guest speakers for it and related groups. As often as she could, she'd reminded herself that she and Mo had Chosens. And for months, she'd limited her time with Mo outside of classes and aviacraft lessons to a mere few hours a week, to prove to herself that life without Mo could be satisfying and enjoyable. But therein lay the problem. It wasn't. She missed Mo and, against her better judgment, wanted to spend more time with her.

Would sharing a room really be weak in the Way? Going to the concert was out of the question—that would be a clear choice of Mo over the Way. But sharing wouldn't interfere with any of her activities; in fact, she could do more and still have daily private time with Mo. Other cadets shared with lovers or friends, so why shouldn't she? She worried that sharing would encourage Mo's fantasy that they were Chosens, that it would feel like a commitment of sorts, but how could it? Not only would Mo continue to hope they were Chosens whether they shared or not, but they couldn't commit to each other—and both knew it.

Someone nudged her arm. "Are you okay tonight, Lesley?" Heather

 DISOBEDIENCE MEANS DEATH

asked, speaking loud enough to be heard over the spirited conversation between three nearby group members. "You were a little quieter than usual."

Great, Heather had noticed that she wasn't herself. That could be another benefit to sharing—she might give meetings her full attention again, rather than daydreaming or agonizing about Mo. "I'm fine," she said, sliding her notes into her satchel. "Just a bit of a headache, that's all."

"Nip over to the infirmary and let them take care of it for you."

If the infirmary could help with what was bothering her, she'd be over there in a second. "Good idea," she said, nodding.

Heather smiled at her. "Great job, getting Phillips. I heard your parents helped."

"Yes, they did." She started to buckle the satchel's straps. "They don't advocate for the Tradition, though." Few advocates did, since most articles in the Tradition were closed to amendments.

"Have you considered inviting one of them to lead the Law group for an evening? I'm sure Jeremy would love—"

Lesley was so focused on her satchel that it took her a few seconds to notice that Heather hadn't finished her sentence. Then she realized the whole room had gone quiet. She looked up. Heather was staring in the direction of the door, a strange expression on her face. Lesley followed her gaze and swallowed. Commander Morton stood in the doorway, his cloak open and his thumbs hooked through his belt loops. "Cadet Thompson!" he snapped. "A word."

Her legs turned to jelly. Trying to look casual, she lifted her satchel and carefully walked toward him.

"Get your cloak and walk with me," Morton murmured. He spun around and started down the corridor.

The skin on her back crawled as she slipped on her cloak. When she stepped through the doorway, whispers arose within the meeting room.

Morton couldn't possibly know what she was grappling with, could he? She'd been careful not to discuss it with anyone, including her counsellor. Commanders were powerful, but they weren't mind readers. She tried to remain calm as she followed him to the building's exit.

Outside, he waited for her to draw even before starting to walk again, his hands clasped behind his back. "Remember me?" he asked.

"Yes, I do, Commander Morton." She couldn't help glancing toward Building D, where the practice rooms were. *Focus!*

"It's hard to believe your evaluation was over a year ago."

"Yes, it is." First year exams were less than a month away, and she'd turned nineteen a few weeks ago. Time was moving quickly—too quickly. She'd be twenty-five before she knew it.

"Are you still planning to choose Defence?"

A cluster of cadets stood on the path that led out of the recreation centre complex. Seeing Morton, they parted and stood quietly as he and Lesley walked past. "Yes, I am," she said as they left the complex.

Morton stopped and faced her. "And still interested in the fighter pilot program?"

She forced herself to meet his eyes. "Yes."

"I think you belong in Interior, but it's your choice." He paused. "You're probably wondering why I'm here."

Lesley nodded.

"As I'm sure you've figured out, your first year is a probationary year. We've become quite adept at identifying cadets who pass their evaluation, but turn out not to be a good fit for the military. We're also adept at identifying cadets who are an excellent fit. Those who could become admirals. Those like you."

Shock stabbed through her. "It's a little early to think about admiral," she blurted.

Morton almost smiled. "Cadet, it's never too early to think about admiral." He motioned for her to resume walking and fell into step with her. "We'd like a mentor to guide you through your remaining years here. Have you met Lieutenant Commander Larson?"

"No."

"He's a former fighter pilot who now teaches here and oversees our domestic patrols. There's also Lieutenant Greeves. She isn't a pilot, but she excelled while a student here and her knowledge of military history is second to none. Would you like a mentor?"

"Yes."

"Good. Along with Larson and Greeves, there are a few other officers

   DISOBEDIENCE MEANS DEATH

you'll want to consider. I'll dispatch a short list to you. When you return from your break, let me know which one you think would be the best fit. You'll also want to develop your public speaking skills. We'd like you to join the group that records announcements for the academy. At first, you'll record announcements for c6 only. Once you have the hang of it, you'll record announcements intended for all academies."

"How often are announcements recorded?" she asked, wondering how much time she'd have left for Mo.

"Daily. But each member of the group is required for only a couple of hours a week. Later on, you'll branch out and perform duties that require you to speak to Rymellans in general, but we'll start with the academy announcements. Lieutenant Griffiths is in charge of the group. Shall I tell her to expect you at the group's orientation meeting?"

Faced with a crossroads, Lesley glanced at Morton. He slowed down, but didn't indicate which path to take. She decided to go left, toward the dormitories. Lights out was approaching.

"Well?" Morton said.

At the same time she told herself that a couple of hours a week would leave hardly any time for Mo, she heard herself say, "Tell her I'll be there."

"Excellent. You'll receive a dispatch with the meeting details. It'll take place sometime during the first week of your second year." He stopped. "I'll be following your progress, Cadet. Good night." Morton nodded to her and strode off.

Lesley quickly continued on, not wanting Morton to catch her gawking at him, should he look over his shoulder. Who would have thought that speaking up at the execution site during her evaluation would lead to this? He thought she could make admiral. Admiral! What would Mama think? What would Mo?

Her excitement died. Mo probably wouldn't care one way or another, but she would care about how any new activities would impact their time together. The question around sharing a room and Lesley's decision not to attend the concert were already causing tension between them. Mo would throw a fit when she found out their time together would be further reduced in their second year. Perhaps that was more of a reason to share a room, but what would Morton think if they did? Now that his attention was focused on Lesley, she had to be careful, not only for the sake of her future career, but for Mo's.

One thing she did know for sure: she'd have to choose the right time to tell Mo about her encounter with Morton, and do it in private. The conversation would probably be a loud one.

MO SLIPPED HER arm through Les's as soon as they left Station C3-8's waiting area and veered onto the path that led to the Thompson and Middleton estates. She'd spent the entire train ride biting her tongue, not only about sharing a room, but about Morton. Did Les honestly believe that her run-in with Morton hadn't gotten around? Mo had hardly believed her ears when Bruce had told her about how Morton had strode right into the middle of Les's meeting and commanded her to report to head office. "It's true!" he'd insisted when she'd rolled her eyes and shaken her head. "Tim told me. He heard it from Sheila. One of her friends knows someone who goes to meetings in the same building and at the same time as Lesley's group. Everyone's talking about it!"

It couldn't have been about anything terrible, since Les was very much alive, hadn't been thrown out of the academy, and didn't seem any tenser than usual. So why hadn't she mentioned it? And would she keep her promise to discuss sharing a room?

"It's nice to be home for longer than an overnight stay," Les said. "This time we'll be here for a few days." She smiled at Mo.

Mo smiled back and reminded herself that pushing Les would be the wrong approach. She had to be patient, wait until Les was ready. Maybe spending a few hours together without talking about anything important would help relax her. A few hours . . . what a luxury that would be! They hadn't sat alone and simply enjoyed each other's company for ages. She squeezed Les's arm. "Do you want to go to the lake tonight? Tomorrow's the supper and then it's the festival. After that, I'm visiting my aunt and uncle. So tonight is probably our only chance to go." Her right hand tightened around the handle of her violin case. She also had to fit in practice, but that was better left unsaid.

"Um," Les said, "well, I'm not sure. I'd like to."

"Then let's do it."

"I might have stuff to do."

"What stuff?"

"Well . . . I have some reading to do for group."

"I don't know about you, but I want to leave the academy and everything associated with it behind for a night," Mo said, trying a different tack. "I want to sit by the lake, relax, and forget I'm a cadet for a few hours. Well, apart from having to wear my cadet cloak."

Les frowned. "I'm pretty sure that if we stay on the estates, we don't have to wear our cloaks."

Mo wanted to believe her, and Les was usually right about such things, but she made a mental note to check exactly what the regulations were regarding the wearing of cloaks. Cuddling wouldn't be the same if they had to keep the flaming things on, but the evening would be ruined if they were caught not wearing them when they should. "Cloaks or no cloaks, let's go. Do you really want to miss a chance to go to the lake?"

"No, I don't," Les said softly. "It wouldn't feel right, going back to the academy without a visit to the lake."

"Then I'll come by right after supper," Mo said, thrilled that they'd spend the evening alone together, even though the topic of sharing a room would be off-limits.

A flash of orange up ahead caught her eye. A military was walking toward them. Odd; usually military patrolled in pairs, and this one was using a branch as a walking stick, as if she were out for a leisurely stroll.

"Mo," Les said, pulling her arm away and stopping.

Irritated, Mo whirled to face her. "What?"

"Look at her sleeves."

She turned her attention to the military's cloak and took in the gold-trimmed sleeves. As the woman drew closer, the insignia sewn onto the cloak's left breast confirmed what Mo had already surmised: Commander, Interior Division. Mo lowered the violin case to the ground and stood at attention, her hands clasped behind her back. Les stepped next to her and followed suit.

The commander stopped in front of them and threw the branch off to the side of the path. She eyed them up and down. "At ease, cadets."

Mo unclasped her hands and let them fall to her sides, but her body remained taut.

"You must be Lesley Thompson," the commander said, nodding to Les.

"Yes, Commander."

"And you must be Mo Middleton." She met Mo's eyes.

A chill ran up Mo's spine. "Well, my name is Ramona Middleton, Commander. But nobody calls me that. Everyone calls me Mo. Commander."

The commander's mouth twitched. "I know. That's why I called you Mo."

Mo wanted to hide her face behind her hands. If there were an article that covered making a fool of oneself in front of a commander, this commander would be reaching for her data collector.

"But I have you at a disadvantage," the commander said. "I'm Commander Finney. I've taken over C3 from Commander Newton."

As of that moment, Mo had seen Finney more times than she'd seen Newton. "How did you know who we were?" she asked before she could stop herself. The sooner her brain re-established its connection with her mouth, the better.

"Everyone I talk to mentions the two cadets representing C3 at the academy, so the cloaks were a giveaway," Finney said. "But even without them, I would have known who you were. I've just left the Thompson estate, so I knew you were due home. You look very much like your papa," she said to Les.

"Is everything all right at the estate?" Les asked. Her voice sounded even, but knowing her as well as she did, Mo detected a trace of apprehension.

"Oh, yes, everything's fine," Finney quickly said. "I happened to be in the area and thought I'd stop by and introduce myself. I didn't mean to alarm you."

"We didn't see much of Commander Newton. That's why I wondered."

"Well, expect to see more of me. C3 is a quiet sector, but complacency is dangerous. Did you know that a few years ago, E8 was a quiet sector? And guess who lived there?"

"The Adamses?" Mo and Les said together.

"Yes. The Adamses." Finney placed her left hand against her chest; the

 DISOBEDIENCE MEANS DEATH

Chosen ring on her third finger glinted in the sun. "Whenever possible, I want to prevent capital violations before they happen. No one likes to be at an execution site, including me. So is there anything either one of you would like to tell me?"

Mo wasn't sure what Finney meant. She glanced uncertainly at Les.

"Anyone you're concerned about, anyone who might be falling from the Way?" Finney said.

Oh. "I'm not concerned about anyone," Mo said, determined to contribute and to show that she wasn't an idiot. "But we've been away at the academy."

"We've had our heads down, studying," Les added. "We're a bit out of touch with what's going on in C3."

Finney nodded. "I guess you'd be more likely to raise a concern with Commander Morton." Mo peeked at Les from the corner of her eye, but Les's expression remained bland. "I went to the C6 academy," Finney said.

Mo found the idea of Finney at any academy difficult to grasp. It was hard to imagine that the confident woman in front of her had once worn a light blue cloak, done homework, shared a room in the dormitories, and been evaluated by the military. Would any of this year's cadets eventually have the power to decide between life and death?

"I chose Interior, and that's where I've stayed. From what I hear, you two will choose Defence."

"We're hoping to enter the fighter pilot program," Les said. Mo stood a little taller.

"I see," Finney said. "That's a tough one to get into, but not impossible. The aviacraft lessons you're taking should help."

Mo stared at her in disbelief. "My parents don't know about the lessons," Les said slowly.

"They won't hear about them from me. You're nineteen. You don't have to tell your parents everything. As for the fighter pilot program, you might want to look into booking simulator time."

"I thought only those in the program were allowed to use them," Les said.

"That's what they like you to think, but it's not true. The student pilots take priority, but you can try. If you're willing to get up early, you stand a better chance." Finney paused. "If you find out when the pilots are away on exercises, you might be able to book time at a reasonable hour. Book time together and you can fight each other."

Fight against Les? Mo would love the opportunity. Not only would it be fun, but blasting lasers at her would be a safe way to vent her frustrations. Don't want to share a room? *Blam!* Can't get together because some long-winded advocate is leading group and you have to prepare? *Blam-blam!* Can't make the concert? *Blam-blam-blam!* "We'll look into that as soon as we get back," she said, hardly able to contain her excitement at the prospect. She was almost glad they'd run into Finney.

"Get in as much practice as you can. How well you perform in the simulator will definitely be part of the evaluation when you apply for the program."

"Thank you for telling us," Les said.

"Yes, thanks," Mo added, a little bewildered that she was standing on a path chatting away with a commander. Finney almost seemed like a normal person. Maybe she could help save the agony of wading through regulations later. "Do you mind if I ask you a question about our cloaks?"

"Of course not," Finney said.

"I know we're supposed to wear our cloaks whenever we leave the academy. But does that mean we have to wear them at home?"

Finney pressed her lips together and studied Mo. "Do you mean inside the house?" she finally asked, a hint of laughter in her voice.

Mo's shoulders sagged. She was back to sounding like c3's resident simpleton. "No, I mean on the estates. We've been home a couple of times, but they were only overnight stays, so I never even went out. But this time we're home for a few days. Let's say I go for a walk around the estate. Do I have to wear my cloak?"

"No. When you're not sure, read Article 18. You have to wear your cadet cloak whenever you're in a public place in accordance with that article. Otherwise, you don't. The rule changes a bit when you're no longer a cadet, but you don't need to concern yourself with that now." She looked down at Mo's violin case. "Are you playing in the concert at the academy, the one that's taking place in a couple of weeks?"

     DISOBEDIENCE MEANS DEATH

"Yes," Mo said, trying not to sound too enthusiastic with Les standing next to her.

"I'll be there. One of my cousin's sons is performing."

"Oh." With her luck, she'd trip on stage or blow her duet, giving Finney even more reason to think she was an idiot.

Finney looked past them. "I want to talk to that patrol, so I'll have to go. I'm sure I don't need to remind you that attendance at all the festival's morning events is mandatory."

"No," she and Les said in unison.

"Good. Enjoy your break." Finney nodded to them.

They nodded in return and moved aside so she could pass between them.

"That was a surprise," Les murmured as Mo watched Finney join the two military down the path.

"It sure was." She picked up her violin case. If she'd also had a knapsack, her back would probably be killing her, but neither she nor Les had packed anything. Half their clothes were still at home, and since they would dress formally for all the festival-related events and visits, the casual clothing back in their academy rooms wouldn't do them much good. They wouldn't dress up tonight, though. Tonight, they'd go to the lake. She couldn't help but smile at Les.

"What?" Les said.

"Nothing." Mo slipped her arm through Les's, and they continued on their way.

LESLEY DODGED SEVERAL caterers whisking food into the kitchen as she made her way to the Thompson home's formal dining room. Festival suppers were always held the night before the festival—nobody had time to prepare a five-course meal on the festival day itself. If past years were any indication, tomorrow's supper would be a cold buffet in the smaller family dining room.

Mama stood at the near end of the long, rectangular dining table, studying a paper she held. "I'm just having one last look at the seating plan before I give it to the hostess," she murmured when Lesley stopped next to her. "She said she'll memorize it, even after I told her we're expecting over thirty." She lifted her head, then gaped. "You're not wearing *that.*"

"Mama, the supper is four hours away. I thought I'd go over to Mo's for a bit, get out of everyone's way."

"Be back in three. But don't go just yet. You should know about a change in the seating plan." She passed the sheet to Lesley. "And before you think I'm completely heartless, Susan and I discussed it. We both agreed it's time."

Lesley read the plan with a sinking feeling. There she was, seated between Karen and Jason, with Mo at the other end of the table. She sighed. "Why now?"

"Because you both have Chosens. We could have done it last year, when we knew for sure that you're a Chosen, but we held off. Now that we know you're both Chosens, it's time to start respecting that, at least symbolically. The chair next to you belongs to someone other than Mo."

"There are two chairs next to me. We don't know if my Chosen will claim the one on the left or the right, but we do know she won't claim both."

"Be that as it may, seating you next to Mo is no longer appropriate." Mama snatched back the seating plan. "It's only for a few hours. You have to start accepting that you have a Chosen."

"I do accept it!"

"Then you must understand that treating you and Mo as a couple at family events is only going to become more awkward. Nobody's saying you should stop seeing each other, but you can't expect to be treated as if you're Joined."

Lesley rubbed her forehead, then ran her hand through her hair. "I know, Mama." She paused. "Does Mo know?"

"Susan planned to mention it to her sometime today, before they arrive. Do you want me to beep her and ask her to do it now?"

"No." It would only take ten minutes to bike to the Middleton home. She'd rather tell Mo than arrive five minutes after Susan had told her.

"I have you down for CT12 tonight. Is that all right?"

Lesley nodded. After supper, those eighteen years and older would stand in turn and read an article from the Tradition. Tonight would be her second time and Mo's first.

Mama's mouth turned up at the corners. "It'll be nice to have you at the table again."

"It's good to be home," she said. They stared at each other. Lesley tipped her head toward the doorway. "I guess I'll go." She turned and walked out of the dining room.

Her cadet cloak hung on a hook near the door, but she reached for her brown one. Wearing the light blue one would only make her feel weak, reminding her of everything she was avoiding with Mo. The change in seating plan had dampened her spirits; she didn't need the cloak mocking her, too.

She set off for Mo's on her bike, looking forward to seeing her again, even though she'd seen Mo the previous evening. The visit to the lake had been idyllic—she couldn't remember the last time she'd taken the time to breathe. Mo had stuck to her plan to leave the academy behind, not raising the subject of sharing a room once, when she must have been dying to talk about it. Lesley had almost managed to forget that she had a Chosen; everything she loved about Mo—her feelings for her . . . everything—had rushed to the surface, and for the first time in a while, she hadn't berated herself. She'd felt alive and rejuvenated, almost seeing her relationship with Mo as something positive, rather than something she had to overcome.

But the conversation with Mama had brought her back to reality. She did have a Chosen; she did have to overcome and eventually cast aside her relationship with Mo. The change in the seating plan was only the first step of many. She understood the reason behind it, but without Mo beside her, the festival supper would never be the same. And how would Mo feel, sitting almost a room away? Mo already felt that Lesley was squeezing her out of her life. Now she'd have another slight to add to the list—now the families were doing it, too.

Sharing a room would run counter to what everyone apparently expected them to do: remain a couple, but publicly behave as friends. On the other hand, perhaps that was an argument in favour of sharing? Perhaps they needed to claim what they could while they could, because tradition, and *the* Tradition, would gradually take it all away from them. Or perhaps that was her way of rationalizing something she knew was wrong. If it was inappropriate for Mo to sit next to her at supper, how could she justify sharing a room? The answer had to be no.

She hopped off her bike at the Middletons' and guided it into the rack that stood to the left of the front door. Mo opened the door seconds after she knocked, saying, "I saw you ride up."

They kissed. Lesley drew back. "Did your Mama—"

"I know about the seating plan," Mo said tersely. "Maybe we can hide our comm units under the table and use them to talk to each other." She smiled, but her eyes remained dull.

"I didn't ask for the change."

"I know."

"I thought I heard your voice," Susan said, coming into the entrance hall from the living room. "It's nice to see you. We haven't seen you for a while, and now we're not only seeing you this week, but the week after next, too."

"The week after next?" Lesley said, confused.

"Yes! At the concert." Susan put her arm around Mo. "We're looking forward to it. Though she won't tell us what she'll be playing," She squeezed Mo and ruffled her hair. "You must know, Lesley. Tell me. Give me a hint."

Her face grew hot. She had no idea what Mo would be playing. They'd avoided all discussion of the concert since Lesley had made it clear she wouldn't be attending. Why hadn't Mo told her parents? Now she was on the spot. "I—"

"Now, now, Mama, that would be cheating," Mo said. "I want you to find out when you read the program. And I told you, I don't want any talk about the concert over the break. It'll only make me nervous."

"She practised outside this morning," Susan said, with a look that indicated she thought her daughter was a bit strange.

"Enough about the concert!" Mo said, ducking out from Susan's arm. "I thought you said you were going to the Indoctrination Academy."

"I am. It's my turn this year," she said to Lesley.

"Mo told me." And since Susan would be at the Indoctrination Academy for the festival, so would Mo, to Lesley's disappointment. Even though she and Mo weren't due back at the academy for three days, they wouldn't have much time alone together for the rest of the break. After the festival, Mo was off to visit relatives and would only return late the next day. The day after that, Lesley had to meet her cousins for brunch, then she and Mo would return to the academy on an early afternoon

  DISOBEDIENCE MEANS DEATH

train. She wanted to see if the academy's library had information about her potential mentors that wasn't available on the public network, and she believed Mo had a concert rehearsal.

"So yes, I'm off to help finish with the preparations." Susan shrugged on her cloak. "I'll see you later."

"What should we do?" Mo asked after Susan had gone. "We could maybe go to the Trading Centre. I want to stock up on those candies the academy's centre never has. Or we could stay here and maybe talk?" she said, hope in her eyes.

They should talk; otherwise, when would they? But Lesley wasn't ready. Every time she thought she'd come to a firm decision, something happened that called it into question. How could she tell Mo she wouldn't share a room when Mo had just covered for her, saving her a ton of embarrassment? And did she want to tell Mo today, after they'd just found out they'd sit at supper like strangers? Perhaps it would be better to wait for Mo to force the issue, or to let the deadline slip by. No, she'd promised they'd talk before they returned to the academy. But how?

She couldn't imagine telling Mo that she wouldn't share a room. Every time she tried to rehearse a conversation about it, something inside wouldn't let her say the words, even in her head. It should be easy. All she had to do was say one sentence, a sentence that would take less than three seconds to say. So why couldn't she say it?

Maybe because sharing a room wouldn't be so bad. They were both at the academy. They didn't intend to split up. If they didn't share, when would they see each other? But then, if they weren't supposed to sit next to each other at supper, should they share a room? Morton and the academy's administration would be scrutinizing her behaviour. Sharing a room with her lover might raise eyebrows.

She couldn't risk it.

So the dilemma that had paralyzed her for weeks was still there: she didn't intend to share a room, but she didn't want to hurt Mo. Once she'd figured out how to not do both, she'd open her flaming mouth and talk about it.

Mo waved her hand in front of Lesley's face. "Well?"

"Let's go to the Trading Centre," she said, cringing. "I'll have to go home to change cloaks first, though."

The hope faded from Mo's eyes. "Fine. I'll go with you." She stepped around Lesley, grabbed her cadet cloak, and marched out the door.

LESLEY PLUCKED A stone from the pile in her left hand and tossed it toward the lake. *Plop.* She transferred another to her right hand—a flat one, one that would be perfect for . . . She whipped it sidearm toward the lake. It skipped along the water four times before sinking beneath the surface. Not bad.

"I had a feeling I'd find you here," Papa said behind her. When he reached her side, she held out her hand and displayed the stones in her palm. He selected several. "I almost didn't recognize you in that cloak," he said as she threw one underhand. "I thought, what's that cadet doing on the estate? Then I realized it was you."

She chuckled. "When it's orange, you'll mistake me for a patrol."

"Seeing you in an orange cloak . . . now that'll take some getting used to." He threw a stone into the lake. "Mama's wondering where you are."

Wanting the goods in the knapsack at Lesley's feet, no doubt. She'd meant to return home as soon as she'd finished trading, but had found herself taking the path to the lake instead.

"We're a bit worried about you."

"Why?" she asked without looking at him.

"You don't seem yourself. I first noticed it during the festival supper."

And her demeanour at the festival itself probably hadn't helped. The skits, music, and food hadn't kept her mind off her dilemma, nor had the conversations with former classmates: *"How's Mo doing? Does Mo like the Military Academy? Which division is Mo choosing?"*

"Mama's worried that you're not happy at the Military Academy."

Lesley rolled her eyes. Hoping, more like.

He tossed three stones into the lake. "There'd be no shame if you decided the military isn't for you. Sometimes you don't know until you try."

"It's not that. I'm happy at the academy." She should be delirious— she expected to finish her first year at the top of her class, was on track to apply to the fighter pilot program, and the military had taken notice

     DISOBEDIENCE MEANS DEATH

of her. Yet she dreaded returning to the academy, where the tension between her and Mo would only increase.

"What is it, then?"

She crouched to look for more stones. "I'm just tired, that's all. It's been a busy year," she said as she scooped some up and looked for more. Papa didn't want to hear about her problems with Mo. He'd only think her weak and indecisive, and he'd probably tell Mama, the last thing she needed. Anyway, what advice could he offer? Had he ever had to choose between a girlfriend and the Way? "Papa, can I ask you a question? And if you don't want to answer it, don't. I'll understand."

"What is it?" he asked, curiosity in his voice.

"Did you have girlfriends before Mama?" Lesley kept her eyes on the three stones she was lifting from the sand. "Well, I'm sure you did, but was there anyone special?" She swallowed and slowly stood. Papa wasn't answering; he'd either decided it was none of her business or hadn't heard. As long as he wasn't angry . . . She selected a stone from her new supply and threw it underhand.

"There was someone," he said softly.

Really? She fought the urge to look at him, instead tossing another stone.

"We met in college, through a study group. I couldn't help but notice her, she picked up the lessons so quickly. I've always liked women with sharp minds, like your mama."

Mama had a sharp tongue to go with hers, though. "Were you still together when your Chosen Papers came?"

"Oh no, we split up long before then—when we left college."

"Because you had to?"

"Well, we didn't have to, not at that point. But we did. She was a Solitary. I was a Chosen. I think we both saw it as a college relationship from the beginning." He paused. "That doesn't mean it wasn't difficult, but you do move on."

She and Mo would eventually have no choice but to move on, but she couldn't imagine never seeing or talking to Mo. "Do you think about her much?"

"Not much, no. Occasionally, when I'm researching a case, I come across a case she advocated. And though I haven't seen her for over twenty-five years, I instantly think of her whenever I smell baking bread." His voice grew wistful. "Her papa was a baker."

Lesley realized she'd stopped throwing, too absorbed in the conversation. She dropped the remaining stones and finally looked at him. "What was her name?"

Papa shook his head. "That, I'll keep to myself. And I meant this to be a conversation about you, not me. Why the sudden interest in my past relationships?"

She scrambled for an answer, but couldn't think of anything that wouldn't sound like a lie. Just curious wouldn't do—he'd ask why she was curious.

"How are you and Mo doing?" he asked when it must have become obvious that she was flailing around for a reply. "She also seemed a little subdued at the festival supper."

"We're doing great. We would rather have been sitting next to each other, that's all."

"Are you sure?"

"Yes."

He studied her; she stared back and concentrated on relaxing the muscles in her face. "If there's a problem . . . if you want to talk . . ."

"Really, we're fine," she said firmly.

"Good afternoon," a man shouted. "Lovely day, isn't it?"

They whirled as two military strode up. Lesley recognized both men: Lieutenant Wilson and Sub-Lieutenant Taylor. "Nice to see you, Alan. And you, Cadet," Wilson said.

She stifled a chuckle. It had been plain old Lesley, last time she'd seen them. "Nice to see you, Lieutenant and Sub-Lieutenant."

"Did you enjoy the festival yesterday?"

Papa nodded. "We did. That new skit about the Adams Incident was quite good. A couple of the masks scared the children, though."

Taylor laughed and elbowed Wilson in the side. "We were just saying that they'll have to make a few adjustments for next year."

Lesley smiled. They'd have to either do away with the masks that suggested the character had been struck with a horrible flesh-eating disease, or not ask the children to gather near the front of the stage.

         DISOBEDIENCE MEANS DEATH

Three of the poor things had run screaming for their parents when the "Adamses" had made their entrance.

"Did you meet Commander Finney yet?" Taylor asked. "She's been making the rounds."

"A few days ago. We were surprised when she beeped us." Papa glanced down at his comm unit, as if he were expecting her to beep again at that moment. "And grateful, of course."

"She always beeps beforehand. Nobody wants to open the door and find a commander on the doorstep unannounced," Wilson said to murmurs of agreement.

"She certainly has a different way of doing things than Commander Newton," Papa said. "He was here for, what—twenty years? I think he visited the estate twice."

"I don't remember him visiting the estate," Lesley said.

Papa frowned. "You were either too young or not even born. That's how long ago it was. Commander Finney said to expect her more often."

"Everyone will have to be on their toes now," Taylor said, wagging a cautionary finger.

"Including us," Wilson said wryly. "Not that I'm complaining. When we heard the rumour that the admiral was considering her for C3, we hoped she'd get it."

"Why?" Papa asked.

"She has an excellent reputation. Several decorations, even though she's only in her mid-thirties. Strong in the Way. Doesn't hesitate to stick anyone who decides the Way isn't good enough for them, but at the same time won't stick someone unless she's sure. Not that I expect she'll load her stick much here, but if you do find yourself teetering on the brink, she'll give you a fair hearing."

Taylor nodded. "Tough but fair, that about sums it up. And military who've served under her have only good things to say. We're glad she's here."

He'd piqued Lesley's curiosity. Why would someone like Finney, strong in the Way and apparently highly regarded by her peers, end up overseeing C3? The sector was so quiet, it almost ran itself. "Was she just promoted to commander?"

Wilson shook his head. "That's another thing. She made commander quite young."

"Which sector did she oversee before?" Lesley asked.

"C4."

"Why did she switch?"

Taylor and Wilson exchanged bemused glances. "I think she's practising an interrogation technique she learned at the academy. I'd be careful," Taylor said. They shared a laugh.

Lesley's cheeks burned. "I'm sorry. I—"

Wilson waved her apology away. "He's only teasing. As for your question, I don't know why she transferred to C3. That's between her and the admiral. All I can tell you is that she's just returned from leave, after having her son."

"Her son?" Lesley blurted. For some reason, she'd never pictured commanders with children.

"Yes. She has two sons and a daughter."

That must be a strain. As far as she knew, commanders worked long days and were on call all the time. Finney would inevitably be summoned at odd hours, even in C3.

"Anyway, if we don't get moving, we'll fall behind on our patrol, and that won't impress our new leader at all." Wilson motioned for Taylor to follow him. "Let's go."

"Enjoy the rest of the afternoon," Taylor said.

Papa nodded to him. "Thank you."

They started to walk off, but then Wilson turned around, still walking. "Oh, I'll give you the same advice I'm giving everyone else," he said. "If you can't think of anything to say when Commander Finney visits, ask her about the history of the Chosen Tradition. She'll talk your ear off."

No wonder Finney's name had sounded familiar when Mo had first mentioned it! A few years ago, she'd given a lecture at the academy about the history of Article CT52. When group had studied the article last month, the suggested reading list had included a transcript of the lecture. Lesley would have to dig it up and read it again.

"I'm heading back, or Mama will start worrying about me, too," Papa said. "Are you coming?"

"I think I'll stay here for a bit, enjoy the peace and quiet while I can."

"Okay." He bent forward to pick up the knapsack and slung it over his shoulder. "You can talk to me if you want. You know that, right?"

"Yes, Papa." She expected him to set off, but he didn't seem to want to leave. "I'm fine. Really."

"If you change your mind . . ."

She nodded. "I know."

"I'll leave you be, then." He pulled out his comm unit. "I should let Mama know I'm on my way back. See you later." She watched him walk away. "Supper's in two hours," he called over his shoulder.

When Lesley couldn't see him anymore, she crouched and gathered the stones she'd dropped earlier. As she tossed them into the lake, her mind returned to Mo, relationships, and sharing a room. Papa had apparently survived a serious relationship and seemed to look back fondly on the experience. How would Mo look back on their relationship? Would she grow wistful, as Papa had, thinking about the times they'd laughed and smiled and danced together, or would she remember the last few months, when their time together was always rushed and everything important turned into a battle? *"We weren't that serious. We didn't even share a room when we were at the Military Academy,"* she imagined Mo saying. *"The relationship fizzled out on its own. By the end of our second year, we hardly saw each other."*

No! That wasn't what she wanted. Their relationship *was* serious, and she wanted to share a room. That was why she couldn't talk to Mo, why "no" wouldn't come out. If only she could justify it, figure out how to show that she was strong in the Way and serious about her future military career, despite caring too much for someone who wasn't her Chosen.

Lesley threw the remaining stones down and walked along the beach. If she intended to keep her promise to Mo, she'd better do her deciding quickly. She had to come up with a solution by the end of the day, or she'd have to break her promise or say no, and she didn't want to do either. Both would disappoint Mo.

Frustrated, she kicked at the sand again and again and again, not caring when the wind blew it back at her. As much as she hated to admit it, as much as she wished she felt differently, she couldn't deny that disappointing Mo would hurt her much more than disappointing the military. She'd go along with Morton's suggestions, but perhaps the military had made a mistake this time. Perhaps Mama would get her wish after all.

MO RUMMAGED THROUGH her closet to see if there were any clothes she wanted to take back to the academy. She'd sort of missed a couple of shirts, but her drawers were already bursting and Kary would flip if she asked for more closet space. Since it looked like she and Kary would share again next year, Mo didn't want to antagonize her.

She backed out of the closet, slid the door shut, and tried to think positive. Okay, so she'd been home for over an hour and had left Les a message, but Les hadn't beeped. The day wasn't over, and there was still tomorrow morning. Yeah, right. Who was she kidding? It was already 22:45. That left tomorrow. But Les was having an early brunch with her cousins; unless she intended to visit at the crack of dawn or to squeeze in a discussion on the train platform so she could claim she'd technically kept her promise, they wouldn't be talking about sharing a room anytime soon, if ever.

Les must still be struggling with whatever was on her mind. Flaming Argamon! Mo appreciated that Les thought every decision through carefully and always tried to do the right thing, even when it hurt her personally—that was one of the reasons Mo loved her. But just this once, she'd take rash and shallow!

She sighed. No, she wouldn't. That wouldn't be the Les she loved, the Les she wanted to scream her lungs out at. Nor would it be the Les who'd always kept her promises . . . until now. Mo hoped Les's silence wasn't a sign of things to come.

Her comm station beeped twice in rapid succession—a dispatch. It could wait. But then it beeped again, this time signalling that someone was trying to reach her. Mo rushed to the station and read the screen, then read it again: *L. Thompson*.

"Hi!" she said as soon as they were connected.

"Is it too late for me to drop by? I want to talk to you . . . about sharing a room," Les said.

"No, come on over," Mo said, working hard to mask her surprise. "I'm still up."

"I'm leaving right now." The connection went dead.

Mo flopped onto her bed, dazed and relieved. Les may have left it to the last minute, but she was honouring her promise. No matter what she said when she arrived, their relationship still meant something to her. But what had she decided? Finally, an answer, but after desperately wanting one, Mo dreaded what she'd hear and imagined the worst.

By the time the tap at the door came, she'd convinced herself that Les was definitely going to say no, but pasted a smile on her face and swung the door open.

Les strode into the room. "I'm sorry it's so late. I know I sent you a dispatch, but I still wanted to talk to you about it in person."

"A dispatch," Mo said slowly, confused. "Wait, you mean just before you beeped me?"

"Yes."

"I haven't read it."

"Oh."

"I would have read it if I'd known it was from you. But right after you beeped me, I had to . . . help Mama with something." Les didn't need to know she'd lain on the bed for the past ten minutes, sweating about this conversation.

"I sent you the room request form, with my half filled in and signed."

"Oh, okay," Mo said, determined not to let on that Les had just made her week. Since Les was treating it matter-of-factly, so would she. "I'm glad. You know it's what I want."

"Well, it makes sense. We're both so busy, and it's only going to get worse. If we don't share a room, we'll hardly see each other."

Mo nodded and said, "I know," while frantically wondering what Les meant by "it's only going to get worse."

"Can we sit down?" Les asked.

"Sure." Mo sat on the edge of the bed, expecting Les to sit next to her. But Les pulled the chair out from under the desk, wheeled it toward the bed, and positioned it directly in front of Mo. She lowered herself into it; their legs touched. When Les took Mo's hands and kissed them, Mo braced herself—she had the feeling she wasn't going to like whatever was coming. Still, her heart sped up when Les gazed at her, and not from apprehension.

"Commander Morton came to see me last week," Les said. "Remember him?"

"Of course I remember him." She wasn't likely to forget the commander who'd taught her that, if she was tense enough, she could pull a muscle while standing still. But even if she'd forgotten about the incident at the evaluation, the recent tales flying around about Les's encounter with him would have reminded her. So, she was about to find out what had really happened. About flaming time. "What did he want?"

"To give me some extra help."

"What do you mean?" Les didn't need help; she was doing well in all her classes, as usual.

"He said I'm an excellent fit for the military. They want to give me a mentor, and they want me to work on my public speaking skills."

"Why public speaking?"

"Well, he said I could make admiral," she said sheepishly.

"Admiral? Um, you do realize that to get to admiral, you have to go through commander, right?"

"I doubt he meant it."

Mo was sure he meant it. If anyone could make admiral, Les could.

"Admiral or no, the first step is to graduate from the academy. If they're willing to help, I won't turn them down." Les's hands tightened around Mo's. "But it means I'll be busier next year."

So that was it.

"I'm joining the group that records announcements for the academy. And I'll also want to volunteer for more activities related to the Way, to show that I'm strong in the Way."

Mo pulled her right hand from Les's and scratched her nose, hoping to hide her dismay. Now it was all clear. Les wanted their relationship, but it was low on her priority list. Impressing Morton and his cronies was most important to her. So how to do that and keep Mo happy? Well, how about share a room with her? What a brilliant idea! Mo could imagine the conversations now: *Les, we hardly spend any time together! Now Mo, that may be true, but just think—every morning when you wake up, you get to see the indentation on my pillow where my head lay all night.*

But what was she supposed to do? Tell Les to limit her career options and throw away a great opportunity because it meant they'd see less of each other? Refuse to share a room, forcing Les to either spend time with her or dump her? Considering that Les probably viewed their relationship as a practice run for the real thing, making her choose between their relationship and her career would be stupid.

If they were Chosens this conversation would be completely different. They probably wouldn't even be having it. But they didn't know if they were. No wonder Les had put their almost five-year relationship at the bottom of her list.

Calm down! Les wouldn't be there if their relationship meant nothing to her. She would have let the deadline slip by or said no. Wait a second—"Why would they think you're not strong in the Way?"

Les hesitated, then shrugged. "I don't know how they'll look upon me being serious about you."

Mo swallowed. "Les, don't share a room if you think it's the wrong thing to do."

"I want to share with you."

"Are you sure?"

Les nodded. "I'm sure."

Now Mo felt selfish, though she wasn't sure she should. Maybe Les was holding herself to too high a standard; maybe she wasn't. Either way, agreeing to share a room when she thought it might tarnish her image was a huge concession on her part. Mo wouldn't throw it back in her face, even though she wasn't thrilled with the way things were turning out. She suspected that Les planned to knock herself out with all these new activities whether they shared or not, so better to move into the same room and then work on their schedules than to refuse the room and never see her.

"Like you said earlier, it makes sense," Mo said. "Right now, it's hard to even study together when Kary or Jackie is around. When we share, we can at least do that. It'll be nice to be together, even if we're just reading." She inwardly snorted. Who was she trying to convince, herself or Les?

"Let's hope the request goes through."

She restrained from retorting that it would have had a better chance if Les hadn't taken so long to make up her flaming mind, and said, "I'm sure it will."

They sat and stared at each other. There didn't seem much else to say—not that night, anyway.

"I'd better go," Les said. "I don't want to fall asleep during the brunch tomorrow." She rolled the chair back under the desk, then held out her arms.

Mo went to her without hesitation. "I'm looking forward to sharing a room," she murmured into Les's ear. And she was, despite her suspicion that Les's full days would soon have them at each other's throats.

Les drew back and kissed her, a lingering kiss that left Mo breathless when they finally parted. "I'll see you tomorrow," Les said.

Mo smiled at her. "Enjoy brunch."

After Les had gone, Mo sat on the edge of her bed and reviewed the conversation. Okay, so she'd got what she wanted—sort of. She'd have to see how much time they actually had for each other after Les had scheduled all her activities, though she wasn't sure what she could do if it turned out that they hardly had any. She couldn't ask Les to risk her dreams and her reputation for their relationship, not when their relationship might not have a future. At the same time, it was a struggle not to feel resentful about Les's current priorities.

Her determination to be patient and understanding while Les tried to impress Morton and company had better turn out to be worth it. She still harboured the hope, the belief, that they were Chosens. If they weren't, she was a fool to be making sacrifices for Les and her career when some other woman would reap the benefits.

"SO YOU AGREE that I should go with Larson?" Lesley said as she followed Mo onto the train platform.

"Yeah, for sure." Mo switched her violin case to her left hand and reached behind her with her right.

Lesley smiled. "They all sound good," she said, grasping Mo's fingers. "But not only has Larson gone through the program, he's still an active pilot."

"According to that biography, he's also in charge of domestic patrols. You can't beat that. He'll help us a lot. Well, you."

     DISOBEDIENCE MEANS DEATH

"Us. I'll tell you everything he tells me."

"You better." They walked through the station's waiting area and entered the courtyard. Mo glanced around. "Not many back yet. Oh, there's David. David!" Mo called, waving as vigorously as she could while holding her violin.

He waved and sauntered over to them. "You two are back early."

"So are you," Lesley said.

"I haven't finished two assignments due tomorrow, and with a house full of screeching cousins, I figured I'd have a better chance of getting them done here." He pointed at Mo's violin case. "You back for a rehearsal?"

Mo nodded.

"The concert's what, just over a week away now?"

"Yeah, don't remind me."

"I'm looking forward to it, and the reception afterward."

Lesley felt like an outsider. Everyone would gather around Mo, congratulating her and sharing her special evening. Everyone except her.

"Our last chance to enjoy ourselves before the exam crunch," he continued.

Mo groaned. "Instead of practising, I'll be cramming. Wish I could relax for a bit. Oh, guess what? The commander of our sector is going to the concert."

"Are you serious? Everyone's going!"

"Well, I'm sure not *everyone* is going," Mo said, for Lesley's benefit, no doubt. "But I don't want to humiliate myself in front of the ones that are, so I better get going. I want to get an hour in before rehearsal."

"You two want to meet at the mess hall for supper?"

"Yeah, let's," Mo said. "Around 18:00?"

David nodded.

"We'll see you later," Mo told him.

"I'm not sure I want to have supper with him," Lesley said when they'd walked out of earshot.

"If he brings up the concert, I'll tell him I don't want to talk about it because it makes me nervous," Mo said. "Which isn't exactly a lie."

"Thanks," she mumbled, feeling small. Along with everyone else,

David had assumed she'd attend the concert. She'd lacked the courage to correct him.

"I want to change before I practice," Mo said. "You going straight to the library?"

Lesley wanted to stay with Mo. They still held hands, but the tension that had lessened at home had risen between them again. A whole five minutes back at the academy—that was all it had taken. "I can come with you if you want, walk partway to the recreation centre."

Mo appeared to think about it. "No, you go ahead. I'll see you later." She squeezed Lesley's hand, then hurried down the path to the dormitories before Lesley could respond.

Lesley stared after her. As much as she'd like to go to the concert, she couldn't—not after she'd already given in to sharing a room. Too bad none of the potential mentors could advise her on how to reconcile Mo, the military's expectations, and the Way. That was where she really needed help, though she'd never admit that to anyone, especially her mentor. *So, Thompson, you think you can make admiral, but you can't even put your girlfriend in her place?*

She was trying, but it was tearing her apart.

MO WIPED HER violin and carefully placed it in its case.

"Remember, 19:00 sharp!" the conductor said.

Butterflies fluttered in her stomach. Tomorrow night she'd be right here on this stage, but facing an audience. Her parents, her siblings, her friends, even Commander Finney—they'd all be out there, listening. But no Les. Mo sighed. It wouldn't be the same without Les.

"I'll see you tomorrow," one of the other violinists said, excitement and anticipation raising her voice an octave. Mo nodded as she picked up her violin.

As soon as she stepped outside, she turned on her comm unit and checked for messages. A couple of dispatches had arrived. She requested the list and almost dropped the comm unit when she saw *RE: Room Request #3432-976*. Her heart raced. Please, please let it be a confirmation.

First things first—she put down her violin. Throwing it into the air with glee or smashing it in disappointment wouldn't bode well for her

impending performance. Her hand shook as she opened the dispatch—
a lot rode on this.

*Your request to share a room with Cadet Lesley Thompson has been
fulfilled.*

Yes! Yes, yes, yes! She danced a little jig around her violin, then read
the message in its entirety. It had arrived almost an hour and a half
ago. Les must have received the confirmation, but she hadn't beeped
and left a message, even though she'd said she'd be in her room all
night, preparing for her group meeting. Well, this news called for an
interruption.

After dropping off her violin, Mo hurried to Les's room and rapped
sharply on her door.

Les opened it; her face lit up with surprise. "I wasn't expecting
you."

"Didn't you get a dispatch?"

"A dispatch?" Les said, stepping aside so Mo could enter the room.

"Les, we got a room!"

"We did? Let me look. I've been ignoring beeps." She grabbed her
comm unit from her nightstand and peered at its display. A smile
spread across her face. "It's in this dormitory. I won't have to carry my
clothes very far."

"No, you won't," Mo said, wondering if Les was smiling because they
had a room or because of the room's location. "I wonder where Kary will
end up. I hope she's in this dormitory, too."

"She might end up next door. I'm pretty sure Kyle and Jeremy are
moving."

"That would be great. We've become good friends."

"We both did well with roommates," Les said. "I wouldn't call Jackie
and me friends, but we get along okay. I wanted a roommate who didn't
snore and wasn't messy, and she worked out that way." Les paused. "At
least with you, I know for sure I'll be sharing with someone who doesn't
snore."

"That's right." Wait a minute . . . "Hey!" She playfully punched Les's
arm.

Les chuckled and pulled Mo closer. "I'm looking forward to it," she
said, wrapping her arms around her.

Mo snuggled against Les. This was more like it.

"It'll be nice, waking up with you every day."

It sure would. So would sharing a bed after lights out.

"We'll be living together! We were under the same roof at the Indoctrination Academy, but that wasn't the same." Les squeezed Mo tighter and kissed the top of her head. "I can't wait!"

"What about the concert? Are you sure you can't go?" Mo said, caught up in Les's excitement. She instantly regretted it; doubly so when Les stiffened.

Les let go of Mo and dropped her arms to her sides. "I can't."

"I know you'd have to miss group, but it's only one night."

"Haven't you been listening? I've already agreed to share a room. I can't do anything more right now." Les turned away and straightened the pile of notes on her nightstand.

"You really think missing group for one night will matter?"

"Yes, I do. And not finishing my assignment will matter, too, so I'd better get back to it."

Mo bit her tongue. She had to get out of the room before she exploded. "I'll see you tomorrow, then." Without a backward glance, she marched from the room and stormed along the corridor.

One night. One flaming night! She'd honestly believed that Les would change her mind, that there was no way she'd miss the concert. She was trying hard to accommodate everything important to Les, so why couldn't Les give up one measly evening and support her for once? Mo shook her head. She was sick of trying to figure it out.

On the way back to her room, she considered what to do with Les's seat. She couldn't give it to one of her siblings, because the others would feel slighted—one of the reasons she'd given the leftover seat to Kary in the first place. Maybe give it to Ben, so he and Kary could sit together? She reached for her comm unit, knowing Kary wasn't in their room, but then shoved her hand into her pocket. She might be a fool and a hopeless, idiotic moron, but she wasn't ready to concede defeat, not yet. Until the auditorium doors closed and the concert began, it wasn't over. Les still had time to change her mind. And if she didn't, Mo would rather see an empty seat than someone in Les's place. Nobody could ever take Les's place.

     DISOBEDIENCE MEANS DEATH

LESLEY SHUT HER room's door with a sigh of relief and set the bag containing her supper on the nightstand. In here, she wouldn't have to listen to someone going on about tonight's concert. In class, in the library, on the paths . . . it seemed like everyone was talking about going. Of course, that wasn't true—the auditorium only held so many. But since all the musicians were first- and second-year students, much of the audience would be as well, and that included just about everyone she knew at the academy. At least she could eat supper in peace, though she'd have to hurry. Dodging everyone between the mess hall and the dormitory had put her behind schedule. She didn't want to be late for group.

As she ate, she thought about Mo. After last night, she'd expected Mo to be angry with her, but Mo had seemed preoccupied, probably with the concert. What would Mo be doing at that moment? She was probably backstage, perhaps squeezing in some last minute practice, or whispering nervously with a fellow musician, the hum of the crowd growing louder as excited family and friends arrived and took their seats. Mo's parents and siblings were probably already there, or rushing from the train station to the auditorium. They'd be at the reception afterward, proud and happy, celebrating with Mo and her friends. And tomorrow, everyone would say what a wonderful time they'd had and how much they looked forward to the next one.

Lesley swallowed the last bit of potato and looked around the room. Suddenly it seemed very quiet and felt very lonely.

Well, she'd be with people soon enough. Time for group. She returned her dirty dishes to the bag, planning to drop them off at the mess hall on the way to the recreation centre. Since both were in the same direction as the auditorium, it would be safe to take the direct route—everyone would assume she was on her way to the concert. She reached for her cloak, then dropped her hand. The recreation centre wasn't far and it was warm outside; she hadn't worn her cloak all day. Instead she cradled the bag against her chest and started to lift her satchel, then stopped as if paralyzed.

What was she doing? Did she honestly think she could skip Mo's concert and everything would remain the same between them? How would she face Mo tomorrow? Would Mo still believe that she cared, that their relationship was important? Tonight was a huge night for Mo. Lesley couldn't miss it, nor did she want to.

She slammed down the satchel, yanked her comm unit from its holder, and punched in a code with her thumb as she hurried out the door. "Heather?" she said, bounding down the stairs two at a time. "It's Lesley. Sorry for the short notice, but I won't be at group tonight."

"Oh." A pause. "Is everything okay? When I ran into you earlier, you were reading Whitner's commentary. I figured you were preparing for tonight."

"I was. But I've decided to go to the concert," she said, too focused on getting to the mess hall to come up with a believable excuse.

"Nobody else has beeped to say they're not coming." Heather said, her tone eloquent with disapproval.

"Sorry. Anyway, I have to go." She'd need both hands to unload the dishes.

"See you next week, then, I guess." The connection went dead.

Lesley winced. She'd beep Heather tomorrow, try to smooth things over. Right now, the concert was her first priority.

Approaching the auditorium from the mess hall, she was relieved to see a few Rymellans still waiting in line. She joined the end of the queue and listened to the excited chatter filtering from the lobby, her own anticipation growing.

"Ticket," said the usher when she reached him.

Ticket? Mo had never said anything about tickets! "I don't have one."

He frowned. "You don't need one if you're on the reserved list. What's your name?"

"Lesley Thompson. But I don't know if I'm on the list." While he entered her name into his comm unit, she stared at her feet, despairing. Half an hour ago she hadn't been planning to attend, but now she'd be crushed if he turned her away.

"Here you are. A friend of Cadet Middleton, right?"

She lifted her head, surprised and grateful that Mo hadn't given her seat away. "Yes."

"Do you know Michael and Susan Middleton and Kary Dixon?"

"Yes, I do."

"They're already here, so look for them. They'll be somewhere in the first four rows. Enjoy the performance."

"Thank you."

The concert would begin in less than five minutes, leaving no time to linger in the lobby and take in the atmosphere. She accepted a program from another usher as she entered the auditorium and scanned those seated near the front as she walked down the aisle. Movement caught her eye—Kary, waving at her from the third row. Lesley smiled and repeatedly murmured "excuse me" as she sidled along the row to the remaining empty seat.

"Glad you could make it," Kary said.

Michael leaned forward and looked at her across Kary. "You cut it a bit close, didn't you?"

Before she could respond, a lieutenant walked onto the stage and motioned for everyone to stand. Lesley held hands with Kary and the man seated to her left. The lieutenant joined the rather rectangular circle formed by those in the first and second rows. He nodded, and everyone present recited, "Disobedience means death. Death to those who commit a Chosen Violation. Death to those who disobey. Death to those who violate the Way. Death to those who violate the Way. Death to those who violate the Way!" Applause filled the auditorium.

The lieutenant returned to the stage. "Thank you, and welcome. Tonight, you'll be treated to a wonderful variety of pieces by our talented first- and second-year musicians. The concert will run for approximately one and a half hours, after which we hope you'll join us at the reception in the main hall off the lobby. And now, please welcome our musicians."

Still on her feet, Lesley watched in anticipation for Mo to appear, her height allowing her a clear view of the stage's wings. The auditorium thundered with another round of applause as the musicians filed onto the stage and took their places. There she was! Lesley willed Mo to look her way, but Mo's attention seemed to be focused on making it to her seat.

Everyone clapped when the conductor entered. She bowed and waited for the applause to die before introducing the first piece. Lesley only half listened, her eyes on Mo. Now that Mo was safely seated, she was scanning the front rows. Her eyes met Lesley's; slowly, she smiled. Lesley smiled in return, so widely that her cheeks ached. For a moment, grinning at each other, they were the only two people in the auditorium.

Then a polite round of applause dragged Lesley back to her surroundings. The lights dimmed, Mo's attention shifted to the conductor, and the musicians launched into the piece. Lesley watched Mo play and wondered how she'd ever thought she could miss the concert. She'd earned Heather's disappointment and put Mo before her commitment to group, but she was sure she'd made the right decision. For once she'd trusted what her instincts had screamed at her—and now that she was here, what she fully believed. Going to group would have been a mistake. Tonight she belonged here, with Mo.

LESLEY WALKED DOWN the wide steps that led to the reception hall and picked up a glass of grape juice from one of the refreshment tables. Beside her, Susan surveyed the selection and chose apple juice. "She did great, didn't she, Mama?" Neil said, joining them.

"She certainly did."

"When she told us she was taking violin lessons, I thought it would be a passing fancy," Michael said, selecting his own glass of juice. "But now she's talking about auditioning for the student orchestra."

"If it accepts her, she'll play at other academies," Lesley said, dismayed but not surprised that this was the first she'd heard of Mo's interest in the orchestra. Now that they wouldn't have to avoid everything related to Mo's violin, she couldn't wait to ask her about it, and to tell her how she'd sat enraptured throughout the concert, her ear to the violins and her heart bursting with pride.

They moved away from the table to make room for others.

". . . looked petrified when he walked onstage," a familiar voice was saying nearby. David. "I thought he was going to faint."

"He was okay once he sat down," Bruce said. "Oh, look who's here," he added as Lesley and the Middletons joined the circle.

"You must be proud of Mo," David said. "She looked totally at ease up there."

"The duet was beautiful," Beth, a fellow first-year student, said. "I think that was my favourite part of the concert."

Susan's face lit up. "When she first started, I was so nervous for her,

I couldn't enjoy it. But once I settled down, all I could think was, 'That's my daughter up there!'"

Lesley grinned, remembering how she'd listened in awe, mesmerized by the movement of Mo's bow. And to be here now, reliving the experience with others . . . hearing about it tomorrow, second-hand, would have been a poor substitute. She couldn't remember the last time she'd smiled so much or felt so relaxed—her inner struggle around how to please everyone seemed to have called a truce for the evening. Perhaps she should trust her instincts more often.

Kary squeezed herself between David and Bruce; Ben hovered behind her, his hand on her shoulder. "When they got to that tricky part in the middle, I was holding my breath. I knew she was worried about it," she said.

"She played it flawlessly," Lesley said, gesturing in Kary's direction with her glass. "And she—"

"Cadet Thompson!" a voice cracked behind her.

She turned. Her fingers tightened around the glass. Commander Morton stopped in front of her. "What are *you* doing here?"

Lesley tried to speak, but her mouth wouldn't move.

"Doesn't the Chosen Tradition group meet tonight?"

She nodded. Those around her fell silent.

"Then I'll ask you again, *what* are you doing here?"

"Um . . ."

"I assume she came for the concert, like everyone else," came an answer from her right in a low, feminine voice. Lesley's heart sank when she placed it: Commander Finney.

Morton's jaw tightened. "I'd like an answer from the cadet."

"Why don't we ask her privately?" Finney said.

He looked past Lesley's right shoulder. "This doesn't concern you."

"This cadet is from my sector. It concerns me."

Morton continued to gaze over Lesley's shoulder for several seconds. Then he looked away. "Very well. Follow me." He whirled.

"Hold onto my drink. I'll be back in a few minutes," Finney murmured to someone, at the same time Susan lifted the glass from Lesley's hand.

Lesley willed herself to move, keeping her eyes on Morton's back and aware of Finney walking behind her. Shame flooded through her. She couldn't feel more mortified, having two commanders march her out of the reception in front of the Middletons, her friends, and many of her classmates. She'd ruined the entire evening, not only for herself, but for Mo. Now everyone would talk about the cadet in trouble, not the wonderful performances.

Morton ushered them into a small office near the auditorium's entrance, startling the Rymellan sitting at the desk. He jerked his thumb over his shoulder. "Out!" The wide-eyed woman scurried from the room.

"What has she done that's so terrible that you had to make a public spectacle of her?" Finney asked after he'd shut the door.

He jabbed his finger at Lesley. "This cadet belongs to a group that studies the Chosen Tradition. She skipped its weekly meeting to come to this concert."

"That's it?"

"What do you mean, that's it?"

Finney shrugged. "I'm sure whatever article they're studying tonight will come up again."

"That isn't the point. And it's not the only reason I'm upset." He pulled his comm unit from its holder and tapped its buttons. "File 3432976, Academy Section."

Finney yanked out her comm unit, presumably to pull up the file. "I still don't see the problem," she said a minute later.

"Would it help if I told you that Cadet Middleton was one of the performers tonight?"

"No, it wouldn't," Finney replied.

"No wonder the admiral has you babysitting C3. Speaking of which, don't you think you should be getting back?" Morton examined the floor around his feet. "Someone might have dropped a piece of litter while you've been here."

Up to that point, Lesley had avoided looking directly at either commander, but now she couldn't help glancing at Finney.

Finney's face was a blank slate. "Cadet Thompson is nineteen. Don't you remember what it was like when you were a student at the academy? Everyone paired up and shared rooms."

Morton's face reddened. "I don't care what everyone was doing or is doing. I care about what *this* cadet is doing. Every year, we handpick a few cadets we think will go all the way. Those we think are different from the rest. Those who hold themselves to a higher standard. Those who don't toss aside commitments without any thought. Those who minimize unnecessary distractions, especially ones that won't lead anywhere. This cadet is on that list, and that makes her behaviour unacceptable."

"I know about the list. But—"

"Then I shouldn't have to explain everything to you." He shifted his attention to Lesley. "You know Heather, the leader of the Chosen Tradition group?"

Lesley nodded.

"She's being mentored. Did you see her at the concert tonight?"

"No."

"Did you see her deciding that she didn't have to bother with group?"

"No."

"You chose to skip group because of Cadet Middleton, didn't you?"

"Yes," Lesley said without hesitation.

"You chose Cadet Middleton over your commitment to the group."

"Yes."

Morton's eyes bored into her. "I'm extremely disappointed with your display of poor judgment. But I'm willing to give you one chance to get your priorities in order. You can start by rescinding the room request and making sure that you attend all of this year's remaining group meetings." He paused to draw breath. "I have a meeting with Lieutenant Commander Larson on Thursday to discuss the possibility of mentoring you. He's a busy man. He'll want some assurance that his time will be well invested, and he may not feel that way when he hears about this. What should I tell him that'll ease any doubts he has about you? What can you tell me that'll ease my doubts?"

Lesley scrambled for something to say in her own defence. But all that ran through her mind was how sure she was that her decision to attend the concert, to be there for Mo, had been right. If arranging her priorities to match Morton's expectations meant turning her back on

Mo and others she cared about, she couldn't do it. If that meant she was weak in the Way, then she was; and if that meant she'd serve her career out as an ensign, so be it. She'd rather wear an ensign's insignia and be at peace with herself than wear an admiral's and cringe at her reflection in the mirror. "Nothing," she said, her voice stronger than she'd expected, given that she was about to jeopardize her future. "You misjudged me."

Shock crossed his face, shock he quickly masked. "Well, then. I'll remove you from the list. One less cadet I have to worry about."

"Removing her from the list would be a mistake," Finney said.

Lesley looked at her in surprise.

"Oh, would it?" Morton said. "Even she thinks I've misjudged her. You don't?"

"No, I agree with her," Finney said, to Lesley's dismay. "But I don't think you should remove her from the list."

"I'm not going to waste my time trying to convince Larson or anyone else to mentor her when even she doesn't think she deserves a mentor."

"Just have them read her file."

"Finney, not all of us have time to lounge around reading files," Morton said, rolling his eyes. "These are busy people, unlike some I could mention."

Finney inhaled deeply and took her time exhaling. "I assume they'll take the time to read the file of anyone they're considering. If they don't, they're not worth having as mentors."

Morton barked a laugh. "If you're such an expert on mentoring, why don't you mentor her? After all, you're the one who thinks it's a mistake to remove her from the list."

"You know, that's not a bad idea. I think I will."

"What? Are you serious?"

"Yes, I am. I'll mentor her. It'll allow me to keep an eye on the situation."

Morton shook his head. "No. Perhaps I was a little hasty about taking her off the list. I let my disappointment get the better of me." He turned to Lesley. "And I can understand why you think I may have misjudged you, Cadet. You're young, and you might find the sacrifices we'll require of you difficult to make. That's why you need a mentor. If

     DISOBEDIENCE MEANS DEATH

you'd already had one, I'm sure your lapses in judgement would have been avoided. With Lieutenant Commander Larson advising you on all your future decisions, we can avoid a repeat of tonight. I'll soothe over any misgivings he might have."

"Why can't I mentor her?" Finney asked. "I thought she could request anyone."

"She can. She requested Lieutenant Commander Larson."

"And now I'm putting my name forward for consideration. Since you haven't talked to Larson yet, it's not too late."

Morton glared at Finney and folded his arms. "I guess it's up to the cadet, then. So, Cadet, do you want to stick with Lieutenant Commander Larson, or take Commander Finney up on her offer to mentor you?"

They both stared at her. Lesley forced herself to look back at them. Who to favour: the commander of her sector, who could oversee C3 for years, or the commander of the Military Academy, who probably held her future in the palm of his hand? Both choices could have dire consequences, and that annoyed her. Did either of them have her best interests in mind, or were they using her to spite each other?

Morton, despite his backtracking, had doubts about her. Well-founded doubts, since she knew that she couldn't meet his expectations and didn't want to. He'd only changed his mind about keeping her on the list to prevent Finney from becoming her mentor. As for Finney, did she honestly intend to act as a mentor, or had she only offered in the heat of the moment? And why had she insisted that Lesley stay on the list, when she'd agreed that Morton had misjudged her? Was it just a way of getting at Morton? At first Lesley had been grateful to Finney for defending her, but now she wondered if Finney would have done so if Morton wasn't involved.

She couldn't be sure of their motives, so she'd have to assume that they both wanted to help. Her instincts were telling her to go with Finney, but they were the same instincts that had landed her in this mess in the first place. Going with Morton wouldn't make sense, though. Two minutes ago he'd been more than ready to remove her from the list, and his priorities weren't her priorities. Plus he'd referred to Mo as a distraction, dismissing her as if she were nothing. Just for that, she'd prefer to deal with him as little as possible.

Finney it was, then, though she hoped she wasn't about to saddle herself with an incompetent mentor. The military at home had spoken highly of Finney, but Morton, who'd have more information, didn't seem impressed. Still, Finney's interest, if sincere, could prevent Morton from sabotaging Lesley's future. She took a deep breath. "I accept Commander Finney's offer."

"Good," Finney said as Morton scowled at Lesley. "And since I'll be mentoring her, I decide if she stays on the list or should be removed. If you have a problem with her, talk to me."

"Oh, don't worry," Morton said, raising his hands in a gesture of surrender. "I'll make sure that everyone knows you're responsible for this cadet."

"I'm sure you have a plan prepared for her second year. I'd like to see it."

Morton whipped out his comm unit and pressed several buttons. "I just dispatched it to you. But I'm responsible for reporting to our superiors about the list, so I expect regular progress reports from you."

"Of course," Finney murmured.

"Apart from that, you're on your own. So I'll let you decide where the cadet goes when she leaves this room. If it were up to me, I wouldn't reward her by sending her back to the reception, but I'll leave it up to you. Now if you don't mind, I'd like to continue with my evening. Good night." He nodded to Finney and strode from the room.

Feeling awkward, Lesley faced Finney. "I'll look over his plan and be in touch to set up a time to meet," Finney told her.

"Is there anything you'd like me to do right now?" Lesley asked, sure that Finney wouldn't tell her to rescind the room request, but asking just in case.

"No." She paused. "It would be prudent for you to return to your room."

"Yes, Commander. And thank you."

Finney nodded. "Dismissed."

Lesley walked as fast as she could, glad that she didn't have to pass through the reception hall to exit the auditorium. She wouldn't think about what had just happened, not until she was in the safety of her room.

Ten minutes later, she shut the room's door behind her. The satchel lying on the dresser reminded her of how she'd raced out earlier, determined to make the concert. At the time, she'd had a bright future with the military. How quickly life could change.

All she'd wanted to do was be there for Mo. Other cadets had attended to support their friends, so why hadn't they been publicly dressed-down and escorted from the reception? Because they weren't on that flaming list, that was why. No, that wasn't it. They hadn't tried to be someone they weren't. Perhaps Mama was right. She wasn't cut out for this.

No! She'd never doubted her dedication to the Way, or her willingness to serve, until she'd known for sure that she and Mo had Chosens. Before then, she'd always been confident in her strength in the Way, even though she hadn't spent every free moment participating in activities with an obvious connection to it. But when she'd known for sure that she and Mo had Chosens, and had still wanted to be with Mo, had still cared for her so much . . . Her feelings for Mo weren't logical; trying to think her way out of them wouldn't work—that had led her to doubt herself and her instincts.

She'd do what the indoctrinators had always advised on the rare occasions when she'd struggled: go back to basics. Realign with the articles. Worry only about not violating them, not about deeper issues, like caring for someone so much that the thought of losing her was terrifying. She'd follow the articles without analyzing them and, once she'd regained her equilibrium, face the problem. If she'd done that in the first place, instead of panicking and trying to prove that she was strong in the Way and that her relationship with Mo didn't matter, Morton might have forgotten about her and tonight wouldn't have happened. Instead, she'd given him the wrong impression about what she believed it meant to be strong in the Way.

Hiding behind the Way, using it as an excuse to treat Mo badly, was about as weak in the Way as one could get. She wouldn't make that mistake again. No matter how her schedule turned out next year, her priority would be to make Mo feel special. No more squandering their time—they'd run out of it soon enough without wasting it themselves. If they were still together in a few years, she'd have to face her fears, but for next year, at least, she'd go back to basics, regain her equilibrium, and breathe.

Someone knocked at the door. "Just a second," she called, but the door opened before she reached it.

Mo rushed into the room, worry etched across her face. Without a word, she reached for Lesley and hugged her. Lesley wrapped her arms around Mo and rested her cheek on the top of Mo's head.

"I got here as soon as I could," Mo said. "Are you okay?"

Actually, she was. Tired, apprehensive about facing everyone the next day and unsure about her future, but okay, especially now that Mo was here. "I'm all right. I guess the entire reception's buzzing about it?"

She felt Mo nod. "I walked everyone to the station, then came straight here."

Lesley sighed; she'd forgotten about them. "I'll expect a beep from Mama tomorrow."

"They won't say anything. They thought Morton was horrible, putting you on the spot like that in front of everyone. If I'd been there, I would have said something."

"Then I'm glad you weren't there."

She lifted her head when Mo drew back. "What happened?" Mo asked. "I mean, I heard about what happened in the reception hall, but what happened after you left?"

"Well, Morton was upset that I skipped group for the concert." She'd leave out the part about the room request; Mo didn't need to know about it, or that their relationship had caught Morton's attention. Or maybe Mo should know—she had the right to decide whether she wanted to stay together and possibly risk her future. "Finney stuck up for me, so much so that she's now my mentor."

"Finney's going to be your mentor, instead of Larson?"

"If she's serious about it, yes. I know that's disappointing. He's an active pilot, she's in Interior and not part of the academy."

"You had no choice."

"No, I had the choice. I chose Finney."

Mo's brow furrowed. "Why?"

Lesley considered the question. At the time, her choice had been more against Morton than for Finney, but now she realized that something else had influenced her decision. "I trust her more than I trust Morton. I suspect Morton's suggested mentors are all loyal to him, so as far as I'm concerned, dealing with them is the same as dealing with him." Especially since he'd given her the impression that she had to choose a mentor from his short list, when apparently she could have requested anyone.

"Okay, so we don't get inside information on the pilot program, but you get a commander for a mentor. That kind of worked out, right?"

She wouldn't call being caught between two commanders working out, but she nodded. "There's something I need to tell you, though."

"What?"

Suddenly overcome with weariness, Lesley backed toward the bed and sat down.

"What?" Mo asked again, softer. She reached out and stroked Lesley's cheek.

Lesley looked up at her. "Morton isn't happy about our relationship. Finney didn't seem to care, but he made it clear that he'd be much happier if we weren't together."

Mo's face fell. "Les, don't do this. I know you're going to be busy, and I'll keep myself busy. I'll stay out of your way, I promise."

"No, no, no," she said, grabbing both of Mo's hands and hanging onto them. "I don't want to break up. I'm telling you in case—well, in case you'll want to split. Staying with me could hurt you." Lesley hoped it hadn't already. She could forgive herself for losing her way over the past few months, but she'd never forgive herself if she'd damaged Mo's future.

"You're worried about me?" Mo said incredulously. "I'm not going anywhere. And you'd think Morton would have more important things to worry about than two junior cadets seeing each other. Is he Joined? Because if he is, I pity his Chosen."

Lesley chuckled. "I don't think so. I don't remember a Chosen ring."

"Well, good for the Chosen Council."

"But he is the commander of the Military Academy, so he has a lot of clout. He could influence whether we're accepted into the fighter pilot program, and who knows what else. He's not impressed with me right now. Perhaps he'll limit his disappointment to me. Perhaps not."

"Les, I'm sorry," Mo said quietly. "You told me what could happen, but I kept pressuring you—to come to the concert, to share a room, to spend more time with me. I should have listened."

"I'm glad you didn't. Because I wasn't saying what I wanted to say, but what I thought I should say, and I'm not going to do that anymore. I'm glad we're sharing a room, and I wanted to go to the concert." She took Mo's face in her hands. "And by the way, you were brilliant. I'm so proud of you. I don't regret going for a second."

Mo's eyes glistened. "That's good," she said, her voice quivering. "Because when I was onstage looking for you, and I saw you were there . . ." Her lips trembled. "I'll remember that moment for the rest of my life."

Lesley's eyes filled. She closed them and touched her forehead to Mo's. In her mind, she saw herself at the lake, one of her daughters at her side. *"Mama, before you were Joined, was there anyone special?"* Yes, she'd say, and tell her daughter about the woman with the dark brown eyes and lopsided smile; the woman she instantly thought of whenever she heard a violin.

 DISOBEDIENCE MEANS DEATH

MISINTERPRETATION

.....

MO GLANCED AT THE SENSOR PANEL. Argamon! Two hostiles were on her tail. The incoming indicator flashed; the earpiece in her left ear emitted an urgent beep. "Where are you?" she snapped as she fired a countermeasure. Direct hit—missile neutralized—but with two hostiles pursuing her, one remaining countermeasure in her arsenal, and no decoys, she'd bought a minute at most.

The comm-piece in her right ear crackled to life. "I'm almost there," David said.

"Hurry up! I can't hold out much longer."

Another incoming missile. Fire the last countermeasure or evasive maneuvers? A second missile appeared on sensors. Okay, this was not going well. Wait! Evasive pattern 23-A at half velocity just might . . .

She keyed a command sequence into the navigation panel and braced herself. The ship spiralled downward, pitched left, then right. The eggs she'd eaten for breakfast slid into her mouth. She choked them down. Through the nausea she focused on the sensors, her thumb hovering over the countermeasure trigger. A friendly appeared on the panel.

"I'm in range," David said.

"Pull one off me."

"Engaging."

One hostile broke off pursuit. Her spirits lifted—they might get out of this!

Wait for the missiles to start converging . . . Ready, and . . .

She pressed the trigger. The countermeasure sped toward the missiles.

"Yes!" she shouted. Now to take care of the hostile still after her. Her eyes widened. Uh-oh. She'd forgotten to—

The cockpit shook and the panels went dark. "Simulation failed," an impassive voice said in her comm-piece as she was slowly returned to an upright position.

No kidding. Thank you very much for rubbing it in. She slapped the navigation panel with both hands and groaned. Argamon! They'd almost had it.

"What happened?" David asked.

"Oh, a move I thought was brilliant turned out to be stupid. I tried taking out two missiles at once by getting them to converge."

"Their programming would prevent them from destroying each other."

"I know. But they were close enough that I only needed to hit one to take both out."

"And you missed?"

"No, I hit." Mo sighed. "But I didn't take the increased damage radius of the chain reaction into account." She'd blown herself up. Idiot. "Sorry."

"It wasn't all your fault. I ran into heavy resistance at the supply depot and took way too long to destroy the weapons cache. I was supposed to be on my way back when that patrol showed up."

"Maybe," she said, unconvinced. He hadn't destroyed himself, and she wouldn't have either, if she'd had more options available to her. The simulation had been completely unfair! How had the designer expected anyone to hold off the opposition with such a measly allotment of missiles, decoys, and countermeasures? She'd been outnumbered three to one, hardly conducive to whittling down a hostile with the fighter's laser weapons.

"Come on," David said. "It's the first time we've tried this one, and it's rated high difficulty. We did good."

He'd done well; she'd committed a huge blunder. But she said, "Yeah, I guess so."

"Do you want to try again?"

She pulled off the helmet and checked her comm unit. "I don't think we have enough time." And she was no longer in the mood. "That's it for me."

"Okay." He paused. "I'll meet you in the lobby. I want to fly a short speed sim."

Mo unbuckled herself, stepped out of the dim simulation booth, and pressed the *Disinfect* button to the right of the portal.

The soft lights in the corridor eased her transition from darkness to light—she didn't even blink when she reached the brightly lit equipment room and handed her helmet to the attendant with a murmured "thank you." If she ever flew an intermediate sim she'd have to suit up, but she hadn't tried one of those yet. The novice ones required only a helmet.

She sank into one of the lobby sofas and stared out the large picture window. Last week the path outside had bustled with cadets hurrying to lectures and exams, but now it was empty. Most were on break; the only cadets remaining were those who'd just completed their second year and hoped to enter a specialized program for their third.

Mo swallowed. The next two weeks would decide whether she'd spend her third year training to be a fighter pilot or enter the general stream, putting herself at the mercy of the military's whims when she graduated. Two years of books, aviacraft lessons, and barely palatable food had come down to this. She better not blow it—she'd rather spend her career flying than performing whatever mundane duties the military assigned to her. She'd hate to be stuck washing floors and cooking meals while Les was out blasting hostiles.

David strolled into the lobby. She pasted a smile on her face, still smarting from her miscalculation in the simulator.

"I can't believe it's only 08:00," David said. "I'm still half asleep." He yawned as if to emphasize his point. "You had breakfast yet?"

She grimaced, reminded of the eggs she'd almost deposited on the simulator floor. "Yeah, I have. But I wouldn't mind a mug of tziva." She had no reason to rush back to the room. Les wouldn't be there, and Mo had just completed the one activity that might give her an edge in the upcoming evaluation. She couldn't really prepare for the essay exam or interview, but the simulator test was a different story. Blowing herself up was hardly encouraging, though.

"When's Lesley due back?" David asked as they left the pilot training complex and walked toward the mess hall.

"She said she'd arrive on the 10:12 train at the earliest."

"She must get up at the crack of dawn for these meetings."

"Normally, yeah, but this time she went home last night."

David drew back in mock surprise. "You mean you managed to get up, have breakfast, and show up for 07:00 all by yourself?"

She couldn't help but smile. "Believe it or not, I did." When Les had beeped her, Mo had already had her shower. Rising early hadn't been difficult—she didn't like sleeping alone. Finney and her flaming 08:00 meetings! At least this time Les had been able to travel the night before, but Mo had selfishly missed snuggling up to her in bed. "Though she did beep me."

"Aha! I knew it."

"I was up! I was up!" she protested, laughing.

"I bet Lesley was surprised."

Mo responded with an absent "Mmm," distracted by a familiar voice off to her right. She felt compelled to look that way, despite knowing what she'd see: Les, talking to the lone Rymellan standing in front of a nearby monitor.

"Hi Lesley," David called, waving at the image on the monitor. Mo rolled her eyes. The first few times had been funny, but the joke had grown stale over the past year. "Will she record announcements over the break?" he asked.

Mo shook her head. "She recorded her last set a few days ago." Unfortunately, Les would have to return from the break a couple of days early to record the announcements that would greet everyone upon their return.

David pulled open the mess hall door and almost bumped into a fellow cadet. "Oh, hi," he said as Ann passed through the doorway.

Ann grinned at him. "Just dragged yourself out of bed?"

"No, I've been up since 06:30," he said, letting go of the door. "Why?"

"Had simulator time booked at 07:00. We've just come from there."

Ann seemed to notice Mo for the first time. "Both of you?"

David nodded.

"I can understand why you'd want to use the simulator, but why would you?" she asked, frowning at Mo.

"Why wouldn't I?" Mo replied.

"Don't tell me you're trying out for the fighter pilot program."

"Um, yeah, I am," Mo said, irritated. She and Ann weren't friends, but her aspiration to become a fighter pilot was hardly a secret. Surely Ann had heard about her plans from someone—what they hoped to do in their third year had been the main topic of conversation among cadets over the past month.

Ann looked down at her. 'No offence, but are you sure you're not too short?"

Blood rushed to Mo's cheeks.

"There's no height requirement," David snapped.

"Well, not officially, but there's a glut of applicants this year, so they can afford to be choosy."

"That doesn't mean they'll reject applicants based on their height," Mo said.

"There's that little thing called an evaluation that'll determine who makes it in and who doesn't," David added.

"Well, you'd better hope you ace every single part of the evaluation," Ann said to Mo. "And even if you do, if it comes down to you and someone . . . bigger, anyone with a smidgen of common sense knows who they'll pick." She smiled tightly. "I'd hate to see you waste your time, so take some friendly advice and go after something a little more suitable for you, okay?"

No, it wasn't okay. Being a fighter pilot would suit her just fine.

"Unless you have more wisdom you'd like to share, we want to eat," David said, pulling the door open again. "See you."

"I'm only trying to help," Ann called as Mo hurried into the mess hall after him.

Help her do what? Drop out of the evaluation? Yeah, that was probably exactly what Ann hoped would happen. Ann was also trying out for the program, so why not narrow down the field of applicants and give herself a better chance?

"Don't listen to her. She's only trying to rattle the competition," David said, thinking along the same lines.

"Yeah! She must be worried her skills aren't up to snuff." Mo wished she'd said that to Ann, instead of thinking of it a minute later. Then she changed her mind; she wouldn't want to stoop to Ann's level. The best way to show Ann would be to make it into the fighter pilot program, exactly what she intended to do.

LESLEY BOUNDED UP the stairs to the station's waiting area and stepped into the late morning sun. The meeting with Finney had gone well, she looked forward to spending the rest of the day with Mo, and she was eager to undergo the evaluation. What a difference from this time last year, when she'd felt confused and tired. Finney could take credit for part of the change—she believed in a balanced schedule. The Chosen Tradition group had been the first thing to go. Lesley hadn't missed it.

Her comm unit beeped; she smiled when she read its display. "Good timing," she said to Mo. "I just stepped off the train. Are you at the dorm?"

"No, I'm in the middle of a round of cards. We're at the mess hall. Do you want to come here?"

She wasn't in the mood for cards and wanted to see Mo alone. Since they'd switched to wearing cadet uniforms at the beginning of the year, they hadn't felt as comfortable expressing their affection publicly. If she went to the mess hall, she'd be lucky to get a peck on the cheek. "I think I'll just go to our room."

"Okay. I should only be another twenty minutes or so."

"I know it's only just gone eleven, but can you bring lunch with you? I had breakfast at six."

"Yeah, I'm starting to get hungry, too. What do you—"

"Mo, your turn," someone said in the background.

"Just get me the usual. I'll see you soon." Lesley terminated the connection and continued on to the dormitory, cringing when she passed a monitor and heard her own voice. Another announcement reader had said she'd get used to it. When?

As in the rest of the academy, the dormitory was quieter than usual. She swung open the room door and hung up her cloak. Her book about the evolution of Article 44 lay on her nightstand. She'd meant to take it with her to read on the train, but in her hurry to leave, she'd forgotten

DISOBEDIENCE MEANS DEATH

it. Well, she had time to read a few pages before Mo arrived. She took off her boots and lay on her side of the makeshift double bed.

The first thing she and Mo had done when they moved in was push the two single beds together. The result was still smaller than her bed at home, but then, her room at home was at least four times the size of this one, richly furnished, equipped with a comm station and several bookcases filled with books, and—well, she had everything at her fingertips there. This room was cramped and drab by comparison. But lying in her bed at home last night, she'd wished she were back here with Mo . . . despite the two pairs of dirty socks inexplicably draped over the back of the chair near Mo's side—though neatly draped, she had to admit.

Her comm unit beeped twice. Over the past year, she'd learned to read dispatches promptly, since scheduling changes often arrived with little notice. She flipped up the unit and leaned forward to peer at its display, then opened the dispatch. Oh good, Finney had thought of two advocates who might be suitable for the Law group's first meeting of the new academic year. The speakers committee had been at its wit's end, trying to find one to speak about Article 223. Even Lesley's parents had drawn a blank. Since the article hadn't been amended for over seventy years, a historian specializing in the Law would have been easier to find, but the new Law group leader had insisted on an advocate. What next—would the Chosen Tradition group want an advocate to speak about an article pertaining to triads?

She opened her book and started to read. Six pages later, the door opened. Mo strode into the room, a paper bag in hand. "Lunch," she announced, setting the bag on the dresser.

"Good, I'm starving." Lesley snapped the book shut, then hastily placed it on the nightstand when Mo rounded the bed, her arms outstretched. She pulled Mo close and breathed in the scent of her hair. Mo's lips and cheeks felt cool. "Weren't you cold without your cloak?" Lesley asked when they finally parted.

"A little. I should have checked the weather bulletin before I left." Mo picked up the bag and nudged Lesley over so she'd have room to sit. "How'd your meeting with Finney go?"

"Good. We can't really plan the year until we know for sure what

I'll be doing, but we tossed around a few ideas. How'd it go in the simulator?"

"Great, if you don't count blowing myself up and almost regurgitating breakfast." Mo reached into the bag. "I don't know if I'll ever get used to some of those evasive maneuvers," she murmured.

"You blew yourself up?"

Mo nodded. "I'll tell you in a minute. Okay, egg for you," she tossed Lesley a sandwich wrapped in wax paper, "and cheese for me." She lifted out two covered mugs. "Tziva, and maybe a little something for dessert." Mo set the bag on the floor.

"Is dessert in the bag, or did you have something else in mind?" Lesley couldn't resist asking.

Mo grinned and wiggled her eyebrows. "I guess you'll have to wait and see."

MO LET GO of Les's hand as they approached the pilot training complex. "Which room again?"

"Conference room two," Les replied, pulling the door open and holding it for Mo. "I think it's down the corridor to the right."

She veered that way, glad the evaluation was finally starting. She'd had enough of playing cards and sitting around speculating about what questions might be asked during the interviews. As Papa would say, time to get on with it.

Though the meeting wouldn't begin for ten minutes, every chair at the long, oval conference table was already occupied, and several cadets stood against the wall. "Nobody wants to arrive late in case it counts against them," Les murmured as they joined the cadets along the wall.

Mo nodded. She searched faces, looking for David. Many of those present were strangers, aspiring pilots from academies that didn't have a fighter pilot program. Kary was off at the F10 academy undergoing the evaluation for the counselling program. Mo couldn't think of a more perfect career for her; she'd be a shoo-in.

She grabbed David's arm as he walked past. "Didn't see you," he said, squeezing himself between her and the cadet to her left. He glanced around. "Quite a few here—what, around forty?"

     DISOBEDIENCE MEANS DEATH

"Forty-five, not counting the lieutenant commander," Les said, "and a few more will probably arrive."

He grimaced. "Not good. There are nowhere near thirty spots, let alone forty."

Mo turned toward him to say something reassuring and saw Ann walk into the room. Great. She watched the other woman move to stand almost directly across from them. Mo briefly met her eyes, then focused on the blackboard behind the lieutenant commander seated at the front of the room.

Two more cadets entered. The lieutenant commander stood and did a head count. "It looks like everyone's here, so we might as well start," she said, closing the door. "I'm Lieutenant Commander Ross, and I'd like to welcome you to this brief orientation meeting." She motioned for those at the table to stand.

Mo grabbed Les and David's hands. Two circles formed, one around the perimeter of the room, the other around the table. Ross nodded. "Disobedience means death. Death to those who commit a Chosen Violation. Death to those who disobey. Death to those who violate the Way. Death to those who violate the Way. Death to those who violate the Way!" Applause echoed around the room.

When everyone had settled down, Ross picked up a piece of chalk. "So, you want to be fighter pilots. Time for a dose of reality." She wrote 232 on the board and circled it. "That's how many cadets applied to undergo the evaluation." Next, 186. "That's how many passed the aptitude test.

The number surprised Mo. Anyone who'd played with blocks as a child or had the slightest notion of how objects related to each other in three-dimensional space should have breezed through.

Ross wrote 48 on the board; Mo shuddered when the chalk squeaked. "This is you, the ones in this room. Your aptitude results ranked in the top twenty percent. And this is how many spots you're competing for." Dismayed murmurs filled the room when Ross wrote 21 on the board. "That means most of you will not enter the fighter pilot program next year," she said to a greatly subdued audience. She tossed the chalk back into the tray.

"Your aptitude results got you this far." Ross scanned faces. "Now the real evaluation begins. Over the next ten days, you'll write an essay exam, be interviewed, and show us what you can do in the simulator." Her eyes paused on those standing across from Mo. "When there are an abundance of applicants, as there are this year, performing well during the evaluation may not be enough. We may consider other factors when deciding who we'll invite into the program." Her eyes touched Mo's as she shifted her attention to those on Mo's side of the room. "Don't take it personally if we don't select you. Making it this far is an accomplishment you can all be proud of." She cleared her throat. "Now, before we tour the facility, I'll quickly go over the evaluation schedule."

Mo couldn't concentrate on what Ross was saying; her mind kept replaying the moment when Ross's eyes had met hers. Was it her imagination, or had Ross deliberately looked at her when she'd spoken about other factors influencing their decision-making process? Had Ross meant height? She looked at Ann. To her horror, Ann smirked and held her hand waist-high. Mo turned away, her heart pounding. She tried to focus on Ross, but couldn't help sizing up the cadet sitting directly in her line of vision, and then the cadet next him, and the one next to her, and the three cadets in her peripheral vision on the other side of the room. They were all taller than her. She could be the shortest one here. She wanted to size up everyone in the room, but no way would she look in Ann's direction again. Ann was probably still staring at her, that stupid smirk on her face.

Mo self-consciously shifted her weight to her left foot and tried to look relaxed by bending her left leg a little, but she felt awkward and probably looked even shorter. Standing next to Les didn't help. She closed her eyes, disappointed with herself, and silently apologized to Les. It wasn't Les's fault that she was tall, any more than it was her own that she was short. And yeah, she was short. So what? Other factors could mean anything—grades, Learning and Indoctrination Academy records, the colour of a cadet's hair.

If she didn't stand a chance, they wouldn't have passed her through to the evaluation, especially given the number of applicants. Ann was only trying to raise her own chances of getting in by rattling others into blowing it. Mo pressed her lips together. Then again, Ross's eyes *had* lingered on her when she'd mentioned other factors . . .

Ross clapped her hands, dragging Mo back to her surroundings. "All

          DISOBEDIENCE MEANS DEATH

right, time for the tour," she said. "c6ers familiar with the facility don't
have to come along, but you're welcome to. Any questions before we go?"
Nobody raised a hand. "All right, then. We'll start in the lobby."

The low murmur of conversation competed with rolling chairs and
shuffling footsteps as everyone prepared to follow Ross out the door.
Ann seemed to have befriended a couple of cadets from other academies;
it looked as if she was planning to go with them on the tour.

"Let's tag along," Les said in the corridor. "We've never had an official
tour of the place."

With Ann staring at her the whole time? No, thank you. "I think I'll
skip it. I'm not really in the mood."

Les frowned. "You sure?"

"Les, it's not like we'll see anything new. I'll meet you back at the
room."

"I'll come along," David said.

"Have fun," Mo said when they reached the lobby. She left the building without looking back and hoped the tour would last a while, since
she had no intention of going to the room right away. Ross's "other factors" still nagged at her. The *How to Apply for the Fighter Pilot Program*
brochure hadn't specified a height requirement, but maybe there'd been
a misprint or someone had forgotten to update the information on the
network—they could have thought it only fair to allow the error to stand
this year, rather than reject applicants like her. Or maybe they'd recently
dropped the requirement on a trial basis and now regretted it.

Half an hour later she leaned back in the wooden chair in one of the
library's study cubicles and placed her hands behind her head. Nothing. Not one mention of height in anything she'd read, and she'd gone
back twenty years. So either height wasn't a factor, or the requirements
had always had a loophole and she was in on a technicality. She could
imagine the conversation:

*"Oh no, another short cadet ranked in the top twenty on the aptitude
test."*

*"Oh dear. Pass her through, and we'll do what we always do—reject her
based on other factors."*

She snorted; now she was being silly. What actually happened during the meeting? Ann had smirked at her and done that stupid thing

with her hand, and Ross had happened to look at her when saying that they might consider more than the evaluation when making a decision. Big deal. She'd just wasted half an hour reading archived brochures—brochures!—when she could have been reading about simulator techniques, interview tips, anything but brochures. If Ann had intended to distract her from preparing for the evaluation, she'd succeeded, but only because Mo had let her.

Mo snapped off the monitor and left the library in disgust, determined to ignore any more of Ann's pathetic attempts to make her feel as though she shouldn't be trying out for the program. She was in the evaluation. If that bothered Ann, too flaming bad.

MO WALKED INTO the classroom and scanned for an empty seat—there, in the fourth row. She threaded her way between the desks toward it. If Les were here, she'd want them to sit in the two empty desks at the front. But she'd been assigned to the other classroom for the essay exam, which suited Mo just fine—no distractions. And she hated sitting right under the proctor's nose.

This should be the easiest part of the evaluation. According to the information packet describing the evaluation process, the interview would focus on why an applicant wanted to become a fighter pilot and on the applicant's career goals, while the essay exam would consist of a series of questions about the applicant "to help us get to know you." How much easier could an exam be? All she had to do was write about herself.

She adjusted the monitor and keyboard on the desk and surveyed those seated in the rows in front of her. Sheila and Ruth were sitting next to each other, as usual. They'd been together for a while and, lucky for them, were Solitaries. Well, sort of lucky. They couldn't have daughters, their relationship would never be officially recognized, and while the military tried to keep Solitaries in relationships together, there were no guarantees. Chosens, on the other hand, would never be separated.

The military could separate her and Les after graduation, especially if the pilot program declined her. Mo was sure that Les would be invited into the program, so she *had* to get in, not only because she wanted to be a fighter pilot, but because it would mean training in the same

 DISOBEDIENCE MEANS DEATH

program as Les next year, and probably serving with her for at least a year or two after that. She'd heard that pilots who trained together flew domestic patrols together after graduation. Another two to three years would be—

"Um, excuse me," someone bellowed behind her. "You, with the brown hair, sitting in the third row. Hello?" The room went quiet.

Mo looked over her shoulder. Flaming Argamon, not Ann.

The cadet sitting in front of Mo, the one Ann seemed to be referring to, turned around.

"Don't you think you should move to another seat?" Ann said. "She can't see."

His face screwed up in confusion.

"The cadet sitting behind you. The short one." Ann enunciated every word. "You're blocking her view."

Mo's cheeks burned; blood pounded in her ears. She shrank in her seat, then thought better of it and sat as straight as she could.

The cadet in front stood and leaned toward her. "Would you like to change seats?" he asked.

"No, that's okay, I'm fine," Mo mumbled.

"You sure?"

"Yes, yes," she said, motioning for him to move away and sit down.

"Mo, switch with him," Ann said. "Then you'll be able to see."

Mo whipped around. "It's a flaming essay exam. I don't need to see," she hissed, then faced forward, feeling foolish and self-conscious. Everywhere she looked, faces stared back, cold and unsympathetic.

"I'm only trying to help," Ann trilled.

Mo's hands clenched. If she heard that one more time . . . Ann said something else, too low for Mo to catch. A gale of laughter rose behind her. She sank lower in her seat, then quickly straightened again and glanced at the neighbour to her right, but for what? Reassurance that they weren't laughing at *her*? She didn't get it—he looked away the moment she met his eyes, his keyboard suddenly fascinating.

For a split second, she had the overwhelming urge to bolt from the room and forget about the whole flaming evaluation. But what would she tell Les? That she was too short? There was no height requirement. No height requirement! She had as much right to sit the exam as everyone else here. She'd applied to undergo the evaluation, just as they had. They wouldn't have accepted her application if they'd known she had no chance, right? Surely someone had noticed how short she was at some point during the application process. Her medical records must have been examined, for one thing.

A lieutenant strode into the room. "Good afternoon, everyone," he said on his way to the front. "I'm Lieutenant North. Welcome to the essay portion of the fighter pilot program evaluation. The exam . . ."

Mo only half listened, the humiliation raw and the laughter still ringing in her ears. Not only Ann thought she was too short; everyone did. For all she knew, she was the laughingstock of the evaluation—the short, deluded cadet everyone whispered about. *Poor thing. Thinks she can be a fighter pilot.* Well yeah, she did. She'd wanted to be a pilot from the moment she'd sat in a fighter. She'd never considered anything else. Maybe she should have.

"Begin!" North's voice rang out, startling her.

She flicked on her monitor and tried to focus. If she didn't do well on the exam, it wouldn't matter if she were a giant—being a fighter pilot would be out of her reach. But then she read the first essay question—*Describe yourself*—and had to restrain from typing *I'm short. Short, short, short!* Her temples pulsed. The next question didn't help: *If your friends were to describe you, what would they say?* How much trouble would she be in if she picked up the monitor and flung it against the wall? Question three—*What would your fellow cadets say?*—made her want to rest her head on the desk and cry.

Half an hour later, she still hadn't written a single word.

MO FLUNG OPEN the room door and stalked inside, almost bumping into Les.

"I was about to come looking for you," Les said, holding her cloak. "I don't know why they gave us ninety minutes to write the exam. I left after an hour, but only because I wanted to triple-check my answers. I think I was the second to last one out." She hung her cloak back on its hook. "When I didn't see you in the hall, I figured you were back here."

No, at that point, she'd been on question two, after frittering away half the allotted time. Not in the mood to blather on about herself,

 DISOBEDIENCE MEANS DEATH

she'd written terse, pointed answers. Whoever read them would probably think she hated herself. Right now, that wasn't far from the truth. She sighed and slipped off her cloak.

Les's face creased with concern. "You okay?"

"I'm tired." Mo sank onto the bed, untied her boots, and pulled them off. "Maybe I'm coming down with something."

"Do you want to go to the infirmary?"

"No." She doubted they had a cure for her condition: the post-delusional blues, often seen in those who'd discovered their career aspirations weren't and never had been attainable. For the first time, she wished she wasn't sharing with Les. She wanted to be alone so she could lie down, pull the blanket over her head, and not go out until the evaluation was over and everyone had gone home for break. Lying down would have to do. She settled on her side and curled up in a fetal position.

Les rounded the bed and looked down at her. "Are you sure you shouldn't go—"

"Les, don't fuss, okay? I'm not dying. I just want to lie down for a while."

"Okay," Les mumbled, though she continued to stare. "Do you mind if I sort through some clothes, then? I want to take home anything I haven't worn for a while, which will probably be at least half of what's here."

"No, go ahead." Anything to distract her for a bit.

"You'll tell me if you're feeling worse, right?"

"Yes," Mo said through clenched teeth.

Les looked as if she had something else to say, but she turned away and slid the closet door open. She lifted out a shirt, examined it, and apparently decided that the shirt would go home—she slid it off the hanger, folded it, and placed it on top of the dresser. Even when doing something so mundane, her movements were graceful. She always looked so cute when her face crinkled up in concentration. And Argamon, she wore a uniform well.

Not for the first time, Mo wondered where she'd ever found the courage to kiss Les, all those years ago at the Indoctrination Academy. Well, she hadn't exactly given it a lot of thought, and if it had backfired, she'd be looking back on it as impulsive and stupid, not courageous.

But it hadn't, and as she watched Les examine another shirt, her mind wandered back to when she was fourteen and in agony.

She and Les had always been best friends. Growing up next door to each other and only five months apart in age, they were always together, at family functions, at the Learning Academy, and at the Indoctrination Academy. Mo knew Les almost as well as she knew herself; she could talk to Les about anything. When they entered the Indoctrination Academy at thirteen for their Level Four, Les had been a fixture in her life for as far back as she could remember—she was like a part of the family. Around Les, Mo didn't have to be polite or pretend to be someone she wasn't. She could be herself.

But then something changed. Suddenly Mo felt self-conscious around Les. Did she sound stupid? Was she laughing in the right places? Did her hair look all right? Did she have a piece of lettuce from lunch stuck between her teeth? Half the time, she couldn't focus on what Les was saying, distracted by Les's blue eyes with their long, delicate eyelashes. Worse, she wanted to reach out and touch her—her hand, her cheek, her hair. Forget the talking; she just wanted to gaze into Les's eyes. She even imagined herself sitting on Les's lap!

At first she didn't understand what had happened, but one day, during class, it all became frighteningly clear. Level Four expanded on the basics of the Chosen Tradition covered during Level Three, and that meant sex education. Sure, she knew about sex, but up to that point, she hadn't thought about it much, nor about whether she was diff- or same-oriented. She certainly hadn't thought about it in relation to Les. They were friends; they knew everything about each other. Her feelings for Les weren't *those* types of feelings, she was sure of it. She didn't plan on having any of those until she met her Chosen—if she had one.

But on that excruciating day, the indoctrinator talked about sexual attraction and how sexual orientation was a discovery, something one learned about oneself, not something one chose. She sat in horror as he described exactly what she was feeling, and watched the large monitor at the front of the classroom in disbelief as several adult Solitary Rymellans, both diff- and same-oriented, recalled their "adolescent crushes." She could hardly breathe; she wanted to crawl under her desk and hide. Most of all, she did not want Les, sitting up front, to turn

     DISOBEDIENCE MEANS DEATH

around; she was convinced that how she felt was plain on her face. She wouldn't be surprised if a bright light suddenly shone down on her and the indoctrinator said, "Now, class, I want you all to look at Mo Middleton. She's another example of a Rymellan with a crush, and on Lesley Thompson, no less."

She left class in a daze, her mind turning over the same question again and again: what was Les's orientation? It had never come up; they'd never discussed boys or girls in that way. Did Les know? Was she experiencing the same sorts of feelings as Mo . . . but for a boy? Would it affect their friendship if she was? Could they be as close, understand each other as much as they did now, or at least as much as Mo thought they did?

Well, that was enough for her. She didn't want anymore of this sexual attraction nonsense. She wanted to feel comfortable with Les again. If she accidentally spat on her while talking, she didn't want to feel as if she'd just done the most embarrassing thing ever. If she stumbled and Les caught her arm, she wanted to laugh and thank her, not blush and wish it hadn't happened. She wanted back that familiar ease between them, along with the certainty that Les would always be her friend no matter how dumb she sounded or how her hair looked. Who would want those other feelings? Not her. They were annoying and inconvenient. From now on, she'd pretend those other feelings for Les weren't there.

Les came out of the classroom and walked toward her. "That was an interesting class," she said, shifting her notebook from her left to her right hand.

"Yeah," Mo mumbled, her heart pounding.

Les stared at her and shifted her notebook back to her left hand. "Do you . . ." The notebook moved again. "Do you know . . . if you're same- or diff-oriented?" she asked.

Mo gulped and tried not to hyperventilate. "No," she managed to say faintly. Les must have the bluest eyes on the planet. "I mean, I'm not sure. I don't know. I've never experienced anything that would help me tell." They needed to open the windows—it must be one hundred degrees in the corridor.

"Oh."

What about you? *What about you?* But the words wouldn't come out. She couldn't ask a question when hearing the answer terrified her.

The moment passed. "Uh, I thought I'd take a walk during break, get some fresh air. Want to come?" Les asked.

"Sure," Mo said. A walk with Les would be great—as long as she didn't spit on her, didn't trip, and didn't forget herself and grab Les's hand. Les must never know that she had those sorts of feelings for her. Ever.

Over the next few weeks, Mo noticed that she wasn't the only one who'd discovered her orientation. Actually, the signs had been there before, but she hadn't put two and two together. Now she understood why Simon and Judith spent most of their time grinning at each other like morons, and why Sheldon had stood and glared at Timothy at lunch one day, until Timothy had surrendered his seat next to Raymond. She'd even seen classmates kissing. *Kissing!*

Feeling like she'd explode if she didn't tell someone about her own discovery, she decided to tell Mama and Papa on the next family visitation day. They nodded knowingly and smiled at each other.

"You already know?" Mo asked.

"We've known for quite some time, ever since your last appointment with the Chosen Council," Papa said. "They know then, you see, and tell the parents. But it's best that you find out yourself, when you're ready."

But she wasn't ready, not if it meant she couldn't have back her old friendship with Les. The comfortable one, not the one they had now. Over Papa's shoulder, she could see Les chatting with her parents. They knew. They flaming knew. Did Les? Is that what she was talking about with them? Did she have a crush on anyone? Did she know how many of her classmates had a crush on her? Mo knew how many: a lot.

She wasn't the only girl walking around in misery with Les the object of her affection. Last week at supper, she'd noticed Caroline staring at Les from a nearby table, and her stomach had clenched when she'd recognized the look in Caroline's eyes. She'd also lost count of the number of boys offering to carry Les's books, squeezing themselves in at the same table at mealtimes, and ogling her during class. Once Les had dropped her pencil, and Mo had almost been trampled in the stampede to reach it first, pick it up, and present it to her.

Mo wondered how Les felt about the attention—whether it bolstered or bothered. They never talked about it. In fact, they never talked about

   DISOBEDIENCE MEANS DEATH

anything related to sex, crushes, orientation, or the like. It was almost as if they had an unspoken agreement to not discuss what ninety percent of their classes were about, or the obvious displays of affection right in front of them every time they went outside on break. Mo lived in fear that one day she'd round the corner of the sports equipment shed and find Les pressed against its side, kissing some pimple-faced idiot.

The chances of that happening were slim, though, since she and Les were pretty much always together. If Les planned to go outside on break, she always asked Mo to go with her. She always wanted to sit together at meals, and she spent more time quietly doing homework in Mo's room than she spent in her own. Mo understood why—Les was using her as a shield against all the attention. She didn't mind. If Les wanted to stick to her like glue, that was fine with her. Despite the constant longing when Les was there, despite the ache to touch her, to feel her skin, to press her body against Les's, the almost physical pain when Les wasn't with her was worse.

She tried not to think about the day when Les decided she no longer needed a shield. Les would have her pick of the boys or same-oriented girls. Mo knew it wouldn't be her. Even if she hadn't been Les's friend all these years and as familiar as an old pair of shoes, she was plain, and she didn't seem to be growing much. Anywhere. Les looked taller and curvier every time Mo saw her. So did most of the other girls. But not her. Sometimes she wondered if she had a defective mirror.

Mo told herself that being Les's friend was enough, but deep inside, she knew that wasn't true. One day, sitting directly behind Les and admiring the nape of her neck as Les peered down at her notes, she considered telling Les how she felt. If she knew Les's orientation, if she heard from Les's mouth that she didn't stand a chance with her, maybe she could let her feelings go, stop irrationally hoping, stop lying in bed at night doing with Les in her mind what she wished she could do with her in reality. Maybe they'd get their old friendship back. Yeah, and maybe she'd wake up tomorrow and the sky would be pink with red polka dots.

Plus, she'd thought of another reason why Les spent so much time with her, and why it would be a disaster to tell Les about her orientation and her feelings. Les was probably diff-oriented and assumed Mo was, too. So Mo was a safe person for Les. Les could be sure that, with Mo, she wouldn't have to deal with unwanted attention, wouldn't have to rebuff unwelcome and awkward advances. The last thing she'd want to hear was that Mo was same-oriented and had a crush on her. Les would find another safe person to latch onto, and that would be the end of their friendship. Nope, it had to stay a secret. Mo would never tell her. Ever.

The months wore on. Nothing changed. Before she knew it, they were due to leave the academy in less than a month. They'd go back to living next door to each other, not down the hall from each other. Mo dreaded it. She hadn't realized it until now, but here at the academy, she'd know almost instantly if Les paired up with anyone. That wouldn't be true, once they left. They probably wouldn't be in all the same classes at the Learning Academy, they'd spend less time together, and she couldn't wander outside her room and bump into Les within five or ten minutes. The prospect of Les having the opportunity to find another best friend, or worse, frightened her more than she cared to admit.

A week later, she stood next to Les and stared out the lounge window, trying to decide if the grass was dry enough to go out and kick a ball around. It had rained most of the day, but the sun had come out a couple of hours ago and had been shining ever since.

"We can go out and feel the grass," Les said.

"Yeah, let's. We've been cooped up all day."

Outside, Les crouched and ran her hand along the grass. "It's a bit slippery."

"We'll be careful," Mo said, wanting to remain outside in the sun. "I'll get the ball." She ran to the equipment shed, plucked a ball from the pile near the back, and stepped back into the sunlight.

Les had moved away from the academy; she motioned for Mo to kick the ball to her. Mo dropped the ball, stepped back, then ran forward and kicked it. Good shot! Les hardly had to move. She kicked the ball off to Mo's right, forcing Mo to race toward it and snag it with her foot. It rolled slowly to Les, who promptly kicked it to Mo's left, then bent over, laughing. Oh, so that was how she was going to play, was it? Mo ran as fast as she could, determined not to let the ball get past her, though she'd have to kick it while still in motion. Almost there . . .

     DISOBEDIENCE MEANS DEATH

She swung back her leg and—*whoomf!* She was on her back, staring at fluffy, white clouds.

Seconds later, Les peered down at her. "Argamon, Mo, are you all right?"

She wiggled her fingers and toes. Everything still worked. She'd had the wind knocked out of her, that was all. "Yeah, I'm okay." She pushed herself upright.

"I'm sorry," Les said, offering Mo her hand. "I forgot about the grass." Mo grasped Les's hand and Les pulled her to her feet. "I'm sorry," Les said again. "I was being stupid."

"Forget it," Mo said, acutely aware of the warmth of Les's hand. "I'm fine."

"Maybe we should go in."

"No." She reluctantly pulled her hand from Les's, not wanting to give her the wrong idea. Well, the wrong idea from Les's point of view. "I want to keep playing." And delay walking through the lounge looking like she'd been run over by a bike. If she timed it right, maybe the other students would be on their way to supper, though she'd definitely have to change before going to the dining room.

"You sure?" Les asked.

"Yeah, positive. Now get back over there."

Mo fetched the ball and dropped it onto the grass. "I'm changing the game," she shouted to Les. She wanted to show Les that she could bounce back from one little fall, and it would be boring if Les always kicked the ball directly to her. "If you want the ball, you'll have to take it off me."

She darted behind the ball and kicked it away from Les—not too far, just enough so she could continue to kick it as she ran. Almost immediately, she realized what a dumb idea this was. No matter how fast she ran, she wouldn't outrun Les. Sure enough, Les's footsteps soon thudded behind her, then Les was next to her. She almost tripped when Les stretched out her right foot and tried to get control of the ball, but she regained her footing and punted the ball away.

Les darted after the ball; Mo drew on every shred of energy she had and charged after her. They reached the ball at the same time. Mo swung back her leg and kicked, but suddenly Les's leg was there, not the ball. Their legs locked. Mo tumbled forward and broke her fall with her hands. Les crashed down next to her.

Silence, then Les said, "We really should go in," much to Mo's relief. Les was okay, and so was she. She rolled onto her side to agree—enough was enough. Les lay on her back, grinning. "We're asking for it otherwise," she said, rolling toward Mo. "I should have insisted that—"

Their faces were so close, their noses were almost touching. Les's smile faded. Their eyes met. Before Mo could stop herself, she moved in and touched her lips to Les's. Les's lips were softer than she'd ever imagined. She pressed harder, slipped her arm around Les, slid closer to her. She wanted to feel Les's entire body; she wanted to hold her and squeeze her and—

It felt as if someone had thrown a bucket of ice-cold water over her head. Was she out of her flaming mind? This was Les, not only the prettiest girl at the academy and probably diff-oriented, but her best friend, the one who'd never shown any interest in her and would probably run into the academy to throw up as soon as Mo let her go. She'd ruined everything. Now her secret was out, and Les wouldn't want anything to do with her.

Mo snapped her arm to her side and drew back. "Les, I-I'm sorry," she said, trying to move away from her, but unable to do so for some reason. "I don't know what came over me. I wasn't thinking. It won't happen again, I promise."

Les gazed at her, her normally pale face flushed. Mo swallowed; Les was probably so angry and disgusted, she couldn't speak. But then Les said, "That's too bad, because I'd really like to do that again."

Mo could hardly believe her ears. "You mean kiss?" she said, wanting to be absolutely sure before she committed herself. Whatever was preventing her from moving away tightened, forcing her body against Les's. She realized with a start that it was Les's arm. Les had her arm around her!

"That's exactly what I mean." This time Les moved in. Their lips locked, and Mo's surroundings melted away.

Later she thought about why she'd finally thrown caution to the wind. Had she seen something in Les's eyes? Had she reached her breaking point and been willing to risk their friendship because the

     DISOBEDIENCE MEANS DEATH

alternative was too painful? Or had it been a completely impulsive act? She'd concluded that it didn't matter. All that mattered was that they were together.

And now years later, lying in their room at the Military Academy, she couldn't help but wonder if Les had ever regretted how she'd reacted that afternoon. Would she have been so quick to kiss back if she'd known that she'd eventually be saddled with a short, flat, plain girlfriend who was the laughingstock of the Military Academy because she thought she could be a fighter pilot? If she'd known, maybe she *would* have run into the Indoctrination Academy and thrown up.

Mo watched Les fold another shirt. She made folding clothes look like an art form. She turned heads wherever she went. And Mo? The only time she stood out was when she happened to be next to a tree stump. She was also selfish and pathetic, because she'd hang onto Les until the bitter end.

Unfortunately, that end could come sooner rather than later. Les's twenty-fifth birthday had always been the looming doomsday date, the day Mo's life would turn into a day-by-day, nail-biting existence until her and Les's Chosen Papers arrived. Turning twenty-five had been the furthest thing from her mind when she'd first kissed Les. It had seemed so far away, some mysterious state that adult Rymellans entered that she wouldn't have to worry about for a long, long time. Now she could fill in the blanks between now and then, and despair at how close it was. But at least it was still a few years away. If she'd blown the essay exam or didn't have a hope of entering the fighter pilot program because of her height, the end could come as soon as their third year. For the first time, they'd spend a significant time apart.

"Les?" Mo said.

Les looked up from the pair of pants she was folding. "What?"

"What do you think will happen if one of us makes it into the fighter pilot program and the other one doesn't?"

"What do you mean?" Les said, adding the pants to the neat stack on the dresser and reaching into the closet.

"To us. What would happen to us?"

Les dropped her hand and looked at Mo. "Nothing. Why would anything happen?"

"The student pilots go away for weeks. We've never gone that long without seeing each other."

Les hesitated. Mo could guess what was running through Les's mind—that the time would come when they'd never see each other at all, so it wouldn't be prudent to admit that being apart for a few weeks would be difficult. Once, just once, she wished Les would say something, anything, to indicate that she'd be upset if they weren't Chosens. That she'd struggle to adjust, that never seeing each other again was unimaginable. Just once.

"You were away a few times with the student orchestra. We survived," Les said.

"Yeah, but I was only ever away for a night or two." And she'd missed Les terribly and had hated sleeping on her own. "You—or I—would be gone for weeks." Plenty of time for Les to grow close to someone else, someone who'd understand more than Mo what it was like to be a fighter pilot. Les would come to dread returning to the Military Academy. "And what about afterward, when we graduate? If we're both pilots, there's a good chance we'll be posted together. If not, who knows?"

"Well, if I'm not accepted into the evaluation, the first thing I'll do is examine all the options and figure out what else interests me." Les walked to the bed. Mo started to move over, expecting Les to sit on the edge, but Les sat on the floor, rested her arm on the bed, and rested her chin on her arm. "From there, I'll figure out which items on the list are closely associated with fighter pilots," she said, her eyes level with Mo's. "Off the top of my head, there's tactical, fighter maintenance, weapons development and testing, um . . ."

"But the evaluation for most programs is happening now."

"True, but there are still the second-round evaluations."

"What?" Mo had never heard of them.

"If you're not accepted into a program now, you can try out for a different one during the first couple of weeks of your third year. Though only for programs that still have open slots."

"How do you know about them? Oh, wait. Finney."

Les nodded. "Well, sort of. Finney only mentioned them in passing, as something we'll consider if we have to. I decided to look into them further. Apparently, if you fail your first-round evaluation, they tell you about the second-round ones during your results meeting. You can't try out for the same program you just failed, though."

Well, at least that was something. Maybe she wouldn't end up cleaning toilets after all. But even if she enrolled in one of these second-round evaluations, she might end up serving with Les in the future, but not necessarily training with her. In fact, she could end up at a different Military Academy, depending on the program.

"I bet tactical will still have a few places," Les said. "I've heard it's not that popular. I don't know why. I think it would be interesting."

"Why didn't you tell me about these second-round evaluations before?"

"There wasn't any point. You only have to concern yourself with them if you fail the evaluation."

"Did you look into them in case I fail?"

Les chuckled. "No. I looked into them in case *I* fail. You know me, I always like to have a backup plan." She paused. "So why are you suddenly concerned about what'll happen if one of us fails the evaluation? You've never said anything about it before."

"I don't know, I guess it wasn't real before. Now that we'll know if we're in or out in a week's time, probably everyone's thinking about what'll happen if they fail."

Les didn't look convinced. "Did your essay exam go okay?"

"Fine," Mo said, though she avoided Les's eyes.

"It's just that it took you a while."

"Yeah, it did, okay? So what?"

"You seemed upset when you got back."

"I told you, I'm not feeling well."

"Come on, Mo. You might get away with that with someone else, but not with me." Les stroked Mo's cheek.

Mo felt herself soften, but Les wouldn't get around her that easily. "Look, like I said, now that we're finally at the point where we'll know if we have a chance of being pilots or not, failing seems like a real possibility."

"And you think you'll fail?"

She remained silent.

"You did well on your aptitude test, and you said the essay exam went okay."

It had in that she'd answered all the questions. Maybe not going on and on about herself would end up working to her advantage, and perhaps the essay exam wasn't given as much weight as the interview and simulator test. She could hope, anyway.

"I'm sure you'll do okay in your interview, and you know you'll ace the simulator part," Les said.

"Not necessarily. Last time I was in the simulator, I blew myself up."

"Yes, but you were with David. You know how he likes to push. Remember that time he said he wanted to try an intermediate sim, just to see what they were like? It took him longer to suit up than he lasted."

Despite her mood, Mo smiled. They'd linked with him just to observe. *Here we go,* he'd said. The next thing they'd heard was *Simulation Failed.* "Yeah, I guess that's true," she said. "And we did fly a difficult sim."

"I bet he chose it."

Mo nodded. "Speaking of the simulator, we should see if we can book another slot before the evaluation sims start. Might be tough, though. I think they're giving priority to cadets from other academies that haven't had much chance to fly them before."

"So if the essay exam went okay, and you're not particularly worried about how you'll do in the interview and simulator, why are you so worried that you'll fail?" Les asked.

Great, Les wouldn't be derailed. If Mo didn't say something, Les would never let it go. Maybe she should tell Les what was on her mind, so it wouldn't be a total shock when she came back from her results meeting and said she'd failed. "Les, I think I'm the shortest applicant this year."

Les frowned. "Maybe you are, I haven't noticed. But it doesn't matter. There's no height requirement."

"Officially, no. But with all the candidates this year, I doubt my height will work to my advantage. Probably the opposite. I probably don't stand a chance. Not this year."

"Mo, that doesn't make sense. If they didn't want someone of your height in the program or if they prefer taller candidates over shorter ones, they would have rejected your application for the evaluation. You would never have made it this far."

"Maybe I'm in on an oversight."

Les's brows rose in surprise. "You don't believe that. You're right, there are a lot of applicants this year. So the last thing they'd do is fill an evaluation slot with someone they have no intention of accepting. I'm telling you, you're in the evaluation because you have the same chance as everyone else of being invited into the program."

Even if Les was right, that wouldn't change the fact that other candidates were laughing at her because she was short. Les hadn't seen Ann smirking during the meeting. She hadn't noticed that Ross had singled Mo out when talking about "other factors." Most of all, Les hadn't been in the essay exam room. Maybe Mo did have a chance, but without the respect of her fellow student pilots, what was the point?

Les tapped Mo's nose. "You were short when you decided you wanted to be a fighter pilot, you were short when you tried out for the Military Academy, and you were short when you put in your application for the fighter pilot program. You've never been concerned about this before. Why now? What gave you the idea that your height might be a problem?"

"Nothing. I just heard it mentioned as a possible problem, that's all."

"Where? Who mentioned it?"

"I don't know, I just heard it around."

Skepticism was written all over Les's face. "Has someone been bothering you?"

"No," she said firmly. The last thing she needed was Les talking to Ann. *Mo, you're so short, someone else has to fight your battles for you. Hey Mo, I thought Lesley was your girlfriend, not your mama.*

"You sure?"

"Yes!"

"Remember what David said when we first met him? Pilots tend to be shorter than average."

Yeah, but how shorter than average? Hadn't she already mentioned that she was the shortest applicant of the bunch?

"If height's a factor, I'm the one who should be worried," Les said.

Mo restrained herself from snorting. Time to surrender, or at least pretend to; the conversation wasn't going anywhere. Trying to talk to Les about this had been a mistake. Les didn't understand. How could she? "You're right. I'm probably worrying about it for nothing. I don't know, I guess I'm more stressed about the evaluation than I thought I'd be. I feel a bit better, now that I've let some of it out."

Les studied Mo's face, then reached for her hand. "Promise me you'll be confident during the interview. It's important that you come across as confident and enthusiastic, so promise me that no matter what doubts you have, you'll go in there and tell the interviewer that you want to be a fighter pilot and that you'll be one of the best fighter pilots they've ever seen." Her hand tightened around Mo's. "Promise me."

"I promise," Mo said, meaning it. She might not be able to muster up much enthusiasm for herself, but she could for Les, for them. She wouldn't let Les down by not giving it her best shot, or Les might think *she* didn't care if they stayed together. "I promise," she said again.

Les's grip relaxed. They stared at each other. Mercifully, the conversation had come to a natural end. "Do you feel up to the mess hall, or would you rather I go and get us supper?" Les asked.

She wasn't ready to face others yet, especially those who'd been in the exam room. "Get us supper."

Les kissed Mo's forehead and used the edge of the bed to push herself to her feet. "I'll beep you when I get there, tell you what the choices are."

"Okay."

Moments later, the door clicked shut. The room felt empty, as it always did when Les left. Mo sighed. If she failed the evaluation, the room would feel empty a lot more often.

MO PAUSED TO take a breath outside the pilot training complex, glad her interview was over. She had a good feeling about it. The interviewer hadn't burst into laughter when she'd entered the room, for one thing. And once she'd started talking, she'd relaxed, almost believing that she had the same chance as everyone else of being invited into the program. A couple of times she'd felt her confidence wavering but,

     DISOBEDIENCE MEANS DEATH

remembering her promise to Les, she'd looked the interviewer in the eye and answered the question with conviction and what she felt was the appropriate level of enthusiasm. If she failed the evaluation, it wouldn't be through lack of trying.

She pulled out her comm unit and beeped Les. "I'm done."

"And?"

"I think it went okay."

"You sounded like you want to be a fighter pilot, right?"

"Yeah, Les, I did." For some reason, she craved an apple turnover. "I'm just going to drop in at the mess hall to get a snack. Do you want something?"

"I'll meet you there, walk with you back to the room," Les said.

Mo smiled. Ever since their conversation after the essay exam, Les had wanted to be with her every second of the day. "No, don't. There's no point, you coming to the mess hall. I don't want to stay, I just want to pick up a snack."

"Aren't you chilly? The sun's gone in. I can bring your cloak."

Well, it was a little breezy, but the mess hall was only a couple of minutes away and then she'd be going straight to their room. "I'll be fine. Do you want anything?"

"No, thanks."

"Okay. See you in a bit."

At the mess hall, Mo requested the largest apple turnover of the bunch and decided to treat herself and have it heated. "Certainly," said the counter attendant. "It'll only take a minute."

Her mouth watered; she couldn't wait to sink her teeth into it. After her sim test, she'd treat herself again, maybe to a gigantic piece of chocolate cake and ice cream with sprinkles. And if she passed the evaluation, as many cookies as she could carry. They'd have to roll her home! Mo grinned. Yeah, she just might pass. Why not?

A spirited conversation drew her attention to her left. She groaned and looked away. Ann, with three of her new friends from other academies, all male. She'd attracted quite the entourage. Their chatter grew closer. Mo peeked at them from the corner of her eye. They were standing near the hot meal section, discussing how hungry they were and whether they wanted a full meal.

"Oh, remember when we were talking about what makes a good fighter pilot?" Ann said loud enough for Mo to hear. "Well, I thought of something else. You have to be at least as tall as me."

Mo's jaw tightened.

"Why?" one of her companions asked.

Come on, come on. How long did it take to warm an apple turnover?

"Let's say auto-navigation fails, so you have to control the fighter manually," Ann said. "To do that, you'd need to see out of the cockpit. Imagine if you were so short, you couldn't see over the control panels."

Several voices spoke at once.

"What?"

"You'd be all over the place."

"It would look like nobody was flying the craft."

Ann shrieked with laughter. When someone made another comment, too low for Mo to hear, Ann sounded like she couldn't breathe.

Idiots. As long as sensors were still operational, a pilot could fly the craft without having to see out of the cockpit. And Mo could see over the control panels, thank you very much.

"Who would you want on your wing if you're in trouble? Someone using a booster seat?" Ann gasped out.

A chorus of laughter this time. Where was that flaming attendant?

As if he'd heard her, the attendant returned, holding the apple turnover between a pair of tongs. He slid the turnover into a bag and held it out to her. "Here you are."

She wanted to snatch it from his hand, but restrained herself. "Thank you," she murmured, then slunk toward the exit.

"Oh, Mo," Ann called, just as Mo thought she'd escaped Ann's notice.

She turned around.

Ann stepped toward her. "I hope you don't think I had you in mind when I was talking about short pilots."

Making fun of them, more like.

"With your skills, I'm sure you'd be fine, flying a craft with no auto-navigation."

"My skills?" Mo squeaked.

"Well, sure. There's a lot more to you than meets the eye, isn't there?"

Mo had the sinking feeling that Ann was setting her up. Ann's new friends stared curiously at Mo. "Oh, that's right, you wouldn't know," Ann said to them. "You know the tall blonde in the evaluation?" She held her hand above her head. "The pretty one? You can't miss her, she's on the monitors."

"Thompson?" one of them said.

Ann nodded.

The other two looked confused. "Who?"

"The blonde." The one who'd matched Les's description with the name traced curves through the air with his hands. Mo's hand tightened around the bag.

Both their faces lit up. "Oh, *her.*"

"Yes, her," Ann said, smirking at them. "But down, boys, because you don't stand a chance. She's same-oriented. Not only that, she's had the same girlfriend ever since she entered the Military Academy. And guess what?" Ann spread her arms toward Mo. "You're looking at the girlfriend. So you see, Mo here must have hidden skills and talents that we can only imagine."

They eyed Mo up and down. She could guess what they were thinking—why would someone like Les be interested in someone like her? Well, let them. What did she care, what they thought? They could stare and snicker and whisper all they wanted.

But her silent, brave words rang hollow. How many others wondered when they saw her and Les together? Argamon, she sometimes wondered herself. She'd never stood in front of a bunch of gawkers who'd calculated her worth and come up with a big, fat zero, though, and she withered under their scrutiny. She should say something, show some spirit, defend not only herself, but Les. Instead she whirled and marched toward the exit.

"Where are you going?" Ann shouted. "I was giving you a compliment."

Did Ann think she was stupid? She may be short, plain, and as curvy as a wooden ruler, but she wasn't stupid. Outside, she fought the tears but lost, their saltiness stinging her tongue as she licked them away. She couldn't go back to the room, not like this. She headed in another direction, not caring where she ended up.

What was she doing here, anyway? Why had entering the military ever crossed her mind? Her account was overflowing with credits; she could sit around and pick her nose all day and still live well. Too bad nobody would respect her, including herself. How could she ever join hands again and say the Words while contributing nothing to her fellow Rymellans? All Rymellans used their skills to support the Way, and that was what she wanted to do. Yeah, right—her skills. Ha! What a laugh!

A cadet was walking toward her. She wiped her nose on her sleeve and peered into the bag at the turnover as she passed him, grunting a hello. Five minutes ago she couldn't wait to eat the dessert, but now she gagged at the aroma wafting from the bag. She rolled it shut and glanced around for somewhere out of the way to sit, before she ran into someone who'd want to talk to her and wonder why her eyes were so red.

The track field was up ahead. She still jogged around it occasionally, and felt drawn to it now. Finding a seat was easy; the field was deserted and the bleachers empty. Mo set the bag on her lap, wiped her eyes, and stared out at nothing in particular.

What was she going to do? Les's backup plan might work for Les, but Mo wasn't sure it would work for her. Tactical would bore her— she wanted to fly, not stand in front of a grid as if she were playing a game. Weapons testing? Shooting at the other side was the extent of the weapons testing she wanted to do. And fighter maintenance would grate. Working on fighters would be a constant reminder that others soared while she stayed behind.

Well, she could fly aviacrafts. Not as exciting as flying a fighter, but flying, nonetheless. She could even fly military aviacraft, and she didn't need to enroll in a special program for that—all she needed was a licence and nothing better to do. But just thinking about it made her want to yawn. Plus, the point was to do something that kept her close to Les.

Maybe she was stupid after all, because she honestly wanted to be a fighter pilot. She'd wanted that ever since she'd sat in that fighter during the tour of the military installation with the Indoctrination Academy, and she'd honestly believed that she could achieve that dream. The first time she'd flown a sim had only confirmed her desire—she'd left the simulator exhilarated and convinced that she'd been born to pilot a fighter. Les wanting to be one too had validated her career choice. It couldn't have been more perfect. Too perfect, as it turned out. She hadn't counted on not having the respect of her fellow cadets, had never thought that others would laugh at her, but what could she do? She couldn't change the fact that she was short, so where did that leave her?

The wind was picking up. Mo shivered and hugged her legs to her chest, squishing the turnover. She should go inside, but she couldn't face Les—not yet. If it weren't for Les, she'd be packing her bags and going home right now, but she didn't want to disappoint her, not by dropping out of the evaluation, anyway. That could wait until she received her evaluation results, when there would be plenty of disappointment to go around for both of them. What in the flaming Argamon was she going to do?

Her lips trembled and a tear rolled down her cheek, then another. She could sit here forever trying to figure it out, but it wouldn't change a thing. The end result would be the same: her dream shattered, and potentially her relationship with Les, too.

LESLEY STRODE ALONG the path pondering where to look next. She'd already checked the mess hall, the library, the pilot training complex, and the recreation centre, including the practice rooms. The latter had been done in desperation; she'd seen Mo's violin propped in the corner of their room. Where was she? Why wasn't she responding to beeps? Didn't she realize Lesley would be worried? Even David was out looking for her. Lesley shifted Mo's cloak from her left arm to her right and looked over at the track field. No joggers, and it would have been odd if Mo had suddenly decided to go for a run. Well, it was odd that Mo hadn't—

Someone was sitting up in the bleachers. Lesley quickened her pace, and swallowed when Mo's familiar figure came into focus. Mo must be freezing up there. She pulled out her comm unit. "I found her," she said to David as she bounded up the steps to the second-last row. She stopped. Mo was at the other end of the row and seemed oblivious to her presence.

"Is she okay?"

That depended on what he meant by okay. "She's all right."

"Where are you? Do you want me to come over?"

"No. I want to talk to her, find out what's going on. Thanks for looking for her."

"No problem. Think you'll be at Ellen's get-together tonight?"

She doubted it, but said, "Maybe. I'll beep you later and let you know." She terminated the connection.

Mo looked up as Lesley approached, then looked away and rubbed her eyes. Lesley's throat tightened. If Mo thought she could hide that she'd been crying, she was wrong. Lesley knew Mo's face too well—every blemish, every mole, every contour; she could close her eyes and bring Mo's face into sharp focus, as if Mo were standing in front of her. The glimpse she'd caught of that precious face had been more than enough to tell her that Mo had shed tears.

"What are you doing up here?" she asked as she draped Mo's cloak around her shoulders and sat next to her. Mo was hugging her legs to her chest. Lesley put her arm around her to help warm her. She covered Mo's hands with one of her own, then rubbed them. They felt like ice.

"Thinking," Mo murmured.

"About what?"

"What to do with my life."

"What do you mean?"

Mo sighed. "Les, I might fail the evaluation. Even if I don't, I don't know if I should be a pilot."

"What?" Not wanting to be a pilot was new.

"Pilots have to work together, be a team. How can I be a pilot when nobody respects me?"

Lesley mentally kicked herself. This was her fault; she should have met Mo at the mess hall. When they'd talked after Mo's essay exam, she hadn't believed for a second that Mo was suddenly jittery about the evaluation. She'd vowed to stick by her side, hoping to deter whoever was bothering her, or at least find out who it was. Mo had sounded fine after the interview, so she must have run into trouble afterward. But with whom? "Who doesn't respect you?"

"Other cadets who'll be pilots."

"But who? I respect you. David respects you. You've linked with a couple of other cadets. They didn't have a problem flying sims with you. So why do you think nobody respects you?"

Mo sighed again and stretched out her legs, revealing a bag on her lap. Lesley gingerly picked it up and peeked inside. If she had to guess, it contained a pulverized apple turnover. She set it on the bench next to her, then stifled a groan at the stain on Mo's pants. It would have to wait. "Mo, if you don't tell me what's going on, I can't help."

"There's nothing you can do," Mo said, buttoning her cloak.

"At least tell me why you don't want to be a pilot."

"I do want to be a pilot!" Mo snapped. "I said I don't know if I should be."

"Well, I don't know if this counts for anything, but I think you should."

Mo gave her a sidelong look. "Why?"

"Because you're good. You're meant to be in a fighter. Anyone who's linked with you would say the same."

"You're just saying that."

"No, I'm not," Lesley said, bristling. Why did her opinion count less than that of whoever was harassing Mo? She'd linked with Mo; her opinion was based on experience. Mo was almost a different person in the simulator—calm, confident, no-nonsense, focused on the mission objectives and on achieving them as efficiently as possible. Lesley wasn't a slouch in the cockpit, but Mo naturally took the lead. She'd grown used to following the clipped orders Mo probably didn't realize she was giving. "These other cadets who don't respect you . . . have you linked with any of them?"

Mo hesitated, then shook her head.

Ah, so someone *was* getting to her. "Then what do they know?"

"They know I'm short."

So it was back to that, and nothing Lesley said would make a difference. She could tell Mo until she was blue in the face that there was no height requirement and that her fellow pilots would care more about her abilities than her height, but it would be a waste of time. "I hope you're not planning to drop out of the evaluation."

"No, I'm not. But you know why I'm not? Because I want us to stay together, not because I flaming care about the program anymore."

Lesley knew that wasn't true, but if Mo wanted to claim that, fine. As for staying together, unbeknownst to Mo, she had two backup plans—the one she'd already told Mo about, and the one she'd kept to herself, the plan for if she passed the evaluation but Mo failed.

She'd arrived at the Military Academy with one goal in mind: to be a fighter pilot. But studying at the academy and following Finney's advice had opened her eyes to other possibilities. She still wanted to be a fighter pilot, but if that didn't work out, two other areas interested her. The first was tactics, as she'd mentioned to Mo, though that would work best if Mo passed and she failed. The second was, surprisingly, Interior. Finney had advised her to take two Interior courses, so she could "see the other side." She'd enjoyed them, to the point that she hoped to take more in her third year. If Mo failed and decided to drop out of the Military Academy, Interior would keep them together, in the sense that they'd both remain on Rymel. Mo would never follow Lesley into Interior, something Lesley might use if they were both pilots and still together when they turned twenty-five.

But that was for later. Right now, she had to make sure Mo showed up for her sim test, and she'd use everything at her disposal to do it, no matter how crummy. "Well, then, you'd better pass the evaluation, because it'll be a lot easier for us to stay together if we're both pilots, and I have every intention of passing."

Mo stared at her, her face tight.

"And I want to remind you of what you said to me when I was waffling about taking the entrance exam. You said I had to think about the rest of my life and follow my dream, not do what others thought I should do. So now I'm saying the same thing to you. I don't know what these cadets are saying to you, but I do know you belong in a cockpit, and you've worked hard to get to this point. Don't throw it all away over a few stupid comments."

"Stupid comments? You don't even know what they said!"

"Why don't you tell me?"

Mo remained silent, her mouth a stubborn line.

"Okay, don't tell me. But I'm not letting you out of my sight until

   DISOBEDIENCE MEANS DEATH

the evaluation is over." She raised a finger when Mo opened her mouth. "Unless you want to tell me who's bugging you. Then I'll keep my eye on them, instead." She waited. "No? Then you'll have to get used to having a shadow."

Mo tutted. "Everyone will wonder why you're always with me."

Lesley squeezed Mo and took her hand. "They'll think I find you irresistible, which is true." She regretted her words when Mo's nails dug into her palm. For some reason, that had been the wrong thing to say.

A gust of wind almost blew the bag off the bleacher. Lesley snatched it up. "Let's go back to the room before we're blown away." And before she put her foot in her mouth again.

Mo mumbled agreement, then groaned. "Is it Ellen's thing tonight? Because I'm not sure I want to go."

"I don't feel like going, either," Lesley said, standing up and offering Mo her hand. "I'd rather spend the night alone with you."

"I don't want to talk about the evaluation, so if that's what you're planning to do, forget it. I'd rather go to Ellen's."

"Actually, I thought maybe we could go to a practice room and play together for a bit."

Mo brightened. "Sure! We haven't done that for a while. Did you have anything in mind?"

"Well . . . yes." Suddenly she had butterflies. "I've had this melody in my head for a while. With all the waiting around, I finally had a chance to write it down."

"You've written music?" Mo said, her eyes widening.

"Just a short piece."

"For flute?"

"And violin. Your violin. But you know what? We probably won't get a practice room at such short notice."

"Les, hardly anybody is here. And I've never had a problem getting one, no matter when I've tried."

"You probably don't feel like playing."

"No, no, a spot of violin will do me good, take my mind off things."

"You sure?"

"Yes."

When they reached the field, Mo turned to her. "I can't believe you wrote a piece and you're going to let me play it."

Neither could Lesley. She hadn't planned to tell Mo about the piece just yet—she'd wanted to refine it further before sharing. But music usually lifted Mo's spirits, and Lesley would do anything to see Mo's eyes dance again. She put her arm around her and steered her toward the dormitories. "Come on. You need to get out of that uniform. I'll take it to the laundry and get us supper."

"And then we'll go to a practice room?"

Lesley nodded, the butterflies fluttering again. Oh well, seeing Mo energized was worth the embarrassment she'd suffer later. If only Mo were as enthusiastic about the evaluation. Mo's refusal to divulge her tormentors' names was wise. Very wise.

MO WILLED HERSELF to hold her head up as she walked through the pilot training complex lobby with Les. Great, one of Ann's airhead friends was sitting near the reception desk, his nose in a book. If he looked up, she knew exactly what he'd think. *Wow, Ann wasn't kidding. That is her girlfriend!*

"You don't have to wait for me," she said to Les. She couldn't bear the thought of Les talking to that moron while he sat and ogled her, not hearing a word she was saying.

"After what happened last time? I'm not going anywhere," Les said.

"Do you want me to pass or not? I'll feel rushed if I know you're out here waiting." What she'd actually do was worry about Les, but the end result would be the same: she'd be distracted in the simulator.

"I really think it's best that I stick around."

"If I promise to beep you as soon as I'm finished and to wait for you to come here, will you leave?"

Les pursed her lips. "Well . . ."

"I'll do better if you go. Honest."

Les slowly exhaled. "Okay. But you'd better beep me as soon as you're done."

"I will."

They reached the entrance to the simulator wing. "You don't need it, but good luck," Les said.

   DISOBEDIENCE MEANS DEATH

"Thanks. Now leave. I'm not going in until I see you pass by the window."

Les rolled her eyes, but squeezed Mo's hand and walked away. A minute later, she waved to Mo from outside. Mo waved back. Once she was satisfied that Les was heading in the direction of the dormitories and hadn't ducked behind a tree, she strode to room 18B.

A lieutenant sat inside the small office; he looked up and smiled. She nodded to him. "Cadet Middleton."

"Oh, yes." He gestured toward the single empty chair in front of the desk. She didn't think it was his desk; the bare walls and absence of any personal items suggested that he was using the room on a temporary basis. "I'm going to give you a written overview of your mission objectives and a summary of the expected opposition," he said when she'd taken the seat. "In other words, what you'll usually have before flying a mission. You can take ten to fifteen minutes to think about your strategy, then you'll fly the simulation. Oh, and if any of the other candidates have told you about their tests, it won't help. Every test is different."

They hadn't. Les and David hadn't flown their tests yet, and she'd avoided everyone else.

"Here you are." He pushed a sheet across the desk. "Let me know when you're ready."

Time to get down to business. She read through the information and inwardly snorted. Were they kidding? Ten to fifteen minutes to come up with a strategy? She could think of two possible approaches off the top of her head, one of which was almost guaranteed to succeed—okay, unless she blacked out, it would succeed. Not only that, the expected time at the bottom of the page said thirty minutes, but anyone could complete the sim in fifteen. Who'd written this thing? She lowered the sheet. "I'm ready."

His brow furrowed. "Are you sure?"

"Yes."

"All right." He pressed a button on his comm unit. "Cadet Middleton is ready to fly her test."

"On my way."

"Lieutenant Commander Ross will escort you to the simulator."

Oh great, just who she wanted to see.

Ross appeared in the doorway and motioned for Mo to join her. "I'll take that," she said, pointing to the sheet in Mo's hand. "And this is for you." She held out a helmet.

"Thank you," Mo murmured, cringing as she accepted it. Size small.

"Good luck," the lieutenant said behind her.

She thanked him and followed Ross to the simulator, her eyes adjusting to the reduced lighting. "I'm looking forward to seeing what you do with this one, Cadet," Ross said, pressing the *Enter* button and moving aside so Mo could pass through the portal.

"Oh, um, good." She didn't know if Ross was being serious or sarcastic. To cover her uncertainty and embarrassment, she busied herself with settling into the pilot's seat, buckling up, and plugging the loose end of the helmet cable into the helmet's port.

"I'll be waiting right here," Ross said. "The simulation is loaded and ready to go, so when you're ready, just start."

"Understood," Mo said, already thinking ahead to the mission. The portal door swooshed shut. Now that Ross wasn't watching, she tightened the seatbelt straps, then placed the helmet on her head and adjusted it so the earpieces were sitting correctly. She swung the mouthpiece out and said, "Ready."

The lights went out. In the blackness, she realized that this could be the last time she sat in a simulator. At least she'd go out with a bang, and it wouldn't be herself blowing up this time. She flexed both her hands, then poised her left over navigation and gripped the weapons control with her right. "Go!"

Thirteen minutes later, she bid Ross good-bye at the equipment counter and beeped Les. "I'm done."

"That was quick. You didn't throw it, did you?"

"It wasn't hard. I'll tell you about it, but everyone flies a different sim."

"I could still learn something. Don't leave. I'm coming over."

"I'll be in the lobby." Mo slid her comm unit back into its holder and looked over her shoulder at the corridor that led back to the simulators. Despite Ann, despite worrying that other pilots would never respect her, she wanted to walk up that corridor again. If only she hadn't let Les talk

     DISOBEDIENCE MEANS DEATH

her into going on that tour of Installation 22; if she hadn't sat in that fighter . . . but there was nothing she could do about it now.

She returned to the lobby. Since the airhead was nowhere in sight, it didn't matter where she sat, so she plunked down in the same place where she'd waited for David after they'd flown that disastrous sim. Then, the evaluation had been ahead of her; now it was over. She felt at a loose end. No more classes, no more exams, no more simulator bookings—all she could do was wait for her results meeting, then go home exuberant or crushed.

If they didn't invite her into the program, she had no idea what she'd do. Despite racking her brains about what else she could do with her life, she'd always come back to being a fighter pilot. She'd come to realize that, for her, the military and the fighter pilot program were intertwined. Until recently, she hadn't seriously considered the possibility that she might not make it into the program.

In hindsight, that had been naïve, but if she'd allowed herself to consider failure, she might not have rolled out of bed all those dark mornings and dragged herself to the simulators when any sane person was still snoring. She wouldn't have slogged through all those books, and she certainly wouldn't have remained focused on her classes and assignments when she and Les were having problems during their first year. If she'd stopped to think about what she'd do if the program rejected her, it would have been easy to give up.

But a part of her had remained steadfast, even during the last couple of weeks. Her wobbles had occurred between phases of the evaluation, not during them. Les's support had been invaluable, but it wasn't the only reason Mo hadn't stopped trying. Somewhere inside, she'd still believed that she could be a fighter pilot, and a flaming good one! Argamon, the part of her that believed she could do it was probably the same part that believed she and Les were Chosens. Ann would probably say that part of her was delusional. Maybe it was. She'd soon find out, at least as far as the fighter pilot program went.

Les's blonde hair caught her eye; she was outside, approaching the entrance. Mo stood and waved when Les stepped into the lobby and paused to search for her. Les strolled over. "You must have aced the sim."

Mo grinned. "I don't know about acing it, but I didn't have any trouble completing the objectives."

"Good. And now you're done. All that's left is your results meeting," Les said, beaming.

Les looked so gorgeous with her face lit up and the sun accentuating her blue eyes. Mo could hardly breathe, and was absolutely certain that she could never feel more for anyone than she felt for Les. If they weren't Chosens, the Chosen Council didn't have a clue what it was doing—not that she'd ever say that out loud.

"I know it's been rough," Les said, her smile fading. "If they invite you into the program, I hope you'll accept."

"Of course I will! I've never once doubted that I want to be a fighter pilot. I've had some doubts about getting into the program, but that didn't stop me from trying. There's no way I'll say no if they invite me in." And if they rejected her because of how she'd performed and not because of "other factors" that she couldn't change or control, she honestly wouldn't know how she could have done better. Okay, she hadn't been as wordy as she could have been on her essay exam, but otherwise, she thought she'd done well. "I'm just worried that the other student pilots won't take me seriously. If I get in, that is."

Les chuckled. "I'm sure they'll take you seriously, but if they don't, what problem would you rather have? Proving yourself to the other pilots, or figuring out what to do with your life because you didn't get into the program?"

She had a point.

"Come on, let's go to David's."

"David's?"

"He wants to hear all about the sim. And so do I."

"I guess it's over for me, but not for you two," Mo said as she slipped her arm into Les's. She'd done her bit—her fate was now out of her hands.

MO FLIPPED UP her comm unit, read the time, and let it drop. She looked toward the mess hall entrance.

"Relax. Her meeting only started five minutes ago," David said from his place across from her.

Already long enough for Les to know. At this point, Les would be smiling and accepting congratulations, or listening to the officer explain why she'd been rejected and what her options were. They'd all agreed to wait at the mess hall rather than in the lobby at the training complex, so they could each have some time alone after their meeting if they needed it. But now, waiting here, Mo wished she could be there for Les, either way.

"I'll barely have enough time to hear if she's in before I have to leave for my meeting," he said, his hand gripping his tziva mug a little too tightly.

Mo envied him. Her meeting was still an hour away—plenty of time to imagine the worst. A rejection would mean not only the end of her dream, but potentially the end of her and Les. Sure, Les said nothing would change, but Mo wasn't convinced. At the very least, they'd see much less of each other, and that would be a difficult adjustment to make after the past year. She suspected more would change, though. Even if they were both rejected, there'd be a problem. She loved Les, but unless another military role sparked her interest, she couldn't see herself remaining at the Military Academy. Staying for Les might hold them together a little longer, but ultimately it would hurt them. Their relationship would have a better chance if she left. That was what she'd tell herself, anyway.

Unfortunately, if she dropped out of the Military Academy and Les stayed, everyone would expect them to split up. "This would be a natural time to end it," they'd say. Natural? The end of her relationship with Les would never be natural. It would be forced, and abrupt, and leave her gasping and dead inside. She hoped—no, believed—it would never happen. If she had her way, they'd stay together until they received their Chosen Papers, which would arrive on the same day if they were each other's Chosen. But her fear right now was that she wouldn't be invited into the program, and Les would say, "Now would be a natural time to end it." Telling Les she believed they were Chosens and should stay together wouldn't do, not for Les. She'd dismiss the notion as a fantasy.

"What are you thinking about?" David asked.

"Les," Mo said, shaking herself.

"Even if she's rejected, she'll be okay. She's mentioned tactics a few times."

"What will you do if you're not accepted?" she asked him, realizing they'd never talked about it.

He sipped his tziva. "I'm not sure. I've talked to my papa about a few ideas, but I didn't want to jinx myself, so I haven't given any of them serious consideration."

"Do they all involve the military?"

"Of course," he said, as if she'd asked a rhetorical question. "What about you? What will you do if you don't get in?"

"I haven't really thought about it." Not beyond leaving the academy and how that would affect her and Les, anyway.

They sat and drank their tziva in silence, the tension palpable. Mo raised her empty mug to her lips for something to do, then said, "I heard from Kary earlier. They accepted her."

"Good. I'm glad things are looking up for her."

"Me too." Ben had been rejected as part of the post-first-year purge and had left Kary behind along with the academy. He'd sent her a dispatch to break it off, claiming that to see her would be too painful because he associated her with his time at the academy. "Painful?" Kary had screeched. "I'll give him painful!" She'd put on a brave face in class, but had spent many of her evenings in tears, swearing off dating until her Chosen Papers arrived and wishing she'd never set foot inside the Military Academy. Mo had worried that she might drop out or even fail her second year, but she'd rallied.

"I'll miss her," David said.

"She'll be in Defence, so who knows, we could serve with her." There, she'd managed to sound optimistic. "And we'll beep each other." Though it wouldn't be the same as having her down the hall.

All thoughts of Kary left Mo's mind when Les walked in. She searched Les's face.

Les smiled. "I'm in."

"That's great!" Mo said, but something about Les's demeanour was off. She didn't seem overjoyed.

"Congratulations!" David said, rising. "I hate to run off, but it's my turn now. We'll celebrate later."

"Good luck," Mo and Les said in unison.

Les lowered herself into the chair on Mo's right. "An acceptance certificate," she said, handing Mo a sheet of paper. "The officer said that some pilots frame them."

"Really?"

"Yes."

Mo read the sheet; a ton weight dropped onto her shoulders. She slid the paper back to Les, then reached for Les's hand under the table. She wanted to hug her, tell her how proud she was, but while the mess hall was quiet, it wasn't empty. Plus, she sensed from Les's mood that an enthusiastic hug might not be welcome. "Is something wrong? You don't seem happy about this."

Les shrugged. "I'll be happier when I know you're in. Then we'll celebrate together."

"And if I'm not in?"

"I'll be very surprised if you're not in."

Sure, no pressure or anything. Now she'd really feel like a disappointment if she wasn't invited into the program. She squeezed Les's fingers. "But what if I'm not? I know you probably don't want to hear this, but I'm worried. About what'll happen to us." Les stroked Mo's hand. It felt nice, but at the same time it irritated Mo. Les was trying to distract her, but this was too important to ignore. "I just—"

"No matter what happens, we'll work something out," Les said, staring down at their hands. "I promise."

"Even if I were to leave the Military Academy?" Mo said, wanting to get that possibility out in the open.

"Yes." Les paused. "The sensible thing to do would be to break up, not work to stay together." She lifted her head and looked into Mo's eyes. "But for some reason, I can't be sensible when it comes to you." Les's cheeks reddened.

If they weren't in the mess hall, Mo would have grabbed her and kissed her and who knows what else. That was probably the closest thing she'd get to an "I love you" until their Chosen Papers arrived, and much more than she'd expected. She raised Les's hand to her lips and kissed it, then quickly tucked their hands underneath the table before Les could protest.

"You'll get in, though," Les said.

"I hope so." She should probably ask Les if she wanted a tziva refill, but she selfishly didn't want to let her go.

Les's comm unit beeped. She flipped it up and groaned. "Mama. She's probably wondering how my meeting went. I'll beep her later."

"Are you sure? I don't mind if you talk to her now."

"I'll beep her after your meeting. And Finney," Les said firmly.

"So what exactly happened at your meeting, anyway?"

Les was halfway through telling her when David bounded into the mess hall. He rushed over to the table and raised an acceptance certificate over his head. "I'm in! I'm in!" he shouted, grinning from ear to ear.

That was how Mo had expected Les to react. Two more ton weights were added to her shoulders. "Congratulations." She attempted a smile that probably looked more like a grimace. She was happy for him, but also acutely aware that she was now the odd one out. Having to tell them she'd been rejected would be more embarrassing and disappointing than she could bear.

"I'm glad you made it," Les said to him. "Congratulations."

"I guess you're stuck with me for at least another year," David said.

"I guess so," Les said.

The lack of enthusiasm in Les's voice gave Mo pause. She was certain it had nothing to do with David. "You heading home now?" she asked him.

"Are you kidding? We're in this together. I'm not leaving until we've celebrated together, which we'll do after your meeting."

She'd been afraid of that.

"You might want to eat something," Les murmured to Mo. "Your meeting's at 12:00. You don't want your stomach to grumble."

Her stomach grumbling was the least of Mo's worries, but she nodded. A snack wouldn't hurt. "I'll get a muffin. Do either of you want anything?" she asked as she rose.

"Bring over a tziva jug," David suggested.

She returned to the table a few minutes later and handed Les the jug. Let her pour; Mo didn't know how steady her hands were. While she picked at her muffin, she did her best to follow the conversation and appear as if she wasn't thinking about her impending meeting. Normally she was the talkative one, but not today. Les was doing an admirable job of engaging David, her left hand on Mo's leg. Mo would thank her later, ideally when they were holding their own private celebration.

    DISOBEDIENCE MEANS DEATH

Too soon, it was time for her to head to her meeting. She wiped her hands with a napkin and stood. "Now, I might need some time after the meeting. Don't come looking for me."

"We won't," Les and David said.

"Just give me some time."

"We will."

She swallowed. "I'll see you later, then."

Les touched her arm. "Good luck."

"Yeah, good luck," David echoed.

"Thanks."

She walked to the exit, breaking stride only to look at Les over her shoulder one last time. Les smiled and raised her thumb. Mo nodded and left the mess hall. She imagined Les and David huddled together, discussing how to react if she was rejected. If it was up to her, she'd leave the meeting, walk straight to the train station, and go home. After a good cry on Mama's shoulder, maybe she'd be ready to face Les and beep David. But that would be cowardly. She didn't want to lose their respect altogether.

She kept her head down as she strode through the lobby of the training complex. She'd either be doing this a lot more often in the future, or she'd never want to step foot in the place again, regardless of Les.

Her meeting would take place in room 22A, which turned out to belong to a group of offices that shared a small reception area. Good, the three chairs in the waiting room were empty, though muffled voices emanated from behind the closed door to 22B. Before Mo had a chance to sit down, Lieutenant Commander Ross stepped into the room from 22A. "I thought I heard someone. Come in, Cadet, come in."

Not her again. Resigned, Mo entered the office and accepted Ross's invitation to sit. Great, her feet weren't touching the floor. If she were anywhere else and for any other reason, she wouldn't think twice about lowering the seat, but not here. Her legs would have to dangle.

A single file lay on the desk. Ross opened it and looked at Mo. "Let's get to it. I have to say, in cases like yours, I always feel I should start by apologizing for putting you through the evaluation instead of just giving you an extra two weeks off."

Mo wanted to bury her head in her hands. Flaming Argamon! Ann had been right all along! She'd never stood a chance of getting in. All that work for nothing. Nothing!

"You see, every year, there are always one or two applicants we know we want in the program before the evaluation even starts. This year, you're one of them."

"What?" she blurted. Okay, Les was about to elbow her in the ribs and tell her to wake up, right? Or maybe this was really happening and she was sitting here gaping at Ross like an idiot. "I'm sorry, Lieutenant Commander. I'm just surprised."

Ross chuckled. "We've followed you ever since you flew your first simulation. We suspected immediately that we had a natural on our hands. The simulation you flew a couple of weeks ago clinched it for us—the one with Cadet Bryson. Do you remember it?"

How could she forget? "I blew myself up."

Ross chuckled again. "Yes, you did. But it was nothing short of incredible that you lasted as long as you did." She paused. "When I watched the replay, I got the impression that Cadet Bryson chose the simulation?"

Mo nodded. "I told him to choose and linked with him."

"He chose a difficult one."

"Yeah, he did."

"I remember him reading the mission objectives to you and suggesting a strategy, but I don't recall him mentioning that the simulation was rated for three pilots, not two."

Three?

"One pilot is supposed to destroy the weapons cache while the other two intercept any incoming hostiles."

David!

"I watched the replay with two other officers. We gave you about, oh, four to five minutes, tops. We never imagined you'd come so close to victory. There was lots of cheering in the viewing room that day," Ross said, smiling. "That little mishap at the end was nothing. Calculations of blast radius and the like will soon be second nature to you. We were amazed that you thought of the maneuver in the first place, given the pressure you were under."

Mo didn't know what to say.

Ross lifted a piece of paper from the file. "Your acceptance certificate.

Normally we give applicants a few days to confirm their intent to enter the program, but I have orders not to let you go until you've confirmed that you'll join us. I hope you do, otherwise I'll have to try to persuade you, and I'm hungry. So what do you say?"

"I'm definitely on board," Mo said, feeling dazed as she accepted the sheet.

"Good. I'm looking forward to training you. See you in a month, Cadet. Enjoy your break, and be ready to work hard when you get back. Dismissed."

Mo nodded and left. She paused in the lobby to read the certificate. There it was—her name in black and white. She traced it with her fingers, to make sure it was real. Outside, she stood blinking in the sun. The buildings were where she expected them to be, the sky was blue, and she recognized the two officers strolling past. Not a dream, then—which meant Les and David were waiting for her at the mess hall, and she had no reason to delay heading there. She folded the certificate and slid it into her back pocket. Other pilots might frame it, but not her. A lot could happen in a year. She'd wait for her graduation certificate.

She set off for the mess hall, her step lighter than it had been in weeks. Not only had she been accepted into the fighter pilot program— no, make that the *elite* fighter pilot program—but she and Les could stay together next year without anyone thinking they were foolish. And if what she'd heard was true and pilots who'd trained together were posted together after graduation, they'd just bought themselves another two to three years without others pressuring them to end their relationship. That "natural end" would have to wait.

Someone let out a loud whoop behind her. Startled, Mo spun around.

Ann ran up to her and thrust an acceptance certificate into her face. "Yes!" Ann shouted. "Yes!"

Mo drew back and waved the certificate away.

Ann fell into step with her. "Just left your meeting? Oh dear," she said with an exaggerated pout. "I don't see an acceptance certificate, so I guess you didn't make it."

"I was accepted," Mo snapped.

"Are you sure?"

She reached for the certificate in her pocket, then stopped. She didn't have anything to prove to this airhead. "I wouldn't say I was accepted if I wasn't."

"I guess they figured it wouldn't be a big deal to raise this year's quota to twenty-one and a half student pilots." Ann doubled over with laughter.

Mo felt her face tighten. She was so tempted to tell Ann what Ross had said, but that would only cheapen it. "I'm tired of you making fun of me," she said instead, surprising herself.

Ann straightened. "Argamon, lighten up! It's only a joke. And just when have I made fun of you?"

Mo gave her a withering look.

"Oh, come on. You didn't think I was serious, did you? Nobody's *that* naïve. We were in competition," she said, as if that explained everything. "So no hard feelings, right?"

Mo couldn't believe it. Ann had humiliated her in front of her peers and now expected her to just brush it off?

"Anyway, I have to go. See you next month, squirt!" Ann let out another whoop and jogged away.

Mo wanted to strangle her. Worse, she'd be stuck flying with her. Well, if Ann ever got into trouble during a mission, Mo might suddenly discover that she couldn't see over the control panels! She shook her head in exasperation and continued on to see Les and David, people who counted.

They both stood as she approached the table. Les stepped forward, her face grim. Of course—Mo wasn't carrying anything. This time, she pulled the certificate from her pocket. She smiled broadly and raised it over her head. "I'm in."

Suddenly they were all jumping and pumping their fists into the air. Not caring that they were in the mess hall, Mo ran to Les and leaped into her arms, almost sending her flying backward.

"Now we can celebrate," Les said, laughing.

Yes, they could! She was in! She was going to be a fighter pilot! Better than that, the part of her that had remained steadfast, that had believed, that had refused to let go of the dream when the rest of her had wanted to—that part of her had been vindicated. She held an acceptance certificate to the fighter pilot program in her hand, and now she believed with every fibre of her being that she was in her Chosen's arms. She pumped her fist into the air again. Yes, she was short, and yes, she was plain, but she was also the luckiest flaming Rymellan alive!

INTERVENTION

·····

ESLEY PAUSED AT THE ENTRANCE TO the pilot training complex and breathed in the fresh morning air. If not for her scheduled practicum session, she'd stay outside and stroll around the academy. While she enjoyed the training stints at Space Station 72, the arboretum and artificial lighting were poor substitutes for the sun, the breeze that coloured her cheeks, the trees lining the paths, and the flowers dotting the dormitory's garden. She couldn't fathom being away on a six-month tour of duty; fortunately, she wouldn't face one for a couple of years. Perhaps by then she'd be used to seeing darkness whenever she looked out a window.

She strode across the lobby and swung open the door to the simulator wing. Only one more practicum before graduation. In three weeks, she'd become Sub-lieutenant Thompson. She'd been surprised to learn that graduating pilots skipped ensign rank. Defence valued fighter pilots more than she'd realized.

Lieutenant Leeds stood near the equipment counter, two helmets in hand. Leeds had taught several of Lesley's classes, but hadn't supervised any of her practicums. Lesley nodded to her, and the lieutenant returned the gesture. "It'll be interesting to see what you can do in the cockpit," Leeds said, smiling. "Of course, I'll see you in action a lot more often from now on."

Lesley didn't know what she meant—a few sessions in the simulator was hardly a lot more often.

Leeds noted her blank expression. "You haven't heard? I'm moving to 72 to supervise its domestic patrols. So we'll be seeing much more of each other, maybe even flying together. I'm not one to sit in an office all day." She handed Lesley a helmet. "Anyway, let's get to it."

"We're not suiting up, Lieutenant?"

"No." Leeds started up the corridor to the simulators. "Once you have the maneuver down, we'll fly an intermediate, but that's at least a session away. Did you remember not to eat?"

"Yes."

"Good," Leeds said over her shoulder as she hit the *Enter* button to one of the training simulators. "I'll take the right."

Lesley settled into the left seat and lifted her helmet.

"Not yet. You haven't logged much time in this model. I'd like to review the controls before we start."

"Yes, Lieutenant." She lowered the helmet. Leeds was certainly thorough. Lesley's other practicum supervisors had only reviewed the controls the very first time she'd flown a particular craft. She may not have flown this model often, but she *had* flown it, and recently.

Leeds leaned across her. "Let's start with navigation."

Annoyed, Lesley pushed herself back against her seat. Why couldn't Leeds point out the controls on her own panel, clearly visible from Lesley's position? Holding her body away from Leeds was uncomfortable and interfered with her concentration. By the time Leeds finished, Lesley's muscles ached.

"Now you can put on your helmet." Leeds lifted hers.

Lesley gladly complied, relieved to have some breathing room.

"Are you ready, Cadet?"

"Yes."

"Ready," Leeds barked into her mouthpiece.

The simulator darkened.

"Go!"

Leeds turned out to be a superb and patient instructor, though reviewing the controls had left them only enough time to run through the maneuver twice. "I'll view the replay, identify areas that need improvement," Leeds said after they'd turned in their helmets. "Why don't we meet in my office before our next session? We can discuss which steps need work."

"That sounds like a good idea, Lieutenant," Lesley said, once again impressed with Leeds' thoroughness and efficiency. Her other supervisors had always used the first five minutes of the following session to review the last one.

"Excellent, I'll book the time. And well done today, Cadet. You're a quick study, and handled the craft well. I'm very much looking forward to seeing you in action again."

Lesley felt herself blush. "Thank you, Lieutenant," she said, embarrassed but pleased. Too bad Leeds had only been assigned as her supervisor for this one practicum—they worked well together. When Leeds had told her about her move to 72, Lesley hadn't cared one way or the other, but now she considered it good news.

MO SURVEYED THE open closet in dismay. All those times she'd tossed something into one of the boxes on the closet floor with the intention of dealing with it later had come back to haunt her. Later was now. She and Les had to be out of the room in three weeks, so if she didn't sort through everything here, she'd have to lug it all home.

Three weeks, and then they'd no longer officially room together. They'd have their own rooms on the space station, a perk she could do without. Nothing would stop them from spending their nights together, but it wouldn't be the same. Les would be glad to have her own closet, though. She probably wanted to scream every time she opened this one.

A pair of boots sat on the topmost box. Mo moved them to the floor, then lifted the box from the pile and set it down near the bed. She opened it with a feeling of anticipation. Several pairs of shoes, what a letdown! They could wait; she wasn't in the mood to sort through them. She shoved the box out of the way against the nightstand and turned back to the pile in the closet. Now that it was shorter, she could see the top of what looked like a rolled-up piece of cloth, propped in the corner behind the boxes. Curious, she reached for it.

Someone knocked at the door. "Come in," Mo shouted, turning. She felt her face tighten when Ann stepped into the room.

"So this is the love nest," Ann said, glancing around.

"What do you want?"

"Charming."

"Well?"

"I want you to link with me." Ann avoided Mo's eyes. "I'm having . . . well, I don't quite have maneuver 16C down. Ross said that if I can't demonstrate that I've got it by graduation, I'll have to stay behind until I do."

"So go practice it."

"I have been. But I need someone to watch what I'm doing, give me a few pointers."

Mo shifted her weight to her right foot. For anyone else, she'd readily agree. But nobody else made cracks about her height whenever an opportunity presented itself, and always when only Mo could hear. Ann had nerve, showing up here, asking for help. "You'll have to find someone else. I'm busy."

"Come on," Ann said. "The only thing we have to do over the next few weeks is the practicum."

"I have other things to do."

Ann put her hand on her hip. "You know, you never link with me."

"I do too!"

"Only when you have to. You help everyone else, so why won't you help me? Lesley links with me."

Yeah, and that grated, but Mo couldn't blame her. She'd never told Les the identity of her tormentor during the evaluation, nor about Ann's continued harassment. Ann made a great show of treating her respectfully when others were around. "Like I said, I'm busy. Find someone else."

"Ross said to ask you."

"Well, you asked me and I said no."

Ann stared at her for a moment, then whirled and marched from the room, slamming the door behind her. Mo winced at the rattling windows. But what had Ann expected, an enthusiastic yes? Now who was the delusional one? And she'd have to stay behind if she couldn't master the maneuver. Ha! Served her right.

But Mo's glee at Ann's predicament didn't last. Like everyone else, Ann was probably looking forward to the break. Having to stay behind and watch everyone else excitedly bound down the stairs to the train would be depressing. She must be desperate to get the maneuver right, otherwise she never would have lowered herself and asked Mo, of all people, for help.

Maneuver 16C was a tough one. Even when it was performed on auto-navigation, the pilot had to fire weapons at precise moments for it to be effective. A significant part of Mo's training over the past year had involved learning to manually fly maneuvers, in case auto-navigation failed or was knocked out. Unlike other maneuvers, 16C had challenged her.

She felt a twinge of regret. Maybe she should have agreed to link with Ann, rather than acting like a petty airhead. Wait a minute! Ann had treated her like dirt all flaming year. Why should she feel guilty because she'd shown some self-respect and not meekly gone along with what Ann wanted? That was exactly what she hated about people like Ann—they trampled over feelings until they wanted something, then made the other person feel bad for not going along. Or maybe what she hated was people like herself, people who were so soft, they felt as if they'd done something wrong because they'd stood up for themselves. She needed to learn not to be such a pushover.

Mo shook her head. Enough of Ann; back to the closet. She lifted out the cloth, unrolled it, and read *Happy Eighteenth, Mo*. Oh yeah, the banner from her surprise eighteenth party. At the time, she'd wanted to forget everything associated with turning eighteen, including the banner, but she'd felt obligated to keep it. Now it reminded her of how kind her parents and friends had been to arrange the party, and how much she missed some of those friends, several of whom had left the academy almost two years ago. But nostalgia aside, she'd never hang the banner, so it was time to get rid of it. Enough time had passed that nobody would be offended. She'd wait until she got home, though, and quietly—

Her comm unit beeped. Oh, great. Ross. "Cadet Middleton," Mo said.

"I'd like to see you in my office, Cadet. Now."

"I'll be right there." She stalked from the room. Why did people like Ann always get their way?

To Mo's dismay, Ross wasn't alone. Ann turned around when Mo tapped at Ross's open door.

 DISOBEDIENCE MEANS DEATH

"Come in, Cadet," Ross said.

Mo stepped into the office and nodded to Ross, then forced herself to nod at Ann. Ann nodded in return, a smug smile on her face.

"That will be all, Cadet Hawkins," Ross said to Ann.

Ann's smile faded. "Yes, Lieutenant Commander."

"Close the door behind you."

Mo focused on Ross and tried not to gloat as the door clicked shut.

Ross gave her a stern look. "Why did you refuse Cadet Hawkins' request for help?"

There was no point in lying. "We don't get along. I doubt she'll listen to me. She'll pick up the maneuver faster if she links with someone else." Someone she respected.

"I want her to pick it up from you. You know that maneuver inside out." Ross folded her hands on the desk. "I'm aware of the tension between you and Cadet Hawkins, but she's willing to put her personal feelings aside to get the job done. I expect you to do the same."

Mo pressed her lips together. Ann had teased her all year, but had somehow convinced Ross that *she* was the gracious one? Flaming unfair!

Ross's face softened. "Look, the other student pilots regard you as their leader, and so do I. I expect more from you than I do from the others. You might not like Cadet Hawkins, but you have to fly with her. Helping her master this maneuver will benefit everyone and set a good example. So I want you to arrange simulator time with her, all right?"

Not really, but Mo nodded.

"Good. If you do find that she isn't listening to you, let me know. But try to work out any difficulties yourselves, first. Understood?"

"Yes, Lieutenant Commander."

"I'll expect Cadet Hawkins to demonstrate the maneuver in a week's time. Dismissed."

Not surprisingly, Ann was waiting outside. "So are we on, then?"

"Yeah, we're on," Mo muttered.

"Try not to sound so enthusiastic."

"Just book simulator time for tomorrow, okay? After 10:00. Send me a dispatch to let me know when it is."

Ann rolled her eyes. "Of course, Cadet. I'll send you a dispatch. I wouldn't dream of beeping someone as important as you."

Mo's hands clenched. "You know what? I'm doing you a favour. If you don't like the way I want to do things, find someone else. And you better listen to me when we're in the simulator."

"I'll be on my best behaviour."

Somehow Mo doubted that. Maybe it was the smirk on Ann's face. Well, one short joke, and she was gone; she didn't care what Ross said. If being a leader meant she had to grin and bear it while someone insulted her, follower would suit her just fine.

LESLEY SANK INTO the chair in front of Leeds' desk, eager to learn which parts of the maneuver she'd performed well and which could use improvement. She waited while Leeds read over the sheet in front of her—notes from the replay, Lesley presumed.

Leeds looked up. "It's nice to have the opportunity to sit down and chat with you. There's never any time when the year is in full swing."

"That's true," Lesley said politely.

"Have you always wanted to be a fighter pilot?"

"I have. Well, ever since I sat in a fighter during a tour of a military installation."

"Really? How old were you?"

"Sixteen."

"It sounds as if you were interested in something else before that. What was it?" Leeds asked.

She'd convinced herself that she was, but . . . Lesley shifted in her seat. She'd rather talk about the replay than answer personal questions. "Advocacy."

"Advocacy?" Leeds repeated, clearly surprised. "Oh, that's right, both your parents are advocates, aren't they? I guess they expected you to follow in their footsteps. Were they disappointed?"

The last thing she wanted to discuss was whether her parents were disappointed with her career choice. "No."

"That's good. I'd be surprised if they were. I can't imagine anyone being disappointed with such an intelligent and pretty daughter."

Her face suddenly hot, Lesley stared at Leeds.

"The military is lucky to have you, given your Learning and Indoctrination Academy records and how well you did during the entrance

     DISOBEDIENCE MEANS DEATH

evaluation. You could have chosen any career you wanted. Is anyone else in your family in the military?"

"No. I'll be the first."

"Really? Then again, we don't get many from C3."

She crossed her legs, surprised at how much Leeds seemed to know about her personally.

"But now we have you," Leeds said, smiling.

"And Cadet Middleton," Lesley added. "She's also from C3."

Leeds' smile wilted. "Oh, yes, of course." She cleared her throat. "Well, then, let's talk about the replay."

Relieved, Lesley listened to Leeds' analysis and felt pleased with her performance during the last session. She was definitely ready to perform the maneuver during an intermediate sim.

When she and Leeds reached the equipment counter and the attendant asked if they'd be suiting up, Lesley nodded.

"No, not today," Leeds said.

Lesley looked at her in astonishment. "But I thought—"

"You did well, but I did say that your transition from steps three to four and steps twelve to thirteen could be smoother."

Yes, but not enough to warrant another novice session. Perfection normally wasn't required to move on to the next level, where the maneuver could be further refined.

"You take the left again," Leeds said when they entered the simulator.

She grudgingly did as she was told, convinced that they should be preparing for an intermediate sim, not a novice one.

"Now, when you transition from step three to four and from step twelve to thirteen, remember to slow your velocity by tapping this area of the panel," Leeds said, leaning across her and tapping the panel.

It was all Lesley could do not to slap Leeds' hand away. She knew where the velocity control was, as she'd amply demonstrated during her last session.

Leeds straightened, lifted her helmet, and nodded. Lesley put on her helmet and gripped the weapons control a little tighter than usual.

"Are you ready, Cadet?"

"Yes."

Leeds chuckled. "You know, I've taught you so many times and seen that pretty face of yours on the monitors so often, I feel as if I know you. Do you mind if I call you Lesley?"

The question caught her off guard. Despite feeling uncomfortable with the idea, she said, "No," not wanting to deny a request from a senior officer. Finney used her first name, but Finney was her mentor—a different type of relationship.

"And you can call me Christine."

Uneasiness snaked through her. Using Leeds' first name wouldn't be right. She didn't use Finney's first name; in fact, she didn't even know what it was, and Finney had been mentoring her for two years. "If you don't mind—"

"Ready," Leeds said. The simulator darkened. "Go!"

Hardly having to think, Lesley executed the first three steps of the maneuver and glided into step four after slowing her velocity.

"Excellent," Leeds said. "You did that well." She patted Lesley's leg.

Lesley went rigid with shock. She tried to remain focused on the simulation, but her mind raced. Leeds must have patted her for emphasis, because she couldn't see her face. Leeds wasn't—no . . . it would be inappropriate. She mustn't have realized, must have absently—

"Lesley!" Leeds snapped.

Too late, she noticed the friendly cargo ship in her path. The panels went dark. *Simulation Failed* flashed on one.

"That's all right," Leeds said. "We'll just start again."

"Can I have a minute first?"

"Of course."

Lesley pulled off her helmet and tried to collect herself. Perhaps she'd imagined it. Or maybe the seatbelt strap had slapped against her leg, though she usually made sure the belt wasn't hanging loose. A quick look down confirmed that it was tightly secured. Still, she hadn't actually seen Leeds touch her. If it had been Leeds, it could have been an accident. They'd been in the middle of a simulation and in motion.

She took a deep breath and put her helmet back on. "I'm ready."

"Good. Stay focused this time."

Lesley bit her tongue.

Even though she couldn't concentrate, she managed to fly the simulation twice without making any mistakes. Leeds didn't touch her again, if she'd touched her in the first place. By the time Lesley turned in her helmet at the equipment counter, she'd convinced herself that she'd blown the incident out of proportion.

Leeds motioned for Lesley to move away from the counter. "I'm certain you're ready to move on to an intermediate sim, but we should still review the replay," she said when they were out of the attendant's earshot. She bit her lip. "I was planning to meet a friend tomorrow for supper, at that new eatery near station C6-12, but she had to cancel. Perhaps you'd like to take her place? We can discuss the replay then. It's only a five minute train ride away."

Lesley struggled to keep her expression neutral. She felt as if she was back at the Learning and Indoctrination Academies, where she'd grown used to politely declining advances. Back then, she'd turned down invitations from her peers, her equals. Leeds was not only an officer, but her supervisor for the last practicum she needed to pass before graduation. Maybe Leeds was looking for a supper companion, nothing more, but given what Lesley now had to concede had happened in the simulator, she doubted that. "An eatery wouldn't be the best place to review a replay," she said, deliberately taking Leeds at face value. "And our next session is a few days away, so there's no need to work over supper on my account. Invite another friend and have a relaxing meal."

Leeds smiled stiffly. "You're right. Why work over supper when I don't have to? I'll schedule a time for us to review the replay. Dismissed, Cadet." She turned on her heel and walked away.

Lesley couldn't understand why Leeds had asked. She must know about Mo, so it didn't make sense. She'd created an uncomfortable situation, and now Lesley wished that Leeds wasn't transferring to the space station.

Back at the dormitory, she swung open the door to her and Mo's room. Mo was in front of the closet, a jumble of shoes at her feet. She swivelled to face Lesley. "Do you think I'll ever wear these again?"

Lesley assumed she was referring to the pair of shoes she held. "Aren't those the shoes you wear when you perform?"

"The shoes I used to wear."

Right. She'd no longer be a member of the student orchestra. "I'd keep them, just in case you decide to audition for the military orchestra."

"Given that I missed half the performances last year, I doubt I will. My schedule will be worse when we're flying domestic patrols." Mo tossed the shoes into a box near the nightstand. "How did your session go?"

"Okay." Part of her wanted to tell Mo what had happened, but the other part worried about how Mo would react. Mo might think she'd done something to attract Leeds' attention or to give her the wrong idea. Worse, Mo's insecurities about their relationship could resurface—she might assume that Lesley secretly wanted a relationship with Leeds, no matter how strongly Lesley denied it. Better to not bring it up, especially since she'd already dealt with it. "You've never had Leeds as a supervisor, right?"

Mo shook her head. "I've heard she's good, though."

She was, when she stuck to business.

"What do you think of her?" Mo asked.

Lesley hesitated; she wanted to choose her words carefully. "She's—"

Mo's comm unit beeped. She read its display. "It's Mama. I better take it."

Relieved, Lesley sat on the bed to untie her boots.

"Guess what? You'll be coming home a little sooner than you thought," Susan said, excitement evident in her voice.

Mo looked at Lesley, her brow furrowing. "Why?" she asked her mama.

"Neil's Chosen Papers have arrived."

"What?" Mo shrieked. "No, I mean, wow! I mean, obviously I knew they'd arrive at some point, but I'm shocked."

Susan laughed. "Everyone's reacting that way."

"When's his meeting?"

"Thursday."

"That's in three days!"

"But you'll need to be home in two, for his notification party. Lesley's invited, of course."

Is he the Principal? Lesley mouthed at Mo.

Mo shook her head and leaned forward. "Just a sec, Mama."

"Is he the Principal?" Lesley whispered.

"Oh, yeah. Mama, is he the Principal?"

"Yes!" Susan said. "So we're hosting lunch. I still need to get hold of the caterers, so I've got to go. Try to be home by two on Wednesday. Your papa wants to make sure that whatever you'll wear on Thursday fits nicely."

Mo rolled her eyes. "Mama, he made just about all my clothes."

"Still, he wants to make sure. It's a special day."

"Yeah, okay."

"And plan to go back to the academy after lunch on Friday."

"After lunch?"

"Yes. Your papa and I would like to talk to you about something, and there won't be time before Friday."

"What do you want to talk to me about?" Mo asked, raising her brows at Lesley.

"Not now, Mo. Friday. Anyway, I've got to go. See you soon." The connection went dead.

"Flaming Argamon, can you believe it?" Mo said, sliding her comm unit back into its holder.

"He's twenty-seven. That's the average age for Papers."

"I know, but I still can't believe it. Just think, someone out there got her Chosen Papers today, and she's getting Neil!" Mo grinned. "You know, she could do worse."

Lesley nodded.

"And she'll be a Middleton, too."

"That's right." Lesley almost added that she wouldn't mind being a Middleton, but stopped herself. Mo would take that to mean that she wanted to be Mo's Chosen, when she meant that the Middletons were a respectable family that anyone would be pleased to Join into. Well, that was mainly what she meant.

"Anyway, I better go see Ross, let her know. I'll have to juggle around a few sessions." Mo rushed to the door, then rushed back to Lesley and kissed her on the cheek. "Sorry, I'm excited," she said, then rushed from the room.

Lesley smiled. So, the first family member in her and Mo's generation had received Papers. It was beginning. She stopped smiling.

MO DRAGGED HERSELF to the pilot training complex and resisted the urge to pull the fire alarm—she didn't want a level three strike on her record. When she'd told Ross about Neil, she'd hoped that Ross would let her off the hook about Ann, but no such luck. *We'll extend the deadline by a few days. There will still be time*, Ross had said.

And there was Ann, standing by the equipment counter. Mo already hated helping her, and she hadn't started yet.

"I was about to beep you to see if you'd forgotten," Ann said. "I checked for you in the lobby, in the bathroom. I even checked underneath that little table over there, in case that's where you were waiting."

"Very funny," Mo mumbled, refusing to rise to the bait. Ann wouldn't win that easily. "I hope your Chosen isn't short," she couldn't help saying as they walked to the simulators.

"I'm a Solitary," Ann said.

Mo's respect for the Chosen Council went up a notch. "Oh."

"What do you mean, oh? I don't mind leaving the breeding to others. I have other things I want to do."

Like what, torment people? Mo bit back the words and remained silent. She'd sound patronizing if she tried to say something nice, and she regretted raising the topic in the first place. "Let's start with a sandbox sim. I'll watch you fly 16C, see if I can figure out what you're doing wrong."

"I didn't say I was doing anything wrong," Ann snapped. "I said I could use some tips."

Mo quietly sighed. The next hour would be a long one. "Okay, fine. I'll see if I can give you any tips."

"So you're just going to watch?" Ann said after they'd linked and initiated the sim.

"Yeah. You fly it, I'll observe from a distance."

Minutes later, Mo understood why Ross had suggested that Ann find help. "Just a sec, I want to review the sensor log." The maneuver had fallen apart at step six. "You're not executing the Hanson spiral correctly in step six. If you don't hit that, you come out at the wrong velocity and trajectory, making it impossible to execute the next step. Once you recovered, the rest of the maneuver looked okay. So . . . I think it's just a matter of hitting the spiral."

"I did hit the spiral," Ann said.

"No, you didn't. I saw you blow it, and the sensors confirmed it."

Silence, then, "Fine, I'll do it again. Pay attention this time."

Pay attention this time, Mo mouthed back. With luck, Ann would hit the spiral, do it a few more times, and declare herself ready to show Ross. Flaming Ross! Anyone could have told Ann where the maneuver was falling apart. Mo had the sneaking suspicion that Ross had thrown them together in the hope that they'd iron out their differences. *Well, keep hoping, Lieutenant Commander, because it isn't going to happen.* "You ready?"

In response, Ann started to fly the maneuver again. Mo watched in disbelief; this attempt looked exactly like the last one. "You missed the spiral again."

"You're wasting my time."

"No, you're wasting *my* time. Do it again. I'll call out the steps, and when I say Hanson spiral, do it." She ignored the loud sigh that emanated from the comm piece in her left ear. "Start again. Please."

Ann silently complied.

Mo called out steps one to five. "Next is the spiral," she said as Ann executed step five. "Hanson spiral!" she said. "Hanson flaming spiral!" she shouted when it became obvious that Ann wasn't entering the spiral.

"I'm doing the flaming spiral!" Ann shouted back.

Okay, that was it. Ann was probably laughing herself silly right now. Mo felt like an idiot. "I'm done." She pulled off her helmet and left the simulator, barely stopping to punch the *Disinfect* button. Flaming waste of time. Forget her suspicion about Ross; now she suspected that Ann had set this whole thing up by convincing Ross that only Cadet Middleton could help her.

Ann caught up to her halfway to the equipment room. "Where are you going?"

"Where does it look like I'm going?"

"I hope it's to tell Ross that you're a lousy teacher."

Mo stopped and pointed to herself. "I'm a lousy teacher? It's hard to teach when the student refuses to listen."

"When didn't I listen?"

Mo shook her head. "No. I've had enough."

"Seriously, when didn't I listen?"

"I told you right away that the Hanson spiral was the problem. You ignored that. Then I said I'd call it for you. You ignored that. So what do you want me to do? Keep trying so you can giggle to yourself every time you ignore me?"

"I was doing the spiral," Ann said indignantly. "What are you trying to do, distract me from the real problem so I'll be stuck here for weeks on end? Or maybe you don't know what a Hanson spiral is."

She flaming-well knew! She could fly the spiral with her eyes shut. If anything, Ann was the one—wait a minute. Only two maneuvers contained the Hanson spiral: 16C and 19A. "What score did you get for 19A?"

"None of your business."

"Look, tell me, okay? I might know what's wrong here." If not for her history with Ann, she would have figured it out earlier and not assumed that Ann was fooling around.

Ann looked at her feet and sharply exhaled. "Well, it wasn't my best score. I passed. Barely."

"Come on, let's go back into the simulators," Mo said.

"Why, so you can scream at me some more?"

"No, so I can teach you how to do a Hanson spiral." Mo raised her finger. "And don't tell me you know how to do one, because you flaming-well don't. You can get away with that in 19A, but not in 16C."

"Whatever you say."

They started back to the simulators. "You're going to listen to me, right?" Mo said. "Otherwise we're both wasting our time."

"I'll listen!" Ann hissed. "I want my full break, and I'll do whatever I have to do to get it. Even listen to you."

Mo restrained herself. "Let's focus on the spiral, then."

Half an hour later, she turned to Ann in the equipment room. "You've almost got it. I figure you'll only need part of the next session to master it. After that, it shouldn't take you long to master 16C. So maybe one more session, two tops."

"That's great." Ann smiled tightly. "I think I can stand another two sessions."

Ann could stand another two sessions? If Mo hadn't been wearing a helmet, she would have torn out half her hair.

Lieutenant Leeds strolled into the room and checked her comm unit. She probably had a session scheduled with a cadet. It wasn't Les; her next session wasn't until Thursday, the same day as Neil's meeting. Speaking of which . . . "Don't forget, I'm leaving tomorrow and won't be back until Friday," Mo said to Ann.

"Do you know when? Maybe we can fit in a session."

"I'm not sure." It depended on what her parents wanted to discuss. She hoped it had nothing to do with her and Les's relationship. "Once I know exactly when I'll be back, I'll book a session, send you a dispatch."

Ann snorted. "Check my schedule first. I also have a practicum." She paused. "I suppose I should say congratulations about your brother. Stand up straight when you meet his Chosen, okay? Otherwise she might not be able to see you." She marched from the room, denying Mo the chance for a witty retort. Not that she had a witty retort—she'd probably think of one on the way back to the room.

"Cadet Middleton." Mo turned to see Leeds stepping toward her. "Did I hear you say that you'll be away until Friday?"

"Yes, Lieutenant. My brother received his Chosen Papers. His meeting's on Thursday."

Leeds smiled. "That's wonderful! Congratulations."

"Thank you."

"Will Cadet Thompson also be away? I have a session with her on Thursday."

Mo would love it if Les could be at the lunch on Thursday, but that would be inappropriate, a word she was starting to hate. Plus, Les had an appointment at the Military Academy on Thursday morning. "She's attending my brother's notification party, but that's Wednesday night. She'll be back in time for her session."

"I was wondering if I'd have to reschedule it."

"No," Mo said, surprised that Leeds would consider that a possibility. Wanting to be in the same sector as your girlfriend while she met her brother's Chosen wasn't an acceptable reason to reschedule sessions.

Sheila, a fellow student pilot, strode into the room. She wiggled her fingers at Mo. Mo waved back, causing Leeds to glance over her shoulder. "There's my 15:00," she said. "Congratulations again, Cadet." Leeds turned to Sheila.

Mo set off for the dormitory, her excitement about Neil growing now that her session with Ann was over. Maybe it was fitting that Les couldn't attend Neil's lunch—the first post-notification lunch they attended together should be their own.

LESLEY SANK ONTO the bed and pulled off her boots. She covered her mouth as she yawned. Neil's notification party the previous evening had finally broken up at 01:30. Six hours later, she'd been on a train back to the Military Academy, arriving just in time to record the last batch of announcements for the year. Staying up late had been worth it—getting caught up in the Middletons' excitement, seeing Mo's parents present Neil with more land, Susan's emotional speech . . . Today they must all be running on adrenaline. Mo hadn't sounded tired when she'd beeped earlier.

Can't talk long, just thought I'd beep you, let you know that Neil's Chosen is named Barbara. She seems nice. Oh, she's a teacher at the Learning Academy, and—okay, have to go. Mama's calling me. I'll tell you more when I see you.

Lesley smiled. Mo could probably go dancing tonight, whereas she was ready to get into bed with a book at 20:00. Yes, she had the entire evening to herself, and she'd probably be fast asleep by 21:00. She'd sleep soundly, too; Leeds had been completely professional during that afternoon's session. Focusing on the replay had quickly dissipated the first few awkward moments, and Leeds had finally decided that Lesley was ready for an intermediate sim.

She was in the middle of unbuttoning her shirt when someone knocked at the door. "Just a minute," she called, quickly refastening the buttons. If it was David, he'd have to find another partner for cards. She opened the door and froze.

Without waiting for an invitation to enter, Leeds brushed by her. "I was just passing by and thought I'd let you know that the replay of this afternoon's session looked great. One or two more sessions and you'll be done."

"Well, uh, thank you for letting me know," Lesley said, trying to get her head around Leeds being there.

   DISOBEDIENCE MEANS DEATH

Leeds walked to the corner of the room nearest Mo's side of the bed and picked up Mo's violin. "Is this yours?"

"No, it's Cadet Middleton's." She fought the urge to grab the violin from Leeds' hands. "It's probably best that you don't touch it."

Leeds chuckled. "Cadet Middleton's? My, you're formal," she said as she propped the violin back in the corner. "Is that what you call her when you're alone?"

Voices drifted into the room from the corridor. Lesley shut the door, not wanting anyone to see Leeds, but then kicked herself. She'd just made it more difficult to get rid of her.

"Are you musically inclined?" Leeds asked.

Lesley hesitated. "No, I'm not." Fortunately her flute was hidden away on the closet shelf.

"But you like to read." Leeds rounded the bed and picked up Lesley's book from the nightstand. She flipped through its pages.

Lesley swallowed. Why did this have to be happening with an officer? If Leeds were another cadet, she'd tell her to leave. Well, she could try asking Leeds if she wanted anything else, and then say, *No thank you, goodnight.* "Is there anything else, Lieutenant, or was the replay the only thing you wanted to discuss?"

Leeds looked up. "It sounds like you're trying to get rid of me."

Yes! And it would be nice if Leeds took the hint.

"Actually, there is something else. I was wondering if—"

Another knock at the door. Oh please, let it be someone who'd save her from having to turn Leeds down again. Lesley opened the door a crack.

Ann stood in the corridor. "Is Mo here?"

"No, she's not," Lesley said, disappointed.

"She was supposed to send me a dispatch about a session tomorrow, but I haven't heard from her, even though I've sent her two. I saw you after supper and thought maybe she'd come back with you. I thought I'd try the direct approach."

"She's still at home."

"If you hear from her, can you ask her—" Something thudded inside the room. Ann tutted. "Oh, I get it. She's not here. Sure." She pushed past Lesley. "I'm coming in, Mo, and you—oh. Lieutenant Leeds." Ann gaped a moment, then clamped her mouth shut.

"Cadet," Leeds said, straightening and setting the book she must have dropped back on the nightstand.

Ann's eyes darted between Lesley and Leeds. "Sorry to interrupt."

"No, no, you weren't interrupting anything," Lesley quickly said, her cheeks burning. "Is there anything I can help you with? Anything at all?" She rubbed her forehead as she willed Ann to come up with something.

Ann appeared to think it over. "I'm still working on 16c."

"We can see if any simulators are available and fly it together," Lesley said, trying not to sound as elated as she felt.

"Isn't Cadet Middleton helping you with that?" Leeds said.

"Yes, she is," Ann said.

"Then wait for her. Cadet Thompson and I are busy . . . discussing her next session."

Ann's mouth twitched. "Of course, Lieutenant. Sorry to bother you. Good night." She gave Lesley a long look as she walked from the room. Lesley listened to her fading footsteps in dismay.

"Helping Cadet Hawkins isn't your responsibility," Leeds said. "Cadet Middleton is supposed to be helping her."

"She is helping her," Lesley said, her teeth on edge. This time, she'd leave the door open. "You were about to say something when Cadet Hawkins knocked."

Leeds nodded. "Shut the door."

Lesley reluctantly did so and turned to Leeds.

"It's early." Leeds moistened her lips. "I was wondering if you'd like to spend some time together."

"No," Lesley said firmly. Then she grudgingly added, "Thank you."

Leeds' face tightened. "Are you sure?"

"Yes. I'm tired. I was getting ready for bed when you knocked."

"Were you?" A smile played on Leeds' lips. "You don't have to go to bed alone, do you?" Leeds stepped toward her.

Blood rushed to Lesley's face; she stepped back.

Leeds chuckled. "I'm sure you get tons of offers. Do you blush like that every time?"

It wasn't the offer; it was the manner in which it was being made. She had to put an end to this, be blunt, and hope that Leeds wouldn't hold it against her when scoring the practicum. "Look," she said with a sigh, "you're my practicum supervisor and that's all you are. I'm not interested in a relationship."

"Neither am I. Not a serious one, anyway. It would be nice to spend some time together, including the occasional night, when we can. That's all I'm looking for."

"I'm not interested."

"Come now, I'm sure Cadet Middleton doesn't always sleep alone when she's away."

Lesley hoped and believed that she did. "What Cadet Middleton does is her business."

"And what you do is yours." Leeds closed the gap between them and reached for her.

She caught Leeds' wrists. "I'm not interested in having any type of personal relationship with you," she said evenly. "You have to leave. Coming here was inappropriate."

Leeds' expression hardened; she yanked her wrists from Lesley's grasp. "Inappropriate? You have the nerve to say that *I'm* being inappropriate? I'll tell you what's inappropriate—you and Middleton, you're flaming inappropriate. You're both Chosens, and you both need to grow up! Clinging to each other the way you do . . . it's unhealthy! I'm sure your Chosen would prefer that you have more experience, you know what I'm saying?"

"My relationship with Cadet Middleton isn't open for discussion. You have to leave." Lesley opened the door and stood aside.

"You're making a mistake."

"Not according to Article 493."

Leeds' jaw dropped. "You wouldn't dare."

"Try me." Lesley hoped Leeds wouldn't push her—it would be her word against a lieutenant's and horribly embarrassing.

Her shoulders sagged with relief when Leeds said, "Fine, I'll leave." She stopped in front of Lesley and jabbed a finger at her. "But I'll leave you with this. I'm not the only one who thinks your relationship with Middleton is inappropriate. I was at a reception last week, one that Commander Morton hosts every year for the faculty. Do you know what he said about you?"

Leeds was obviously going to tell her, so she tried not to look too interested and waited.

"He said that your priority is your girlfriend, not the Way. So you might want to consider being seen out with someone else on occasion, to show that you're not too attached to anyone. Otherwise, people will talk, and all it takes is a few whispers to sink a career. Think about *that* when you're lying alone in bed tonight." Leeds glared at her, then strode from the room.

Lesley shut the door and stood shaking; she hadn't expected such a venomous reaction. The entire situation was surreal. Had she finally got through to Leeds? Perhaps angering her would turn out for the best—Leeds might wonder why she'd ever been interested and stick to being her practicum supervisor. On the other hand, Leeds might go on a vendetta against her. But what else could she have done? She'd already tried to politely turn Leeds down—twice. That hadn't worked. She'd had to be blunt.

Then there was Ann. What conclusions had she jumped to? More importantly, would she say anything to Mo? Probably, given how the two of them hated each other. Lesley had better tell Mo what had happened.

She reached for her comm unit, then sat on the bed and buried her face in her hands. She couldn't beep Mo now, interrupt a family celebration—make that two family celebrations. And she'd rather tell Mo in person. Mo might think she was interested in Leeds, or had said or done something to give Leeds the wrong idea. Lesley was sure she hadn't, but Mo might assume otherwise, as she had in the past.

Another knock at the door. She didn't want to answer it, in case it was Leeds, but forced herself to stand. Leeds knew she was in the room; no point trying to hide. She slowly swung the door open. Leeds. Lesley didn't try to hide her displeasure. "Yes?"

"I owe you an apology. You're right, I behaved inappropriately," Leeds said.

Lesley closed her eyes. Finally.

"You'll soon be a sub-lieutenant. I should have waited until then."

Her eyes snapped open. "What?"

"And I came on too strong. I assumed too much, and I can see I frightened you. I also see that Commander Morton was right and that you do need to get over your dependence on Middleton. So I want you to take some time to reconsider you and me. I could be good for you, in more ways than one."

Lesley couldn't believe it. "I don't need any time. "

"Take some time, Lesley. There's no rush. We'll be seeing a lot more of each other on 72. Come to think of it, I can schedule you and Middleton on different rotations, give you some time for yourself."

"No!"

"Well, I'll be less inclined to do that if you show signs of being less dependent on her. So think about it." Leeds smiled; she looked as if she were baring her teeth. "We can talk about it again before our next session. Good night."

Without a word, Lesley shut the door and collapsed against it. What a flaming nightmare! Why was Leeds being so persistent? She wasn't doing it to impress Morton, was she, because of what he'd said? Maybe she saw it as serving the Way, though Lesley could make a case for the opposite. Leeds' behaviour was disturbing and dangerously weak in the Way.

Perhaps Lesley should report her. No; she couldn't prove anything. Leeds could deny it, even turn it around and make it sound as if Lesley were the one who refused to take no for an answer. But Lesley had to do something, not only for the Way, but because the thought of sitting in Leeds' office, of being in a simulator with her when the lights went out . . . the thought sickened her. And if Leeds went through with her threat to tinker with the schedules on 72 . . .

She flopped onto the bed. Forget about being sound asleep by 21:00 — she had some serious thinking to do.

MO WALKED WITH her parents along a path on the Middleton estate, her patience wearing thin. They'd said they wanted to talk. They'd insisted on going for a walk. And so far, they'd discussed . . . the weather and yesterday. "So are you going to talk, or what?" she blurted.

"About what?" Papa said.

"Oh, come on. I need to get back to the Military Academy." She hoped to fit in a session with Ann, and she wanted to see Les. When they'd spoken that morning, Les had sounded distracted, though she'd insisted that nothing was wrong. "You said you wanted to talk to me about something. So talk."

"I think they're a good match," Mama said. "I couldn't believe it when Barbara said she enjoys bird watching. Did you see them talking about it? It was as if they'd known each other for years."

Papa grinned. "It won't be long before there are little Middletons running around."

"There are a few details to take care of first," Mama said with a chuckle. "They have to Join, he has to be reversed—"

Mo wheeled around. "Okay, that's it, I'm going home." She drew the line at discussing Neil's privates. "You can talk to me after the graduation ceremony."

"No," Papa said, grabbing her arm. "We're almost there."

"Almost there?" He'd piqued her curiosity. "Where?"

Papa pointed ahead, to the right of the path. "There."

She squinted into the distance, shielding her eyes with her hand. Something was reflecting the sun. They moved closer. It looked like . . . no, it couldn't be, but . . . "What's an aviacraft doing in the field?"

"Not an aviacraft, *your* aviacraft." Papa swept his arm toward the craft, an ear-splitting grin on his face.

"What do you mean, my aviacraft?"

Mama threw an arm around Mo's shoulders and squeezed her. "Congratulations, soon to be sub-lieutenant. We're so proud of you!"

They weren't serious. "You bought me an aviacraft?"

"Do you like it?" Papa patted the craft's side. "Perfect gift for a pilot, don't you think?"

"I hope you don't mind that we didn't give it to you yesterday while everyone was here, but we didn't want to upstage Neil," Mama said.

"No, you did the right thing." She would have been mortified if they'd presented it to her in front of everyone. "I mean, I appreciate it and all, but don't you think it's a little extravagant? I can't accept this."

Their faces fell. "You only graduate from the Military Academy once," Papa said.

"You've been complaining about how long the train ride is to the shuttle—um, thingie you have to leave from to get up to the space

     DISOBEDIENCE MEANS DEATH

station—remember? Over three hours by train, but—what did he say it would take by aviacraft, Michael?" Mama looked at Papa.

"Twenty minutes," Papa said.

"Well, yeah, it would be faster, but I wasn't hinting for a craft or anything," Mo said. "I hope you didn't get it because of that."

Papa dismissed her concern with a wave of his hand. "No, no, we ordered it months ago, when you told us you'd passed the exam for your full licence."

"What's the point of having an aviacraft licence if you don't have an aviacraft?" Mama asked.

"Mama, most fighter pilots occasionally fly military aviacraft, so most eventually get aviacraft licences. Les and I mainly took lessons to help us get into the program. It was a head start, that's all."

"That may be, but that doesn't mean you can't have your own craft." Papa beckoned to her. "Take a look inside."

"Take us for a ride," Mama suggested.

Mo inwardly sighed. She was fighting a losing battle. Maybe she should humour them today and then wear them down until they finally saw sense and agreed to return it. "I wouldn't mind checking out the interior," she said, then felt guilty when their faces lit up. "What's the code?"

"The code?" Mama repeated, confusion plain on her face.

"The entrance code. So I can unlock the craft."

Mama's eyes widened. "Why would it be locked?"

"Safety regulations."

Papa nodded. "The pilot who delivered it gave me quite a stern safety lecture. They don't want just anyone climbing in and pressing on the panels in case they accidentally take off on automatic pilot. Listening to him, it sounds like any idiot could fly one of these things."

Mo placed her hands on her hips. "Thank you very much."

"Not you!" Papa said with a pained expression. He pulled out his comm unit. "I'll dispatch the code to you."

"Thanks. I'll need to hang on to that dispatch until I memorize it."

Mo entered the code and slid the aviacraft door open. They climbed inside. "Don't touch anything," she said as she sat in the pilot's seat and ran her hand along the control panel and then along the back of the seat next to her. She had to admit, it certainly felt nice sitting in a brand new craft. Not that she'd keep it. "When did it arrive?"

"You mean on the estate?" Mama asked from one of the seats behind her.

Mo twisted around and nodded. Room for eight, including the pilot, she noted. She could fly people home for their breaks. Well, she could if she kept it, but she wouldn't. Seriously, she couldn't.

"Do you remember when Papa and Andrew went out for a walk? Then."

And Andrew hadn't told her? He'd been more useful when he couldn't keep a secret.

"Adelaide and Alan saw it delivered," Papa said. "I guess they noticed it land and came over to see what was going on." He paused. "I doubt Lesley will be getting one. Adelaide called it a monstrosity."

Mama snorted.

Papa nudged Mo's arm. "Oh, I know—let's fly over the Thompson estate."

"I'm not flying over the Thompson estate," Mo said.

"Michael!" Mama said. But then she smiled. "It would be fun, though, wouldn't it?"

Papa gleefully clenched his hands together. "Let's do it! How close can you get to the house?"

Mo opened her mouth to protest, but her comm unit beeped, forestalling her. She stifled a groan when she read its display: Ann—again. She'd already beeped once that morning, and sent numerous dispatches. If Mo didn't answer this time, Ann would probably beep her every five minutes. "I'll just step outside and take this," she said, rising from her seat. The last thing she needed was her parents overhearing Ann making fun of her. "Don't touch anything."

"We won't," they both said.

Outside, she pressed the connect button. "Yeah, I know, I was supposed to let you know about the next session, but I was waiting until I knew for sure when I'd be back. Sorry."

"Do you know if you'll be back in time to do one tonight?"

"Should be."

"How about 19:30?"

"Yeah, okay."

"So everything went okay with your brother?"

"Yeah, fine," Mo said, surprised at how pleasant Ann sounded.

"Have you talked to Lesley today?"

"Why?" Mo asked, instantly guarded.

"I was just wondering if she mentioned Leeds."

"Leeds?"

"Yeah. I went by your room last night to see if you were back, and Leeds was there."

"Oh. Well, Leeds is her practicum supervisor." Though even as she said it, Mo wondered why Leeds would need to see Les in their room.

"They didn't look like they were discussing a practicum," Ann said.

Mo could hear the smirk in Ann's voice. "What do you mean?"

"Let's just say that when Lesley answered the door, she was in her socks and her shirt's top buttons were undone. And she looked a little flushed. I don't know about you, but practicums don't excite me that much." She chortled. "Leeds seemed really anxious to get rid of me. Who knows when she left? Last night, this morning . . ."

"You're such a liar! Stick to your short jokes."

"Hey, I'm just telling you what I saw, okay? I thought you should know. I don't care if you believe me or not."

"Just be at the simulators at 19:30," Mo snapped.

"I'll be th—"

Mo terminated the connection and rammed the comm unit back into its holder. She could hardly think; she grabbed her head with both hands. How could Les do this? No, consider the source: Ann flaming Hawkins. But why would she tell a lie that Les could easily refute? And Les *had* sounded distracted earlier—had Leeds been with her when Mo had beeped? Why hadn't Les said anything about Leeds being in their room? *How could Les do this?*

No, she shouldn't jump to conclusions. She'd assumed the worst before and been wrong. She wasn't a child anymore—she'd give Les a chance to explain. There was probably a perfectly logical explanation for why Leeds had been in their room, and why Les had answered the door to Ann *half-naked!* So she'd remain calm. Calm, calm, calm. Return to the Military Academy, talk to Les, sort it out. Les would explain—and that explanation better be flaming good.

The train ride would be excruciating and feel like hours, so the sooner she left, the better. Mo turned back to the aviacraft. Then again . . .

"I just want to check something," she said as she slid back into the pilot's seat and entered a set of coordinates into the navigation panel. Estimated time to the Military Academy: seven minutes. "Something's come up. I have to go back to the academy right now."

Mama and Papa groaned.

"I know, I'm sorry. Do you mind if I fly the craft there? I mean, I still don't know if I can accept it, but I'm in a hurry."

Papa nodded vigorously. "Take it! Take it!"

"Is everything all right?" Mama asked.

Mo nodded. "Everything's fine." Fine, fine, fine. "I'll take you on a ride after the graduation ceremony, okay?"

Papa narrowed his eyes. "So you'll hang onto the craft until at least then."

"Uh, well, I guess so. I owe you a ride, right? And a thank-you."

Papa grinned. "I knew you'd want it as soon as you sat in the pilot's seat."

"No, no, I'm just in a hurry," Mo said feebly.

She joined them outside and hugged them. "An aviacraft . . . such a wonderful thought. But extravagant."

"You think about it." Mama cupped Mo's chin with her hand. "You'll make us very happy if you keep it."

Mo embraced her again. Making her parents happy was important, right? Keeping it for that reason would almost be noble. Not that she would keep it. She couldn't.

"You don't need anything at the house?" Mama asked when they parted.

"No."

"What about the candies you picked up at the Trading Centre?"

"I'm not going back just for them." She sighed when Mama's face creased with concern. "I'll beep you later." Before Mama had a chance to respond, Mo climbed into the craft and slid the door shut. A minute later she waved to them as the craft ascended, quelling the guilt she

     DISOBEDIENCE MEANS DEATH

felt over running out on them. She'd deal with it later. After Les. Right now, she had to focus on remaining calm. Calm, calm, calm.

"I'LL SEE YOU at 15:30, then," Lesley said.

"Don't be late." The connection went dead.

Lesley slid the comm unit back into its holder.

"Who was that? Your girlfriend?"

She spun around. Mo stood in the doorway. "I didn't hear you come in," Lesley said.

"I *bet* you didn't." Mo pushed the door shut and flung her cloak onto the bed. She glared at Lesley.

"You've spoken to Ann."

"That's it? That's all you have to say? It's a good thing I spoke to Ann, otherwise I wouldn't have a clue what goes on around here. She told me what you forgot to mention this morning."

Lesley sighed. "I didn't tell you because I was afraid of this."

Mo's hands went to her hips. "Afraid of what?"

"This!" Lesley thrust her arms toward Mo. "Your reaction. I figured in person I'd stand a chance of explaining what happened."

Mo folded her arms. "I'm all ears."

She'd better start from the beginning. "Leeds asked me on a date a few days ago."

"Oh, great. Flaming g—" Mo stared at her. "Don't tell me last night was a date with her."

"Of course not. I turned her down. I thought that was the end of it. But then she showed up here last night and barged into the room."

"And stayed, from the sounds of it."

"Not for long. I told her to leave, and she did."

Mo snorted. "You expect me to believe that's all that happened? Ann said you looked pretty comfortable, with your boots off and your buttons undone."

"My buttons? I don't think so."

"Oh, but your boots were off," Mo said, pointing at her.

"Yes, they were. This is my room, right? I don't go to bed in my boots." She winced. "I was getting ready for bed when she showed up. I'd already taken off my boots."

Mo folded her arms again. "Why would Leeds come here when you'd already turned her down?"

"There's a problem."

"What problem?" Mo said, her eyes betraying the deadly calm of her voice.

"She's being persistent. Now she's saying we should get together on 72."

"I don't flaming believe this!"

"Neither do I."

"So what are you going to do, get together with her on 72?"

"No!"

"Because this whole thing sounds a little odd to me. She asks you on a date, you turn her down, she comes here, you turn her down, but, oh no, she still wants you. Come on, do you think I'm stupid?"

Lesley blinked back tears of frustration and disappointment. Though it wasn't Mo's fault; she was assuming Leeds was a reasonable person, as Lesley initially had. "It's true! I want nothing to do with her. If I had my way, I'd never see her again, but it'll be tough not to because she's my practicum supervisor, the practicum I have to pass to graduate."

Mo stared impassively at Lesley, her arms still folded.

"Are you listening to me?" Lesley placed her hands flat against her chest. "I'm telling you the truth! She asked me out, I said no. She came here and made a pass at me, I said no, and in no uncertain terms."

Mo's eyes bulged. "She made a pass at you?"

"Yes! And I told her no and to leave, even though she's an officer and can stop me from graduating and can stop us from seeing each other. Maybe if you trusted me and listened to what I'm saying, you'd realize why there's a problem. A huge problem. Listen to me!" Lesley turned away, struggling for control. Why wouldn't Mo listen? Maybe if she kept repeating it, Mo would eventually hear. She drew a deep breath and looked back at her. "She asked me on a date. I said no. The last thing I expected was for her to show up here. She must have known you wouldn't be around, but I don't know how. No, I didn't tell her."

Mo unfolded her arms. "I told her."

"You?"

"Not on purpose." Mo pressed her lips together and shook her head. "I thought she was being nice, taking an interest."

"When?"

"A few days ago at the simulators. She overheard me telling Ann about Neil and came over to ask when I'd be away. She asked about you, too. Now I know why."

"Mo, I don't like her. I don't want anything to do with her. I hated her being here last night." She felt her lips trembling, but willed herself not to turn away. "I need you to believe me."

Mo stepped toward her. "I do. But if something like this happens again, you tell me right away. Even over a comm unit. I want to hear it from you first, not someone else."

Lesley wrapped her arms around Mo and fought tears of relief when Mo squeezed her back.

"I'm sorry," Mo said into her shoulder. "But you have to admit, it sounds unbelievable. I mean, if what you're saying about Leeds is true . . ."

"I know," Lesley said, drawing back. "But I'm not sure what to do about it. My instinct says to report her. She could be falling from the Way. Not only will she not take no for an answer, but she's completely ignoring you, our relationship."

"That doesn't surprise me. After all, I'm nobody, right?"

"That's not true," Lesley murmured, stroking Mo's cheek.

"It is in the sense that everyone sees us as temporary," Mo said, a little too casually. "According to the Way, this isn't a real relationship."

She had to admit that was true.

"So while it bothers me that she's acting as if I don't exist, I don't see her asking you out as worrisome, as far as the Way goes. It's her persistence . . ."

"That's why I need to do something."

"It will be your word against hers."

"Ann can corroborate that she was here last night, to prove that I'm not making the whole thing up."

Mo sneered. "The same Ann who made it sound like Leeds spent the night? I wouldn't count on her."

"It's a capital violation to lie to the military during an investigation.

And I find it strange that Ann made it sound like I wanted Leeds here. Last night, I had the impression that she was trying to help me out of the situation." Lesley waited, hoping that Mo would finally tell her about Ann's harassment. She'd stood on the sidelines all year, knowing that Mo wanted to handle it on her own. It would be nice to get it out in the open so she could stop pretending that she didn't see the daggers shooting from Mo's eyes whenever Ann was around.

Mo didn't bite. "Still, it would be her word against Leeds'." She paused. "What did you mean when you said she could stop us from seeing each other?"

"She threatened to schedule us on different rotations on 72. But right now, my immediate concern is graduating. I have to figure out what to do before my next practicum. That's why I'm seeing Finney this afternoon."

"You're going to tell Finney?"

Lesley nodded. "At 15:30. That's who I was talking to when you walked in. Do you have a better idea?"

"No. What's the point of having a mentor if you can't talk to her about stuff like this?"

"I'm not looking forward to it." An officer making a pass at her wasn't on her list of comfortable topics.

"It'll only get worse. It doesn't sound like Leeds will give up."

"That's why I'm doing it, anyway."

"Leeds mustn't know about Finney," Mo said. "Or at least I hope she doesn't, because if she does, she's definitely falling from the Way."

"I thought the same thing." Lesley let go of Mo. "I hate to do this, but I should probably get going. I don't want to be late. Finney's being good, fitting me in at such short notice."

"You don't have to run off right away if you don't want to. I can go with you."

"That wouldn't be a good idea. Even if it was, we'd still have to leave now to make the next train."

"I meant I can drop you off."

Lesley frowned. "Drop me off?"

"Um, yeah. I have an aviacraft. I flew here." Mo shifted her weight.

     DISOBEDIENCE MEANS DEATH

"Remember my parents wanted to talk to me? Well, they gave me an aviacraft. For a graduation present."

"They gave you an aviacraft?" Lesley said, wondering if she'd misheard.

"Yeah. I'm not keeping it, though. I flew it here, and I'll fly you wherever you're meeting Finney, and then I'll fly home and take the train back."

"It would probably be easier if you just flew back here."

"Yeah, it would. But since I'm not keeping it, I shouldn't keep flying it around." Mo shifted her weight again. "Though it would make my parents really happy if I kept it."

"Why don't you keep it? I would, if I got one. Not that I will. I'm pretty sure I'm getting a complete set of Law books."

Mo gaped. "Law books? How do you know?"

"I overheard them talking about it last time I was home."

"They never give up, do they?"

"Mama never gives up." Lesley wished her parents were as proud of her as Mo's parents were of Mo. Papa tried; sometimes she believed he'd accepted that the military suited her. But Mama . . . no matter how wide the smile, Lesley could still see the disappointment. "You're very lucky, Mo."

Mo nodded. "I need to properly thank them. It was a great idea, even if I can't keep it. Though I guess me having an aviacraft would benefit you too, wouldn't it?"

"It certainly would." Lesley slipped on her cloak.

"If I'm flying you, we don't have to leave yet."

"I'd like to see it. And we don't have to go straight to the military outpost. Take me for a ride."

Mo grinned. "You sound like Mama and Papa."

"Have you taken them for a ride yet?"

"Not yet. I rushed over here when Ann beeped me," she said sheepishly.

"Then after you drop me off, fly home and take them for a ride. I'll beep you when I'm done. Maybe by then you'll have finished talking yourself into keeping it and can come and get me."

"What if I decide not to keep it?"

Lesley shrugged. "I'll take the train." She lifted Mo's cloak from the bed and held it open for her. "Let's go."

LESLEY WALKED TO the window and peered outside. Nothing had changed in the last twenty seconds. "And then she marched down the corridor. And that was it." She moved away from the window and looked at Finney.

"Has she communicated with you since then?"

"No. The last thing she said was that we'd talk about it before our next session."

"'It' being getting together on 72?"

"Yes." Lesley rubbed her forehead; she felt exposed.

"And she said you'd talk about it in her office?"

"Not explicitly, but that's where we usually meet before a session."

Finney lifted a mug to her lips and sipped, watching Lesley over its rim. "Do you think you can sit down now or do you want to keep pacing?"

Lesley stiffly lowered herself into the chair in front of the desk. Her mug was still full. She didn't trust herself to reach for it.

"I know this has been difficult," Finney said, lowering her mug, "but you did the right thing. I'm glad you came in."

"You don't think I'm overreacting?"

"No. This is definitely an Interior matter." Finney paused. "She hasn't violated any articles, though I agree that she was pushing 493. Hard. But her behavioural pattern indicates that she's slipping. Your instincts are sound."

"I wish it hadn't come to this. She's a good teacher."

"Don't feel bad. You've done her a favour. The best time for us to intervene is before she falls, when we can still help her. That's why the indoctrinators teach that you should contact the military the moment—*the moment*—you suspect that someone is having a problem," Finney said, slapping her hands together. "It can mean the difference between a refresher stay at the Indoctrination Academy and an execution site."

"If she hadn't been so persistent—"

"Then you wouldn't be here. If she'd accepted your answer when she first asked you out, would there be a problem?"

   DISOBEDIENCE MEANS DEATH

"No."

"Exactly. It's not unheard of for officers to date cadets, though chasing one of your own students is definitely a show of poor judgment. Having said that, if someone were to complain to the administration, the Military Academy would deal with it, not Interior. But Lieutenant Leeds went beyond that. That's why you're here." Finney tipped her head to the left, then the right. "I could try to strike her under 662 for what she said about scheduling you and Mo on different rotations, but that would be extremely difficult to support."

"If she hasn't violated any articles, what can you—oh. Article 998."

Finney nodded. "Very good. But we have to build a case that she'll be a potential threat to the Way unless we intervene." She swivelled the desk's comm station until the keyboard was directly in front of her and started to type. "Now, are you sure you've never had a problem with her before, when you took classes with her?"

"No, never."

"She never wanted to talk to you after class or anything like that?"

"No. That's why I was surprised when she started to get personal in her office. She knew what my parents do, my sector of residence, she knew a bit about my Indoctrination and Learning Academy records."

"She probably read your military file, the sections available to instructors, anyway. However . . ." Finney tapped away at the station's keys. Lesley heard the familiar click of a connection being established.

"Yes, Commander," a voice said from the station.

"I've just dispatched a file identifier to you. I want you to check all accesses of that file over the past year. Look for anything unusual and get back to me within an hour. Understood?"

"Yes, Commander. I'll look into it right away."

"Thank you." Finney terminated the connection and looked at Lesley. "Did Lieutenant Leeds ever say anything to you over a comm unit about, um, getting together?"

"No."

"Did she ever say anything while you were flying a sim?"

"No. Never during a sim."

"Cadet Hawkins is the only one who saw her in your room?"

"Yes."

"And she handled Mo's violin case and a book on your nightstand?"

Lesley nodded.

"Is the book still on your nightstand?"

"Yes."

"When do you next meet with Lieutenant Leeds?"

"Tomorrow at 14:00, but I don't want to—"

Finney raised her hand. "You'll have to trust me. Go to her office tomorrow, but don't initiate a conversation with her about anything related to this."

"I won't. It's the last thing I want to talk about."

"Good." Finney leaned forward. "I'll have to bring Commander Morton in on this."

Lesley grimaced. She couldn't imagine telling Morton what she'd just told Finney.

"It would be discourteous of me to investigate one of his officers without telling him. And it will be easier to build a case with his cooperation."

"Do you think he'll cooperate when he finds out I'm involved?" Lesley asked.

"Yes. He's done exactly what he said he'd do and left us alone. He hasn't interfered with my mentoring. He hasn't tried to hold you back in any way. Now, he's probably done that because he figured we weren't worth his time, but that's fine. It's been better than having him on our backs."

Finney leaned back in her chair and sipped her drink again. "But even if he had been causing trouble, he wouldn't let something like this go. The worst thing that could happen for him would be that Lieutenant Leeds eventually commits a serious violation, and it comes to light that he was warned and refused to cooperate with an investigation. So don't worry about him. I'll deal with him."

"Thank you." Lesley sat quietly while Finney typed, the overwhelming compulsion to ask the question at the back of her mind growing stronger. She had to know. Shifting in her chair, she asked, "Do you think my relationship with Mo is inappropriate?" The vulnerability in her voice made her wince.

The typing stopped. Finney picked up a pencil from the desk and twirled it in her fingers as she looked at Lesley. "Inappropriate is the wrong word. It implies that you're doing something wrong, when you're not. You're not violating any articles. You're not even pushing any. Many twenty-one-year-olds are in relationships."

"What word would you use?" Lesley asked, sensing a "but."

Finney inhaled deeply and slowly exhaled. "Most young Chosens try not to get too serious with anyone, for obvious reasons. You and Mo aren't typical in that you've been together for some time. You're not an academy romance or a casual relationship. Given that you'll serve with Mo for at least the next couple of years and perhaps beyond, you'll probably still be together when you're approaching twenty-five. I'd be careless not to keep my eye on you. Having said that, I've come to know you, and I'm confident that you'll do what the Way expects of you without much prodding from me."

Lesley swallowed. "I know what I have to do."

"I know you do. And I know it won't be easy. You'll both need time to recover before you meet your Chosens. That's why you don't want to leave it too late. You probably won't receive Papers the moment you turn twenty-five, but you never know. You can't count on not receiving them until you're twenty-nine." She tapped the pencil on the desk. "When you decide it's time, I can help, if you want me to."

"How?" Finney wouldn't put one of them in the Indoctrination Academy, would she?

"I assume you'll want to stop serving together at that point. Let's say you want to transfer to another ship, so you won't be on the same tour together. I can whisper a word in the right ear to make sure that happens. Things like that."

"I see." That would be useful if she were to put in a transfer request and Mo tried to follow her, though if she stuck to her plan, she'd request a transfer to Interior. She couldn't see Mo doing the same.

"When the time comes, just let me know if you need my help."

Lesley nodded and hung her head. Actually thinking and planning and talking about their eventual breakup saddened her almost more than she could bear, but at the same time, she felt as if a weight had been lifted from her shoulders, a weight she hadn't realized was there. She wanted to believe that she'd have the strength when the time came, but if she faltered, Finney would help. In fact, Finney would force them apart, if it came to that—she could put a word in the right ear whether Lesley wanted her to or not. She must never forget that Finney was not only her mentor, but the commander of her sector, and Mo's.

"So to get back to your original question, I don't agree with Lieutenant Leeds," Finney said briskly. She put down the pencil and resumed typing. "I'm glad you didn't let her intimidate you."

Lesley's comm unit beeped twice—a dispatch.

Finney looked up. "I think I have everything I need," she murmured.

"Then I won't take up anymore of your time. Permission to leave."

"Permission denied. I want to take another minute of yours." Finney clasped her hands on the edge of the desk. "I was going to talk to you about this after the graduation ceremony, but I might as well do it now, when it's quieter."

Lesley waited, her heart pounding. Finney had never denied her permission to leave before. Did she have more to say about Mo?

"You're graduating, but that doesn't mean you'll stop needing a mentor. In fact, you'll need one more than ever. Most of the cadets on Morton's list will continue their relationships with their mentors after graduation."

Lesley's heart sank—she could guess what was coming. Finney wanted to stop mentoring her, and who could blame her? Despite offering to be her mentor on the spur of the moment and probably regretting it later, Finney had honoured her commitment for two years. She'd done enough.

"You're a special case. We were sort of thrown together. On paper, I'm not the best mentor for you. You're pursuing a career in Defence, and in a couple of years you'll be away from Rymel for months on end. I'm in Interior. I'll always be stationed here." Her face hardened. "The committee that oversees the lists at all the academies, the one Commander Morton reports to, contacted me last week with a list of potential replacements for me. I just dispatched it to you. You should read it over, consider the choices carefully, and let me know if you're interested in meeting anyone on the list before making a decision."

"I will." How unfortunate that she was losing Finney at the same

   DISOBEDIENCE MEANS DEATH

time she'd needed her for more than the usual advice on classes and extra activities!

"Mentoring you over the past two years has been a positive experience for me. I hope it's been a positive experience for you. No matter whom you choose to guide you through the next few years and beyond, you'll be a fine officer."

"Thank you," Lesley said, though a sense of loss tempered Finney's praise. "The past two years *have* been a positive experience."

"Good." Finney cleared her throat. "If Lieutenant Leeds talks to you about what we've discussed before you meet with her tomorrow, contact me immediately. And remember not to initiate a discussion with her."

"Yes, Commander."

"And about what we talked about, about you and Mo, you beep me anytime if you want to talk about it or need my help. Understood?"

"Yes."

"You did the right thing, coming to see me about Lieutenant Leeds. Dismissed."

Lesley nodded to her and left the outpost, relieved that the meeting was over and confident that Finney would resolve the problem with Leeds in the best way possible, for all concerned. But losing her as a mentor . . . she'd gladly show up for more of Finney's 08:00 meetings, if only she could. After today, she felt like she could talk to Finney about anything. Her next mentor would have a lot to live up to.

She beeped Mo. "So am I taking the train?"

"Only if you don't trust my flying."

"I knew it!"

"Papa was right. If I didn't want to keep it, I should never have sat in the pilot's seat. But forget that, how did it go?"

"She agreed that Leeds' behaviour indicates a potential threat. She's trying to build a case under Article 998."

Mo sucked in her breath.

"It's better than an execution site. Anyway, I'll tell you all about it when I see you. Should I go to the same place where you dropped me off?"

"Yeah. You know, it'll take me longer to walk to the craft than it will to pick you up and fly back to the academy. I'll be there in about fifteen minutes."

"See you then."

Five minutes later, Lesley stood in a field and searched the sky, even though she knew Mo couldn't possibly be in the area. She decided to give the list of Finney's possible replacements a quick look while she waited. Heavy with disappointment, she pulled out her comm unit, opened the dispatch, and started to skim names. She didn't recognize the first five, all in Defence. According to the blurbs after their names, they were all involved with fighter pilots in some way. The sixth name was familiar: *Lt. Cmdr. J. Larson, Defence Division*. Morton had pushed him when he'd first approached her about being mentored. Larson might be suitable for the next two years, since he oversaw domestic patrols, but she wasn't sure he'd be the best choice long term. The next four names meant nothing to her.

She moved down to the last name on the list and blinked. *Cmdr. L. Finney, Interior Division*. Underneath, the following: *I persuaded the committee to add my name to the list. Finney*. She laughed; she couldn't believe it! But Finney had said she wasn't the best mentor for her. Actually, no. She'd said *on paper*. That sounded more like an explanation of why the committee didn't consider Finney the best mentor, not Finney's thoughts on the matter.

Despite wanting to stick with Finney, Lesley planned to spend her remaining free time at the academy researching the others on the list. Finney would expect that of her. She read over Finney's note about persuading the committee and chuckled. She wouldn't have wanted to be on the other comm unit for that conversation. Her mirth died. Nor would she want to be Leeds.

MO PASTED A smile on her face and sauntered over to Ann, standing near the equipment counter. "I'm not suiting up because I'm only going to observe."

Ann seemed surprised to see her. "I wasn't sure you'd make it tonight."

"I would have beeped you if I wasn't coming."

"So everything's okay between you and Lesley?"

"Yeah, why wouldn't it be? Anyway, sim time is slipping away here."

Mo checked the board behind the counter. "It looks like five is free. I'll grab it. Link to me when you're ready."

"Sure."

Mo accepted a helmet from the attendant and headed up the corridor without a backward glance. Ann would just love to know what had happened when she'd returned to the academy and confronted Les. Too bad she'd never get the satisfaction.

She'd just settled herself into the simulator when her comm unit beeped. She frowned at its display. "What?"

"I have to cancel," Ann said. "Can we reschedule for tomorrow morning?"

"What do you mean, you have to cancel? You were just about to suit up."

"Mo, some Interior officer just beeped me. They want to see me." Her voice quavered. "They're over in administration."

Mo's grip tightened around the comm unit. Finney didn't waste any time.

"Do you know what they want?" Ann asked. "Have you heard anything?"

"No, nothing." It was probably about Leeds, but she didn't know for sure. "You better go. I'll reschedule for 11:00 tomorrow, okay?"

"Okay." The connection went dead.

Her mood sombre, Mo returned to her and Les's room. Les looked up from her book when Mo entered.

"Interior beeped Ann. She's with them now," Mo told her. "I hope she realizes it's not a game and answers their questions honestly."

"I'm sure she realizes it's not a game," Les said.

Considering how nervous Ann had sounded, Les was probably right. Mo pulled off her boots and snuggled up to Les on the bed. "What if she makes it sound like you wanted Leeds here?"

"She might make it sound like I didn't." Les squeezed her. "Don't worry. Interior probably wants to confirm that Leeds was here, nothing more. They might ask her to describe what she saw and heard, but I don't know how much weight they'd give to her interpretation of events."

"What if she says she didn't see Leeds here?"

"That would be really stupid. They can pull her recent comm conversations."

Mo hoped they didn't. She'd sounded like an idiot when she'd spoken to Ann earlier that day, and Ann had made it sound like she'd caught Les and Leeds in the act. "Do you think they'll want to see you?"

Les took her time responding. "I've already talked to Finney. I can't see them talking to me unless they have a strong reason to doubt either her record of what I said, or me."

"Why would they doubt you?"

"I could be lying. Maybe I hate Leeds and want to get her into trouble."

"But you're the one who'd end up in trouble," Mo said.

"Yes, but if I was the one falling from the Way, I wouldn't care."

Speaking about Les falling from the Way, even in hypothetical terms, made Mo uncomfortable. "Why couldn't she have accepted it when you said no? Why did she have to come here and get all weird?"

Les shrugged. "I don't know. I hope I never understand what goes on in someone's head when they're starting to fall."

"Me neither." To think that someone who might be falling had been here, in this room. Someone she'd actually spoken to. She held Les a little tighter.

Les kissed the top of Mo's head. "You okay?"

"Yeah." And ever so grateful for Interior. "Things are moving quickly."

"They would. Interior won't wait around until Leeds decides she'd be good for a Joined Chosen."

Mo shuddered and silently recited the Words.

LESLEY PULLED ON her cloak with a sigh and grasped the doorknob, then hesitated. She felt Mo's hand on her back. "This probably doesn't help, but I'll be thinking of you," Mo said.

"It does help. Thanks."

"Do you want me to walk over with you? I'm meeting with Ross and Ann at 14:30. I can fly a sim until then."

"No, I'll be fine on my own." If she could, she'd keep Mo away from Leeds—the thought of Mo anywhere near that woman made her feel ill. "I'll see you later."

Her dread grew as she crossed the lobby of the pilot training complex and entered the wing that contained Leeds' office. Finney had said to trust her. Even so, when she spotted Leeds at her desk through the open office door, she wanted to turn and bolt.

"Right on time," Leeds said, gesturing toward the chair in front of her desk.

Lesley lowered herself into it and glanced around. Everything looked exactly as it had the last time she'd been here. Well, what had she expected, the office to be crawling with Interior officers?

"The replay looked good." Leeds gave Lesley a pointed look. "As I mentioned the other night. So there isn't anything to discuss as far as your last session goes. But we have other things to discuss, don't we?" She rose from her chair. Lesley's skin crawled when Leeds walked by her to shut the door. Leeds returned to her desk. "Have you given any more thought to what I said?"

"I told you, I don't need to think about it." So much for trusting Finney!

"And I told you that I think you do. Do you want people whispering about you? What will it take to get through to you, Lesley?"

She wanted to ask Leeds the same question.

"Being seen out with someone else will be good for you. I'll be good for you. I don't understand why you can't see that."

Lesley remained silent.

"Are you just going to sit there?"

"I've told you several times that I'm not interested in having any type of personal relationship with you. Can we go to the simulators now?"

"Tell me you'll give some thought to seeing me on 72 and we'll go to the simulators."

They stared at each other. The awkward silence lengthened. Lesley jumped when someone knocked at the door.

Leeds frowned. "Yes?" she called.

The door opened. "I'd like to see you, Lieutenant. In my office."

"Yes, Lieutenant Commander." Leeds rose. "Wait here," she said to Lesley as she walked past.

A moment later, Lesley risked a look over her shoulder, and saw

Leeds turning the corner at the end of the corridor. She darted out of the office and stood outside. When Leeds returned, Lesley would start walking toward the simulator wing; hopefully Leeds would follow, not order her back into the office. But then what? Would Leeds continue to badger her in the simulator—or worse? What had been the point of seeing Finney and having her initiate an investigation, if nothing was going to happen? Had Interior decided that Leeds wasn't a problem? How could she not be a problem?

Forget 998; Lesley was certain a case could now be made under 662. Leeds' continued pressure to become personally involved with her was no longer just persistent—it was harassment. But Leeds always made sure that she didn't say or do anything when it could be recorded, and things were only going to get worse. Leeds would have more power over her on 72. She'd be in charge of—

"Cadet Thompson."

Startled, Lesley jerked her head toward the lieutenant approaching her. "Yes, Lieutenant Browne."

"I'll be supervising the rest of your practicum. Let's go to the simulators."

Lesley fell into step with him.

"I reviewed your last two sessions," he said. "It looks like you have the maneuver down. Did Lieutenant Leeds explain why she wanted you to attend another session?"

Not explicitly, though Lesley could guess, and it had nothing to do with the maneuver. "No."

"I see. Well then, you can fly the maneuver for me, and if it looks good, I'll score you and that will be it."

"Thank you." She paused. "Where is Lieutenant Leeds?"

Browne turned to her and smiled. "I'm afraid I don't have any information about Lieutenant Leeds. I was asked to take over your practicum. That's all I know."

He couldn't possibly have reviewed the two sessions since Leeds had been called from her office—they each ran for about an hour. "Do you mind if I ask when you were asked to take over my practicum?"

"Not at all. This morning. I was told to collect you from Lieutenant Leeds' office at 14:10."

MO STOOD WITH Ann in front of Ross's desk, relieved, and surprisingly proud, that Ann had executed 16C to Ross's satisfaction. "I'm pleased that the two of you worked together," Ross said. "It only took two sessions for you to accomplish your goal. You see what you can do when you put your differences aside? Keep it up on 72. Dismissed."

"I suppose I should thank you," Ann said as they strode down the corridor to the lobby.

"I didn't do much. It was all about the spiral."

Ann swung open the door to the lobby; Mo followed her through. Time to get rid of her. She wanted to beep Les, find out if anything had happened with Leeds. Les's session must be over by now. "Anyway, see you at the ceremony. I'm heading—" She bumped into Ann, who'd stopped dead. "Sorry," she said, to head off the inevitable *Watch where you're going, pipsqueak!*

"Look!" Ann said, her voice low, urgent.

Mo sidestepped her to see what was happening. Everyone stood frozen, their attention on a small group marching toward the exit: Leeds, surrounded by four Interior officers, the ring of their boots echoing around the lobby. The moment the group left the building, everyone rushed to the window and craned their necks. The whispering started as soon as Leeds and her escorts could no longer be seen.

"Argamon," Ann breathed.

Mo had been dying to ask Ann what Interior had wanted the previous evening, but had restrained herself, since the question was personal and they weren't exactly friends. But now . . . "Is that what they wanted to see you about last night? Leeds?"

Ann turned to her. "Yes, it was. I guess it's okay to tell you. They didn't tell me not to tell you, and I guess you know anyway."

"I wasn't sure."

"You weren't? I assumed Lesley reported her." She leaned forward and stuck her face close to Mo's. "Or maybe you did."

"I didn't."

"So it *was* Lesley."

"She didn't report her. She asked an officer for advice. And, uh, that officer took it from there. I wasn't sure that's what Interior wanted to see you about, though. What happened?"

"Not much. I was only with them for five minutes. If I'd known it would be that short, I would have told you to fly a sim until I came back."

"Five minutes?"

Ann nodded. "All they wanted me to do was confirm that Leeds had been in your room."

Then why had Ann jumped to the conclusion that Les had reported Leeds? If Ann's interpretation of what she'd seen had been accurate, Les wouldn't have had any reason to report her. "Why did you think Les reported her?"

"Because of what they asked. They asked me if Leeds had been in your room, and when I said yes, they asked me to describe what I saw. Of course I gave them my impression of what was going on, too."

Of course. "I'm glad they didn't listen to you."

Ann's brow furrowed. "Who says they didn't listen?"

"We just saw them take Leeds away."

"Which means my impression of that evening was correct," Ann boomed. Then she elaborated in her normal tone. "I told them that Lesley wanted to get away from Leeds." She started to laugh. "You should have seen her. I thought she was going to pass out! I took pity on her, tried to give her an excuse to go to the simulators with me, but Leeds told me to get lost."

Mo wanted to slap the smile off Ann's face. "Then why in the flaming Argamon did you make it sound like they were all over each other when you told me about it?"

"Because it's fun to pull your strings and make you dance," Ann said, moving her body as if she were a puppet.

"You know what? I've had enough of you." Mo walked away.

"But we work so well together," Ann called in a sing-song voice. "Think of what we could accomplish."

"I don't understand you," Mo said over her shoulder. "I hope I never do." If Ann replied, she didn't hear her. Forget about beeping Les; she wanted to be with her, hug her, tell her what she'd seen. Tell her that Leeds wouldn't bother her anymore.

LESLEY CAUGHT A glimpse of herself in one of the mirrors that lined the corridor to the reception hall. Was that really her, in an orange cloak, a sub-lieutenant's insignia on her left breast?

Someone slapped a hand onto her right shoulder. "Did Mama tell you I passed the Advocacy Entrance Exam?" Jason asked.

"Yes." Several times. "Congratulations. Oh, and if you ever need a specific Law book for a paper or presentation, check my room." That was where she planned to store her graduation present. A set of Law books wouldn't be in high demand on the space station.

"I have my own set," he said with a grin. "Mama got it for me, for passing the exam."

She forced a smile. "Great. No need to use mine, then." He'd received a better gift than she had for passing the Military Academy entrance exam. Nothing wasn't difficult to beat.

They checked their cloaks, entered the reception hall, and surveyed those gathered below them. "Lesley!" a voice rang out. "Or should I say Sub-lieutenant Thompson?"

She peered in the direction of the voice. Neil waved and beckoned to her. She waved back, then descended the wide steps and threaded her way through the crowd to him.

"Congratulations!" Neil said.

"Thank you."

He proudly presented the woman at his side. "I'd like to introduce Barbara, my Chosen. And this is Lesley Thompson."

Barbara smiled. "Neighbour and Mo's girlfriend. Sorry, I'm meeting so many people lately, I have to label everyone and keep repeating the labels, otherwise I won't remember who's who. You'll be easy to remember, though. Your name comes up a lot, especially when Mo's around. I'll be seeing a lot of you, I'm sure."

Over the next couple of years, perhaps, but after that, she and Mo would be away for months at a time. And once they received Chosen Papers . . . Lesley didn't want to think about that yet, beyond knowing that she'd be incapable of living next door to Mo. She preferred to honour tradition and always strove to do so, but if Mo and her Chosen ended up living on the Middleton estate, Lesley and her Chosen wouldn't live on the Thompson estate, even if Lesley was the Principal. In fact, she'd have to avoid the estate unless she knew that Mo wouldn't be around. Running into her would be too dangerous, for both of them. Ideally, Mo would remain in Defence and often be away on tour. "Will you live on the Middleton estate?" she asked, her gaze taking in both Neil and Barbara. Mo hadn't mentioned their plans in that regard.

Neil nodded. "Mama and Papa said we don't have to build on the land, we can use it for whatever we want. But we've decided to build."

"The estate is lovely." Barbara slipped her arm into Neil's. "The climate is a little warm for this time of year, but I'll get used to it."

"She's from L9," Neil explained.

"It's not this warm all the time," Lesley told her.

"That's what Neil says." Barbara's eyes lit up. "Jason, neighbour."

"You remembered," Jason said, joining them. "You'll be at my eighteenth next month, right?"

"Yes, Jason, we'll be there," Neil said, sounding like he was saying it for the twentieth time.

"You'll be there, right?" Jason said to Lesley.

"Of course I'll be there. Why wouldn't I be there?"

"Mama says you'll hardly be around now."

"Mama's wrong." Perhaps she should forget tradition and plan to live somewhere other than the Thompson estate, regardless of where Mo lived. "I'll be around more than I have been for the past three years. I'll be home between rotations." Over Neil's shoulder, she saw Finney accept a glass of juice from one of the servers. "Excuse me, I need to speak to someone. Nice meeting you, Barbara. I expect I'll be seeing you again soon."

She skirted around them, anxious to catch Finney before someone else did. Unfortunately she didn't get to Finney first, but Finney acknowledged her with a nod and pointed to the floor with her left hand. A familiar signal, one Finney often used—*I'll come talk to you when I'm finished here.*

While she waited, Lesley scanned the room for Mo. They should have stayed together after the ceremony, but Mo had needed the bathroom. Though Lesley had just left them, she couldn't help looking at Neil and Barbara again. They were getting along well. Lesley doubted they'd wait the full year to schedule their Joining Ceremony. Barbara would become a Middleton, live on the Middleton estate, be there for all the family celebrations, meet Mo's Chosen, know Mo's daughters . . . And there was Mo, walking toward them. Lesley watched her smile and shake Barbara's hand. Well, she would—Barbara was family. Barbara had known Mo all of five minutes, but she was family.

"Congratulations, Sub-lieutenant."

Lesley turned to Finney. "Thank you. Did you read my dispatch?"

"I did. Are you sure? Building a relationship with some of the Defence officers on that list could be very advantageous for your career."

"I understand that." She hesitated. She wanted to tell Finney that she respected and trusted her, one of the primary reasons she wanted Finney to continue as her mentor. Her experience with Leeds had taught her that even military could go astray; she'd naively never considered that possibility. From now on, military would have to earn her respect and trust—she wouldn't give it by default. Finney had it; the others on the list didn't. But Finney might scoff if Lesley were to tell her that, and ask for a better reason, one related to her career. As it happened, she could provide one. "But you're a better fit for my long-term plan."

"Your long-term plan?" Finney said, her brows shooting upward.

"Yes." Lesley took a deep breath. Saying it out loud would feel like a commitment. "I'm looking forward to flying domestic, and it'll be interesting to go on a couple of deep tours. But after that, I'll probably be ready to stay on Rymel. We've talked about how much I enjoyed the Interior courses."

"Are you saying you'd want to transfer into Interior after a few deep tours?"

Lesley nodded.

"You'd be a good fit for Interior. Not only that, we value officers with knowledge of both Interior and Defence procedures. I'm glad you told me. It'll definitely affect who I introduce you to and how I advise you. If you're willing, I can help prepare you for the transition. You can study Interior material when you're on 72, get a head start."

"I'd like that," she said, smiling to herself. Finney would continue as her mentor.

"Good." Finney sipped her juice. "So if your rough timeline is to transfer after two or three deep tours, that would make you how old when you come over to Interior?"

"About twenty-five."

Finney studied Lesley over the rim of her glass. "About twenty-five." She took a long drink this time, probably weighing what to say. "I think that would be the perfect time." A passing server relieved her of her empty glass. "Of course, twenty-five is a few years away and things can change. So I won't hold you to it if it turns out you don't want to transfer to Interior, or there's," she waved her hand around, "less of a reason to. We'll plan for it, but we won't neglect the possibility that you might remain in Defence."

Lesley selfishly wanted the next few years with Mo, wanted to be a part of Mo's life until it became unbearable and, yes, inappropriate. Unless Mo decided to end their relationship, there wouldn't be less of a reason to transfer when Lesley turned twenty-five.

"I hope you didn't feel that you had to come up with a plan because of what we talked about. I wasn't trying to apply any pressure," Finney said.

"No, I've been thinking about it for a while."

Finney looked her in the eye. "I can understand why you didn't mention this to me before. I'm only your mentor."

Blood rushed to Lesley's face. "I'm sorry, I—"

Finney sighed and shook her head, but she was smiling. "I'm joking, Lesley. I don't expect you to tell me everything the moment it crosses your mind."

Since Finney seemed to be in a good mood, Lesley decided to ask a potentially risky question. Nothing terrible had happened when she'd asked about her relationship with Mo. If anything, talking to Finney had been a great relief. With that in mind . . . "Can I ask what happened to Lieutenant Leeds, or is that something you can't tell me?"

"Not here," Finney said. "Let's go for a stroll."

Lesley expected it to take forever to maneuver their way through the packed room, but everyone quickly moved out of the way when they realized it was a commander saying "excuse me." At least this time Finney wasn't escorting her from a reception in disgrace. Finney had to stop and promise to speak to two officers, but otherwise they reached the room's exit without much trouble.

"Lieutenant Leeds is in the adult wing of the Indoctrination Academy," Finney said as they walked along the deserted corridor. "The indoctrinators will remind her of what we consider appropriate behaviour. I expect she'll spend quite a bit of time with a counsellor, too."

"I passed by her office yesterday. Her name is still on the door."

"Of course it is. She's on an unscheduled break, that's all. Once the indoctrinators are satisfied that she's regained her equilibrium and respect for the Way, she'll be back. As you said, she's a good teacher. Though I doubt she'll be permitted to supervise one-on-one for a while, if ever."

Lesley didn't need to ask what would happen if the indoctrinators weren't satisfied. "I gather that Commander Morton cooperated with the investigation."

Finney chuckled. "Do you remember me asking that accesses to a particular file be checked?"

She nodded.

"Those sorts of things are always monitored. I only had to ask because any anomalies for your military file would be reported to him, not me. And they were."

"You mean she accessed my file when she shouldn't have?"

"More than she should have, and he knew that. But that alone wasn't enough to initiate an investigation. It's not a violation for an officer to be interested in a cadet. However, it meant he was receptive when I beeped him and told him about what was going on, probably more than he would have been if he hadn't already had the nagging suspicion that she'd developed an unhealthy interest in you. You provided the pieces he was missing."

Finney stopped walking and faced Lesley. "So you see, coming forward early is always the right thing to do. We're helping Lieutenant Leeds, rather than executing her. I'll teach you how to spot worrisome situations and behaviours before they escalate to the point of no return. When we have to execute a Rymellan, everyone has failed, not only the criminal. So it's always better to be proactive, anticipate, recognize potential problems before they occur," she said, slicing her hand through the air as she made each point. "Always keep your eye on things. Don't wait for something to happen. Anticipate."

Perhaps advanced Interior courses covered how to anticipate who could fall from the Way—she'd only had room in her schedule for basic courses. "It sounds like I have a lot to learn." And who better to learn it from than Finney? "Thank you for telling me what happened. I didn't know if you would."

"Well, you're one of us now," Finney said. "Anyway, I should go speak to those officers before they come looking for me. Let's go back."

As soon as Lesley reentered the reception hall, she spotted Mo, standing with David. "Look at us," Mo said with a sweep of her arm. "Remember when we met? Now we're sub-lieutenants. Time flies."

"And so do we," David said.

Mo groaned.

"Did she tell you that she wants to pick you up and take you to the shuttle base for our first rotation?" Lesley asked David.

"You mean that she wants to show off her aviacraft?" David said, winking. "Yep, she did. She's agreed to let me fly it."

"What?" Mo shrieked.

"Oh, my mama's waving to me. Be back in a minute." He darted away.

Mo raised both her hands, palms up. "His mama's waving to him. How convenient."

Lesley stifled a laugh. "I'm sure the sub-lieutenant will be back soon."

"I can't believe it," Mo said, looking down at the insignia on her uniform. "And you, too." She stepped forward and traced her fingers along Lesley's insignia. "But you know what the best thing is about today? It's official. We'll be flying domestic patrols and then going on deep tours!" Mo squeezed Lesley's fingers. "And I'm so glad we'll be doing it together, experiencing so much for the first time."

"So am I," Lesley said, though she felt guilty, and hoped the shadow she felt hanging over them didn't show on her face. Would it always feel this way, now that she'd drawn a line in time and called it the end? Unable to look Mo in the eye, she looked past her and noticed Finney watching them. Their eyes briefly met, then Finney shifted her gaze back to the officer in conversation with her.

"What is it?" Mo asked, glancing behind her.

She refocused on Mo and managed a smile. "Nothing." Just Finney, keeping her eye on things.

THE ACCIDENT

·····

MO GAZED AT THE FRAMED IMAGE in her hand and traced the faces smiling back at her: Mama and Papa, relaxed and happy next to Mama's garden. The image had sat on the fireplace mantel for several years, always drawing her eye whenever she entered the living room. When Mama had asked if she wanted to take any family mementos with her on tour, she'd instantly thought of it. But would seeing it in her quarters on the *Falcon* warm her, or make her homesick? For six months, the only contact she'd have with her family would be dispatches that arrived hours after they were sent. She'd never been in that situation.

A knock at the bedroom door, then Mama peered into the room. "Can I come in?"

"Sure." Mo turned and slipped the image between two shirts in the open bag on the bed, then transferred the bag to the floor.

Mama sat where the bag had been. "Packing already?"

"Just a few things I don't want to forget."

"I can't believe you'll be gone in two weeks."

Neither could she. The thirty months she'd flown domestic patrols had whipped by.

"Are you looking forward to it? You used to talk about going on tour all the time, but lately, you've been quiet."

Because time was moving too quickly. She could count the number of tours until Les turned twenty-five on one hand. "I'll miss everyone, especially you and Papa. I've never been away from you for that long."

"Yes, you have. At the Indoctrination Academy."

Mo crouched and made a pretense of fussing inside the bag to hide her face. "I saw you once a month, and you weren't far away."

"I'll write to you every chance I get. I'll record my dispatches, if you like."

"It won't be the same as seeing you." Mo looked up. "Will you miss me?"

Mama tutted. "Of course I'll miss you. Not being able to beep you whenever I feel like it will take some getting used to. You won't be able to beep me, either. So if you want to talk to me about what's really bothering you, you'd better do it before you leave. Now would be a good time."

Mo sighed. Mama knew her too well. Maybe talking to her would help—it had to be better than lying awake at night, thinking the same thoughts over and over. She plunked down on the bed next to Mama. "It's Les."

"What about her?"

"She seems excited about the tour and everything, but . . ."

"But what?"

Mo couldn't shake the feeling that Les was slipping away. She'd hoped that Les would want to stay together until their Chosen Papers arrived and confirmed they were Chosens, but lately she'd started to wonder if Les had other plans. Why had Les been reading Interior cases on Space Station 72? *I mentioned to Finney that I would have taken more Interior courses if I'd had room in my schedule. She offered to give me some reading material,* Les had explained. A perfectly logical explanation— so why did Mo have the nagging suspicion that Les hadn't told her the whole story?

Maybe because Les hadn't told her anything until she'd noticed an Interior file on Les's station display and asked about it. Or maybe because Les would attend an Interior reception with Finney next week. Why would Finney take her to an Interior reception? Okay, Finney wasn't in Defence, but she was a commander—surely she could get her hands on a couple of invitations to a Defence reception. Wouldn't that make more sense for Les's career? Mo figured she must be missing a piece of the puzzle—a piece Finney had. "I don't know, Mama, I just feel as if we're not as close as we used to be. She spends a lot of time with Commander Finney."

     DISOBEDIENCE MEANS DEATH

Truth be told, she was jealous of Finney's influence with Les, hated that Finney might know things about Les that she didn't. Les was with Finney right now; who knew what they were discussing? Well, she'd soon be out of Finney's clutches for six months. A good thing, as far as Mo was concerned.

"Lesley has ambitions," Mama said. "Commander Finney is helping her."

Mo stared at her lap. "I know, but . . ." But she was afraid that some airhead would end up on Les's arm, nodding and smiling at all the receptions and telling everyone how proud she was of Admiral Thompson and how she'd supported her dream. Would she be as proud to be on Lieutenant Thompson's arm in thirty years? Mo would. She'd be proud of Les, and respect and love her, no matter what insignia was sewn on Les's uniform. All she'd ever wanted was to love Les, to support her, to be by her side, always. But would the Chosen Council let her? She bit her lip to stop it from trembling.

Mama slipped her arm around her. "You know, your papa and I, we've stayed out of it. We didn't want to interfere. But now I can see it's starting to hurt." She paused. "Maybe it's time to think about breaking up."

"No!" Mo leaped to her feet and crossed to her desk, keeping her back to Mama. "We're only twenty-three."

"Mo, you don't want to wait until you're twenty-five. The longer you wait, the harder you'll make it for yourself, and Lesley."

It was already impossible. They could break up tomorrow and it wouldn't make a difference; she'd always long for Les. Oh, she'd do her duty and Join with her Chosen, but she'd never love her. She'd struggle to not resent her, despite knowing it wasn't the poor woman's fault. No, Les had to be her Chosen. Too many lives would be ruined if she wasn't. "Mama, let me deal with this in my own time." Mo turned to face her. "I understand what you're saying, but I'm not ready yet."

"I'm not suggesting that you break up right now, not when you're about to go on tour with her. But you have to start thinking about it, for your sake and hers." Mama pursed her lips. "Maybe you can transfer to another ship after this tour. You'll be almost twenty-four at that point. It'll be rough, but you'll have at least a year to come to terms with it before your Papers arrive." She wagged a finger. "You definitely don't want to wait until Papers force you into it. It wouldn't be fair to your Chosen."

But Les is my Chosen. Saying that to Mama would probably alarm her. "I don't know."

Mama frowned. "At least promise me you'll think about it while you're away. It'll ease my mind."

Mo felt a pang of guilt; she'd had no idea that Mama was worried. "I will," she said, the desire to reassure winning out over honesty. She'd never break up with Les—not unless she had to.

"Your papa and I will always be here for you," Mama said, rising. She pulled Mo into a hug. "You can lean on us. We know how hard it'll be . . . when you decide it's time."

Tears stung Mo's eyes; she clung to Mama. If Les turned out not to be her Chosen, Mama and Papa would be her lifeline. She wouldn't survive without them.

Mama drew back and smiled. "So are we going to the C5 Trading Centre? That's the one that has my seeds. You said you'd take me."

"Oh, right," Mo said, brightening. She loved flying her parents around. Their faces shone with excitement every time the craft lifted off, even though she'd taken them for dozens of rides. They seemed so proud of her. Her eyes welled up again; she felt silly. Brooding about Les was turning her into an emotional wreck. An afternoon with Mama would be a welcome diversion. She'd rather think about which candies to take with her on tour than about the future of her and Les's relationship. "Well, yeah, let's go. And hey, why don't we take the train?"

Mama laughed.

LESLEY READ THE list Finney had just dispatched to her and gulped. Was Finney serious? There were over a hundred articles here. "So you want me to read and comment on at least one analysis of each article on the list?" In six months?

Finney shook her head. "Of course not. They focus on those articles in the Advanced Chosen Tradition course, but the students have a year to do it and they're cadets, not officers on duty." Her brow furrowed. "And I believe they only have to hand in forty to pass. I've highlighted the critical ones, around fifteen. The others are optional.

          DISOBEDIENCE MEANS DEATH

Do what you can. I sent you the entire list so you can see what they usually cover."

Relieved, Lesley scanned the list again, paying more attention to the article numbers. Good; the Chosen Tradition group she'd belonged to during her first year at the academy had covered a number of the critical ones. She'd dig up her notes, see what she could reuse. "There aren't any articles between CT120 and CT230." And for some reason, she couldn't recall what those articles were about—oh, wait. "They all pertain to triads."

"That's right. There's no point studying them when we don't have one. Most of the articles just clarify how other articles apply to triads, anyhow."

No wonder they hadn't been at her fingertips—the Indoctrination Academy had spent half an hour on triads, if that. "I remember the indoctrinator saying that there hasn't been a triad for . . ." Had it been 200 years? No, 210 years.

"For 228 years," Finney said, impressing Lesley. Finney had known off the top of her head; she hadn't touched the comm station on her desk. One of her interests was the history of the Chosen Tradition—she sometimes lectured about it at the Military Academy—but still.

"One seems to show up about every 350 years, so I doubt we'll see one in our lifetime," Finney continued.

"Maybe I should study one or two, just in case we do."

Finney snorted. "If the Chosen Council gives us a triad, the only officers who won't be scrambling to brush up on those articles are historians and people like me. So don't waste your time on them. You have enough to do already."

That was certainly true.

Finney leaned forward and clasped her hands on the edge of her desk. "Have you told Mo yet? About your plans?"

"Not yet. I didn't want to tell her while we were flying domestic, in case she wanted time alone. It's hard to get away from someone on a space station, and we only had a few days at home between rotations."

Finney lifted an eyebrow. "As opposed to getting away from someone when you're on a ship with her for six months?"

"That's why I'm going to tell her tonight, while we still have two weeks off," Lesley said, knowing how feeble that sounded. However, the truth would sound worse: that she was so terrified of telling Mo, she'd delayed the conversation too long. Her unspoken plan hung between them, mocking every word and making everything she said about the future feel like a lie. She'd never lied, but at the same time, she'd held back the truth—and hated herself. Lately it had become easier to draw back from Mo and avoid the issue altogether.

Mo must have sensed it. She hadn't said anything, but she'd grown subdued over the past month. Lesley wanted to bridge the widening chasm between them; she wanted the rest of their time together to be honest—if Mo wanted to stay together. She desperately hoped Mo would.

Finney's comm station beeped three times in rapid succession. "I have to go. My son's giving a presentation at the Learning Academy and I promised I'd be there." She rolled back her chair and stood. "Are you heading to the train station?"

Lesley nodded.

"We can continue this conversation on the way, then."

They put on their cloaks and Finney flicked off the light. Though Lesley was half a head taller than Finney, she had to hustle to keep up with her as she strode to the train station.

"Don't forget to wear your dress uniform for the reception," Finney said.

She hated her dress uniform; it always felt tight around her neck.

"I'll be introducing you to quite a few officers, including a couple of admirals."

Lesley's stomach fluttered. "I'll try not to say anything stupid."

"You don't have to say much. We want them to become familiar with your name, that's all. Many of them probably already are, given how often you're on the monitors."

After graduation, she'd moved on to recording announcements available to all Rymellans. Much to Lesley's embarrassment, people were starting to recognize her wherever she went.

"We'll meet you at station B2-3 at 19:30."

We? Right—she'd meet Finney's Chosen. She'd seen him from a distance, but had never spoken to him.

"And don't worry about the reception. Stick close to me, follow my lead, and you'll be fine."

Despite her apprehension at meeting powerful members of Interior, the reception was the least of Lesley's worries. Telling Mo about her plan to transfer to Interior intimidated her more than conversing with admirals. If she survived the conversation with Mo, she could survive anything.

MO SLID OPEN the aviacraft door and looked down at the two bags stuffed with candies. Climbing aboard would be difficult with them weighing her down. Mama wasn't empty-handed, but several seed packets and a gardening book wouldn't hinder her momentum. "How about you get on first and then I'll pass the candies to you?"

In response, Mama entered the craft and put the seeds and book into one of the cargo holders, then motioned for Mo to pass her the candies. "Are you sure the craft will lift off with these on board?" she said with a smile as she lifted the bags from Mo's hands. "I thought this tour was for six months, not six years."

Mo grinned and hoisted herself into the craft. "I want to take a selection with me, just in case. I have no idea what the *Falcon*'s Trading Centre carries." She slid into the pilot's seat. "Seatbelts," she said, fastening her own.

"Yes, Lieutenant."

Mo grinned again, so glad she'd decided to spend the afternoon with Mama instead of moping around in her room, dreaming up all sorts of doomsday scenarios about her and Les. Worrying about it all the time was skewing her perspective. Okay, Les was reading Interior material, but she was still in Defence. Mo had seen Les's orders to report to the *Falcon*, so there was nothing to worry about. If she didn't stop blowing everything out of proportion, she'd squander away the next two weeks with everyone and regret it the moment she left the planet. She wanted to start the tour on a positive note, not a remorseful one.

And what a tour it would be! She'd see Argamon. Argamon! She sometimes forgot it was an actual planet; she couldn't wait to see it up close. And serving aboard a research ship would be a whole new experience—for her, Les, David, several pilots she'd flown with on 72.

Once again, they'd be the new recruits, learning their way around the *Falcon* and adjusting to a new lifestyle. Too bad Ann would be on board. Oh well, she couldn't have everything.

She entered the coordinates for the Middleton estate and engaged the automatic pilot. The craft ascended, rotated, and burst in the direction of C3. After checking the navigation panel to ensure they were on course, Mo leaned back in her seat. Five minutes and they'd be home.

"You seem less tense," Mama observed.

"I am. It's a glorious day, I'm in a pilot's seat, and I'm with my mama." If Les were here, things would be perfect. She turned to Mama. "I'll help you plant the flowers, if you like."

Mama nudged Mo's cheek with her knuckle. "You've never shown any interest before."

"Yeah, well, I've never been out of reach for six months before, either. If I plant them with you, they'll remind you of me."

"Don't be silly," Mama said, rolling her eyes. "I won't need anything to remind me." She paused. "I guess I'll have to limit myself to Trading Centres near home, or spend hours on the train."

"Oh, so that's it. You'll miss having your personal pilot around."

"Exactly." Mama winked, then grew serious. "You know I'll miss you."

Mo's throat tightened. "I'll miss you too, Mama. And Papa. I'll even miss Nathan and—"

She shot forward when an alarm sounded, both audibly and in her mind. They should be over C4 by now, but the navigation system hadn't chimed when they'd crossed the border. Shock coursed through her when she read their current coordinates. The craft had drifted off course—they were heading toward B5!

"What is it?" Mama asked.

"Autopilot acting up," Mo said casually, even though the auto-navigation system had sounded the alarm. "I'll switch to—"

The craft suddenly dropped. Mama shrieked. "What's happening?"

Mo disengaged auto-navigation and grasped the navigational control with both hands. She rotated the altitude dial with her thumb to ease the craft to a higher altitude. Nothing happened. She rotated it again. Nothing. The altitude readout continued to fall. She tried to steer the craft, to see if it would respond. No response. The navigational control system had failed. They were going down. And there was nothing she could do.

She hit the emergency communication button on the comm panel. "This is Lieutenant Middleton, aviacraft 7652. Navigational control has failed. Current coordinates C5-885-227. Altitude 443 and falling. Advise."

"Lieutenant Kent. We have you, Lieutenant," came a reply moments later. "Dispatching tractors. Intercept two minutes, thirty seconds."

She glanced at the altitude readout. "They won't make it in time."

"Projecting impact coordinates and conditions."

Mo waited impatiently. If the craft continued its somewhat controlled descent and they came down in a wooded area, they might survive.

She heard Kent suck in his breath. "Lieutenant, you're on an impact course with the B5-1 Learning Academy!"

No! "Estimated time to impact?"

"Ninety seconds."

"Mo, that academy is filled with children!" Mama shouted.

"Contact the B5-1 Learning Academy and tell them to evacuate immediately," Kent barked, sounding more distant than he had previously.

"They don't have enough time." Her voice sounded far away, but Mo felt calm and in control of herself, at least. Somehow, she had to alter the craft's course. "Impact coordinates?"

"Roughly B5-072-235. Unless you change course, you'll hit the eastern wing. Do you have any nav control at all?"

"None." But there had to be some way to change the—yes, that might work. However . . . "One moment." She muted her side of the comm connection and looked at Mama. "I might be able to miss the academy by—"

"Seventy seconds," Kent said.

"—venting some chemicals and ejecting parts of the craft. Important parts. Once I do that, the craft will probably go into a spin. We'll go down. Hard. Do you understand?" She stared at Mama's ashen face and willed her own not to tremble.

Mama gulped. "I understand," she said with only a slight tremor. "But all those children . . . we have to save the children. Do what you have to do."

Mo reopened her side of the connection. "I'm going to vent energy cells one through five and eject cells six through twenty. That should push the craft east, altering its course enough to miss the academy."

"But you'll lose all power! And it might not work."

"It's that or the academy."

Silence, then, "I've already dispatched medical."

"Time to impact?"

"Forty-five seconds. Are you sure about this?"

"Yes. Middleton out." Mo terminated the connection and punched in the override code that would allow her to disable the craft in flight. To her relief, a beep signaled success. Only navigation, then. "I'm sorry, Mama," she said as she rapidly queued up a series of directives. Sorry they'd never plant those flowers.

"I'm proud of you," Mama said, her voice breaking. "Proud."

With a lump in her throat, Mo braced herself. One tap on the panel and the craft would commit suicide, taking them with it.

"Mo, the academy!"

Yes, she could see it now, hurtling toward them. Again, that calm. She held out her right hand and felt Mama's slip into it. With her left, she tapped the panel. At first nothing happened, but then the craft started to veer east.

"It's working!" Mama exclaimed. "Mo, it's working!"

The academy disappeared from view. Mo opened her mouth to whoop, but suddenly it felt as if the bottom had dropped out of the craft. Mama screamed; Mo's grip tightened. She was thrown back against her seat. Pressure on her chest. *Can't . . . breathe.* Ears—bursting. She tried to cry out—Mama! Les! *I'm sorry, Les. Had to save the children. Had to sa—*

LESLEY GAZED OUT over the lake and sighed. Two hours of pacing the beach while rehearsing what she'd say to Mo, and she still wasn't ready. Perhaps she should wait until she was satisfied that she'd found the right words. If she gave it more thought—no. No more excuses. She'd already left it too long. It had to be tonight.

She pulled out her comm unit and punched in Mo's code. Mo didn't answer. "Um, it's me," Lesley said after listening to Mo's message. "Do you want to go for a walk tonight? I want to talk to you about something,

   DISOBEDIENCE MEANS DEATH

something important. I know you mentioned the lake, but maybe we can do that tomorrow." They'd never argued here; she wanted to keep it that way. "Beep me, okay?"

There, she'd committed herself. Mo would be bursting to find out what she wanted to discuss; she'd probably ask when she beeped. Lesley would promise to tell her as soon as they got together, and Mo would pester her until she did.

Her comm unit beeped before she'd slid it back into its holder. Expecting to see Mo's name, she smiled at the display, then frowned. "Yes, Mama."

"Where are you?"

"At the lake."

"Come home."

The urgency in Mama's voice set Lesley's heart pounding. "Why?"

"Just come home, Lesley, as quick as you can." The connection went dead.

She broke into a run, slipping the comm unit into her cloak pocket instead of its holder. With her feet sinking into the sand, it took forever to get off the beach. She'd ridden her bike to the train station on her way to see Finney, and then to the lake when she'd returned; she'd left it leaning against a tree at the side of the path. Practiced at mounting a moving bike without catching her cloak in its wheels, Lesley grabbed the bike's handlebars, ran with it, and hopped on. She pedalled as fast as she could. Her legs ached and her breath grew ragged with the effort of feeding her hungry lungs, but she kept up the pace. Something was wrong. She could feel it.

But as she rode up to the house and slammed on the brakes, sending a spray of dirt into the air, she wondered if she'd read something into Mama's voice that wasn't there. Nobody rushed out to greet her. Everything seemed quiet.

After maneuvering the bike into the bike rack, she entered the house. Her heart pounded again, but not from exertion. Someone was crying. She peered into the living room—Andrew! Why was he crying? And why was he crying here? Should she go in and comfort him? What in the flaming Argamon was going on?

"Lesley," a voice hissed behind her.

She turned around. Mama beckoned to her and walked into the dining room. Lesley followed, her apprehension rising. A close look at Mama's face didn't reassure her—Mama had shed tears. Mama! "What's going on?" she asked, fear making her voice harsh.

"There's been an accident." Mama drew a deep breath. "Lesley . . . Mo's aviacraft went down."

No. No, no, no. It couldn't be—Mo was an excellent pilot, she—there was no way. "Are you sure?"

Mama closed her eyes and nodded.

Andrew was crying! Andrew was flaming crying! She hugged herself, braced herself. "How is she?" *Don't say it, Mama. Don't say it.*

"She's alive, but critical."

Critical. She started to shake. "What happened?" she shrieked. "Why did the craft go down? What flaming happened?"

"I don't know, Lesley. All I know is that it went down somewhere in B5."

"B5? What was she doing up in B5?"

"I don't know. I overheard the military say it crashed in B5. That's all I know."

"The military?" Asking clipped questions was all she could manage. Half of her was holding the conversation; the other half was holding a tidal wave of panic at bay.

"They were with Michael. They flew him to the infirmary."

"Was Susan with him?"

Mama's hand went to her mouth. She stared at Lesley.

"Don't tell me Susan doesn't know. Where is—" She went cold with dread. Mama was trying not to cry. "Mama, what is it?"

"Susan was with her, on the craft," Mama whispered.

Lesley swallowed and gripped the back of one of the dining room chairs. "How is she?"

Mama's fingers trembled. "She's dead."

Her mouth moved, but nothing came out; she felt as if all the air had been sucked from her. Susan, dead? Dead! *No. Argamon, no.*

The front door slammed. "Adelaide," Papa called.

Mama turned. "In here."

Papa strode into the room. "I got here as fast as I could." He held out his arms to Mama.

The sight of them embracing threatened Lesley's fragile composure. He let go of Mama and reached for Lesley. His reassuring presence, the feel of his stubble against her cheek, brought tears to her eyes. She used every shred of willpower to not cry unabashedly into his shoulder. She'd cry later, once she knew Mo would be all right. And Mo *would* be all right. She had to be. "Do you know which infirmary she's in, Mama?" Lesley asked when she trusted herself to speak.

"The one in B5-1."

Almost two hours by train. "I need to be there."

"You'd better go with her, Alan. Michael's in a terrible state. I tried to get him to stay until you arrived, but he wanted to go right away. I'm not sure he knows what he's doing."

Papa frowned. "Will you be all right? Why don't you come with us?"

Mama shook her head. "I can't. Michael dropped Andrew here because he didn't want him at the infirmary."

"Andrew's here?"

"Yes, and we can't leave him by himself. He said he wanted time alone, but I should see how he's doing." She covered her mouth with her hands.

"What?" Papa said, grasping Mama's shoulders.

"As far as I know, only Michael and Andrew know. Nobody else knows! Michael wasn't in any condition to tell them."

"You'd better beep them before they see it on the monitors."

"Beep Neil," Lesley said. "No, Barbara." Neil shouldn't hear about Susan and Mo over a comm unit. The news would upset Barbara, but Susan was Neil's mama and Mo was his sister. "He'll probably beep everyone else or ask you or Barbara to do it." Enough of this. She wanted to be near Mo, will her to survive. "We should get going."

Papa hugged Mama again. "We'll beep you, let you know how she's doing."

"All right. I'll check on Andrew." Mama paused. "Then I'll beep Barbara." Her face left no doubt that she wasn't looking forward to it.

"Come on," Papa said to Lesley.

They decided to ride to the train station, both anxious to get to the infirmary as quickly as possible. They joined several c3 residents on the train platform; Lesley managed to return their waves, but not their smiles. Look at them, going about their business as if today were just another day. It wasn't. Susan was dead. Mo was fighting for her life. Yet everyone and everything looked so normal. Didn't they realize that Mo was dying? Argamon, she was dying!

No, she was fighting for her life! *Fighting!* Those other thoughts—not allowed. Lesley had to stay positive, for Mo, and to hold herself together. That tidal wave of panic was still roiling beneath the surface; she wouldn't burden Papa with a hysterical daughter right here on the platform.

On the train she stared out the window, even though there was nothing to see. The more she tried not to think about Mo, the more Mo entered her mind. She pushed away the negative thoughts and desperately searched for something—anything—remotely positive or reassuring. Whatever had happened, it must have happened quickly. Given that Mo was critically injured and Susan was . . . dead, the craft must have gone down hard. Susan probably hadn't known they were crashing, and Mo? Perhaps seconds before the aviacraft crashed. At least that was something. They hadn't suffered long, if at all.

But what *had* happened? Had the craft just dropped from the sky? Mo could have handled most emergencies—done her best to descend in a controlled manner, or even ditched in an area with a high probability of survival.

"I can't believe it," Papa said, breaking into her thoughts. "Poor Michael."

She turned to him and noted his drawn face. "I've known Susan almost as long as I've known your mama," he said. "She made me feel welcome when I was adjusting to a new sector—well, a new life, really. I can't believe she's gone." He sighed. "I don't know how Michael will cope. At least he won't have to deal with the loss of his daughter, because Mo will survive. She will."

Lesley didn't think she could talk about Mo right now. Instead she asked a question for which she already knew the answer. "Were Susan and Michael Joined when you met Mama?"

"Yes. They received their Papers a few years before we did. And I think Neil was three when Karen came along. In fact, Mary was—"

"Excuse me, Alan." Alice Timson, a C3 resident who lived three estates south of the Thompsons, stood in the aisle, her comm unit in hand. "My Chosen just beeped and said Susan and Mo were in an accident. Do you know if it's true?"

Papa nodded. "I'm afraid it is."

"Oh dear," Alice said, placing her hand against her chest. "How are they?"

"Didn't Paul tell you?"

"No. He didn't know."

"Oh." He swallowed. "Mo's in an infirmary in B5. That's where we're going now. I don't know how she's doing. Susan . . ." He gripped the arm of his seat. "I'm sorry to have to tell you this, Alice, but she didn't make it."

The blood drained from Alice's face. "Oh no. Oh, that's terrible. Oh no." She made a beeline for the bathroom at the rear of the car.

Lesley met Papa's eyes. "I had to tell her," he mumbled. "It'll be on the monitors soon."

She turned back to the window. Argamon, the crash had actually happened. It wasn't that she hadn't believed Mama, but now it was starting to sink in. Soon everyone would know; everyone would be talking about it. She rubbed her forehead. Arriving at the infirmary, seeing Michael, hearing details about Mo's injuries—that was when it would really hit home. She'd have to control herself, remain strong for Mo. To keep her mind busy, she recited articles of Law.

They were directed to the critical care section when they arrived at the infirmary. "She said waiting room 3A," Papa said as they hurried along a corridor, scanning room numbers.

They hesitated outside 3A. Once they opened that door . . . Papa pushed it open.

Michael started to rise from his chair, then lowered himself back down. "Oh, it's you. I thought it was a physician. In surgery—that's all they keep telling me. In surgery. I've been here over three hours and I don't know any more than I did when I arrived." He exhaled sharply.

Lesley decided to follow Papa's lead, grateful that she wasn't facing Michael alone. All thoughts of peppering him with questions about Mo and the crash fled her mind. She'd never seen him so pale, nor so small.

"We're so sorry about Susan," Papa said. "A terrible, terrible loss. If there's anything we can do—if there's anything you need from us, don't hesitate to ask."

"Right now, all I need is to know that Mo will be all right. I can't lose both of them . . . I can't. Losing Susan . . . the only thing holding me together is knowing that she'd want me to be here. That's what she'd want. I'm doing what she'd want." He twisted a handkerchief in his hands. "I keep hoping someone will walk through that door and tell me it's all been a mistake, that my Chosen isn't dead and my daughter isn't in surgery. Because I don't know what I'll do without Susan, Alan. I don't know what I'll do without her. And if Mo dies . . . I . . ." He shook his head and covered his eyes with the handkerchief.

Papa sat next to him. "You'll get through this," he said in a soothing tone. "You have your children, your friends, your extended family. . ."

Lesley moved away from them. Though Michael hardly seemed aware of her presence, she wanted to give him privacy. She felt awkward—under normal circumstances, he wouldn't allow her to witness him in such pain.

Her comm unit beeped. Finney. She motioned to Papa that she'd take it outside and stepped into the corridor.

"I just heard," Finney said. "How's Mo?"

"She's in surgery. We're waiting for a physician to come see us."

"I'm sorry about Susan. I know your families are close."

"Thank you." Perhaps she'd feel Susan's death later. At the moment, all she could think about was Mo. "Do you know what happened? I don't know anything except that they crashed."

"I spoke to one of the military at the scene. I don't know if what he told me is accurate, though. He's not one of the crash investigators, he just overheard snippets of conversation between them."

"What did he hear?"

   DISOBEDIENCE MEANS DEATH

"Well, he said Mo intentionally crashed."

What?

"Something about ejecting energy cells. Apparently they would have hit the B5-1 Learning Academy if she hadn't done that."

Hit the—navigation must have failed. Argamon, Mo had known exactly what would happen to them, and Susan might have known, too. They'd known—they'd sacrificed themselves for the academy. Lesley's composure started to crumble. No, not here, out in the corridor. Not before she'd heard the extent of Mo's injuries.

"They're calling Mo a hero," Finney said. "Hundreds of children were in that academy, and their instructors."

She pressed her lips together and struggled to stem the tide.

"I gather that ejecting the cells resulted in an instant loss of power?" Finney said.

If she opened her mouth to reply, she'd lose the battle and collapse into a weeping heap. As it was, she brushed away an escaped tear.

"Lesley?"

Focus on Finney. Answer the question. "Um . . ." Her voice was shaking. From the corner of her eye, she caught a flash of gold as a Chosen Council courier strode past.

"Think about it and beep me later, let me know how Mo is doing," Finney said.

"I'm sorry, I'm . . ."

"It's okay, Lesley. Beep me later, or tomorrow." The connection went dead. She slid her comm unit into its holder and wiped her eyes.

Matthew was coming up the corridor. "Lesley! How is she?"

"I don't know. We're waiting for a physician." She followed him into the waiting room.

Papa and Michael had both stood, hoping for a physician. "I can't believe Mama's gone," Matthew said, embracing Michael and holding him tightly. "I can't believe it."

Lesley felt Papa's arm slip around her shoulders. She leaned into him, grateful for the support. His comm unit beeped. She shifted position so he could slide it from its holder.

"How's Mo?" Mama said.

"She's in surgery. That's all we know."

"Word is spreading. I'm telling people to come here."

Papa glanced at Michael and Matthew. "I think that's best."

"Mary's here. So is Barbara. Neil has gone to get Nathan."

"Nathan!" Michael exclaimed, letting go of Matthew. "How could I forget Nathan? It's visitation day next week. He'll be looking forward to seeing his mama." His Adam's apple bobbed.

"Neil will tell him," Matthew murmured.

Michael sat with a thud and buried his face in his hands.

Someone knocked at the waiting room door and swung it open. A physician stepped into the room.

"A physician just arrived. I'll beep you later," Papa said, quickly terminating the connection.

Michael and Matthew were already on their feet; Matthew held Michael's arm. Lesley could hardly breathe. If the physician said Mo had died—no. Don't even think it.

"Michael Middleton?" The physician's gaze shifted between Michael and Papa.

Michael stepped forward. "I'm Michael Middleton."

The physician nodded and shut the door. "I'm Physician Sands. I'm coordinating your daughter's care team. First of all, I want to express my condolences for the loss of your Chosen."

"Thank you," Michael said. "But what about my daughter?"

"She's just come out of surgery. I'm pleased to tell you that she's going to be all right."

Lesley hugged Papa and blinked back tears. Mo would be all right. She'd be all right.

"We've moved her to an accelerated healing chamber. Depending on how her body responds, she'll remain there anywhere from three to five days." He paused. "The right side of her body suffered most of the trauma. She broke several bones, her right lung collapsed, and she has chemical burns on her right side. In addition, we stopped some internal bleeding during the surgery. Despite all that, she was very lucky—she didn't suffer a head injury. I'll provide you with detailed information about her injuries tomorrow, after you've had a chance to digest what I've just told you."

Lesley held Papa tighter. The summary of Mo's injuries was bad enough.

"Will there be any scarring?" Matthew asked quietly.

"Not if we do our job properly. Dermagenesis has already received her genetic material from the Chosen Council and is growing new skin."

Michael had grabbed Matthew's arm for support. "Can I see her?"

"Not while she's undergoing accelerated healing. The chamber is sterile, and even if you could enter it, you wouldn't see much of her. The body requires a lot of support while it's undergoing the process, and since her broken bones will be knitting, it's important that she remain absolutely still. That's why she'll remain sedated until the process completes. And she'll be extremely tired once she's brought around. In fact, she'll experience fatigue for the next month or so."

The next month or so? But Mo was due to report to the *Falcon* in two weeks. Lesley had feared for Mo's life; now she worried that she'd be separated from her sooner than she'd anticipated.

"You said she'd be in the chamber for up to five days," Michael said. "But my Chosen's farewell ceremony . . ."

"I'm afraid she'll have to miss it. I'm sorry."

"No. I . . . understand."

"Is there any reason for us to remain here?" Papa asked.

Sands shook his head. "I'll beep you immediately if there's any change. Otherwise, there's really no reason to be here until we bring her around." His gaze shifted to Michael. "Would you like to be present when that happens?'

Michael nodded. Lesley wanted to be there too, if Michael would let her.

"That's all I have to say for now. Do you have any further questions?" Nobody spoke. "I'll dispatch updates to you on a regular basis. I'll also dispatch my comm code to you. If you have more questions later, don't hesitate to use it. I'll beep you tomorrow to provide you with more details about Ramona's injuries." His mouth turned up at the corners. "Don't be alarmed when you see my name on the display."

"Thank you," Matthew said. Michael nodded to Sands, unable to speak.

"I'll leave you, then. Please, take your time and leave when you're ready." He nodded to them and left the room.

"You heard what he said," Michael said gruffly the moment the door shut. "There's no point hanging around here. I can't do anything for Mo right now." He pulled out his comm unit, then collapsed back into a chair and grabbed his head, his comm unit still in his hand. "I was just about to beep your mama, to let her know we're leaving," he said to Matthew. "But she'd be here, wouldn't she? She wouldn't be at home." His eyes widened and he reached up to Matthew. "I don't know where she is. I don't know where they've taken her. I've been so worried about Mo, I forgot about her. How could I forget about her? Where is she? Where have they taken her?"

"The military who brought you here must have told you, or at least given you a code to beep," Papa said, using the same soothing tone he'd used earlier. "Let's go. When we get home, we'll take care of Susan."

Matthew helped Michael to his feet. "Come on, Papa. We need to go now."

As they walked down the corridor, Lesley couldn't help wondering if Mo was nearby. She wanted to go to her, hold her, tell Mo how grateful she was that she was still alive. But it would be days until Mo came around; days until she found out her mama was dead.

LESLEY SLIPPED OUT the Middletons' back door and strolled away from the house, glad for a moment of solitude. Most of the guests had trickled away, leaving a mess the caterers had started to clear. She'd only be in their way.

Apparently she wasn't the only one who'd sought a bit of peace and quiet. Mama stood on one of the paths that led south into the Middleton estate. Lesley stopped next to her and looked up at the dark clouds. "At least the rain held off," she said. It had threatened throughout that morning's farewell ceremony, held at the Middleton crypt's entrance.

"Mmm," Mama murmured.

"I'm glad the weather didn't discourage anyone from coming." Mourners had jammed the area outside the crypt, leaving only a narrow path for the undertakers. They'd gingerly carried the closed casket to the entrance, where the Middleton family waited.

     DISOBEDIENCE MEANS DEATH

A closed casket was unusual; Lesley had tried not to think of the possible reasons for it. She'd focused her thoughts on Mo, who still lay in an accelerated healing chamber, "progressing as expected." Perhaps it was silly, but she'd felt as if she were at the ceremony not only for herself, but to represent Mo. Others would scoff if they knew—she and Mo weren't bound to each other in a manner Rymellans recognized—but she'd felt that way, all the same.

Mo would have been proud of her papa. Despite the dark circles under his eyes testifying to a lack of sleep, and the pallor of his skin, Michael's voice had been strong when he'd read his prepared words. Mo's siblings had struggled to appear stoic, an occasional flash of a handkerchief the only sign of their grief. Even little Jacob had remained quiet for the most part. When he'd started to fuss, Barbara had gently rocked him in her arms and he'd settled down, unaware of the tremendous loss he'd suffered. He'd understand later, when he listened to stories about the grandmama he'd never know.

Enough! Lesley had felt gloomier than the sky all day; these maudlin thoughts weren't helping. She turned her mind back to the practical. "Did you invite the Middletons to supper?" she asked Mama. "You said you were going to."

Mama didn't respond; she continued to stare up the path.

"Mama?"

Mama's eyes focused on her. "It's so final, isn't it, when the crypt door closes. Then everyone has their sandwiches and tziva and goes home, and that's it. The end. We're all expected to get on with our lives, as if nothing's happened."

She realized that Mama hadn't heard a word she'd said.

"It doesn't seem all that long ago that Susan and I were skipping down this path. And now she's gone."

Lesley felt her throat tighten. She and Mo had used the same path—it led to another path that, in turn, led to the lake. When they were young, they'd skipped. Later, they'd done a couple of other things along the way, things Mama and Susan wouldn't have done. Not with each other, anyway.

"We may have had our differences, have wanted different things for our children, but that didn't stop us from being friends," Mama continued. "We still talked just about every day. Do you know what had been on Susan's mind lately?"

Lesley shook her head.

"You and Mo. She was worried. We all are." Mama gazed back into the distance. "When you and Mo first showed an interest in each other, we all thought, 'How cute! Our daughters are dating.'" She paused. "It's not cute anymore, Lesley. It hasn't been cute for a while. We keep hoping you'll sort things out yourselves, but there's no sign of that happening."

"Do we have to talk about this today, of all days?" Lesley asked with an exasperated sigh.

"Yes, we do. Your papa would rather stick his head in the sand, Michael will be distracted for a while, and Susan's gone. That leaves me to make sure you do what you have to do. And I do mean you, because you know Mo won't do it."

Lesley hesitated, then decided to be honest. Mama would only badger her, otherwise. "I am dealing with it, but . . . well, I haven't talked to Mo about it yet, and I want to do that before I tell anyone else about my plans. I was about to tell her, but then the accident happened." She swallowed. "I'll have to wait for a bit. You can't expect me to dump it on her now."

Mama studied her. "No, I suppose not. But you can't leave it too long."

"I won't."

"And you'd better not be lying to me." Mama's face hardened. "If you disgrace the Thompson and Middleton names, I'll never forgive you. I loved Susan, as much as friends can love each other. I've shed tears for her, several times. You're my daughter, and I love you. But if you end up at an execution site, I won't shed a single tear for you. Do you understand? Not one tear."

Lesley shook with rage. Her hands balled into fists; she couldn't speak. Rain splattered onto the path. She felt a drop hit her head, then another.

"Don't disappoint me," Mama said as she wiped a raindrop from her cheek.

She was about to say that she couldn't believe Mama would even consider the possibility that she'd die at an execution site when a cacophony of voices rose behind her. She spun around.

"What now?" Mama snapped, looking toward Susan's garden, where the commotion seemed to be originating. Lesley followed Mama over to Neil, Barbara, and Mary, who were huddled near it.

"It's raining, Papa. Come inside," Neil was saying.

Now Lesley could see Michael kneeling in the dirt, pulling at a weed.

"Papa, please! Come inside," Mary said.

"There are weeds. She wouldn't want weeds," Michael said.

"There are only a few." Neil carefully stepped around flowers to grasp Michael's arm, then frowned when Michael pushed him away.

"We'll come over tomorrow and weed the garden," Barbara said. "I promise."

"I have to do it now." Rain dripped from Michael's hair and nose. "She wouldn't want weeds. If she were here, there wouldn't be any."

Lesley's vision blurred.

"Michael!" Mama's voice cracked. "Get up! You'll catch cold. Susan wouldn't weed in the rain, you know that. So come on—inside! You're getting your clothes dirty and we're all getting soaked."

"We'll keep up the garden," Mary said. "Matthew said he'd tend to it."

"All of us will." Mama leaned over and looked Michael in the eye. "So come on. Inside."

Neil grasped his arm again. Michael struggled to his feet and allowed Neil to steer him into the house. Mama, Mary and Barbara shook their heads and followed them. Lesley stayed outside, letting the rain wash away her tears.

MO SLAMMED THE door to her and Les's room and marched down the dormitory's corridor. Why did Ross want to see her? She didn't have time for any nonsense—she had an exam tomorrow.

She bounded down the stairs to the first floor, swung open the lobby door, and stepped into Ross's office. "You wanted to see me?" she said to the back of Ross's chair.

The chair spun around. A broad smile spread across Ann's face. "Guess who just made lieutenant commander." She placed her hands behind her head, leaned back in the chair, and plunked one foot on top of the desk, then the other. "What, no congratulations? Did you hear what I said? Can you hear me, Ramona? Can you hear me? Ramona, can you hear me?"

No flaming way! She whirled and ran into the simulator.

"Ramona, can you hear me?"

"I told you, nobody calls her Ramona," Papa said. "If you keep calling her that, she'll never come around. Call her Mo."

Papa? She tapped the earpiece in her left ear.

A panel beeped—incoming hostile. She glanced at the sensors and gasped. A look out the cockpit window confirmed her worst fear. A learning academy! And it was heading her way. "This is Lieutenant Middleton, requesting assistance. I repeat, requesting assistance. A learning academy is on an intercept course. Advise."

Static crackled in her left ear.

"Can anyone hear me?"

Another beep. The academy was arming missiles!

"Mo, can you hear me?" said an officer she didn't recognize.

"Yes, I can hear you. Advise."

"Engage."

"No, there are children inside. I have to save the children. Advise."

"Mo, can you hear me?"

"Yes! Advise!" Funny, she was sure she was shouting, but it sounded like a whisper.

"She must be dreaming," the officer said.

"She wants you to tell her what to do." *Les! But where was she? There were no friendly craft in the vicinity.*

"Oh." The officer again. "Open your eyes, Mo."

"What?" Mo murmured.

"Open your eyes."

She opened her eyes.

"I think she's awake"—Papa, peering at her. Then Les was there, staring over Papa's shoulder. What was the matter with them? Les looked like she could burst into tears at any second, and Papa looked haggard and pale, as if he hadn't slept for days.

 DISOBEDIENCE MEANS DEATH

They drew back; suddenly Mo was looking up at a stranger. "Welcome back," the stranger said.

She wanted to pull the blanket up to her chin, but her right arm felt heavy and lethargic, as if she'd lain on it too long. Actually, the entire right side of her body felt that way. And though she'd apparently just awakened, she felt like closing her eyes and drifting off again. But not before she found out what this strange man was doing in her bedroom. She turned her head slightly. No, this wasn't her bed—hers didn't have bars attached to its side. "Where am I?" Her raspy voice shocked her.

"You're in the B5-1 infirmary," the stranger said. "I'm Physician Sands."

Infirmary? "What am I doing here?"

"I think I'll let your papa explain that to you." He said something to Papa, too low for her to catch, then left the room.

Papa sank into a chair near the bed; Les stood next to him. He took Mo's left hand. She waited, but he seemed reluctant to talk. "Papa—"

"Your brothers and sister wanted to be here, but I knew you'd be tired. I didn't want you to feel overwhelmed." He started to play with her fingers.

Yeah, okay. But . . . "Where's Mama?" She almost cried out when his grip tightened. "Papa?"

"You have no idea why you're here?" Les said.

She slowly shook her head.

Les looked at Papa, then back at her. "Mo, your aviacraft crashed."

What?

"You were badly hurt. You've just come out of an accelerated healing chamber."

Was that why her right side felt funny? "How long?"

Les hesitated. "Four days," Papa murmured.

Four days!

"Do you remember anything, anything at all about what happened?" Les asked. "What's the last thing you remember doing?"

Well, she'd been at the Trading Centre, choosing candies. No, she'd already traded for candies. And was . . . *She slid into the pilot's seat.* "Seatbelts," *she said, fastening her own . . . on the craft. Navigational control has failed. Current coordinates C5-885-227. Altitude 443 and falling.* She stared at Les. "Navigational control failed."

Papa's hand left hers. He covered his mouth.

"Mo, that academy is filled with children!" Wait. Mama had been there—in the craft with her. Mama had been in the craft! *We'll go down. Hard.* "Where's Mama? Where's Mama!" She tried to roll toward Papa, but didn't have the strength. His eyes glistened. *No!* She looked at Les. *Please, please say Mama's here at the infirmary, in another room.*

Les drew a deep breath. "Your mama was killed in the crash." Her voice broke. "I'm sorry."

Argamon, she'd killed Mama. She'd killed Mama! "Papa, I'm sorry. I'm so sorry."

"No, no," Papa murmured, shaking his head. "It was an accident. I'm just so grateful you're alive." He took her left hand again and touched it to his cheek.

It wasn't a flaming accident! She'd intentionally crashed the aviacraft, killing Mama. A tear rolled down her cheek. She wanted to brush it away, but her flaming, useless, stupid right hand wouldn't obey her.

Les gently wiped away the tear for her. "You saved all the children in that Learning Academy."

Yes, and killed Mama! Were they both stupid? Were they flaming imbeciles? They must be, all of them. Mama was dead. Hotshot pilot Lieutenant flaming Middleton had killed her. Yet here she was, fresh out of an accelerated healing chamber, all patched up, with her whole life ahead of her. *Idiots!*

They shouldn't have saved her. They should have let her die.

LESLEY'S ANTICIPATION GREW as she climbed the stairs to the infirmary's third floor. She'd last seen Mo three days ago, when Mo had come around. Mo was never awake for long, so Lesley had wanted to give others, especially Mo's siblings, an opportunity to visit.

Being separated from Mo, unable to even beep her, had been excruciating, and a frightening taste of what was to come. No matter what she'd been doing or who she'd been talking to, Mo had always been at the back of her mind. Everything else had been a distraction, to keep her busy until Mo was on her feet and life stopped being on hold. Was that what it would be like for the rest of her life? Would her Chosen, her daughters, and her career be one long distraction, a way to dull the pain until death ended it? Was going through the motions all she had to look forward to?

She forced a smile and walked into Mo's room. "You're sitting up!"

"Propped up, more like," Mo muttered. "They're threatening to walk me around the floor tomorrow."

"You think you'll be up to it?" She sat in the guest chair nearest the head of the bed and leaned forward.

"Maybe. My right side is starting to feel like it's mine again." Mo lifted her right hand and flexed her fingers. Her sleeve slid down to her elbow, revealing a patch of grafted skin. She pointed at it. "Neil said it's pinker than Jacob's bottom."

Following Sands' instructions for visitors, Lesley resisted the urge to touch it. Instead, she gently squeezed Mo's fingers, afraid of doing anything more, lest she hurt her. Mo squeezed back, but didn't meet Lesley's eyes. "Your papa said two crash investigators came to see you yesterday," Lesley said.

Mo closed her eyes and nodded. Lesley waited for her to elaborate, but Mo remained motionless. The silence lengthened. Just as Lesley started to suspect that Mo had fallen asleep, Mo spoke. "Did Papa tell you I'll be reporting to the *Falcon*?"

"Yes, he did." Much to her relief. "You won't be on duty for the first couple of weeks, but that's better than being assigned to another tour." Apparently Commander Baker, the officer in charge of the *Falcon*'s pilots, had consulted with Mo's care team before deciding that Mo would remain on the roster. The desire to have pilots who'd flown domestic together on the same tour had also factored into his decision. "And your papa also said they're going to let you out of here a few days before our report date." She tapped the top of Mo's hand. "So you'll have a few days at home, too."

"They also said they'd be willing to transfer me directly to the *Falcon*," Mo said. "I haven't decided what I want to do yet."

"You don't want to go home?" Lesley asked, surprise raising her voice.

Mo shrugged.

"I think your papa's assumed you'll be home." He'd been lamenting how empty the house felt with only Andrew and him in it, now that Nathan had returned to the Indoctrination Academy. He was looking forward to having Mo home, if only for a few days. "He started to see clients again today, only a couple, though. He said there's no point working full days until after you've left on tour, since he'll want to be home with you." Though she suspected that wasn't the only reason Michael was easing back into his regular routine. He wasn't ready to work a full day. He was still in shock—functioning, but barely.

"I don't see the point of going home."

Mo's words dismayed her. "I just thought that—well, I don't know, I thought you'd want to be with your family." And with her. "You won't see them for six months."

"I can see them here," Mo said flatly.

"But what about your mama? Don't you want to visit the crypt? You missed her farewell ceremony—"

"It'll take me all day to walk there."

Considering it normally took half an hour, Lesley doubted it would, even in Mo's weakened condition. Still, she said, "Then it'll take all day. I'll go with you. We'll take it as slow as you want. We can pack a lunch, have a picnic on the way. You can even nap if you want. I'll bring a book."

"No."

"If you let me know what article you'd like to slot, I can have it prepared."

"I said no!" Mo reached for the cup of water on a tray next to the bed and gulped some down.

"You won't have another opportunity for six months," Lesley said.

"You know, I was thinking about what happened." Mo set the cup back on the tray and closed her eyes again. "Maybe I shouldn't have ejected all the cells I didn't vent. Maybe ejecting only some of them would have lightened the craft enough, and we wouldn't have lost all power. The craft might not have spun if we'd still had power."

Lesley didn't know any details about the crash and Mo's actions in the cockpit, beyond what Finney had told her. She wanted to hear them, but not now, when Mo could fall asleep at any second. "From the little I know about what happened, it sounds like you didn't have much time to make a decision. Whatever you did worked. You missed the academy."

"I might have missed the academy if I'd ejected fewer cells."

"There's no point thinking about 'what ifs.'"

Her eyes still closed, Mo didn't reply.

"Let the investigators sort it out."

"What if they conclude I did the wrong thing?"

"Did they say anything to give you that idea?"

"No," Mo said, her face taut.

"Then don't worry about it." She'd expected Mo to be sombre and tired; she hadn't expected her to doubt her actions in the cockpit. She wanted to hold Mo, tell her that it hadn't been her fault. Navigational control had failed; Mo had made a difficult decision and saved hundreds of children. But Sands had been clear about the permitted level of physical contact. Again, Lesley had to be content with squeezing Mo's fingers.

The investigation would confirm that Mo had taken the appropriate action. Mo was a superb pilot with sound instincts. If she'd ejected all the cells, then that had been the only way to avoid hitting the academy, Lesley was sure of it. But Susan had died. Perhaps it was only natural for Mo to second-guess herself so soon after the crash.

"I think I'm going to fall asleep," Mo said.

"Oh," Lesley said, disappointed. "I guess I'll go, then. I'm not sure when I'll see you next." More long days of keeping herself occupied. "Your papa and Andrew are visiting tomorrow afternoon, and others want to visit, too. I'll try to squeeze myself in as soon as I can."

No response. Mo hadn't been joking when she'd said she was about to fall asleep. Lesley touched her lips to Mo's hand, then tucked it under the blanket. She rose and tip-toed away.

"Les," Mo said.

She turned.

Mo's eyes were on her. "I almost forgot. They delivered a new comm unit this morning, so you can beep me."

"That's great! I'll beep you later." It would be a struggle not to beep her every five minutes.

"If it's off, it means I'm asleep or have a visitor." Mo paused. "I had a

few messages. One was from you. You said you had something important you wanted to talk to me about."

Blood rushed to Lesley's face; she turned away. "Um, yeah," she said,
thinking furiously. "But it seems so trivial now, after what's happened.
Just me blowing something out of proportion. We can talk about it
later." Much, much later.

She snuck a look at Mo. Mo had closed her eyes again. Lesley crept
from the room, wanting to escape before Mo opened her eyes and saw
the guilt on her face.

MO ACCEPTED PAPA'S arm and leaned on him as they walked down
the medical aviacraft's exit ramp. She'd boarded it filled with dread,
expecting those final moments in her craft to come rushing back. But
medical equipment had jammed the craft's interior, leaving the pilot's
seat barely visible to passengers. Still, she hadn't dozed, despite being
overdue for a nap. She'd never relax in an aviacraft again.

"Let's get you inside," Papa said after he waved the craft off.

Her heart pounded as they approached the house. If she'd had her
way, she'd be back in her bed at the infirmary, not here. But Papa had
wanted her home, and she'd acquiesced, not wanting to add to the hurt
she'd already caused him.

The moment they stepped through the front door, the rest of the
family streamed into the hallway. Everyone spoke at once.

"Do you need help?"

"Do you want tziva?"

"Welcome home."

"Don't crowd her!"

Everyone was there. No, not everyone. Nathan had gone back to the
Indoctrination Academy. And . . . though she knew it was pointless, she
searched for her, expecting her to be hovering behind Neil, or to suddenly bustle in from the living room and hold out her arms. But that
would never happen again. The house would never be the same. The
family would never be the same. Her life would never be the same. *I'm
sorry, Mama.* Mo's eyes filled; she quickly looked at her feet.

"She's tired," Papa said. "Move out of the way so we can go into the
living room and sit down."

"No." She looked up. "I think it would be better if I went up to my room. I want to lie down." And get away from everyone. "I appreciate that you all came, though."

"We'll still be down here if you need us," Barbara said.

Neil stepped to her side. "Let me take your other arm." She didn't need his help in addition to Papa's, but nodded anyway.

A vase of limp flowers sitting on a table just inside the living room caught her eye. The dried petals surrounding its base and the curled edges of those still clinging to life condemned her. "I'm sorry, but I need to get into bed now." She cringed at the brave faces that peered back at her. Despite everyone's show of concern, they must blame her. How could they not? She'd survived; Mama hadn't. Maybe they were asking themselves the same question she'd had on her mind since she'd first awakened after the crash: had she subconsciously sacrificed Mama to save herself? She was the pilot—*she* should have died in the crash.

With Neil and Papa supporting her, she climbed the stairs, and averted her eyes as they passed Mama and Papa's bedroom. "I can make it from here," she said outside her bedroom door, but they remained at her side until she reached the bed.

Neil covered her with a blanket. "Do you want me to sit with you for a while?" he asked.

She shook her head. "Can you close the door?" They glanced at each other. "I'll be fine. I'll probably be asleep before you reach the bottom of the stairs."

"Wait." Papa fumbled in his cloak pocket, reminding her that she'd soon receive a new military cloak to replace the one she'd worn that awful day. She'd waved away the cloak Papa had brought to the infirmary, knowing that she'd only be outside for a few minutes. He still had it over his arm. "Here." He set her comm unit on the nightstand. "Beep me if you need anything."

She wouldn't—she'd feel silly beeping him when he was only downstairs, and she wanted to be left alone.

The door clicked shut. Footsteps receded along the hallway, then thumped down the stairs. The journey home had tired her. She closed her eyes and started to drift . . . *Lieutenant, you're on course to impact with the B5-1 Learning Academy! . . . They don't have enough time to fully evacuate . . . I'm going to vent energy cells one through five and eject cells six through twenty . . . Mama screamed, Mama screamed, Mama screamed!*

Her eyes snapped open; she covered her ears. Why had she ejected so many cells? If she'd ejected only nine through sixteen but vented one through eight, the extra force could have compensated for the extra weight and they wouldn't have lost all power. Or maybe venting one through five had been okay, but ejecting six through twenty had been unnecessary. If she'd only ejected six through eighteen, maybe the craft still would have altered course, but not gone into a spin.

She blew out a sigh and rolled onto her left side. If she'd kept her eye on the control panels instead of talking to Mama, maybe she would have noticed earlier that they'd drifted off course. A few extra seconds could have made all the difference. Or what if she'd vented the cells on the other side of the craft? If she'd vented eleven through fifteen and ejected one through ten, they still would have had sixteen through twenty. No, the craft had been on course to impact with the eastern wing of the academy. Venting the other side . . . too far west . . . still would have hit . . .

She closed her eyes.

Mo opened her eyes and squinted into darkness. A light flashed in her peripheral vision. She turned her head toward it and could just make out Les, sitting hunched over the desk. "How long have you been here?" Mo asked.

Les spun around and snapped off the cylindrical reading light in her hand. "Around half an hour. Can I turn on the light? I'm starting to go cross-eyed."

"Sure."

"I came earlier, when I saw the medical aviacraft," Les said as she pressed a button on the desk and bathed the room with light. "But they told me you'd gone to bed, so I went home for a couple of hours and then came back. At least I can sit with you while you sleep." She placed a bookmark in her book and snapped it shut. "I couldn't do that at the infirmary."

Mo swallowed. Les still cared.

"How are you feeling?" Les sat on the floor next to the bed and touched Mo's cheek. The tender gesture brought tears to Mo's eyes. She closed them. "I'm sorry, I should have beeped before I came over," Les said softly. "I hope I didn't wake you."

"You didn't." She opened her eyes. "Do you think I could have saved her? I keep thinking that if I'd reacted differently, come up with another plan . . ."

"I'm sure you took the right course of action."

"You weren't there."

"No, I wasn't. But you were, and you're a good pilot, with excellent instincts."

"I crashed the craft." Her voice quavered. "I killed her."

"No, you didn't. You did not kill her." Les shifted to a kneeling position. "Can you handle a hug?"

In response, Mo slid over and reached out with her left arm. Les cautiously embraced her, murmuring, "I don't want to hurt you."

Mo leaned into her, comforted by her warmth.

"You did what you had to do," Les said into Mo's ear. "It wasn't your fault, it was a horrible accident."

One in which she'd lived and Mama had died. Why had she survived? Had it been a fluke? Had the way she'd hit the ground or her position in the craft protected her? Had she somehow placed Mama in harm's way to save herself? She squeezed her eyes shut and let go of Les. "I'm sorry, Les, but I'm tired. Now's not a good time for a visit."

"So I did wake you up. I'm sorry." Les kissed Mo's forehead and stood. "I'll come again tomorrow. I'm going with Finney to that reception tomorrow night, but otherwise I'm free. Actually, no—I have to run an errand, but it won't take long." She paused. "I need to ask you something."

Mo cracked an eye open. "What?"

"I know you don't want to go to the crypt," Les raised her hands as if expecting an argument, "but I want to visit one more time before leaving on tour. I've prepared an article. I'm picking it up tomorrow afternoon. Do you want me to put your name on it, too?"

"Which article?"

"CT30."

She inwardly winced. CT30 belonged to the set of articles that addressed the obligations parents had toward their children. What about the obligations children had toward their parents? If there were such a set of articles, Mo was sure that not killing one's parents in a crash would be right up there on the list. Too bad it wasn't—Finney could put her out of her flaming misery and that would be that.

Rymellans often slotted CT30 for their parents, so she could understand why Les had chosen it. Their families were so close and they'd spent so much of their childhoods together that it had sometimes felt as if they each had two sets of parents. By slotting that article, Les would honour Mama. Mo would respect that, not make a mockery of the gesture by adding her name to it. "Don't put my name on it."

Les frowned. "Are you sure?"

"I'm sure. I want to slot an article myself." *Liar!* "Eventually."

"And you don't mind me slotting CT30?"

"No. Mama would like that." She pulled the blanket above her waist; she wished she could pull it over her head and hide beneath it for the rest of her life.

Les collected her book and reading light from the desk. Mo felt oddly detached when Les leaned over and gently kissed her on the lips. "I'll beep before I come tomorrow, see how you're feeling. And, of course, you can beep me."

"I know I'm not good company right now, but I'm glad you came, Les."

Les's answering smile didn't mask her concern. "Me too. Now get some rest."

She left the room. Mo could hear her talking to someone at the bottom of the stairs, then the front door thudded shut.

Moments later, Barbara poked her head into the room. "Do you want something to eat?"

She supposed she should, even though she wasn't hungry. "Something light, maybe?"

"I'll take a look at the list they gave your papa," Barbara said. "Do you want to come downstairs or would you rather I brought it up?"

If she could, she'd stay in her room until she had to report to the *Falcon*. "Can you bring it up?"

Barbara smiled. "Sure."

"Thanks." She didn't deserve Barbara's kindness. Not only had she killed Barbara's Chosen mama, but her son would never know his

    DISOBEDIENCE MEANS DEATH

grandmama. Mo rolled onto her side. There had to have been another way. If she'd vented cells six through ten instead of one through five, maybe the craft wouldn't have spun. Or maybe venting one through ten and not ejecting any cells would have been enough. No, the craft still would have been too heavy. But if she'd only ejected cells eleven through fifteen . . .

LESLEY TUGGED AT her collar for the umpteenth time and leaned over the safety railing to survey the reception below her. Finney must have introduced her to half the room; now the names and faces were nothing but a blur. Not long ago, the prospect of rubbing elbows with admirals and other high-ranking officers had intimidated her, but the accident had put everything into perspective. Mo had been at the back of her mind all evening. She'd seemed more alert that afternoon and mildly interested in the reception, but had only lasted about twenty minutes before declaring that she was tired.

Michael had said he'd had a terrible time persuading her to go for a walk, something she was supposed to do at least three times a day. He was still fragile and barely coping. Mo's behaviour—first not wanting to come home and now shutting herself away in her room—wasn't helping. He'd mentioned perhaps taking her to the crypt, but when Lesley had told him about Mo's reaction when she'd suggested it, he'd abandoned the idea. *She hasn't asked about the farewell ceremony*, he'd said in bewilderment. Nobody had expected her to come home with a smile on her face and a bounce in her step, but they hadn't expected her to be so withdrawn, either.

Perhaps they should give Mo her space. Everyone was concerned and wanted to be there for her, but if she truly wanted to be alone, buzzing around her was probably the worst thing they could do. It made them feel better, but not her.

Lesley knew she was floundering; she wanted to support Mo, but didn't know how. She'd never lost someone close to her, and in Mo's case, the circumstances under which that loss had occurred must be devastating—almost too much to bear. She couldn't imagine what Mo must be feeling. Instead of assuming that Mo needed her and wanted her around, she should follow Mo's lead, be there when Mo wanted her company and accept it when Mo didn't. Less than two weeks had passed since the crash, so it was still early days. Mo wouldn't want to be alone forever.

Finney stopped beside her and propped herself against the railing. "You all right?"

"I'm just thinking about Mo. She doesn't seem to want people around right now. She doesn't want to go to the crypt, either. I'm going by myself tomorrow."

"Give her time. It's still raw."

"That's why I'm not telling her about my plan to transfer—not yet." She'd wanted to tell Finney all evening. "I'm sorry if you find that disappointing, but I can't do it when she's so low."

Finney snorted and tapped her breastbone. "There is a heart beating in here, you know. Of course you can't tell her. It's not the right time." She shifted position and scanned the crowd below. "I think I've introduced you to everyone on my list. No, you haven't met Commodore Parker. Morton's been hogging him all night. I'd rather you not meet him at all than meet him with Morton present."

"You think he'll say something bad about me?"

"No, he'll likely have a dig at me. Normally I wouldn't care, but I want the focus to be on you, not me."

"Morton's opinion of you seems to differ from everyone else's." Lesley wanted to ask why, but doubted Finney would tell her.

Finney gazed expressionlessly ahead. "When I was at the Military Academy, Morton was a lieutenant. He hasn't changed much—he had the tendency to loudly berate cadets back then, too. One day I'd just left the dormitory and was walking to Building 5C when I heard someone shouting near the point where you veer left. You know where I mean?"

Lesley nodded.

"Well, as I got closer, I could see the path was blocked with people. Then I recognized Morton's voice. He was ripping someone apart, right in front of everyone. That someone turned out to be my roommate. From the sound of it, she'd left a public monitor without turning it off, but from the way he was going on, you would have thought she'd committed a Chosen Violation."

　DISOBEDIENCE MEANS DEATH

Finney shook her head. "I didn't even like the woman—she was a bit too vacuous for me. On a breezy day, you could hear the wind whistling between her ears, so I could certainly see her forgetting to turn off a monitor. But I don't like bullies, and he'd reduced her to tears."

"What did you do?"

"I didn't think, that's what I did. I steeled myself, marched up to him, and suggested that he'd made his point and it was time to stop, probably less diplomatically than I should have. You should have seen his face." Finney pressed her mouth into a thin line and bugged out her eyes, much to Lesley's amusement. "He turned his wrath on me, started railing on about how disrespectful I was, daring to tell him, a lieutenant, what to do. Remember, I was a cadet then. The gawkers were on my side, though, and he knew it. So he slunk off. And since then, he's never passed up an opportunity to put me down."

"Fortunately, nobody pays any attention to him," Brian, Finney's Chosen, said from behind them. They both turned. He must have overheard the latter part of the conversation. "Everyone knows that he'll still be the commander of the Military Academy when he retires, whereas you'll be an admiral," he said to Finney. "He must understand you better than he lets on, though. Otherwise, he'd stop. You'll eventually be in a position to crush him."

"I'd never use my position to hurt someone just because I don't like them."

"Exactly. And he must know that. Either that, or he's an idiot."

"Well, he is an idiot," Finney said, to laughter. Then, "No, I shouldn't have said that. He's good at what he does. The c6 Military Academy has an excellent reputation, mainly due to his knack for recognizing and grooming good teachers. But he knows nothing about what it's like to be an Interior officer on the outside, so he's not in a position to judge anyone's performance. That's why nobody takes his remarks about me seriously."

"Would you still have spoken up if you'd known that he'd hold a grudge against you?" Lesley asked. She could guess the answer, and Brian's nod indicated that he could, too.

"Oh, probably," Finney said. "Protecting the Way and protecting Rymellans go hand in hand. And despite how it turned out, I learned something important. I never reprimand anyone publicly. If I have something to say, I say it privately."

"Too bad Morton didn't learn anything," Brian muttered.

"What happened to the roommate?" Lesley asked. "Is she still in the military?"

"No," Finney said with a chuckle. "She was ejected as part of the first-year purge." She turned to Brian. "Had enough?"

"I'm ready whenever you are," he said.

Finney scanned the room again. "I don't think we'll get to Parker tonight, but that's all right, we'll catch him next time. Let's go."

They walked to the train station, only a couple of minutes away from the reception hall, in silence. When they reached the waiting area, Finney said, "It'll seem strange, not seeing you for six months. When you send me your analyses comments, let me know how you're doing."

"I will." She hoped Finney would reply. Now that they were saying good-bye, she realized how much she'd miss her.

"It was nice to finally meet you," Brian said. "I have the feeling we'll be attending more receptions together."

"It was nice meeting you, too." Lesley meant it—his relaxed manner had immediately put her at ease.

Finney nodded to her. "Enjoy your tour, Lieutenant. Good night."

She returned Finney's nod. "Good night, Commander."

The Finneys headed down to the train that would take them home. She waited until she couldn't see them before descending to her platform.

LESLEY HEFTED MO'S bag onto the bed and unzipped it. She lifted out a shirt and walked over to the closet. Though she'd already unpacked Mo's other bag and hung her uniforms, the closet and drawers were still half-empty. "Our quarters have more storage than I'd expected," she said to Mo.

"Mmm," Mo said absently.

She glanced over her shoulder. Mo was sitting at the comm station; she'd walked over and flicked it on the moment they'd entered her quarters. "What are you looking at?" Lesley asked.

"Oh, I just wanted to see what level of network access we have," Mo

     DISOBEDIENCE MEANS DEATH

said, her eyes still on the display. "It looks like we have the same access we had on 72."

"Good." Lesley hung the shirt, pleased that Mo was finally showing an interest in something other than lying in bed. Perhaps surviving her first aviacraft ride since the accident—well, the first ride in a craft similar to the one she'd lost—had lifted Mo's spirits. Lesley had flown them to the shuttle base in one of the Military Academy's aviacrafts. *Forget a three-hour train ride, I'll find you an aviacraft*, Ross had said when she'd beeped a couple of days ago to see how Mo was doing. *One of the 72 or 73 pilots can fly it back.*

She'd picked it up that morning, and had held her breath as she'd helped Mo into it and settled her into the passenger seat. She needn't have worried. Mo had sat quietly, albeit with her eyes closed for most of the journey. Lesley wasn't sure whether Mo had really been dozing, and it didn't matter. The important thing was that she'd done it.

She returned to the bag and pulled out a pair of badly folded track pants. This must be the bag Neil had finished packing—Michael had done a better job with the other one. She slipped the pants into a drawer, pulled a sweater from the bag, and hung it. Back to the bag, to lift another shirt—she dropped the shirt on the bed and stared at the framed image that had lain beneath it. Susan and Michael, near Susan's garden. They looked so happy . . . but now . . . The image had been on the mantel in the Middletons' living room! Mo loved this one. "Where do you want this?" she asked.

"What?" Mo said, still focused on the screen in front of her.

"This image." Lesley held it out to her. "Where do you want it? On the nightstand?"

Mo turned to look; her face tightened. "Put it back in the bag."

Back in the bag? "Don't you want it out?"

"I'll deal with it later."

"If you let me know where you want it, I can—"

Mo leaped to her feet. "Put it back in the flaming bag!" she screeched. "I don't want it out!"

"Okay, okay," Lesley said, taken aback. She made a show of putting the image back in the bag, then picked up the shirt. "When's your first appointment with the counsellor?" she asked casually as she hung it in the closet.

"Why?"

"Just wondering."

"The day after tomorrow, at 23:00."

"So you're shifting your sleep cycle with the rest of us?"

"Yeah, I figured that was best."

Lesley turned away from the closet. Mo was sitting again and had spun the chair to face her. "You better go," Mo said. "The orientation meeting is in half an hour. I can finish unpacking."

"I don't mind doing it. It'll only take me five minutes to get to the meeting room."

"You haven't unpacked your own stuff yet. Plus, I'm tired. By the time I've finished unpacking, I'll want to lie down."

Lesley was starting to wonder if Mo was really tired, or just claimed she was to get rid of people. "Does that mean you're not coming to the meeting? I know Baker said you don't have to, but we'll be getting a tour of the fighter launch area."

Mo shrugged. "I'll only slow you all down. I can check out the launch area another time."

"I'll drop in after the meeting, let you know how it went."

"I'll be in bed, so there's no point." Mo spun to face the station and tapped a key on its keyboard.

"Okay, but the ship's undocking at 19:00. David suggested we go to one of the observation decks." They'd watched numerous ships undock from 72. This time, they'd be on the ship. "I can come get you. You have time for a nap before then."

"I'd like to, but it's already been an active day. I don't want to push it."

"You won't see Rymel close up again for six months." No response. "How about I drop by after we've undocked, then?" Lesley was trying hard to keep exasperation out of her voice. "We can have a late supper."

Mo finally showed interest. "Can you bring us supper here?"

"Sure! And if you want, I'll stay over tonight."

"My right side's still tender."

"I didn't mean—"

"I know what you meant. I'm just saying that I can only sleep in certain positions right now. Sometimes I have trouble getting comfortable. I might keep you awake."

"I'll take my chances. We're supposed to try to stay awake until 03:00 tonight, anyway."

"Then maybe you better stay, to help keep me awake." Mo turned back to the comm station. "Now go, already."

Lesley stepped toward her, hoping for a parting kiss, but Mo continued to gaze at the station's display. She settled for patting Mo on the shoulder, then reluctantly left the room. Even though she'd have supper with Mo and stay overnight, she felt disheartened. Mo hadn't exactly been enthusiastic about spending time together. But what did Lesley expect? She was being selfish, expecting too much too soon after the accident. Mo was right—compared to the last two weeks, today had already been a busy day for her. *Patience, remember? Give her time.* She went to her quarters, on the deck below Mo's, and managed to unpack one bag before the orientation meeting.

The meeting room was half full of former 72 pilots when she arrived. David waved her to the empty chair next to him, in the middle of the second row—she would have preferred to sit in the first. She nodded and waved to everyone as she made her way to the seat.

"Is Mo coming?" David asked.

She shook her head. "She's tired. I doubt she'll watch the undocking, either."

David frowned. "That's too bad. I wanted to tell her how sorry I am about her mama. And that I'm glad she's okay."

"She'll surface soon."

They sat in silence as the room filled. Not everyone she'd trained with at the Military Academy and flown with on 72 was on the *Falcon*. A couple of pilots had opted to continue flying domestic patrols and others had been told that they weren't ready for a deep tour just yet.

A lieutenant commander strode into the room, a clipboard under his arm. "Lieutenant Commander Monahan," he announced. "And I assume you're all 72 and 73 pilots on your first tour, otherwise I'm in the wrong room," he added, eliciting a few chuckles. He motioned for everyone to stand.

Two circles formed and everyone chanted in unison, "Disobedience means death. Death to those who commit a Chosen Violation. Death to those who disobey. Death to those who violate the Way. Death to those who violate the Way. Death to those who violate the Way!" Lesley clapped, though the Words didn't lift her spirits as much as usual.

Monahan waited for everyone to sit down before continuing. "I know you want to get to the launch area tour, so I'll keep this short. I oversee the night rotation, and since new pilots always start on the night rotation, that means you all report to me. If you have a problem or a question, you come to me. Understood?" Everyone nodded.

"Did everyone receive the steps we suggest to shift your sleep cycle?" he asked. Again, Lesley and the others nodded. "Do follow them. I know it'll be tough in the beginning. You might find yourself dozing off when you're on patrol, but that's what automatic pilot is for." More laughter. "No, seriously, we'll be in Rymellan space for most of the tour and in Jessimite space for the rest, so if you're not at your sharpest for a week or so, don't worry about it."

Monahan removed the clipboard from under his arm and slid a pen from his breast pocket. "You'll patrol in pairs. There are four shifts. You'll cover the first two, and the pilots in the next meeting will cover the others. When I point to you, state your last name." He pointed at the pilot sitting at the end of the first row.

"Harris."

"Next," Monahan said, pointing to the pilot to Harris's left.

"Reid."

"Harris and Reid, you'll fly together on shift one." He made a note on the clipboard. "Next."

Lesley waited for her turn. Monahan was Joined; she caught a glimpse of the Chosen ring on his right hand when he pointed to the pilot directly in front of her. Not the Principal, then. His Chosen would be on the ship—about thirty percent of those on board were non-military Chosens, filling non-military positions. When placing military on tours, finding positions for their Chosens was as important as finding positions for them. The *Falcon* had an extensive medical research centre and Learning and Indoctrination academies. Yes, the children were along, too. Most decks were off-limits to them.

 DISOBEDIENCE MEANS DEATH

She straightened as Monahan pointed to her. "Thompson," she said.

He pointed to David. "Bryson," David said.

"Thompson and Bryson, you'll fly together on shift one."

David grinned and gave her a thumbs-up.

Lesley smiled back, despite her disappointment. She would prefer to fly with Mo. Perhaps that could be arranged later. Since Mo wasn't here, she probably wouldn't be assigned to anyone.

Minutes later, Monahan proved her wrong. "And you appear to be the odd one out," Monahan said, pointing to someone in the back row. "But you're not. Lieutenant Middleton isn't here. I'll pretend she's next to you."

She glanced over her shoulder to see who Monahan was talking to. Oh no!

"Your name?" Monahan said.

"Hawkins. H-a-w-k-i-n-s."

"All right, Hawkins, I'll temporarily assign you a pilot from another rotation. When Middleton returns to active duty, you'll fly with her on shift two."

Ann pulled a face. "Looks like I drew the *short* straw."

A chorus of gasps filled the room. Lesley stared at her, open-mouthed.

"Argamon, Ann," someone said.

"What? It was a joke."

"Is there a problem?" Monahan asked.

Ann folded her arms. "Only that nobody in this room has a sense of humour."

"They laughed at my jokes."

"Yours were funny," David said.

Ann glared at him.

"Lieutenant Hawkins, do you have a problem, flying with Lieutenant Middleton?" Monahan asked.

"No."

"Good. That's it, then. I'll dispatch these assignments to you." He stepped back and surveyed them. "With that out of the way, let's proceed to Deck 12. Oh, and don't forget the meet and greet next week. I know it's at an odd time, but we want as many pilots to attend as possible."

As everyone filed from the room, Lesley fought the urge to pull Ann aside and suggest that she stick to business when flying with Mo. There wasn't any point—Ann would ignore her and Mo would be mortified. No, talking to Ann was out of the question. She'd settle for fantasizing about ripping Ann's arms and legs off instead.

MO THREW THE pencil down on the desk when her comm station beeped. Her hands clenched. She took several deep breaths to calm herself. It wasn't Les's fault; it was hers. If she'd paid more attention during math classes, she'd have completed her calculations by now. The station's calculator didn't help when the formulas befuddled her and she kept losing her place. In the cockpit, she could somehow visualize the numbers and answers, but not here. "Yeah, Les."

"Oh, you're there. I wasn't sure you'd be back from your session," Les said.

She stifled a snort. "I've been back for about fifteen minutes."

"How did it go?"

She'd been trapped in a room with an airhead for an hour, but said, "Fine." At least her counselling sessions didn't require her full attention. She could get away with nodding and grunting most of the time, while she mentally analyzed her decision to vent and eject the energy cells and considered what else she could have done. On the few occasions she'd missed her cue to make the appropriate noise, Counsellor Airhead had chuckled sympathetically and asked if she needed a break. Yes, please—a permanent one.

"That's good," Les said, dragging Mo back to the present. "I'll be up in a few minutes."

"Up in a few minutes?"

"Yes. You haven't forgotten, have you?"

"Um . . ."

"We're approaching Argamon."

"Oh."

"You are coming, I hope. We won't be this close again, and practically nobody has seen you since you boarded. There's a whole ship outside your quarters, you know."

Despite Les's light tone, Mo's jaw tightened. She scrambled for an excuse to stay exactly where she was, but quickly realized that none would do. She had to go—everyone would expect her. "Yeah, I'm coming," she said, making an effort to show some enthusiasm.

"Great! I'll be right there." The connection terminated.

She picked up her pencil and tried to ignore the butterflies in her stomach. Well, she had to face them all sometime. None of them had ever crashed a craft. Nope, she was the only one with that distinction, and she'd killed her mama, too. How many pilots could make *that* claim?

Who flaming cared about Argamon, anyway? It was just a planet— she could see it from Rymel using a telescope. She had more important things to do than stand around the observation deck pretending she cared. Then again, making an appearance this time meant she could pass up the next few gatherings, like that stupid meet and greet, without raising eyebrows.

She chewed the end of her pencil and studied the schematic on the station's display. What if there'd been only six seats? She scribbled on the paper in front of her, then crossed out what she'd written. No, they weren't heavy enough. Plus, they'd have been bolted down. Okay, what if— The door indicator chimed. She pressed a button on the desk.

Les strode into the room, smiling. "Ready to go?" Her smile faded when she looked at the display, then at the stack of papers next to it. "What are you doing?"

"I'm trying to figure out if I could have lightened the craft enough without ejecting all the cells."

"Why?"

Mo gaped at her. "What do you mean, why? I need to know if I could have done something else. I might be in that situation again."

"Mo, the chances that you'll ever be in that situation again are pretty low."

"But not impossible."

"Well, no, but—"

"I need to be prepared. If I'd been prepared, Mama might be alive."

Les sighed and sat on the bed. "Look, I've never asked you for details about what happened. I thought I'd wait until you brought it up."

"I crashed the craft, Mama died. What other details do you need?" Her face and chest felt tight.

"I meant details about the situation you were in, and exactly what you did to crash the craft." Les paused. "When I picked up the aviacraft, Ross told me you vented one through five and ejected six through twenty. You were going to hit the Learning Academy, so you lightened the craft by ejecting the cells, vented the remaining cells to alter the craft's course, and then went into a spin due to losing power while rotating."

"Yeah, that about sums it up," Mo said flatly.

"She said she couldn't believe you did it."

Mo could hardly breathe. "What do you mean?" she gasped, clutching her shirt.

Les frowned. "You okay?"

"Tell me what Ross said." She rose from the chair. "What did she think I should have done? Tell me!" she shrieked.

Les's eyes widened; she raised both her hands. "Calm down. She meant that she couldn't believe you thought of it. Most pilots would have smashed right into the Learning Academy because it never would have crossed their minds to do what you did, especially in the time you had. I don't know if I would have thought of it."

She thudded back into the chair, her chest heaving.

"Ross sounded impressed. And proud."

Mo wanted to cry. Why didn't anyone understand? She'd killed Mama! Were they all flaming stupid?

"Let the investigators do their jobs," Les said. "If they think you could have done something else, they'll say so. But honestly, I doubt they will."

No, there must have been some way to save Mama. She'd survived— why hadn't Mama? But Les obviously didn't understand. Nobody did. "Let's go, or we'll miss it."

"We can talk for a few more minutes if you—"

"I don't. Let's go." She flicked off the monitor and rubbed her eyes.

Les offered her hand. "You haven't been to the observation deck, have you?"

Mo shook her head as she slipped her hand into Les's and allowed Les to hoist her to her feet, even though she didn't need the support. In the six days since they'd undocked, her strength had returned. Her sleep cycle was out of whack—she still slept more hours than usual, and shifting her bedtime in preparation for returning to active duty wasn't helping—but merely thinking no longer fatigued her, and she didn't doze off in the middle of conversations.

Her breath quickened when they reached the entrance to Observation Lounge 2. Les punched the *Open* button. They stepped into laughter and the buzz of conversation—the excitement in the room was palpable. Mo waited for her eyes to adjust to the dim light—the window shields were closed, though there wouldn't be more light if they were open.

"Mo!" David came over, several other pilots trailing behind him. "Good to see you."

"Hi Mo."

"How are you?"

"Can I get you a drink?"

She nodded and smiled. It felt unnatural, forced.

A lieutenant commander joined the group. "So you're Lieutenant Middleton," she said. "I've been wondering when I'd meet you."

Mo swallowed.

"This is Lieutenant Commander Quinn," Les said. "She flies day rotation."

"Yes, this is a little late for me. I'll be tired tomorrow," Quinn said, grinning. "But seeing Argamon never gets old. And I love being here when you greenies see it for the first time."

"Oh," Mo said as someone pressed a drink into her hand.

"She's on her fourth tour," Les said.

"Fourth tour?" Mo said, trying to sound interested.

Quinn nodded. "Second on the *Falcon*. My first two were on the *Hawk*."

Suddenly Ann was there, just behind Quinn. Mo tensed. Their eyes met. Ann nodded and moved on. Mo caught only part of something Quinn had said: "—so far?"

Mo stared at her. "Um . . ."

A loud clap drew everyone's attention, much to Mo's relief. An officer waved his hand above his head. "All right, everyone. I've just received word from navigation that we've exited the hyper-route, which means we're here."

A mix of applause and cheers assaulted her ears.

"Argamon is our closest neighbour and the first planet we ever visited, way back when," he said. "The entire planet is uninhabitable. One hour on Argamon and you'll never complain about the weather at home again." Laughter filled the room. Mo drained her drink and set her empty glass on a nearby table. Could he just get on with it so she could get back to her quarters?

"In a moment I'll open the window shields and you'll get your first glimpse. I'll then ask navigation to maintain position over . . ." He pointed at nobody in particular.

"Argamon's flaming valleys!" several people, likely old hands, shouted.

"That's right. Okay, everyone, get ready." He hovered his hand over the window shield control.

Mo stepped to her left to get a clear view and tried to muster up some excitement.

"I present you, Argamon!" The window shields lifted. And there it was, looking like a bald person with a skin condition who'd been out in the sun too long. Silence, then thunderous applause. Mo clapped too, even though she couldn't have cared less.

Les smiled, her eyes alight. "That's Argamon! Can you believe it?"

Mo nodded, but felt empty inside. She'd looked forward to this, sharing moments with Les that they'd remember for the rest of their lives. But what about Mama, lying in the crypt back home? What had she been looking forward to when her life had been cut short? What would she never experience?

"Here come the valleys," the officer shouted.

The planet turned angry; red blotches dotted its surface. One suddenly intensified and appeared to leap out, as if reaching for the ship. Everyone gasped, then exclamations rang out and several people clapped in delight, including Les. Mo was unmoved; she felt detached from the entire experience, as if she were in a bubble, an impassive observer to a phenomenon she didn't understand. She tugged on Les's sleeve. "I'm tired."

Les leaned toward her. "What?"

"I'm tired. I'm going back to my quarters."

"Already?" Les dragged her eyes away from the windows. "Stay a bit longer. We'll be resuming course in five or ten minutes."

"No." Every second here worsened her mood.

"I'll go with you."

That was the last thing she wanted. "Stay here, Les. There's no reason for you to miss out. I'm only going to get into bed, and you're flying soon."

Les's face creased with concern. "But—"

"I'll beep you later, after your shift."

Mo walked away. Another round of applause set her teeth on edge as she stepped through the doorway.

Back in her quarters, she plunked into her chair, flicked on the monitor, and studied the schematic. Maybe she was approaching the problem from the wrong angle. Maybe shifting weight, rather than ejecting it, was the answer. What if Mama had put the candies in the other cargo container? What if Mama had been sitting behind her, rather than next to her? What if . . .

Two Months Later

LESLEY DABBED UP the last of the egg yolk with a bit of bread and popped the bread into her mouth. The officer at the next table was working his way through a huge piece of chocolate cake. The thought made her stomach roil. She'd become used to eating breakfast at 19:00.

A shadow fell across her plate. "Mind if I sit down?" David asked.

"No, go ahead."

He set a mug of tziva on the table and sat opposite her. "No Mo today?"

"Uh, no. You know how she likes her sleep." She inwardly cringed. Covering for Mo had become a habit, one she didn't like. Lying to her friends and peers didn't sit well, but telling the truth would be disloyal to Mo. She couldn't win.

David sipped his tziva. "How long are we going to play this game?" he asked quietly.

She picked up her napkin and wiped a crumb off her upper lip. "What game?"

"Come on, Lesley. I can't remember the last time I saw you having breakfast with Mo. Or lunch or supper, for that matter. Argamon, I can't remember the last time I saw Mo. Well, okay, I see her in meetings and pass her in the corridor occasionally, but that's it." He set his mug down again. "I hate to ask this, but I've been wondering. Are the two of you still together?"

"Yes, we are." Well, they were in the sense that they'd never explicitly broken up, often spent time together in the same room, and often shared a bed, though if someone were to ask if Mo had scars on her body from the accident, she'd have to make up the answer. "But since the accident, she's not been herself. She prefers to stay in her quarters."

"It's only been, what—nine, ten weeks? People handle grief differently. Some bounce back quickly, some don't."

No, it was more than not bouncing back quickly. She wouldn't be concerned if there were signs that Mo would eventually return to her former self. But there weren't any. Mo was obsessed with the accident; more specifically, with whether she could have saved her mama. Nothing else mattered. Her life consisted of going through the motions until she could get back to reliving the moments before the crash and questioning her every decision. Her duties were nothing more than an obligation to fulfill. And their relationship . . . Lesley didn't know what their relationship meant to Mo anymore. But she wouldn't say that to David. She already felt guilty for suggesting that Mo might have a problem. "So you think I should just give her time?" she said, figuring that agreeing with him would be the fastest way to move on to another topic.

"Yes, give her time. I'd like to see her out and about a bit more, but if she wants to be alone right now, I understand. I can wait."

Easy for him to say.

"Hey, you two." Quinn stopped at their table. "A bunch of us are hanging out at the Dance Hall tonight." Her brow furrowed. "Though I guess it's morning for you, isn't it? Anyway, do you want to join us? You have a few hours before you go on duty."

David looked at Lesley. "Er . . ."

"Go ahead," Lesley said. His eyes always lit up when he saw Quinn, and she suspected that Quinn was interested in him, too.

"What about you, Lesley?" Quinn asked. "I can think of a couple of officers who wouldn't mind giving you a tour of the dance floor."

"No, that's okay. I have a few things to do before my shift."

"You sure?"

"Yes. Enjoy yourselves."

"See you later," David said as he stood. "Oh, wait." He reached for his half-full mug.

"I'll take care of it," Lesley said, then chuckled when he rushed off with Quinn without giving her an argument.

She placed his mug on her tray and walked everything over to the dirty dishes rack. Now to order Mo's breakfast, the reason she was here in the first place. Most evenings she ate breakfast with Mo, in Mo's quarters. But occasionally she ate in the canteen, wanting a change from the same four walls and feeling the need to be among people. She'd always enjoyed her own company—Mo was the more social one, or had been. She never felt lonely when she was alone and reading a book, studying an Interior case, or writing music or a dispatch. But lately she felt lonely when she was with Mo, and would rather eat alone than eat while Mo ignored her. The latter left her demoralized. Sometimes she could bear it; other times, like today, she couldn't face it.

Mo had woken her at about 14:00 with another one of her nightmares and had tossed and turned for an hour afterward. Lesley had finally dropped off again around 15:45. Perhaps that was why she'd eaten breakfast here—she wouldn't have the energy to rally herself in the face of Mo's indifference.

"Here you are," the counter attendant said, handing her a bag.

She thanked her and returned to Mo's quarters. Outside the door, she braced herself, then hit the *Open* button, as Mo had told her to do several weeks ago. *Stop pressing the Chime button, Les, it breaks my concentration. Just come in.* Though she'd known what to expect, her heart sank. Mo was in front of the comm station, as usual. "Breakfast," Lesley announced, her cheerfulness ringing false to her ears.

"Just put it there," Mo mumbled, gesturing to the corner of the desk, her eyes still glued to the display.

She set down the bag. "Listen, on the way to the canteen, I checked to see if any practice rooms are available after our shifts. There are a few open slots. Do you want to play together later?"

"I don't know. Go ahead and book one if you want. You can always play alone."

"I don't want to play alone." Despite an overwhelming sense of futility, Lesley pushed on. "Do you even know where your violin is?"

Mo tapped a key.

"Mo! Do you know where your violin is?"

No response.

"I know where it is," Lesley said. "It's exactly where I put it the day we came on board. You haven't touched it."

"I'm not in an orchestra anymore," Mo said.

So she *was* listening. "You haven't been in an orchestra since we graduated from the Military Academy. That's never stopped you from playing before."

"I'm busy now."

"Doing what? Reviewing the same thing over and over again?"

Mo ignored her.

"Fifteen minutes. We'll play for fifteen minutes and that's it."

"I don't want to, okay?" Mo pressed her lips together.

"How about flying a simulation, then? You haven't done that for ages. Have you even flown one since we boarded?"

Silence.

Lesley gave up; she wouldn't get anywhere today. "Eat your breakfast." That was another concern; Mo was losing weight.

She stifled an exasperated sigh at the clothes heaped on the floor at the foot of the bed. Time for another trip to laundry. As she stuffed the clothes into a laundry bag, she remembered the dispatch she'd recently received from Michael. She'd promised to talk to Mo, but now would be a bad time to bring up Mo's three-line dispatches to her family and gently suggest that Michael would appreciate more. But when would be a good time? And if she couldn't get through to Mo, how would she tell Michael that receiving three lines of communication from Mo on a regular basis was more than Mo gave to everyone else?

She tied the bag shut and slung it over her shoulder. "I'm just taking this to laundry."

No response.

"Mo?" Apparently she was back to talking to herself. At least Mo was showing interest in her breakfast—she'd eaten a bit of muffin.

"I'll be back soon." She left without waiting for a reply—there wasn't any point.

In the corridor, a passing officer nodded to her. "Good evening, Lieutenant." He smiled when she met his eyes and returned his nod. A lump formed in her throat. She'd just shared a more meaningful exchange with an officer she didn't know than she was likely to share with Mo for the rest of the day.

MO HURRIED TOWARD the launch area's elevator, eager to return to her quarters now that she'd completed her shift. Her plans for the rest of the day filled her with excitement. No more studying her craft's schematics—she knew them so well, she could visualize the entire set in her head. She'd checked, rechecked, and triple-checked every calculation, and then done it again. But the schematics hadn't yielded an answer. It was time to move on . . . to another set of schematics. She couldn't wait to bring up those for her craft's predecessor to see what changes the engineers had made, especially for safety reasons.

"Hey, Mo!"

She turned around in dismay; she'd almost made it to the elevator.

"We need to talk," Ann said, blocking Mo's path.

"About what?"

"Talking! I've tried, I've really tried. I've kept my mouth shut for two months, but I can't take it anymore." Her hands went to her hips. "Do you know how boring it is out there, flying around in circles in complete silence? Every time I try to start a conversation, I get dead air in return."

Mo resisted the urge to roll her eyes. As if she cared. Let Ann vent— the sooner she said her piece, the faster she'd shut up.

"See, this is exactly what I mean. Do you even know how to hold a conversation anymore?" Ann pointed to herself. "I say something, and then you," she pointed at Mo, "say something back. Or how about a snort every once in a while? Or a cough or a burp. Snore, for all I care. Anything!"

"I'm too busy to talk."

"Doing what?"

"Flying the craft," she said in a tone she usually reserved for two-year-olds.

Ann gaped. "Are you flaming serious? Since when can't you talk and fly at the same time?"

Since she'd learned that the slightest distraction could lead to disaster. "Instead of gabbing, we should focus on what we're doing, in case something happens."

Ann snorted. "What do you think is going to happen? Hello, are you sleeping through all the meetings? There's a reason we were assigned to the *Falcon* for our first tour. We're in Rymellan space."

"We weren't a few days ago."

"No, we were in Jessimite space. You know—the Jessimites, our closest ally. Argamon!" Ann forcefully exhaled. "They call this a deep tour, but it isn't, not really. Those last for years."

Yeah, maybe she should apply for one. There was nothing for her at home anymore, and she could get away from all the naggers. Unfortunately, they probably wouldn't accept her for a lengthy tour until she was Joined. "Still, we need to stay focused."

Ann looked as if she were about to explode. She muttered under her breath, then said, "Okay, so you don't want to talk. Do you mind if I play a little music over our channel, then? You might be okay with sitting in a stupor for hours on end, but I'm going crazy."

Mo shifted her weight. "I'd rather you not."

"You can't have it all your way."

"I don't want any distractions, okay? If you don't like that, tough." She sidestepped Ann and strode to the elevator.

"What's wrong with you?" Ann said, chasing after her.

"Nothing."

"Mo, there's something wrong with you."

"Just because I won't go along with what you want?"

"No, because you're not you. You'd talk. You'd want music. Remember when we flew together on 72? That's you. This isn't you."

And Ann thought there was something wrong with *her*? She stepped into the elevator. "No music. If you don't like that, talk to Monahan and ask him for another flying partner," she said as she pressed the *Close* button.

"I just might do that," Ann said. "Hey! Wait—"

The elevator door slid shut. Mo breathed a sigh of relief, then frowned at the time on the elevator's control panel. Talking to Ann had wasted two minutes, two minutes she could have been studying schematics. And how long would she have before Les showed up and started bugging her about eating supper, or until Papa sent her yet another dispatch? How did everyone expect her to figure it out when they kept interrupting her, nagging her, telling her what to do? Sometimes the constant interruptions frustrated her so much, she could cry. If everyone just left her alone, she'd figure out what she'd done wrong, understand why she'd lived and Mama had died. She had to know, so she'd be prepared next time. And if they couldn't understand that, she didn't need them. She didn't need any of them.

LESLEY STEPPED OFF the elevator and dragged herself to Mo's quarters. Mo's nightmares had kept her up three days in a row; the lack of uninterrupted sleep was catching up with her. She'd sleep in her own quarters today—Mo hardly noticed she was there, anyway. If she could, she'd have a quick supper in the canteen and then go to bed. But Mo's quarters needed tidying, and if Lesley didn't bring her supper, Mo would probably skip the meal, something she couldn't afford to do.

"Oh good, you're here," Mo said, her eyes alight. "I want to show you something."

Her spirits instantly lifted. Mo hadn't been this animated since the accident. Was she finally snapping out of it?

"Look." Mo rolled her chair away from the comm station to give Lesley a clear view of its display.

Lesley felt like screaming. Not another schematic! She wanted to pick up the display and hurl it into the flaming corridor. Instead, she swallowed her anger and disappointment and started to gather the remains of Mo's lunch. "What's special about this one?" she asked, trying to show some interest.

"It's the precursor to my craft. Newer models must be safer than older ones, right? So I'm going to study the differences between my craft and this one."

"Why?" she asked as she activated the recycling chute and threw in what Mo hadn't eaten. She set the dirty dishes on the small table near the door, to take with her when she fetched supper.

"Maybe it'll give me some ideas."

Her temples pulsed. "Ideas about what?" Perhaps making the bed would head off her growing frustration; she hadn't had time earlier.

"Ideas about what I could have done differently."

Lesley dropped the blanket she'd just whipped off the bed and whirled toward Mo. "I'm sure they improved the safety of the craft, but I don't understand how knowing what they did will help you. If there were further safety improvements to make, ones so obvious that you can figure them out by comparing your craft to its predecessor, don't you think they would have figured them out and incorporated them into your craft's design? After all, we're talking about aviacraft design engineers, here." Now that she'd started, she couldn't stop. "And the design document for your craft would list the safety improvements they made. I'm sure you could locate that and just read about them, rather than trying to puzzle them out by studying schematics, but then you wouldn't have an excuse to sit in front of your comm station all day instead of dealing with what happened."

Mo's face reddened. "What do you think I'm doing? I am dealing with it."

"No, you're not. If you were dealing with it, you'd face up to it and accept that there wasn't anything you could do." She pressed on, determined to get through to Mo. "Has it occurred to you that you haven't figured out the exact steps you could have taken to save your mama because they don't exist? That what you did was the best thing, perhaps the only thing you could have done to avoid hitting the Learning Academy?"

"The best thing? Mama died!"

"I know. But it wasn't your fault. It was an accident."

Mo shot up from the chair. "I am so sick and tired of people saying it was an accident! I crashed the flaming craft!"

"Mo, you were going down. If you hadn't done anything, the craft still would have crashed. And you probably would have died, along with your mama and half the Learning Academy."

"But I didn't die. Only Mama did. And I have to understand why."

Lesley rubbed her forehead. "Things don't always make sense. Sometimes there isn't a logical explanation." She gestured toward the comm station. "When will you stop? At what point will you say, yeah, okay, I understand? What if you do discover that you could have handled it differently? Do you think that'll make you feel better? You had to make a decision within a very short period of time. You made it, and saved hundreds of Rymellans. You were willing to sacrifice your own life."

"But Mama died." Mo sat back down. "You know, I'm really disappointed with you."

"What?"

"Disappointed. I thought you'd be on my side. I thought we understood each other. But I guess we don't. And that's disappointing."

Mo's words left her speechless. She had to get out of there. Now. "I'll go get us supper."

Outside, she paused to collect herself as the door swooshed shut behind her. *Disappointed.* She blinked back tears and headed for the elevator. Fortunately the corridor was deserted—not many were up and about at 05:30. *Disappointed.*

She was at her wit's end. Was she selfish because she wanted the old Mo back? The one who readily smiled and grinned, the one who had to drag her to parties, the one who doubled over with laughter when she hit a sour note on her violin? The one who made Lesley feel as if she could do no wrong and that she was the most special woman alive—where was that Mo? Was she trapped and desperately trying to get out, or was she gone?

Lesley had always counted on Mo for reassurance when Mama made her feel like a failure or she doubted herself. No matter what, Mo would still care—that was what she'd always told herself. But now she couldn't do anything right in Mo's eyes. She was running herself ragged covering for her, caring for her, and worrying about her, but Mo didn't see that. *Disappointed.*

Perhaps she should stop, let Mo sink until she had no choice but to start caring again. But what if she didn't? What if she continued to neglect herself and started to neglect her duties? What then? Lesley couldn't stand by and watch. But as she accepted their supper from the counter attendant, she realized that she'd been doing just that, hoping, irrationally, that one day she'd wake up and the old Mo would be back. *Give her time*, everyone had said. So she had. In the beginning, that had been the right thing to do. Now, it was avoiding reality. Mo wouldn't suddenly snap out of it. She wasn't well. She needed help.

But was it up to Lesley to ask for it? What would the consequences be? Would it negatively affect Mo's career and reputation? Would Mo understand why she'd sounded the alarm? No, she should talk to Mo first—it would be better if Mo recognized her problem and asked for help herself. So far, talking to her, trying to get her to see reason, hadn't worked, but one more try wouldn't hurt.

She returned to Mo's quarters. "Supper," she announced.

Mo acknowledged her with a grunt and ignored the food and drink that Lesley set next to the keyboard. Had the circles under Mo's eyes always been that dark and her face so pinched? She looked so tiny in that sweater—Michael would be horrified.

Lesley put her own meal on the nightstand and sank onto the bed. She'd long given up on trying to engage Mo in supper conversation— she'd talk to her later about getting help. No. No she wouldn't. She wouldn't start lying to herself on top of everyone else. Talking to Mo would be an exercise in futility. Mo wouldn't listen—she'd probably become angry. And after this schematic, there'd be another one, and then another. She'd spend the rest of the tour in her quarters, sitting in that chair, staring at that display, while her life crumbled around her ears. Lesley could sit and rack her brain for reasons to not do what she now knew she had to do, but they'd only be excuses to not act.

She picked at her supper and finally cleared her plate, but the food wasn't sitting well. "I'll drop my dishes off at the canteen and then go to my quarters to get some sleep." The lid still sat on Mo's plate. "I'll pick up yours later, take them back with the breakfast dishes, okay?" Probably after throwing out her supper.

"Yeah, sure," Mo mumbled.

Though Lesley knew Mo wouldn't care, she put her arm around Mo's shoulders and kissed her cheek. "Good night." Her composure wavered. *I'm sorry, Mo, but I have to do this.*

Again, her vision blurred as the door closed behind her. Would Mo understand that she'd done it because she cared? If Mo didn't forgive her, their relationship would probably end, but Lesley was willing to pay that price if it brought the old Mo back. Since the accident, their relationship had been nothing but a habit, and they'd always known that it had no future. If Mo's eyes danced again, if she picked up her violin, beat everyone soundly at cards, and stopped tormenting herself, losing their relationship would have been worth it.

After dropping off her dishes at the canteen, she took the elevator to the launch area, hoping that Monahan would still be in his office. Now that she'd reached her decision, she wanted to see him before she lost her nerve.

"Come in, Lieutenant," Monahan said when she hovered in his office doorway.

She stopped in front of his desk. Her mind went blank. She should have rehearsed what she'd say.

Monahan leaned back in his chair and pressed his fingertips together. "What can I do for you?"

"I want to talk to you about Lieutenant Middleton."

He looked at her expectantly.

How to start? "You know she was in an accident just before boarding the *Falcon*?"

"Yes."

"Well, she's not doing very well."

He frowned. "What do you mean?"

"I know she flies her shifts, but that's all she does. She's neglecting everything else—her hobbies, her family, her friends." Her girlfriend. "She's not eating or sleeping properly. She's obsessed with the decision she made that day, or rather, with what decisions she could have made." Saying it all out loud in one go sounded awful. "But I'm not suggesting that she can't perform her duties," she quickly added. "She can. And I'm not here because I doubt her commitment to the tour."

"You're here because you're worried about her," Monahan said.

"Yes."

He pursed his lips. "I'm going to be up front with you. Lieutenant Middleton has come up during the senior officers' weekly review." He tapped his left temple. "She set off my alarm bells a few weeks ago. She rarely speaks in our meetings and she hasn't put any time in at the simulators. Not only that, I've yet to see her at a social event. Now, nothing says that everyone has to be an extrovert and a social butterfly. Off the top of my head, I can think of several excellent officers who don't say much and keep to themselves. But they've always been that way. She hasn't. I've read her file. Abrupt, significant behavioural changes almost always indicate a problem.

"But when do you step in, especially in a case like this?" he mused aloud. "That crash . . . the decision she had to make and then losing her mama under those circumstances . . . horrible, horrible." Monahan shook his head. "We expected her to be subdued for a bit, but lately we've become concerned. And it sounds like you're concerned, too."

"Yes, I am. That's why I'm here."

"Not an easy step to take, I'm sure. As I said, I've read her file."

Her face felt hot.

"You're the second pilot to express concerns about Lieutenant Middleton in so many days," he said, shocking her. "Given how close you are to the lieutenant, I'm inclined to give your assessment of her a lot of weight. Thank you for coming to me with this. You did the right thing."

Perhaps, but hearing him say it didn't make her feel any better. If anything, she wanted to run to her quarters, throw herself onto the bed, and weep. She felt as if she'd just betrayed the person who mattered to her more than anything.

MO'S HANDS CLENCHED when the door indicator chimed. It couldn't be Les—she'd only just left to fetch them breakfast and wouldn't activate the chime. Why couldn't they all leave her alone? She flicked off the monitor, then punched the intercom button. "Yes?"

"It's Commander Baker. I'd like to talk to you."

Flaming Argamon, what did he want? She opened the door and stood at attention.

"At ease, Lieutenant." Baker said, stepping over the threshold. After the door closed, he clasped his hands behind his back and cleared his throat.

Her heart raced; she felt trapped.

"I'm here to tell you that I'm removing you from active duty and placing you back on medical leave," Baker said.

   DISOBEDIENCE MEANS DEATH

Medical leave? "All my injuries are healed, Commander. Physician Collins cleared me for duty."

"Yes, she did. But it's not your physical injuries that concern me. They're often the easiest to deal with. Sometimes it's the emotional and psychological wounds that linger."

She didn't understand.

"I like my pilots to be healthy, on all levels. Based on our observations and on concerns expressed by your peers, it's clear that you're no longer mentally fit for duty."

What?

"Your new orders are to report to the infirmary at 21:00. That's in two hours. I'm advising you now that Article 844 will apply to your situation, so if you need to do anything before you report, please do it before then."

Article 844 . . . She started to tremble.

"You'll be working with Counsellor Willis. He's dealt with the type of depression that you're apparently experiencing and has agreed to shift his sleep cycle to match yours. I want you to follow his directions. I want you to listen to him. I want you to treat your time with him and at the infirmary as seriously as you treat your duties in the cockpit. You won't return to active duty until he says you're fit to do so." He paused. "I want to make it clear that I'm more than satisfied with your performance in the cockpit and that I'd like to see you back out there as soon as possible. Understood?"

She nodded.

"Good. And Lieutenant, it would be best for you to report to the infirmary on your own initiative. I don't want to have to send someone to escort you."

"Yes, Commander," she managed to whisper.

He nodded to her. "Good night."

Her trembling progressed to shakes the moment the door swooshed shut. Not mentally fit? Article 844? Her peers had expressed concern? Yeah, she knew exactly who'd expressed concern. Ann! Ann had flaming tattle-tailed, all because Mo wasn't a chatterbox and wouldn't agree to music in the cockpit. Mo hated her. Hated! Jokes were one thing; this was quite another and had gone too far. What lies had Ann told them? She wasn't depressed—depressed people lay around in bed all day. Morons!

They couldn't do this to her—she still hadn't figured it out, and now she wouldn't have access to a comm station. The infirmary would have stations, but with 844 in effect, she'd be forbidden from using one or someone would be looking over her shoulder the whole time. Her throat constricted and her heart pounded. She felt dizzy; she grabbed the edge of the desk to steady herself, then sat on the end of the bed. It wasn't fair! Why were they doing this to her? Baker was satisfied with her performance, so why should he care what she did when she wasn't on duty? It was none of their business! If they understood, they'd leave her alone.

Maybe joining the military hadn't been such a good idea after all. Being a pilot had brought her nothing but grief. And now the military was poking its nose into her affairs and telling her what to do, even when she was performing her duties well. So fine! She'd report to the infirmary and endure yet more wasted time with another airhead counsellor. She'd tell him what he wanted to hear, and once he'd patted her on the head and cleared her for duty, she'd finish out the tour like a good little girl. And then? She'd quit.

"BREAKFAST," LESLEY ANNOUNCED as she strode into Mo's room. She stopped dead. Mo wasn't in her habitual spot in front of the comm station; she sat slumped at the end of the bed. "You all right?"

Mo looked up. "You won't believe what just happened. Baker was here."

"Commander Baker?"

"Yeah, right where you are. He's relieved me of duty and placed me back on medical leave. Can you believe that?"

Yes, she could, but Mo wouldn't appreciate that answer. However, she didn't want to lie, so—

"Oh, well, thanks for the flaming support!" Mo said in response to Lesley's silence. "You don't even look surprised that Baker was—" Her eyes widened and her mouth dropped open. "It was you! You went to them!" Her voice grew shrill. "How could you do this to me? How could you humiliate me like this?"

   DISOBEDIENCE MEANS DEATH

Lesley set their breakfasts down on the table next to the door and stepped toward her. "Mo, I—"

"Don't you come near me," Mo shouted, standing and holding up her hands to create a barrier. "Stay away from me!"

"I was trying to help."

"Oh, so that's what you think you were doing? Helping? Helping who? Me? Or you?"

"You!"

"Don't kid yourself." Mo blinked rapidly. "If you wanted to help me, you would have supported me. You wouldn't have gone to them and made it sound like I've lost my mind." A tear rolled down her cheek.

Lesley swallowed. "I didn't make it sound like you've lost your mind. But since the accident . . . since your mama died . . . you don't care about anything anymore."

"Of course I do! I still get up, don't I? I fly my shifts. What do you want from me?"

"I want you—"

"I know exactly why you went running to them," Mo shouted, pointing at the door. "You don't want your reputation harmed, because that would compromise your chances of becoming admiral."

"*What?*"

"Better get Mo help, otherwise they'll think I've lost my mind, too."

Lesley couldn't believe it; she wanted to grab Mo's shoulders and shake some sense into her. "That has nothing—"

"Or did you do it because I won't sleep with you? Is that it? Let's get Mo out of the way for a while so I can find someone else."

Trembling with anger, Lesley whirled and marched to the door. If Mo wanted to throw her life away, let her. They had no future together anyway—it wasn't her problem. Let the military deal with it. Not her problem.

But she couldn't bring herself to press the *Open* button and stood there, struggling for calm as she listened to Mo cry, every sob tearing into her. She couldn't walk out, not on Mo. Yes, Mo's words hurt—they wounded her to her very core. But Mo wasn't well, hadn't been well for a while. And right now she was distraught, probably frightened. If they were Chosens, Lesley wouldn't have the luxury of deciding that enough

was enough, of washing her hands of the entire situation; she'd have
to stay, support Mo, be there for her as she clawed her way out of the
abyss. Wasn't that what love was about? Yes, love—*love!* She loved Mo,
she'd always loved her. So she'd act as if they were Chosens and remain
at Mo's side. Walking out wasn't an option—she wouldn't be able to look
at herself in the mirror if she did.

She turned around. Mo had sunk to the floor and sat slumped
against the bed, sniffling. "Mo, your mama loved you," she said, taking a tentative step forward. "She'd want you to go on with your life,
be happy. You know she always wanted you to be happy. She wouldn't
want to see you like this."

Mo slowly shook her head. "Just before we crashed, she said she was
proud of me. Or at least I think she did." She grabbed her hair with both
hands. "I've gone over it so many times in my head, I'm not sure what
actually happened anymore. It doesn't matter anyway. If she'd known
what was going to happen, she wouldn't have said it."

Lesley sat next to Mo but didn't touch her. "She still would have
said it."

"No," Mo whispered. "I let her down. I let her down." She hugged her
knees to her chest and buried her head against them, hiding her face.

Lesley knew nothing she said would get through, so she didn't try.
She cautiously put her hand against Mo's back, prepared to pull away.
But Mo either didn't notice or didn't care. "Did Baker say anything
about seeing your counsellor more often?" Lesley asked, presuming
he must have.

"I'm getting a new one," Mo said, her voice muffled.

Good.

"I have to report to the infirmary at 21:00." Mo turned her head
toward Lesley. "Will you go with me?"

Overcome, she almost couldn't speak. "Of course I'll go with you."

"He said Article 844 would be in effect." Mo's chin trembled. "So you
won't have to bring me supper tonight."

That meant they planned to put her on medication. Mo would be
confined to the infirmary, and under supervision, to ensure that she
didn't commit any violations—particularly capital ones—due to the
medication. They'd lift 844 when she came off the medication or when

    DISOBEDIENCE MEANS DEATH

the physicians and her counsellor were satisfied that it wasn't impairing her judgment, whichever came first. "I'll visit you after I've eaten. I'll visit you as often as I can. If . . . you want me to."

"I do. But that doesn't mean I forgive you. You shouldn't have done this, Les. You shouldn't have done it." Mo hid her face in her knees again.

Lesley wanted to explain why she wasn't sorry that she had. And one day she would, when Mo—her Mo—had emerged from the abyss.

Three Months Later

MO MADE HER way down the shuttle's aisle, searching for two empty seats. "Over there, on the left," Les murmured behind her. They stowed their cloaks and bags in the overhead cargo container and sat down. The shuttle was filling quickly; everyone was eager to get home.

David came up the aisle and stopped when he saw them. "Dress uniforms? What's the occasion?"

Mo tensed.

"Oh, we've decided to start a tradition," Les said. "We're going to wear them home after every tour."

"Interesting," he said, though his face clearly indicated that he thought the notion odd. He glanced over his shoulder. "I'd better move, I'm holding everyone up. I'll see you next week at the Military Academy reunion."

"Now he'll expect us to wear them every time," Mo whispered to Les.

"Don't worry, he'll have forgotten by the next time."

Les was probably right. Mo's comm unit beeped twice. She almost deleted the dispatch when she saw Ann's name, but then decided to read it. *See you in three weeks, squirt. Oh, and mind the gap when you get on the train. You're so tiny you might fall in.* She sighed and deleted it. Things were definitely returning to normal.

"I'll probably doze on the train," Les said.

"Me too." In preparation for the break, they'd shifted their sleep cycles as much as possible while still flying their shifts. Sleeping odd hours would be difficult at home, though they were both going to try. They were on nights again next tour.

The comm system crackled to life. "Welcome aboard, everyone. Before we launch, I want to remind all Chosens twenty-five and over who aren't yet Joined that you must proceed to conference room three when we reach the shuttle base. Again, all Chosens twenty-five and over who aren't yet Joined, proceed to conference room three when we reach the shuttle base. Thank you. Prepare for launch."

Mo fastened her seatbelt. A minute later, the shuttle left 72 and started its journey to Rymel. She stared out the window, hardly believing that the tour was already over. It hadn't turned out the way she'd expected. Three weeks in the infirmary, then five more on medical leave while she continued to undergo intensive counselling. She'd been on active duty for the past month, though she'd still seen Willis every second day. He was returning to day shift next tour, but she had a standing appointment with him every Monday, Thursday, and Saturday at 08:00—late evening for her. *By the end of the tour, we'll have that down to once a week*, he'd confidently stated. She believed him.

Willis had gained her trust during their first session. She'd plunked herself in the chair, folded her arms, and boldly announced that since she'd decided to quit after the tour, seeing him was a waste of time. *I see*, he'd said without blinking, much to her disappointment. *Well, I don't want the session to go to waste, so why don't I help you write your release request to Commander Baker?* He'd invited her to stand where she could see his comm station's display, and then had created a new dispatch, typed in the date and time, and seeded it with the standard *I'm writing to request my release from the military* line. *Now, they'll want to know why you want to leave*, he'd said, looking at her. *You're a good pilot—your performance is stellar—so you'll have to explain. Why don't you want to be a fighter pilot anymore?*

Her pathetic attempt at an answer had provided him with the opportunity to question and challenge. But most importantly, he'd listened, without passing judgment, without telling her that she was wrong, that she shouldn't think this or shouldn't feel that. In the next session, he'd brought up the schematics for her aviacraft and its precursor and invited her to sit next to him and talk about them. Many sessions later, she'd realized that most of his questions had nothing to do with schematics—their discussion had slowly shifted from energy cells and

          DISOBEDIENCE MEANS DEATH

weight distribution to guilt and fear. She'd finally seen how it had been easier to study schematics and do math, of all things, than let herself feel. Why else would she have willingly sat and done math if not to numb herself? Seriously.

So she'd made strides, but still had work to do. Nightmares still haunted her, though they were less frequent, and the image of Mama and Papa still lay hidden away in her closet on the *Falcon*. She no longer cringed every time she thought of Mama, but she wasn't ready to be reminded every time she returned from her shift, climbed into bed, and woke up in the morning. And she still felt guilty—but not about the crash, not really. The accident report had helped assuage her guilt about that, especially its concluding paragraphs:

Our simulations have shown that Lieutenant Middleton took the only viable course of action to prevent the aviacraft from impacting with the B5-1 Learning Academy. Anything else would have failed, resulting in great loss of life. Among the alternatives we tested, Simulation 18A (see pg. 42) would have resulted in the least number of casualties (projected 132 losses, mostly children). Due to Lieutenant Middleton's skill and presence of mind, the number of casualties was limited to one.

We recognize that Lieutenant Middleton was willing to sacrifice her life to save the lives of others, and that Susan Middleton did just that. We also recognize that few pilots would have taken the same course of action as Lieutenant Middleton, and we are grateful that a pilot of Lieutenant Middleton's skill was in the cockpit that day. As such, we have recommended to the military that Lieutenant Middleton receive the Medal of Service to the Way, and we have recommended to the government that Susan Middleton be awarded (posthumously) the Commendation of the Way for her bravery and selflessness.

Mama's commendation had been presented to the family last month—Mo had told Papa to go ahead without her, that there was no need to reschedule the awards ceremony on her behalf. And when she'd heard that Monahan was planning to present her with the medal in the presence of all the pilots, she'd requested, through Willis, that she receive the medal privately. Despite knowing that she'd been awarded it to recognize her role in saving lives, celebrating it with her peers wouldn't have felt right, not when Mama had died. The medal was in her bag—she'd throw it into a drawer in her bedroom for now. Maybe someday she'd look at it and feel something other than sorrow. Maybe not.

Now she felt guilty about how terribly she'd treated everyone, especially Les. In the past, she'd sometimes wondered if Les's feelings were genuine and whether Les would rather be with someone else. Never again. Les might not speak of love, but she sure knew how to show it. Mo didn't know where she'd be without her. And then there was Papa and the rest of her family. Reading over her terse, sometimes angry, dispatches to them had horrified her; she hadn't recognized herself in them. She'd also ignored all her friends, taken them for granted. Given how she'd behaved, she didn't deserve the kindness and understanding everyone had shown her since her release from the infirmary.

The comm system crackled again. "Arrival, two minutes."

A cheer broke out, and she felt herself smile through a burst of panic. As soon as the shuttle touched down, Les unfastened her seatbelt and lifted down their cloaks and bags. Mo's stomach churned, despite the three-hour train ride ahead of them. She followed Les into the packed waiting area, busy with families waving eagerly to loved ones and calling greetings. Several gold cloaks stood out amidst the pandemonium—Chosen Council couriers on their way to conference room three, no doubt. In just two more tours, she and Les would be among those in the conference room, wondering if their Chosen Papers were ready. Where had the time gone?

She didn't bother scanning for her family. At her request, they wouldn't be here at the shuttle base. Neither would the Thompsons, for the same reason. "Do you think everyone will be at the house?" she asked Les on the train.

Les squeezed her hand. "I'm sure of it."

Well, she hadn't received responses from Mary and Matthew, but that wasn't unusual. *Please, let them be there.*

Mo managed to doze off and on, but the closer they came to C3, the more agitated she became. She'd spent much of her recent sessions with Willis talking about this day. When she'd told him that she'd wear her dress uniform for the entire journey home, he hadn't laughed. Neither had Les, when Mo had asked her to do the same. Willis and Les had understood that changing into it at home would give her an opportunity

     DISOBEDIENCE MEANS DEATH

to back out. And so here was Les, sitting stiffly next to her, pulling on her collar. She hated the feel of the dress uniform against her neck, yet she'd readily agreed to wear it for hours. Mo loved her for it.

As they walked to the Middleton estate, she felt herself withdrawing. Would they be angry? Would they ask what in the flaming Argamon she'd thought she was doing, sending them horrible dispatches like that? Did they blame her, despite the report? She'd soon find out. The house loomed in the distance.

When they reached the front door, Les gave her a reassuring smile. Mo felt like pushing Les in first and hiding behind her, but that would be cowardly. She grasped the door handle, blood pounding in her ears. As soon as she opened the door and stepped through the doorway, everyone streamed into the hallway. She flashed back to the day she'd come home from the infirmary, except this time Nathan was here and the flowers in the vase were blooming.

She met Papa's eyes, but held back, not sure if she should hug him. He didn't hesitate. "Welcome home," he said, reaching for her. "I missed you, Mo. Very much." Despite promising herself that she wouldn't cry, she buried her face in his shoulder and let the tears flow.

Everyone gathered around her, their love and support palpable. She wanted to tell them how sorry she was and how much she loved them, but that would have to wait. First things first. She stepped back, sniffling, and wiped her nose on her sleeve. "I guess we should go." So heavy was the sense of dread hanging over her, she almost couldn't breathe.

"Are you sure?" Papa said. "We don't have to rush there."

"I'm sure." If she didn't go now, she might never go. "Do you have the article?"

"Here." Neil handed it to her, his eyes bright.

She slipped off the cloth ring and unrolled the parchment. Article CT30, beautifully calligraphed. "Thank you," she said, rolling it up and slipping the ring back over it. "Oh, he's standing," she exclaimed, noticing Jacob for the first time.

Barbara laughed. "With my help." Jacob, clutching Barbara's hand, suddenly pointed to Mo and looked up at Barbara.

"Yes, that's your aunt Mo. Aunt Mo," she repeated slowly.

Mo drew herself up, then felt silly. But who knew what he was thinking? Maybe he was trying to decide if he should be impressed or wish that he'd been born into another family.

Papa glanced at the others. "We thought we'd have a bit of time before we went. We want to give you something, and I guess now is as good a time as any." He removed a small case from his top sweater pocket. "We talked about it, and we all agree that this should belong to you." He handed the case to her.

Curious, she undid its clasp and lifted the lid. Inside lay a silver badge. In its centre, an engraved circle. Underneath the circle, the words *Susan Middleton, for bravery and selflessness*. Mama's commendation. Her lips trembled as she formed the words to tell them she couldn't accept it; that she was the last person who should have it.

But then she realized that it was their way of telling her that they didn't blame her and that they still loved her. She couldn't refuse it— she'd caused them enough pain already. At least she'd feel pride along with sorrow whenever she looked at it. Her mama had earned the highest civilian commendation. Her mama. "Um . . . I don't know what to say," she said, not at all embarrassed by her quavering voice. "Thank you. I'll always cherish it."

Their faces lit up in delight. And as she looked from one to another, her heavy sense of dread about visiting the crypt lifted. Mama wasn't there. She was here, and always would be. She was in the tilt of Neil's head, in Mary's smile, in Nathan's baking. She was in Matthew's love of gardening and Andrew's mischief. She was in Les and Barbara's memories. And Papa . . . she'd never look at Papa without thinking of Mama.

Most of all, Mama was in her—she saw her every time she looked in a mirror and felt her whenever she laughed. That wouldn't stop Mo from desperately missing her, but knowing that Mama would live on in all of them offered her some small comfort.

Mo closed the case and slipped it into her inner cloak pocket. She'd cry over it some more in private.

"Shall we go?" Papa said.

She reached for Les's hand. "Yes. I'm ready now."

   DISOBEDIENCE MEANS DEATH

GOOD-BYES

. . . . .

MO UNCROSSED HER LEGS AND DREW them up to her chest. Her bum was starting to hurt. Maybe she should have booked a meeting room; then everyone could have sat around a table instead of on the floor in her quarters. But she hadn't planned on holding a gathering to mark her twenty-fifth birthday—she wasn't in a celebratory mood. She'd grudgingly agreed to an impromptu party to appease Les and David, who'd insisted that spending her birthday alone, or with only Les, could draw the wrong type of attention from her superiors. After all, it *was* her twenty-fifth. She was supposed to be beside herself with joy at the prospect that a Chosen Council courier could be waiting for her when the *Falcon* docked in two weeks' time. Just last week an airhead in the Dance Hall had blabbered on to anyone who'd listen that she couldn't wait to Join and start having babies. Ugh.

When Les had turned twenty-five a couple of weeks into the tour, she'd invited her close friends to a five-course supper. She'd booked the room and ordered the food weeks beforehand, at the tail end of their last tour.

Mo, on the other hand, had frantically beeped everyone last night to see if they'd drop in for a couple of hours, sit on the floor, and listen to music blaring from a comm station while they snacked on leftovers scrounged from the canteen. To her surprise, all those not flying a shift had agreed to come, including Ann. Mo hadn't wanted to be rude by leaving her out. She'd braced herself for a string of jokes about her age, her Chosen not being able to see her, or other such nonsense, but Ann had been quiet all evening. Come to think of it, Mo couldn't remember the last time she'd seen Ann with that new pilot she'd hooked up with. Maybe they'd broken up. Ann couldn't seem to hang onto a boyfriend for longer than five minutes.

"I'm getting bored of the *Falcon*," David said, dragging Mo back to the conversation. "The mock battles are fun and you guys are great, but I wouldn't mind a change. Most of the pilots we started with have already moved on. Steve's transferring to the *Osprey* after this tour, so that'll be one more gone."

"I hadn't heard that," Les murmured as she carefully dunked a piece of carrot into the vegetable dip that sat in the middle of the circle everyone had formed. Mo stifled a giggle. Les would probably prefer to eat with her right hand, but Mo was holding it and had no intention of letting it go.

"Most pilots only spend two or three tours here," Jackie Quinn, who'd come with David, said. They'd been seeing each other casually for almost two years. David didn't seem bothered that his Chosen Papers, or hers, could be ready when they returned to Rymel. *It's not as if we're in love,* he'd said when Mo had asked.

"I'm surprised you're still here," David said to her. "You even transferred here. Don't you ever wish something would happen?"

She tipped her head from side to side as she considered his question. "Sometimes I think I want to see real action, but if it happened, I'd probably wish it hadn't, if you know what I mean."

Several heads bobbed in agreement.

"I'll definitely be on the *Falcon* for a while," Sheila said.

David's gaze shifted to her. "You've never thought about transferring?"

"Well, I have, but . . ." She reddened and glanced around. "Well . . . I wasn't going to say anything, but . . . well, you know Ruth went into fighter maintenance when she didn't make it into the fighter pilot program. We've been trying to get assigned to the same ship, and we finally managed it. She'll be on the *Falcon* next tour."

"That's great!" David said. Mo echoed the sentiment along with everyone else, but she couldn't help feeling envious and understood why Sheila would have preferred to avoid the subject. Sheila and Ruth would reunite and could stay together as long as they liked. She and Les, on the other hand, could face the end of their relationship every time they stepped back onto Rymellan soil. Nobody was talking about that tonight, but it must be on everyone's mind. They all knew why she'd only wanted a quiet gathering for her birthday—they weren't stupid. She squeezed Les's hand, but didn't look at her.

"You must both be Solitaries," Jackie said.

"Oh, sorry—yes, we are," Sheila said. "I forgot you weren't in the program with us. I made it into the fighter pilot program, but she didn't. So she went into fighter maintenance, hoping we could serve together. That worked out okay until I was accepted to the *Falcon* but she wasn't. She kept applying, but there never seemed to be a position for her. Then all of a sudden, there was." She snorted. "All of a sudden. It only took four years."

"Four years," Jackie repeated, shaking her head.

"Yeah." Sheila paused. "I heard a rumour that if your relationship lasts longer than three years, they make more of an effort to place you together. But I don't know if Ruth finally got a position because of that. It could be a coincidence."

If Les had been a Solitary, Mo wouldn't have minded being one; she could take or leave children. But four Solitaries probably would have disappointed Papa. Mama too . . . if she were alive.

"Being separated from Ruth when you're on tour must be difficult," Les said.

Sheila nodded. "It was fine when we were both on 72. Sometimes our off days didn't coincide, but for the most part, we were together. It's been rough since then. The last few weeks of the tour are always excruciating. Every day feels like a week."

Mo swallowed.

"Why didn't you keep flying domestic?" David asked. "Then you could have stayed together."

"We considered it, but she didn't want to hold me back." Sheila shrugged. "I wouldn't have minded, but it would have bothered her. So I started going on tour, and we just hoped that it would eventually sort itself out. And it finally has."

"I might apply for a three-year tour in a couple of years," Keith, a former 73 pilot, said. "My brother . . ."

Ann waved to Mo, catching her eye. "I'm going," she mouthed, pointing at the door.

Mo nodded to her and started to rise, but Ann motioned for her to remain where she was and crept away. Moments later, Mo's comm unit beeped twice. She glanced at its display, in case the dispatch was from one of her superiors, but it was from Ann. What witty joke had she sent this time? *Thanks for inviting me. Happy birthday.* Perplexed, Mo slid the comm unit back into its holder. Maybe the joke was that it wasn't a joke?

David was going around the circle, asking about everyone's future plans. Mo half listened, wondering what she'd say when he reached her. As long as she was in a cockpit and with Les, she didn't care what ship she served on. So she'd say something vague about wanting to go on a longer tour at some point. Nobody was taking notes.

Les pulled her hand away. "We're running low on drinks. I'll go to the canteen and get some." She pushed to her feet and headed for the door.

"Wait!" Mo called. "Tim said to beep him if we need anything and he'll bring it up."

But Les didn't hear her—and twenty minutes later still hadn't returned. Mo was about to beep her when the door slid open. "Drinks," Les announced, setting a bag on the table near the door.

"Did you get lost?" David asked.

Les smiled. "Uh, no, I ran into someone and we talked for a bit."

Her answer satisfied David, but not Mo. Les was lying; her smile was too broad and she hadn't met David's eyes. But it would be rude to rush everyone out so she could find out why Les had really taken so long.

An hour passed before she thanked the last guest for coming and turned with relief to Les. "I'm glad that's over."

"It wasn't so bad."

"No, I suppose not."

Les started to gather the dirty dishes. She pointed to the dip bowls. "Can you deal with those?"

"Sure." She'd wait until after they'd tidied up to ask why Les had lied

   DISOBEDIENCE MEANS DEATH

to David. "Maybe we should think about transferring to another ship," she said as she stacked the bowls. "A change could be nice. Do you want to see if any other six-month tours have open pilot positions? We still have a few days before the deadline."

"They'd never transfer us to another ship, not together."

Mo scraped the remains of the vegetable dip into the recycling chute. "They haven't forced one of us to transfer to another ship, so maybe they would."

"We're both twenty-five now."

"I know. But they let us go on this tour and they haven't asked one of us to leave the *Falcon* for the next, so obviously they're not concerned, right?" She wiped a napkin around the bottom of the vegetable dip bowl, put it on the floor, and lifted the next bowl from the stack. "Right?"

"They're not concerned because I won't be on the *Falcon* next tour."

Funny, she could have sworn that Les had just said she wouldn't be on the *Falcon* next tour. "What?"

"I won't be on the *Falcon* next tour."

Mo didn't want to look at her. She wanted to continue scraping cheese dip into the recycling chute; she wanted this instant in time to go on forever so she could continue living under the delusion that Les hadn't said anything about not being on the *Falcon* next tour. But her hands were shaking and she felt sick.

"I'm sorry, I didn't mean for it to come out like that."

In her mind, Mo whirled and threw the bowl at Les. In reality, she clung to it and turned around. Les, paler than usual, stood several feet away, her hands clasped in front of her. "How long have you known?" Mo asked.

"I wanted to tell you—"

"How long?"

"I was waiting for the right time, but I—"

"How long?" she roared.

Les grimaced. "The transfer went through last month."

Anger, disbelief, disappointment, fear, hopelessness, disillusionment—all clamoured for her attention. Her rational mind took over. It wasn't too late to fix this. "Which ship?" She instinctively held the bowl in front of her when Les stepped forward.

"Not another ship. I transferred to Interior."

The bowl slipped from her fingers and hit the carpet with a thud, even though Les's answer hadn't surprised her. She'd just never imagined that Les would actually do it, not without . . . "Why didn't you talk to me? I don't understand. I mean, this is us, Les. This is our relationship. And you went ahead and transferred to Interior without even talking to me about it? What I might think didn't count for anything?" Her voice sounded strained. Swallowing didn't help; her mouth was too dry.

"Mo, I wanted to talk to you, honestly I did. But then the accident happened, and everything associated with that, and then—"

"Wait a second, wait a second." Mo narrowed her eyes. "You knew before the accident? That was almost two flaming years ago! Why didn't you tell me? Did you think I'd have a breakdown or something?"

"No, no," Les said, vigorously shaking her head. "I didn't want to spoil things. I didn't want it hanging over us."

Now Mo understood why Les had fled the room and taken her time returning when David had been quizzing everyone about their plans. Oh sure, she wouldn't lie to them, but she didn't mind lying to her girlfriend. Well, she hadn't exactly lied—she'd held back an important piece of information. For two flaming years! "So you went ahead and made a huge decision that affects both of us without talking to me. You know, frankly, I would have preferred it hanging over us. At least then I would have felt that you cared about how it would affect me, instead of just doing what you wanted."

Les gaped. "Doing what I wanted? This isn't what I want. If it was up to me, I wouldn't be transferring."

"Because you don't really want to be in Interior?"

"No, because I want to stay with you."

"Then why in the flaming Argamon are you doing this?" Mo shouted.

"Because it's not up to me."

"Finney put you up to this."

"Finney didn't force me to transfer into Interior, no. But she did make it clear that she expected us to end our relationship around this time. If she hadn't known that I planned to transfer, she probably would have forced one of us to another ship a couple of tours ago."

 DISOBEDIENCE MEANS DEATH

Now only one emotion ran through Mo, and that was hate. Pure, unapologetic hate.

Les drew a deep breath and slowly exhaled. "I'm not going to lie to you. Interior appeals to me. But that's not the only reason I chose it. Our . . . bond is so strong, that we have to make a clean break. Half measures won't work. I'm not just thinking about now, I'm thinking about the future. If we both remain in Defence, we could run into each other."

Panic surged through her. "You're not seriously suggesting that we completely cut each other off in five weeks?"

"The whole point is to prepare for our Chosen Papers. We can't stay in touch. We can't see each other. We've left it too late already."

No writing? No seeing each other between tours? "I don't think I can do that. It's too sudden."

Les rubbed her forehead. "Mo, in two weeks' time we'll be in that conference room. If either of our Papers—"

"Then we'll break up," she said, not believing it would happen. Since the accident, her conviction that they were Chosens had only grown stronger. "But right now, we don't have to. We can't do anything about the next tour, since you went ahead and transferred without talking to me," she said with a glare, "but we can stay in touch, figure out what to do after that."

"We can't stay in touch. It'll look bad."

Mo put her hands on her hips. "Oh, so that's what it's about. What others think is more important to you than our relationship."

"That's not true! If it was up to me, we'd stay together, but it isn't. We're twenty-five. Our Chosen Papers can end our relationship at any time, just like that." Les snapped her fingers. "So we can't carry on as if we're Solitaries. They won't let us. Not anymore."

"David and Jackie will both be on the *Falcon* next tour."

"They're not like us. Everyone knows they could drop each other tomorrow and accept their Chosens. And everyone knows we'd struggle." Les sighed. "Our relationship is too serious. We have to split."

"If we're told to split, we'll split."

"We need to break up now, of our own accord. We don't want it on our records that Interior had to step in and force us apart."

"You won't even try. All you care about is your flaming record!"

"Yes, I care about my record!" Les shouted, her eyes blazing. "If I can't have you, can I at least try to have a career so I'll have a reason to get up in the morning? Can I try to salvage something from the wreck my life will be without you? And is it so bad that I want you to do the same, that I'll want to imagine you out there flying, on a tour you chose, because you didn't have any black marks on your record limiting your options? Is that so bad?" She bit her lip and looked at the floor.

"Do you really think that breaking up is the only way to satisfy people like Finney?"

"Yes," Les said, her eyes still on her feet.

Mo wanted to go to her, but to say what? That it was all right? It wasn't! "You should have told me sooner. You should have given me more time. You've had how long to get used to the idea? And I'm supposed to get my head around it by the end of leave?"

Les looked up. "I'm not used to the idea. I'll never be used to it. I don't want to do it."

"Then don't! What will Finney do? Monitor our dispatches? Have military stake out the estates when I'm on leave? Come on."

"This is Finney we're talking about," Les reminded her. "Do you honestly think we'd get away with staying in touch and seeing each other behind her back? She may be my mentor, but she wouldn't let that get in the way of doing her duty. She'd come down on us so hard our heads would spin."

And to think she'd liked Finney when she'd first met her. So much for first impressions.

Les took another step toward her. "But you're right. I should have told you sooner. And I shouldn't have just blurted it out, especially on your birthday."

Mo would have laughed, if she hadn't also wanted to cry. When she'd woken that morning, she'd expected to fly her shift, spend a few hours with friends, and then spend the night with Les. Happy flaming birthday! "I want you to talk to Finney and find out if she'd be upset if we stayed in touch."

"No." Les pressed her lips together and shook her head. "I know what she'll say."

"Les, do this for me. Please."

  DISOBEDIENCE MEANS DEATH

"I can't. We can't beg for more time. It's too late."

"Well, I guess you better go, then. It's over, right? No point you hanging around here." Mo pointed toward the door. "Go!"

They stared at each other in heavy silence. "If that's what you want," Les finally said.

"No, it's not, actually," she said, the hysteria she felt creeping into her voice, "but apparently we'll no longer do what we want to do. We'll do just the opposite." Needing to move, she bent over to pick up the bowl. Cheese dip had splattered onto the carpet. "Look at this mess." Suddenly life—everything—overwhelmed her. She sank to her knees.

"I'll take care of it," Les said.

"No. I'll do it . . . I have to get used to not having you around." The dam burst. "Why, Les?" she wailed as she hunched over and hugged herself. Why had they fallen in love? Why had they stayed together? Why?

Her shoulders shook—then her entire body. When Les's arms encircled her, she let herself go and grabbed Les, clung to her, pressed her cheek against Les's and felt Les's tears mingle with her own.

MO ZIPPED UP her bag with a sigh. Two weeks had passed, just like that. Time always dragged when she was looking forward to something; why couldn't it drag when she wasn't? If she could freeze time now, she would. No, she'd wait until she was with Les—then she would.

Les . . . Mo still couldn't believe she'd transferred. When she returned to the *Falcon*, reality would slap her around with the realization that she wouldn't see or contact Les for six months, perhaps ever again. But right now, she couldn't comprehend that Les would no longer be a part of her life. She had no point of reference for it. None whatsoever.

Since learning of Les's transfer, she'd struggled to not lash out, rage at her, ask her how she could have been so flaming stupid. She understood, on a rational level, why Les had transferred. But her heart wanted no part of it and engaged her mind in a constant tug-of-war. One minute she wanted to hug Les and tell her how much she'd miss her; the next she wanted to shout at her for ruining their lives. And in the background, time ticked away, infusing every word, every tender gesture, every moment with a crushing sense of futility. Les had done her a favour by telling her so late—she couldn't have stood years of this.

The door indicator chimed. She pressed the intercom button on her station. "Yes?"

"It's Ann."

What did she want? "Come in."

The door slid open. Ann stepped over the threshold and dropped two bags to the floor. "I'm on my way to 72. I'm on the first shuttle." She shoved her hands into her cloak's pockets. "I just came to say good-bye."

"Oh." This was new—Ann had never bothered before. "Well, yeah, enjoy your break. See you in a few weeks." She tensed. Ann would have a field day when she found out about Les. *So she finally dumped you, eh? Took her long enough. Wonder who's keeping her bed warm now.*

"No, I mean good-bye. I won't be back."

"What do you mean?" Mo blurted in shock.

"I'm going back to flying domestic."

"Why?" Defence wouldn't have removed her from the *Falcon*'s roster. Despite what Mo thought of her, she couldn't deny that Ann was a decent pilot.

"It's my mama." She removed her hands from her pockets, then shoved them back in again. "She needs someone around right now. All my siblings are Joined, so I'm the winner." Her sombre expression contradicted her words. "Domestic is kind of a compromise. She wanted me home all the time."

"What about your papa?"

"He died years ago."

"Oh," Mo said, suddenly struck by how little she knew about Ann personally. "I'm sorry." And sorry for her mama, too. Ann acting as some kind of caregiver? Good luck.

Ann shrugged. "I'd better go. Uh . . . do you mind if I send you a dispatch every once in a while, to see how things are going?"

The question took her by surprise. "No, of course not," she said politely. The chance that she'd actually hear from Ann was slim. Better than the chance that she'd hear from Les, though. Sure, Ann could send her dispatches, but not Les.

"See you, then." Ann picked up her bags and turned toward the door.

"Ann," Mo called.

Ann looked over her shoulder.

"Take care of yourself."

"You too." She punched the *Close* button as she stepped over the threshold. The door swooshed shut.

Had someone asked Mo how she'd feel if Ann left the *Falcon*, she'd have said that she'd jump up and down on her bed with glee. Instead, the news saddened her. Not long ago, they'd all been at the Military Academy, then learning the ropes on 72. What happened? Where had the time gone?

She picked up the image of Mama and Papa from the nightstand and hugged it to her chest. Why did everything have to change? When she'd flown domestic, her life had been almost perfect, marred only by her and Les's uncertain future. Then Mama had died and now Les was leaving.

She hoped—no, believed—that Les's absence from her life would be temporary. But how much solace would that offer her in the lonely months, maybe years, ahead? How long would she have to fight the temptation to slip back into the darkness she'd experienced after Mama's death? Because the temptation to withdraw from life would be very strong indeed. Reminding herself that she was Les's Chosen and that it was only a matter of time before she took her rightful place at Les's side would be her only defence against it. She had to remain strong—for both of them. If she felt herself faltering, she'd see Willis.

Her station beeped. Mo set the image back on the nightstand. "I'm ready," she said to Les. "I'll meet you on Deck 3."

"Okay."

"Oh, I had a visitor. Ann. She won't be back next tour. She's flying domestic again."

"You didn't tell her about me, did you?"

"No." They'd agreed to keep it to themselves for the remainder of the tour. Over the break, they'd tell those they cared about the most, like David. The rest would hear about it when she returned to the *Falcon* without Les; the news would quickly spread. "See you in a bit."

She terminated the connection and lifted the bag from the bed. Next time she entered her quarters, she'd be in a new phase of her life, one she'd never wanted to experience. With luck, their Papers would be there today, waiting for them, but she'd barely turned twenty-five. Receiving Papers this early was rare. Six months on was a real possibility, though, so maybe she'd only have to bear one tour without Les. Six months would be excruciating, but better than the rest of her life.

MO SIDLED HER way to an empty seat in conference room three, more a small auditorium than a meeting room. Les folded down the seat next to her and sat. They briefly touched hands, but didn't look at each other. A Chosen Council courier strode down the aisle and joined the end of the line of those already assembled at the front. The last shuttle would arrive in ten minutes. Once everyone on the *Over twenty-five and not yet Joined* list was present, they'd start announcing names.

David and Jackie took the two empty seats next to Les. "Doubt I'll get mine, but you could get yours," David was saying to her.

Jackie nodded. "I'm already a year over the average age."

Mo wished she could be as casual about the whole thing as they apparently were. Before she left this room, her dream could be realized, or she could be reduced to a weeping heap, barely able to function. Why did they have to gather everyone together to announce Papers? Learning in private that she and Les weren't Chosens would be devastating enough; she could do without an audience.

How would everyone expect her to react if one of them received Papers and the other didn't? Paste a smile on her face? Hug Les and wish her all the best? Forget it. If she could think—if she could move—she'd flee to the safety of her aviacraft, wait for Les . . . and then what? Her mind refused to visualize what would happen next.

She snuck a sidelong glance at Les. To anyone who didn't know her well, Les would appear relaxed and at ease, as if this meeting were about a trivial matter, not potentially about the rest of her life. But the set of her mouth and her rigid posture spoke volumes to Mo. Plus, Les hadn't protested when Mo suggested that they not sit in the front. Les was as terrified as she was, but had always been better at masking her feelings.

Fortunately David and Jackie were carrying on a silly conversation about flying a speed sim blindfolded. Welcoming the distraction, Mo listened and mentally threw in a comment here and there while trying to control her breathing. If she looked down, would she really see her heart leaping out of her chest, or did it just feel that way?

Too soon, those on the last shuttle streamed into the room and settled into seats. Mo did a quick head count: around forty people and eighteen couriers. She didn't like the odds, especially since a single courier could have Papers for more than one person. No, she had to believe! They'd both receive Papers, or neither would.

A female officer stepped up to the microphone. "Welcome home, everyone. Please stand."

Mo grabbed Les's hand and that of the person in front of her. Les's hand felt clammy, another sign that her outer calm was a lie.

"Disobedience means death," she chanted along with everyone else. "Death to those who commit a Chosen Violation. Death to those who disobey. Death to those who violate the Way. Death to those who violate the Way. Death to those who violate the Way!" She joined in the clapping, though today the reality of the Words sobered her, and frightened her a little, too.

"If your name is announced, please come forward and accept your Chosen Papers," the officer said when everyone had sat down. "Then return to your seat and wait until all the Papers have been distributed before reading yours. I know the first thing you'll want to do is rip open the envelope, but please respect your peers and celebrate their moments with them. There will be plenty of time afterward to read your Papers and celebrate with your families and friends. Any questions?" When no hands went up, she smiled. "Then let's begin."

She moved away from the microphone to allow the courier at the front of the line to take her place. He removed an envelope from the satchel slung across his shoulder and read its front. "Lieutenant Kenneth Neilson."

Mo knew of him; he was in navigation. She watched as he rose from his seat in the second row and bounded to the front. The courier presented the envelope to him with a bow. "Congratulations."

Neilson turned to those assembled and waved the envelope above his head, a broad smile on his face. Mo half-heartedly clapped. She hoped they didn't expect her to wave the envelope around like an idiot.

The next courier stepped to the microphone. "Lieutenant Commander Sylvia Moore."

Mo winced at the shriek behind her. Had everyone in here suddenly turned stupid? A minute later, she winced again—another envelope waver. The next courier stepped up. She swallowed and reminded herself to breathe, then relaxed slightly when the courier announced a lieutenant commander's name.

Four more names were called, none of them anyone she knew. She shifted, and grimaced when her shirt peeled slowly from her back, soaked with sweat. Good thing she'd left her cloak at the back of the room with her bag, rather than wearing it.

The courier at the microphone peered at the envelope in his hand. "Lieutenant David Bryson."

Mo felt as if she'd been struck by lightning. David was younger than Les! He was flaming younger than Les! If his Papers were here . . . While everyone else applauded, she gripped the arms of her seat and tried not to hyperventilate. She had to get out of this room. But she was trapped. They were trapped.

"I can't believe it," David said when he returned. Jackie didn't seem bothered; in fact, she smiled at him. How could she smile at him?

Mo could no longer focus. She applauded when everyone else did, but without registering the names and reactions. They hadn't called her or Les's name—that was all that mattered.

"Lieutenant Commander Jacqueline Quinn," a courier announced.

"Finally," Jackie said as she rose.

"What are the chances?" Les murmured.

If Mo read David's face correctly, he wasn't thrilled at the prospect. She shifted her gaze back to the front of the room as Jackie returned to her seat. Two couriers were left. Mo clapped when the courier at the microphone called a sub-lieutenant's name. Now only one courier remained.

Please, please, please! If they were Chosens, the same courier would have their Papers. The Chosen House in the Principal's sector always issued the Papers for both Chosens. So please, if this courier read one of their names, please let her read the other one afterward.

The courier stepped to the microphone. Mo shrank against her seat, closed her eyes, and dug her fingernails into her legs.

"Lieutenant Louise Murphy," the courier said.

Mo let out the breath she'd been holding and listened to the applause.

"Congratulations to those who received Papers," the officer who'd opened the meeting said. "Dismissed."

Tears stung Mo's eyes. Her hands trembled, then her body shook. Her throat felt tight; she wasn't getting enough air.

"Mo, are you okay?" Les sounded far away. "It's okay. We didn't get them. Neither of us got them."

No, it wasn't okay! She didn't know if she could go through this again. And next time she'd be sitting here fighting to breathe by herself! "I'm fine," she said, though her paper-thin voice betrayed her. "Let's get out of here." But then she heard the sound of paper tearing—David and Jackie opening their envelopes. As much as she wanted to, it would be rude to rush off.

David slid out his Papers and skimmed the top page. "I'm the Principal."

"So am I," Jackie said.

Neither seemed upset. "What about our notification parties?" David asked. "Our guest lists will overlap quite a bit."

Jackie pursed her lips. "When's your meeting?"

Mo couldn't believe it. If she and Les had just learned they weren't Chosens, the last thing on her mind would have been to coordinate her notification party with Les's. She would have been incapable of holding a conversation. They would have been carrying her out right about now.

She tugged on Les's sleeve. "Let's go."

"Congratulations, both of you," Les said.

"Oh, yeah—congratulations," Mo mumbled.

David smiled. "Expect invites."

"From me, too," Jackie said.

Not wanting to be insincere, she nodded and moved toward the aisle, trusting Les to follow. She wasn't in the mood to celebrate new beginnings, not when she was facing the end of her own relationship. She could probably come up with an excuse to politely bow out of Jackie's party, but not David's. He'd consider it a slight, and rightly so. Close friends didn't miss notification parties.

So, they were safe for another six months. What a relief! Mo collected her cloak and bag and watched as Les slipped into her cloak, slung a knapsack over her shoulder, and picked up two bags. Then it hit her. Relief turned to anger.

By the time they reached her aviacraft, Mo felt as if she'd explode. She punched in the security code and slid open the door. Even though she'd bought the craft over a year ago, it was still new, having spent most of its time parked at the shuttle base while she was on tour.

"I'm glad that's over," Les said as she slid into the passenger seat.

Mo bit her tongue and fastened her seatbelt. She started to enter the coordinates for the Thompson estate, then stopped. If she didn't get it off her chest, it would only eat at her.

Les looked at her. "What's wrong?"

"I'm so angry with you right now," Mo told her.

Les's brow furrowed.

"Our Papers aren't here. We could have had another six months together. But no, you had to go and transfer."

"It doesn't matter that our Papers aren't here. They can come anytime now. That's what matters."

"You keep saying that, but it's not true! Nobody receives Papers on tour." She pointed above her head. "Up there, we're safe. What are the chances that our Papers will arrive in the next three weeks? If they wanted us to have them, we would have received them today, when there's time for meetings and notification parties. They wouldn't wait until we're about to go back on tour."

Les shook her head. "Not necessarily. Remember that sub-lieutenant who got his Papers during the last week of leave? Those couriers had Papers that would have been delivered over the past six months. They only hold Papers back, they don't move them forward."

"I don't care!" Mo shouted, making Les jump. "What are the flaming chances that we'll get Papers within the next three weeks? Possible? Yes. Probable? No. So we could have had another six months. If you hadn't gone and ruined everything." She unfastened her seatbelt and shot up from her seat.

Les's eyes widened. "Where are you going?"

"I'm too upset. You fly us home."

"Mo—"

"Fly!"

"Okay, okay." Les moved to the pilot's seat.

Mo slammed herself into the passenger seat, did up her seatbelt, and folded her arms. The craft lifted off. She closed her eyes to signal that she didn't want to talk.

Why did Les always have to do what was expected of her? Why wouldn't she try to stay in touch? They wouldn't be violating any articles. Finney could intervene, but at least Les would have tried, shown that she was willing to risk a mark on her record for their relationship.

She inwardly snorted. What a nice fantasy—Les defying Finney. It would never happen. Mo would accept a mark on her record and only realize the consequences later. But she let her emotions rule her more than she should. Les thought things through, anticipated consequences, and acted accordingly. Trying to argue with her, trying to persuade her to reconsider, would be futile. Les would have already considered all the options; she must honestly believe that ending their relationship and cutting each other off—in three weeks!—was the best thing to do, for both of them.

Again Mo's heart and mind waged a battle. The very traits she admired about Les—her loyalty, dependability, and determination to do the right thing—were forcing an end to their relationship. But that was Les. It grated that Les seemed to be doing exactly what Finney wanted without so much as a peep, but truth be told, Mo would have been shocked, even horrified, if Les had told her they'd thumb their noses at Finney. That would have been someone she didn't recognize, not the woman whose loyalty to the Way guided her more than her emotions and desires.

She loved that woman, but at the same time, she wanted to flaming strangle her.

SWEAT TRICKLED DOWN Lesley's left temple as she strode along the path to the Thompson house. A heavy cloak had been suitable when she'd left on tour, but now it was too warm. Next time she went out, she'd wear a light civilian cloak. She was technically between assignments, and tomorrow she'd hand in her military cloaks so they could be altered. When she picked them up next week, they'd have Interior insignia on their chests.

When she saw the house in the distance, she stopped walking and dropped her bags to the ground. This was home now, not just the place she hung her cloak six weeks of every year. No more going on tour. She'd drift through life here until her Chosen Papers arrived.

She fought a wave of melancholy; she couldn't allow herself to grieve, not yet. They couldn't both be in despair. One of them had to remain strong . . . until they parted. It had to be her. Mo was justifiably shocked and upset. Lesley would have found it a bitter pill to swallow if Mo had suddenly informed her of a transfer and dictated the terms of how they'd end their relationship. But Mo would never have done that. Lesley had always known the responsibility for ending it would rest on her shoulders.

Discussing her transfer with Mo beforehand would have been a mistake. Mo would have resisted her every step of the way and potentially damaged their reputations for nothing. They couldn't win this one. They didn't have a choice. Mo didn't see that now, but perhaps in time she'd come to understand, even forgive. Lesley hung her head. How could she expect Mo's forgiveness when she was struggling to forgive herself? She'd transferred into Interior to protect Mo, to ensure that Mo wouldn't harm her reputation and career by trying to follow her. Telling Mo sooner wouldn't have lessened the shock. But still . . .

Her comm unit beeped. She pulled a handkerchief from her cloak pocket and wiped her sweaty hands, then slid the unit from its holder. "Thompson."

"Welcome back," Finney said.

"Thank you."

"I thought I'd beep you to see how things are going. Did you receive your Papers?"

"No."

Finney grunted. "You mentioned in your last dispatch that you'd told Mo about your transfer. How did she take it?"

Was Finney genuinely concerned, or checking up on them? Lesley suspected a little of both. "She's upset. It was a huge shock, not just my transfer, but . . . everything. She knew we'd break up at some point." If they weren't Chosens. Mo was still clinging to the faint hope that they were. "But she didn't expect it to be so abrupt. She thought it would be more gradual, that we'd start by physically parting, but still stay in touch."

"Why would she expect that? You couldn't have done it gradually when one of you received Papers."

Lesley started to pace. "I know. But that's not the situation right now."

"But it could be at any moment." Finney's voice hardened. "If she wanted gradual, she should have taken the initiative and transferred to another ship a year ago. Then she could have had gradual until you turned twenty-five. But not now. It's too late for gradual."

Finney's reaction didn't surprise her; she'd known it would be a waste of time. But for Mo's sake, she wouldn't let it go just yet. She had to be careful, though, not to make it sound as if Mo were weak in the Way. "You have to understand that, for her, it's come out of the blue. I've known for a while. She only found out two weeks ago and needs time to come to terms with it."

"It did not come out of the blue!" Finney snapped, sounding angry now. "She's known from the moment she turned eighteen. She's had seven years to come to terms with it. If she chose not to, that's her fault. That goes for you, too."

Lesley couldn't argue with that.

Finney blew out some air. "I know this is difficult, but tough. If you can't do it now, what makes you think you'll be able to do it when one of you receives Papers? You have to make a clean break now, start building lives without each other."

"I've gone through with the transfer on my own initiative," Lesley said, irritated that Finney was overlooking that point. "And I know we have to cut each other off." She didn't want to do it, but she would. "I was just telling you how Mo reacted."

"And I'm telling you why she'll have to accept that, once she leaves on the *Falcon*, that's it. No contact. She wouldn't have had any warning, any time to come to terms with it, if one of you had received Papers today. As it happens, she's had the last two weeks and has the next three. That'll have to do. I know it'll be rough, but that's too bad."

She'd expected Finney to resist any suggestion that they remain in touch, but not to be so callous about it. Had Finney not grasped what a traumatic and life-changing event this would be for her and Mo? Perhaps she had and knew that if she wavered and gave even the slightest hint that she was sympathetic, Lesley would try to persuade her to let them write to each other. She wished she could see Finney's face.

"I have to go," Finney said. "I'll see you next week."

All right, then. Discussion over. "I'm taking my cloaks and uniforms in tomorrow. Do you expect me to be in an Interior uniform when we meet?"

"No. I'll give you your uniforms and cloaks when I see you."

"I thought I'd have to pick them up from Supply."

"Not this time. Finney out." The connection went dead.

Lesley slid her comm unit into its holder. Well, she'd tried, not that it mattered. They were still breaking up. Mo would still be angry with her. And she'd still make a great show of enjoying her new career in Interior while she withered away inside.

She picked up her bags and resumed her walk to the house. She'd been wrong before. This wasn't her home. Nowhere would ever be home again, without Mo.

MO TRIED TO follow Les's lead on the impromptu dance floor without bumping into anyone. The Brysons had moved the larger pieces of living room furniture into the dining room and had pushed the rest against the walls, but the dance area was still cramped. Everyone was making the best of it—nothing would dampen the enthusiasm of those who'd gathered to offer David congratulations and wish him well during what would probably be the most important meeting of his life.

Usually Mo would be as boisterous and excited as those around her, but not tonight. She'd worked hard to hide her dour mood, smiling so wide that her cheeks hurt. And she'd nodded in agreement whenever someone waxed optimistic about David's future with his Chosen, even though she wasn't feeling all that optimistic about hers. But she found it a strain to keep up the charade as the evening wore on.

When Les had asked her to dance, she'd quickly accepted. If she let the mask slip while in Les's arms, nobody would notice. But glimpses

     DISOBEDIENCE MEANS DEATH

of other dancers—a tender gesture here, a head resting on a shoulder there—made her dance with Les feel like a farce. What were they doing, trying to pretend that everything was wonderful and they were happy, happy, happy? They'd spent the entire evening lying to others through their polite words and smiles. Mo didn't have the energy or the desire to do the same with each other. She drew back. "I can't do this, Les. I'm going to step outside, get some air. Give me a few minutes on my own, okay?"

Les let her go without protesting.

She fled to the back garden, not wanting to weep in front of everyone. The weariness and pain on Les's face had finally broken through her defences. But then, everything hurt these days. Talking to Les, touching her, seeing her, dancing with her—it all hurt. And that flaming clock ticked loudly away in the background, counting down the days, hours, and minutes until Les would disappear from her life. Sometimes she managed to tune it out, but never for long. Did Les hear it too?

The back door squeaked open; someone stepped onto the patio. "Hey, what's up?" David said. "I saw you rush out."

Mo quickly wiped away her tears, but not fast enough. David peered at her. "You're crying! What's wrong?"

If she lied to him, he'd catch her in that lie later, when he found out that Les wouldn't be returning to the *Falcon* and realized what had really been bothering her. Her lips trembled. This would be the first time she'd be telling someone outside her family. "Les isn't going back to the *Falcon*." She swallowed and wiped away another tear.

David's mouth dropped open. "What?"

"She's not going back. We're splitting up."

"I can't believe it! What ship is she going to?"

Mo shook her head. "Not another ship. She transferred to Interior."

David whistled. "Are you serious? When did you decide all this?"

As much as she'd have liked to tell him how Les had decided all of it and dumped it on her, she wouldn't. Despite her anger and disappointment at the way Les had handled it, she wanted to protect her. Everyone siding against Les would be terrible. "A few months ago. But it's really hitting home now."

"I bet."

"I was hoping we could still write to each other, but our sector commander is breathing down our necks. She wants a clean break."

"Not even a dispatch every once in a while to ask how you're doing?"

"Nope."

Sympathy softened his voice. "That's rough. I know you're twenty-five and your Papers can come now, but you would have broken up the moment they came."

As he and Jackie had? If he'd said that, she would have been furious with him.

"I guess it's smarter to do it now, but no contact?" He shook his head. "I can't believe it. It'll be weird, not seeing you together."

"When I rushed out, what did Les do?" she asked, hating herself for caring.

"She looked a little lost, then sat down." He paused. "I've known something's wrong all night. You might be fooling everyone else with those dazzling smiles, but not me. I've known you too long. I could have asked her what's up, but I figured I'd have a better chance of getting it out of you."

He did know them well. "I'm sorry."

"For what?"

"Telling you this tonight, at your party."

"Don't worry about that. It means a lot to me that you came. You must feel awful."

Awful didn't quite cover it. "So you won't take it the wrong way if we leave soon?"

"No. And I'm sorry this is happening, Mo. Seems to be one thing after another for you."

It certainly felt that way. She drew a deep breath. Okay, now David knew, but she still had to tell everyone else. Did Les realize that she'd left it up to her to let everyone know, that she'd be the one who'd have to face all the questions when she returned to the *Falcon* and everyone realized that Les hadn't? Had Les thought of that when she'd come up with her plan? The first few days back on board would be a nightmare, answering the same questions over and over and spinning her answers so Les wouldn't look bad, while trying to make it through her

　　　DISOBEDIENCE MEANS DEATH

days without breaking down. Maybe David could help. "Can you do me a favour?" she asked.

"Anything."

"Can you start mentioning to people that Les transferred to Interior? Not tonight. But you'll beep everyone to let them know how your meeting went, right? If you could just mention it. At least then they'll know before I see them next."

"Yeah, sure."

She would still face questions, but at least the conversations wouldn't start with *Where's Lesley?*

David touched her arm. "We'll all be there for you."

"I don't want to shut myself away in my quarters . . . like I did last time."

"We won't let you."

Her eyes welled up again. Without her family and friends, she'd never survive until she reunited with Les. "I noticed Jackie isn't here," she said, wanting to change the subject before she became too weepy. Jackie's party had taken place the previous evening. She and Les had declined their invitations, saying they had a previous family engagement. The excuse wouldn't have seemed far-fetched—military often visited family during leave.

"You know things were completely casual between us, so we could have attended each other's parties and enjoyed ourselves. But we didn't think it would look good."

She stifled a sigh. For once, could someone please do something that wasn't a violation but didn't look good? "Ann and Kary aren't here either."

"Kary wanted to come, but it's her cousin's eighteenth birthday today. I was a little disappointed, but what can you do? As for Ann, I sent her an invitation, but never heard from her."

That didn't surprise Mo. She couldn't remember Ann ever showing up for a social event when on leave. "You know she's not going back to the *Falcon*, right?"

His eyes widened. "No, I didn't know."

"Really?" Odd that Ann had told her and nobody else. "She's going back to domestic. Something about needing to be close to home."

"We weren't exactly friends, so I can't say I care all that much."

The back door swung open. "David! What are you doing hiding out here? There's a lineup waiting to dance with you. They won't get another chance."

David rolled his eyes. "Coming, Mama." He looked at Mo. "Sorry."

"It's okay. I should go back to Les."

She followed David into the house. If she walked into the living room and saw Les dancing with someone, she'd never speak to her again. Ha! Talk about an idle threat. She'd upset Les more by threatening to send her a dispatch from the *Falcon*.

A woman latched onto David and led him to the dance floor. Mo scanned for Les, saw her standing alone in a corner, sipping a drink. "I think we should go," Mo said as soon as she reached her. "I can't go on pretending that we're not saying good-bye in two weeks."

"We might offend David."

"I told him about your transfer. He won't be offended if we leave."

"You told him?"

"Yeah, I did. But don't worry, I made it sound like we were both in on the plan."

Les's brows drew together. "Why?"

"I don't know. Some of us remain loyal no matter what, I guess." She narrowed her eyes. "And some of us don't." She immediately regretted the jab when Les flinched. "Anyway, I'm leaving. Are you coming or not?"

"I'll just return this glass," Les mumbled.

"I'll meet you out front." She looked around for David's parents and saw them dancing—she'd send a dispatch to thank them for the party, rather than interrupt.

Outside, she pushed away the guilt she felt over taking that shot at Les. If Les expected her to constantly suppress her anger, she expected too much. Les wouldn't have to put up with her mood for long, anyway. She'd soon be rid of her, exactly as she'd flaming planned.

LESLEY FOLLOWED FINNEY through a maze of brightly lit, carpeted corridors and tried to muster some enthusiasm. Her first visit to head-quarters. Any other time she would have been thrilled to be here; she would have soaked up every detail and peppered Finney with questions.

 DISOBEDIENCE MEANS DEATH

But the reason for her visit had driven a wedge between her and Mo, perhaps forever. Normally a transfer would mean a new beginning and new responsibilities, but not this one. She'd always associate this transfer with an end, not only to her relationship with Mo, but to any hope of a happy and fulfilled life. What could have been would always overshadow what was.

They finally reached their destination. "This is my real office," Finney said with a sweep of her arm after inviting Lesley to sit. "I have an office in a couple of the C3 outposts, like the one we usually meet in, but this is home."

The office had a personal touch the others lacked. Images of Finney's Chosen and children hung on one wall, and perhaps sat on her desk—the backs of the frames faced Lesley. On the opposite wall, several drawings with *To Mama* scrawled in their top left corners were tacked up near a bookcase. She scanned the book titles. Not surprisingly, many were about the Chosen Tradition.

"You should become familiar with the military aviacraft routes," Finney said. "I zip between here, C3, and an outpost near home in no time."

When Mo had thought she might fail the pilot program entrance evaluation, she'd considered flying military aviacraft—for all of five seconds. She would have been bored out of her skull. Lesley could use the military's transit service, but perhaps it was time she bought her own aviacraft. Mo's craft had spoiled her.

Finney sighed. "Let's talk about your duties in Interior." She clasped her hands on the edge of the desk. "C3 covers a large area, but has a low population. It's quiet. It doesn't need a full-time commander."

Morton had intimated that Finney oversaw C3 because it was all she could handle, but Lesley had never believed that.

"Admiral Hall assigned me to C3 precisely because it wouldn't occupy all my time. I also head a small group of Interior officers who specialize in investigating potential Chosen Violations. We investigate tips about residents in sectors A1 to D8—Admiral Hall's sectors."

Lesley struggled to maintain a bland expression. Was Finney insisting that she and Mo sever contact because she headed this group? "Did this group spark your interest in the history of the Chosen Tradition?" she said, posing a safe question instead of the one she wanted to ask.

Finney's face tightened. "No."

She'd blundered. The question had hit a nerve.

"When we receive a tip about a potential Chosen Violation, we investigate it quickly and discretely," Finney continued. "We don't want gossip, rumours, or hysterical Chosens. Just about all tips turn out to be false alarms, which is fine. We *want* Rymellans to err on the side of alerting us to potential violations." She paused. "I'd like you to join this group."

And all the group's members would have to be above reproach when it came to the Chosen Tradition. Finney wouldn't tolerate even a whiff of inappropriate behaviour, including writing to former girlfriends while waiting for Chosen Papers. And so she and Mo were being wrenched apart.

Lesley mentally shook herself. She had to stop making Finney out to be a villain to justify her desire to stay in touch with Mo. Finney wasn't being unreasonable; she was doing her duty. Forcing them to build separate lives had nothing to do with this group. "I'd noticed that, for the past while, all the cases you gave me to study were related to the Chosen Tradition."

"And now you know why," Finney said, her mouth turning up at the corners. "Now, if you'd rather be assigned to a sector and a regular patrol rotation, just say so. I don't want people in the group who don't want to be there."

"No, this group sounds interesting." She crossed her legs. "Does this mean I'll report to you?"

"Yes. But not only to me. I'll be your primary report, but you'll have a secondary report, too."

"What do you mean?"

"We receive a fair number of tips, but not enough to keep everyone busy full-time. We all have other roles. When we arranged your transfer with Defence, we agreed that you'll go onto the supply list for domestic patrols and that you'll maintain your readiness to fly, should they need you."

"I don't want to fly out of 72."

"I've already made that clear to Defence." Of course she had. "Defence won't need you very often. You'll have time for other duties. So I have

     DISOBEDIENCE MEANS DEATH

something else in mind for you." Finney picked up a pencil and tapped it on the desk. "You might not like it, but try to keep an open mind."

She waited, more curious than apprehensive.

"We monitor all cases that go before the overseers. We—the military—aren't permitted to advocate in cases. But we can offer an opinion, which we'll do when we think an amendment will be difficult to enforce in practice, or when the presiding overseer asks us for one. Commander Blair heads the group that writes opinions. Based on the analyses you've written, you'd be a good fit for that group."

"Advocacy? Are you serious?" Lesley blurted.

Finney held up her hand. "Not advocacy. Advocacy deals with the theoretical. You'd be concerned with the practical. Advocates debate. You'd submit your written opinions directly to the overseers."

"But it's essentially advocating."

"Well, I hate to break it to you, but you're good at it. And unless you hated writing those analyses, and your sometimes zealous responses to my comments would indicate that you didn't, you might actually like doing it."

Her responses hadn't been zealous!

"I can sort of see why your parents thought you might pursue advocacy as a vocation," Finney said with a pained expression.

Lesley rejected a comeback that would have boiled down to *You're wrong, I'm not good at it and don't like it*. She had to keep her emotions out of this and respond logically. "I don't think I'm a good fit for the group. You said the opinions focus on the practical. I don't have any practical experience enforcing the Way."

"You did well when you analyzed the commentaries. Sometimes your analyses were better than the source material."

"But I had something on which to base my analyses. I wasn't starting from scratch."

"You wouldn't be starting from scratch here, either. You'd have access to every opinion we've offered. And you'd be assigned a case because the group that monitors cases believes an amendment would be problematic for us. You'd be able to contact them to find out why."

Then why couldn't someone in that group write the opinion? "What if an overseer made the request?"

"Then the overseer will have specified exactly what concerns him or her and will likely have provided background material."

Finney seemed to have an answer for everything. "None of that changes the fact that I don't have any practical experience," Lesley said.

"If that's important to you, we can put you on the supply list for Interior so you can go out on a patrol every once in a while. I was going to suggest that anyway. But frankly, I think you'll get enough appreciation for how theory sometimes differs from practice when you investigate tips for me."

But it would still be advocacy. Mama would love it: *If you'd listened to me, you'd be a real advocate, not a pretend one!* "I don't know."

"Lesley, you can directly influence the Way by writing opinions. Granted, most amendments aren't significant, but still. Do this, and it won't be a matter of if you'll be an admiral, it'll be a matter of when." Finney dropped the pencil into a mug that contained several others. "But if you don't want to do it, I won't force you. You can take on longer supply assignments to fill your time, for both us and Defence. Oh, and when Lieutenant Commander Grant heard about your transfer, he said he'd love to have you back on the announcements team."

"No." Announcements were broadcast not only on Rymel, but on Defence ships. Having her smiling face on the monitors wouldn't be fair to Mo. "I'm not interested in doing announcements. I'd rather write opinions." She'd rather not hurt Mo. "I'll join Commander Blair's group."

Finney nodded. "That's settled, then. I'll let her know. You'll probably assist others before you write opinions on your own, but I'll let her fill you in on the details." She flicked on her station's display. "So you'll report to Commander Blair and myself," she said absently as she typed, "and the appropriate superior officer when you're subbing, of course. I hope you like having a variety of duties."

"I want to be busy, and it sounds like I will be." In fact, if her work occupied her every waking minute, she wouldn't mind.

Finney peered at her over the display. "When would you like to start?"

"You're leaving my report date up to me?" Lesley asked, surprised.

"I thought you might like some time after the *Falcon* leaves."

So Finney wasn't oblivious after all. "I'd like to start the day after it leaves." The sooner she could throw herself into her duties, the better.

"Are you sure?"

"Yes. And when you add me to the supply lists, you can set my availability to always."

"Commander Blair and I might need you occasionally," Finney said dryly.

"I meant I'll always be available when you don't need me."

Finney stared at her. "You probably think I have a heart of stone because I want you and Mo to end it, completely, right now. I don't. I don't enjoy having to break up a relationship. I won't enjoy seeing you run yourself to the point of exhaustion to cope. But I'm doing this for your own good, and Mo's. I know you don't believe that right now, but it's true."

Suddenly overcome, Lesley lowered her head and closed her eyes.

"If you think it's hard now, imagine how hard it would be if you were dealing with this at the same time you were meeting your Chosen and her family. That could still happen, because your Papers can come anytime now. We can only hope you'll have time to adjust to life without Mo before they do."

If adjusting meant learning to live with yearning for another person while struggling to build a family with a Chosen she'd never love, she'd adjust—somehow. If it meant forgetting about Mo, never thinking about her, never lying awake at night wondering about her and wishing Mo was lying next to her instead of someone else, then it would never happen.

"You both have promising careers ahead of you. Risking them to stay together would be foolish. In the end, you'd end up right where you are now, but with damaged reputations."

Lesley raised her head, even though her eyes were moist. "I said as much to her when I told her about the transfer. I understand that. I think she does too. But it doesn't make it any easier."

"I know. I just wanted you to know that some duties are more difficult to perform than others."

"I appreciate that." Not only the truth of it, but Finney admitting it.

Finney cleared her throat. "I'm now your commanding officer. If I tell you to take a day off, you will. Understood?"

She nodded.

"Well then, I'll schedule you on a short training course before I put you onto the Interior supply list. I'll also see what Commander Blair initially has in mind for you. Report to me at 08:30 in the C3-1 outpost office and we'll go from there."

"Yes, Commander."

"And I guess it's time for your cloaks and uniforms and then we're done." She pressed a button on her comm station and instructed someone to bring them in. A minute later, a frazzled-looking officer entered and nodded to Finney as he hung them on Finney's rack.

Finney walked over and unzipped one of the bags. "You should try this on, to make sure these are yours and not someone else's." She pulled the cloak off the hanger and held it out to Lesley.

Lesley rose to accept it, then groaned. "They made a mistake. It has a lieutenant commander's insignia on it."

Finney turned it toward herself. "So it does. But it's not a mistake. You're joining Interior as a lieutenant commander. Congratulations."

"Thank you." She forced a smile, but doubted she was fooling Finney. When she'd been promoted to lieutenant, she couldn't stop smiling, but this promotion meant nothing.

"Would you like to go for lunch, to celebrate?" Finney asked.

Any other day she would have quickly accepted. Sharing a meal with Finney would be a privilege. Lesley respected her and valued her opinions, and knew that any resentment she currently felt toward her was temporary and unfair. But she'd be terrible company and didn't want to be dishonest. Every time she smiled, laughed, or showed interest in what Finney was saying, she'd be lying. "I'd like to, I really would. But . . ."

"Not today?" Finney said. "How about in a few weeks' time, then?"

"Yes, please."

"I'll schedule it, so we'll be sure to go."

"Thank you."

"Dismissed, Lieutenant Commander."

Lesley nodded to Finney and collected the rest of her clothing. She'd just achieved another career milestone, but it felt hollow. She'd feel

   DISOBEDIENCE MEANS DEATH

this way from now on, she realized with despair. To give her life a modicum of meaning, she'd throw herself into her new duties with enthusiasm. Lieutenant Commander Thompson would be the most hard-working, dedicated, and loyal officer Interior had ever seen. And an empty shell.

MO LIFTED THE lid off the cookie jar and peered inside. Cinnamon, ginger, and . . . She replaced the lid with a sigh. Not even her favourite oatmeal raisin cookies could entice her today. She wandered into the study and eyed the comm station sitting on one of the desks, but didn't feel like reading announcements. She didn't feel like doing anything—that was the problem.

Three days—three flaming days!—until she returned to the *Falcon*. Yet here she was, wasting away an afternoon on her own. Les hadn't beeped her all day. Mo couldn't blame her. She wanted to be with Les, but no matter how hard she tried, Les's transfer and their impending separation always came between them. Mo hadn't given much thought to what her last few weeks with Les would be like—she'd honestly thought they'd never arrive. She would have imagined them spending every last second in each other's arms, comforting each other, not at each other's throats to the point that they almost couldn't stand to be together. Okay, only she constantly went for the jugular, but then, she was the one who'd been wronged. She found it impossible to put her hurt feelings aside.

So here she was, wondering what to do with herself while fighting the urge to beep Les and pedal over to the Thompsons'. Going over there would be a bad idea—she'd end up reduced to a snapping, snarling, insensitive moron who'd hate herself every time she hurt Les, while hurting her anyway. Until she figured out how to control her anger and resentment—and she didn't have much time—loving Les meant staying away from her.

The comm station beeped. After glancing at its display to see if it was Les, she pulled the chair from under the desk and sat. "I've been expecting to hear from you," she said.

David chuckled. "It's been a busy two weeks."

"So? What's she like?"

"Her name's Angie. Well, Angela, but everyone calls her Angie. She's twenty-eight and lives in B6."

"That's only two sectors away from you."

"Still a ways away, but at least she won't have to adjust much to the weather."

"So what does she do?"

"She's a physician."

"Really?" Mo had expected his Chosen to be a little less . . . cerebral.

"But she's into research."

"Just like Karen! Maybe they know each other."

"Who?"

"Les's sister. Where did Angie study?"

"Somewhere in B5, I think."

"Oh. Karen studied in C2, so they probably don't."

"Speaking of Lesley, I, uh, mentioned her transfer to a few people. I figured I'd beep them before I beeped you."

Mo tensed. "What did they say?"

"Everyone's shocked. I think they expected something to happen, given that you're both twenty-five now, but a transfer to another ship, maybe? And since neither of you mentioned anything before you left the *Falcon*, everyone figured you'd both be back."

Until Les had dumped her surprise news on her, Mo had figured the same.

"I told Angie about the two of you, about how we met and how long you've been together. She said it'll be a rough time for you and that you'll need your friends around—"

Mo liked her already.

"—so we should invite you to supper. How about the day after the *Falcon* undocks?"

"She's going on tour with you?"

"Mo, we have to hold the Joining Ceremony within a year. It wouldn't be smart to not see each other for six months. I could have dropped from the tour. I checked into it and they allow that under these circumstances."

It should have occurred to her that David might drop from the tour because of his Chosen Papers, but she was too wrapped up with her own life at the moment. At his party, he probably hadn't wanted to add to her misery by mentioning that he might not be returning to the *Falcon* either.

"But she's a great fit for the *Falcon*," David continued. "I'll be moving to quarters with two bedrooms."

Well, that answered the unspoken question that had popped into her mind.

"Though I'm sure she won't be able to resist this dashing pilot for long."

Mo snorted and rolled her eyes. "Is Jackie dropping from the tour?" Or would they both be on board with new people on their arms?

"Yes, but not because of me. Anyway, Angie's looking forward to meeting you, so you'll come for supper, right?"

She wanted to say no. She wouldn't be in the mood for light chit-chat, and socializing without Les would feel strange. Obviously she'd done it before, but Les had still been a part of her life. Everyone had spoken of her in the present tense, but now they'd refer to her as someone Mo used to be with. For people like Angie, her relationship with Les would be a thing of the past. Les wouldn't be a real person; she'd be someone they only knew of second-hand, someone who used to serve on the *Falcon*.

Supper with David and Angie could be a struggle. Being with people, trying not to talk about Les too much, appearing interested in others' lives, smiling—it would be so much easier to stay in her quarters and avoid them all. So she had to accept their invitation. "Yeah, I'll come." She'd also beep Willis the moment she stepped back aboard the *Falcon*.

"Great! Um, I hate to run, but I'm meeting her soon. Have to get ready. Oh, will you tell Lesley about her?"

"Sure." She didn't need to ask if he liked Angie; the eagerness in his voice offered the answer.

"Thanks. See you in a few days. I'll drop in on you, see how you're doing." The connection went dead.

At least someone was happy. Mo rose from the chair with a sigh and strolled into the hallway. Now what? Maybe some fresh air would invigorate her. She collected her comm unit from her bedroom and left the house through the back door. "Oh, I didn't realize you were out here."

Papa jumped. The book that had been lying open on his chest slipped to the grass.

"Sorry, I didn't mean to wake you," Mo said as she bent to pick it up.

"I wasn't dozing, I was thinking," Papa spluttered.

She read the book's title: *The Rymellan Government: Organization and Responsibilities*. Definitely sleeping. She set the book on the table next to his lounge chair, taking care not to tip over a jug of juice and Papa's half empty glass.

"Heading over to the Thompsons'?" he asked.

"No, I'm not." She sat cross-legged on the grass, picked up a twig, and rolled it between her fingers.

He studied her from under his wide-brimmed hat. "If your mama were here, she'd know what to say to make you feel better."

Mo shook her head. "Even Mama couldn't have made me feel better."

"I don't get it. I thought you'd want to be with Lesley right now."

"Me too." She threw down the twig and started plucking blades of grass. "I'm mad at her, Papa. How could she do that to me? Just transfer like that?"

"Now come on, Mo. You knew you couldn't stay together forever."

Why not? Why couldn't they choose to be with each other? Why did the flaming Chosen Council get to decide for them?

A chill ran up her spine. Not only would thoughts like that lead straight to an execution site, but she didn't much like them. She desperately wanted to be with Les, but she would never violate the Chosen Tradition. The Way came first, not her. Easy in theory, sometimes flaming difficult in practice, but she wasn't weak in the Way. She believed in the Way, and so did Les. She'd joined the military to protect it, and so had Les. And according to the Way . . . "We wouldn't be violating any articles if we stayed together until our Chosen Papers arrive."

"That's not the point. You're twenty-five. You're supposed to be ready to meet your Chosen. How can you be ready if you're still with Lesley? People would talk."

She couldn't care less if people talked, but Les might.

"One of you had to make a move," Papa said. "Can you blame her for not telling you until after she'd transferred? Look at how you're reacting now."

"Yeah, I can blame her! I should have had a say."

"Maybe she didn't tell you earlier because she was afraid you'd talk her out of it."

"I would have tried."

"See?"

She picked up another twig and snapped it in half. "Okay, maybe I can understand why she waited." At least her head did. "But no matter how many times I tell myself that she didn't do it to hurt me, I can't get past it. Every time I see her, I end up being mean to her, and I don't like being mean to her."

Papa raised his eyebrows. "And that's why you're here instead of over there?"

Mo nodded. "I don't know what to do. I mean, what'll happen if I can't get past this before I go back to the *Falcon*? I don't want to leave things like this."

He gulped down some juice and smacked his lips together. "Did I ever tell you that your mama came to see me at the workshop the day she died?"

"No," Mo said, puzzled and a bit shocked at the abrupt change of subject. Maybe a glance at Mama's garden had reminded him.

"She did. It was a half day at the Indoctrination Academy for her. She dropped in on her way home to see if I wanted to go for lunch. We went to that new eatery near station C3-1. Well, it's not new now, but it was then."

Mo couldn't believe that Mama had been dead for almost two years. Sometimes it all came rushing back as if it had happened yesterday.

"I've always been grateful that we didn't bicker over lunch. We had a leisurely meal and enjoyed each other's company. We talked about Neil and Barbara and when they might have another baby."

Barbara was due with their second child, a girl, in two months. "Did you guess right?"

"Mmm . . . we thought it would be a bit sooner." Papa sipped his drink again. "We talked about you going on your first tour, and Andrew's eighteenth and whether he'd be a Chosen . . ." He stared into the distance. Maybe he was back in that eatery, enjoying his food and laughing with Mama.

Mo waited, not wanting to intrude on his thoughts. At times like this, she always felt as if she should apologize for the accident, even though she'd accepted that it wasn't her fault.

Papa's eyes focused on her. "We didn't say good-bye at the eatery. She went back to the workshop with me. A client was waiting, a little too early for his appointment, I might add. He was suddenly more important than your mama." His eyes glistened. He topped up his glass, drained it in one go, and set it back on the table. "So instead of a proper good-bye, your mama got an absent-minded one. You know how it goes," Papa said, waving in one direction and facing another. "Your mind's already onto the next thing. I didn't even kiss her." He shook his head. "I wish we'd said good-bye at the eatery. I would have taken more time. If I'd known . . ." His shoulders slumped.

"Papa, everyone does that."

"Does what?"

"Says good-bye without thinking about it. You can't treat every good-bye as if it's the last time you'll see the person. Nobody lives like that."

"Maybe not, but I wish I could live those few minutes at the workshop over again. Five minutes, that's all I'd want. I'd take my time, especially since that client was early. I'd look your mama in the eye, talk to her, make sure she knew I loved her. Five minutes. That's all I'd want."

A lump formed in Mo's throat.

Papa met her eyes. "Do you know how lucky you are? You have three days. Three whole days. What I wouldn't do for three days with your mama."

Mo swallowed. "Les isn't going to die in three days, Papa."

"She is for you, Mo. She is for you."

Her chest felt tight. She shook her head. "No."

"Yes. You'll never see her again. You'll never talk to her again. She'll be gone. And if you let these three days go to waste, you'll regret it for the rest of your life. You'll never be able to put it right. It'll hang over you, hurt you every time you think of her or someone mentions her name. You don't want that, do you?"

"Of course I don't," she whispered.

"Forget how she handled the transfer. Don't let it erase all the years you had with her. Don't let it dictate how you say good-bye."

Mo couldn't answer him, not when she was pressing her lips together to stop herself from crying.

"You're still young, Mo. Your Chosen, your daughters, furthering your wonderful career doing something you enjoy—you have all that ahead of you. Don't spoil your chances for happiness. Let Lesley go gracefully. Think about all the good times and all the times she stood by you."

She didn't want to; it would only hurt more if she did.

"Mo?" Papa swung his legs off the lounge chair, sat up, and peered at her. "Oh no, you're crying," he moaned. "Oh, I'm no good at this. I knew I shouldn't have tried." He leaned forward and rubbed her arm. "I should have been gentler. Your mama never made you cry."

"Sure she did." Mo lifted her sleeve to wipe her nose, but then accepted the handkerchief Papa held out to her. She blew her nose into it and shoved it into her pocket. "I'm not crying because of what you said, okay? I've been holding this in all day. If you'd said supper's ready, I probably would have cried."

"I doubt that." He paused. "My cooking's not *that* bad."

Mo almost smiled.

Papa pointed at her, his finger nearly touching the tip of her nose. "I saw that."

She struggled to her feet and hugged him. "I understand what you're trying to say," she murmured. "And I don't want to leave feeling angry with her." She wanted them to part on the best possible terms, so they could pick up where they'd left off the moment they reunited. This breakup would be temporary; in fact, she didn't see it as a breakup at all. They'd be physically separated and out of touch, but still in a relationship. Les would still be her girlfriend, or at least that was how Mo would feel inside—she'd never tell anyone. Would Les feel the same way, or would she consider the relationship completely over once the *Falcon* undocked? Probably the latter. Les didn't believe they were Chosens. Mo would have to believe for both of them . . . and so she could survive.

"Go see her," Papa said, patting her back. "Don't waste any more time."

No, she wouldn't rush over to Les just yet. She needed to be with her, but at the same time, being with her would be unbearable, maybe worse than after Mama had died. This time she knew in advance when her life would undergo a devastating change, but she couldn't do anything to prevent it. She had to accept that it would happen. No hiding within herself—there wasn't time. No letting her anger get the better of her and turning on Les—there wasn't time. Before she saw Les, she had to somehow put aside her hurt over the transfer and figure out what she'd say to her.

She let go of Papa and brushed the grass off her behind. "Why are you reading that book, anyway?" she asked.

"I'm going to run for the government," Papa declared.

Not this again. Since he hadn't talked about it for several years, she thought he'd wisely given up on the idea.

"Dan's retiring after this term, so I thought, why not? I wish I'd done it while your mama was alive. I kept saying I would, but I never did."

"Mama didn't care if you ran for the government."

"She probably got sick of hearing me talk about it all the time. She probably wanted to say do it or shut up."

Mo silently agreed. "What about your clients? Wouldn't you have to give up the business?"

"Dan says the position isn't full-time for the C3 representative. And Andrew can handle things when I'm not there."

Andrew had helped out at the workshop for over a year now. He'd made her a pair of pants during her last leave. Amazingly, they'd fit.

Her comm unit beeped; she glanced at its display. "It's a pilot, I better take it."

Papa nodded and lifted his book from the table. She moved away and hit the connect button. "David told us about you and Lesley," Sheila said after they'd exchanged greetings. "We're sorry. And surprised. Interior? That's quite a change."

"We thought it best." There she went again, protecting Les. "If she'd transferred to another ship, I would have been tempted to transfer too."

   DISOBEDIENCE MEANS DEATH

"They probably wouldn't have let you."

But she would have tried, and appeared weak in the Way. The transfer, the separation, not communicating with each other—it was all about appearances now. And that rankled.

"Sorry, this is probably the last thing you want to talk about. I just wanted to say that Ruth and I were sorry to hear about it."

"Thanks."

"I beeped Lesley to tell her the same, but she didn't answer. Will you tell her?"

"Sure," Mo said absently as she wondered why Les was ignoring beeps.

"Oh, and we were wondering if you'd like to come for supper and maybe play a little cards? Ruth wants to catch up. Maybe a few days after we undock?"

"Sure," Mo said again.

"I'll send you an invite. Take care, okay?"

"You too." She terminated the connection. Apparently she was on the top of everyone's pity-invite list. No, that wasn't fair. Her friends were rallying around her, trying to help. Wait a minute. They were Les's friends too, but they wouldn't be there for her. Les wouldn't have anyone; she was leaving behind everyone and everything she'd known for the past seven years.

At David's party, Mo had resented that she'd have to explain Les's transfer to everyone, but now she realized that she'd be in a much better position to cope with their separation than Les. She'd be doing what she knew and loved while surrounded and supported by friends she trusted. Les would face new duties in a new division and have to readjust to being home all the time. And whose shoulder would she cry on? Finney's? Adelaide's? Alan's, maybe, but he might follow Adelaide's lead. Karen would normally be there for her, but she'd recently Joined. Forget Jason—Adelaide's golden boy would never cross his mama by propping up a sister who should just grin and bear it. So Les wouldn't have anybody. She'd have to cope on her own.

Suddenly Mo feared for her. Les was strong, but everyone had a breaking point. Leaving on an angry note, letting Les believe that she'd destroyed them, would add a burden Les didn't need. Mo hadn't had a say in the timing of their separation or the details of it, but she was flaming-well going to influence how they parted. This wasn't the time for temper tantrums, tears, and cheap shots. She had to make sure Les knew how much she loved her and that she forgave her. Les would need something to sustain her until they reunited.

But first she had to purge herself of her anger, disappointment, and resentment—all the negative emotions that had swirled within her since the night of her twenty-fifth birthday. So she'd find a private spot in the woods on the estate and let it all out. She'd scream at the top of her lungs, throw rocks, stamp her feet, tell Les exactly what she thought of her and her stupid transfer and this farce of a separation. She'd collapse into a heap and cry, beat her fists against the ground, and rage about how unfair it was. And then she'd do it again, until she got so sick of it that she wanted to throw up. Only then would she be ready to see Les.

She strolled back to Papa. "I'm going for a walk. When I come back, let's have supper together."

Papa frowned. "I thought you'd be going to see Lesley."

"I will later. I want to have supper with you first. After that, I don't think we'll be seeing much more of each other before I go back to the *Falcon*."

"I should be offended." His face softened. "But I understand."

"I'll see you in a bit, then." She stalked off. Some tree out there was about to get it.

LESLEY STUCK HER spoon into her pudding and stirred it—again. Even though disappointment and regret had killed her appetite, she'd managed to force everything down but dessert. Ever since she was a child, dessert had been the fun course, a treat after the harrowing ordeal of eating Brussels sprouts or broccoli. But tonight she wasn't in the mood for fun. She doubted she ever would be again.

Why hadn't Mo beeped or dropped by? Yesterday Mo had stormed away after a tense evening that had left them both in tears. Lesley's first impulse had been to go after her, to try to smooth things over. She desperately wanted Mo to forgive her for the transfer and for keeping it to herself for so long, but Mo could hardly stand to look at her right

    DISOBEDIENCE MEANS DEATH

now. So she'd restrained herself and had decided to wait for Mo to beep her, to give Mo time to cool off. She hadn't considered the possibility that Mo wouldn't beep her at all.

So now what? Continue to wait, or cave in and beep her? She didn't want to squander away their remaining time together, but a repeat of last night wasn't appealing. How would they resolve the rift between them when Mo couldn't bear to be with her? How would she live with herself if Mo left angry with her? If only they had more time . . .

Mama walked into the dining room. "Still not finished?" she asked as she buttoned her cloak.

Lesley pushed away the pudding. "I'm full."

"Are you sure you don't want to come to Karen's with us? You barely know William."

"I'm not in the mood." She'd have plenty of time to acquaint herself with Karen's Chosen after Mo had left.

"Why don't you trust the Chosen Council like everyone else does?" Mama said, frowning. "They just might match you with someone you'll like and eventually love."

Like, perhaps. Love, never. She loved Mo. Period.

"If they weren't good at what they do, there would be lineups at execution sites. They probably know you better than you know yourself. They'll match you with someone you'll love, you'll see."

Only if Mo were right and they were Chosens. But she couldn't let herself believe that. She had to prepare for the worst.

Mama tutted. "What is the point of talking to you? If you'd done what every other Rymellan does and dated others, you wouldn't have this childish notion in your head that only Mo will do. But no, you knew better. And now look at you." She jutted her chin toward Lesley. "You're in Interior now. Rymellans expect their military to be strong. We don't want weak people protecting the Way. So pull yourself together. You'll be home a lot more now. I don't want you moping around the house all day."

"Adelaide?" Papa called.

"I'll see you later," she muttered, then turned on her heel and strode from the room. Moments later the front door shut.

Lesley stared at the pudding until her eyes lost focus, then glanced around the empty table. This dining room seated ten; the formal dining room could seat forty. But here she sat, all alone. Well, she'd better get used to it. Even if every chair at the table were occupied, she'd still be lonely, still long for Mo.

The front door slammed shut. Lesley straightened. Her parents must have forgotten something. She'd get an earful if Mama came in and found her crying into her pudding.

"Les?"

Her spirits instantly lifted. "I'm in the dining room," she shouted.

Mo pulled out the chair to Lesley's left and plunked herself into it. She eyed the pudding, then looked at Lesley. "Okay, I know I've been a pain, but your transfer knocked me sideways."

"I'm sorry," Lesley said, relieved and elated. "I should have told you sooner. I put it off because I didn't want to hurt you." And because she'd struggled to face and accept it herself. Every step of the transfer process had seemed surreal.

"Can I have that pudding?" Mo asked, pointing at it.

Lesley slid it over to her.

Mo scooped out a spoonful and lifted it to her mouth. "You know, I thought we'd stay together until our Papers came."

"We always knew we'd have to split up around this time, like everyone else does."

"But we're not like everyone else."

"What do you mean?"

Mo waved the spoon at Lesley. "You'll hate what I'm about to say, because you'll think it's silly and that I'm setting myself up for a gigantic fall. But I'm going to say it anyway." She swallowed and dipped the spoon into the pudding again. "We're Chosens. Each other's Chosen."

Mo was right; Lesley thought she was setting herself up for heartbreak. "Mo, you can't count on that. I know it's what you want." She hesitated, then decided it wasn't the time to hold back. Anything left unsaid would remain that way for the rest of their lives. "I'd like that too."

"Really?" Mo said around a mouthful of pudding.

"Yes. If the Chosen Council were to ask me who I want, I'd say you. But it doesn't work that way. The Chosen Council chooses for us. We

     DISOBEDIENCE MEANS DEATH

have to trust it." She hated parroting Mama, but it was true. Only those weak in the Way doubted the Chosen Council.

"I am trusting it! Don't you see? I trust that the Chosen Council will choose the best match for me. That's you. You're my best match. If the Chosen Council chooses someone else, it will have failed. But I know it won't, because I trust it. I trust the Way. That's why I believe you're my Chosen. See?"

What she saw was convoluted logic based on a single assumption. "Every Rymellan who's ever been in this situation must think that."

Mo scraped out more pudding and licked it off the spoon. "How many Rymellans do you know who've been in this situation?"

Well, nobody, really. She knew of a few couples who'd broken up as they approached twenty-five, or had even stayed together beyond that point, but they'd been casual pairings. David and Jackie were a typical example. There had to be serious couples hanging on to the bitter end somewhere on the planet, but they'd be the exception, not the rule, and their commanders would know exactly who they were.

"Like I said, we're different," Mo said, interpreting Lesley's silence as agreement. "We've stayed together for years. And we'd continue to stay together if we could, right?"

"We can't stay together," Lesley said, wondering where this was leading.

"If nobody cared if we stayed together—if it wouldn't damage our reputations and Finney and everyone else wouldn't bat an eye—then we'd stay together, right?"

"Well, yes."

"You said it yourself—we have a strong bond. We're not struggling with this because we're weak in the Way and should have broken up months ago without blinking, but because we're Chosens. We're meant to be together. We'll never break up. We're not supposed to." She dropped the spoon into the empty pudding cup.

Lesley's heart sank. Now the conversation would degenerate into an argument and Mo would storm out. They'd be right back where they were after she'd marched out last night, but with one less day together. "I can't go back on the transfer, Mo. We have to split now. We have no choice."

"I know," Mo said, surprising her. "I went for . . . um, a quiet walk earlier and had a bit of a think. Everyone's working on the assumption that we're not Chosens, and we're supposed to assume that, too. So fine, we'll force ourselves apart. You'll be here, I'll be on the *Falcon*. We'll be out of touch. We won't see each other for a bit. But as far as I'm concerned, we'll still be together. You'll still be my girlfriend. That's how I'll see it." She gazed at Lesley.

The unspoken question—*Is that how you'll see it, too?*—hung between them. Mo had verbalized exactly how Lesley would feel, even after her Chosen Papers arrived. She'd always feel bonded to Mo. Her life with her Chosen would be one long betrayal, her Joining something to endure, not embrace. And that was why she and Mo had to part and could never, ever see each other again.

The vulnerability in Mo's eyes frightened her. She should tell her that she wouldn't see it that way; that their relationship would end the moment Mo left for the *Falcon*. But Mo had been brutally honest and deserved honesty in return. Again, this wasn't the time to hold back. She took Mo's hands in her own and kissed them. "That's how I'll feel, too. That's how I'll feel for the rest of my life."

Mo's eyes shone. "Then I don't want to hear the words breakup, split, or anything like that again. That's not what's happening here. We'll be separated for a little while. It'll be tough, but temporary. If we're lucky, we'll reunite in six months." She drew a quavering breath.

"The average age for Papers is twenty-seven."

"Aha! You're starting to believe what I believe."

"No, I'm just saying that it could be a while before either of us receives Papers. I'd like to believe we're Chosens, but I can't."

Mo caressed Lesley's cheek. "Yeah, I know, that logical mind of yours is getting in the way."

Actually, her logical mind had a habit of disappearing when Mo was involved. But when it came to the probability of her and Mo being Chosens, it refused to budge. Yes, they had a strong bond. Yes, if it was up to them, they'd stay together for the rest of their lives. But the Chosen Council had considered every same-oriented female within five years of their ages when determining their best matches. She couldn't take the same leap Mo had taken. Sometimes her inability to throw rational thought out the window was a curse, but this time, it was protecting her. If she embraced the belief that Mo was her Chosen and it turned out to be untrue, she'd never recover. She worried that Mo wouldn't, either.

At the same time, she knew it would be pointless, and perhaps cruel, to try to dissuade Mo from her conviction. Mo might need to believe they were Chosens to cope, to see her through the bleak months until she no longer needed to believe or Papers forced her to accept reality. Lesley wouldn't take that away from her, not when she wouldn't be there to deal with the consequences. But she dearly hoped that Mo would have abandoned the notion by the time one of them received Papers. If she hadn't . . . Lesley couldn't bear to think about what might happen. It would probably be better if she received her Papers first; then Mo would have time to grieve before she met her Chosen. If Mo received hers first, a stranger would have to support and help her, while Lesley lay awake at night, worried and resentful.

"Will you promise me something?" Mo said.

"What?"

"Will you beep me when you receive your Papers? If you get yours first, I mean. And don't leave me a message or send a dispatch. Talk to me. I'll want to hear it from you, not read about it or hear it second-hand."

"I'll beep you if you're here on Rymel. If not, I'll have to send you a dispatch. I won't be able to talk to you after my notification meeting. It would be too risky."

"If you have to do it by dispatch, promise me you'll read my reply. If we're not Chosens, I'll want to say a proper good-bye." Mo's chin trembled.

Lesley's eyes filled; she wrapped her arms around Mo and squeezed her. "I promise," she said against Mo's ear. "And I want you to promise that you'll do the same. If you get yours first, tell me. You'll definitely be here, so beep me." She'd want to hear Mo's voice one last time, to know that Mo would be okay. If she suspected that Mo was struggling, she'd beep Willis, corner Mo's siblings, talk to Michael, do whatever it took to see that Mo received the support she needed. Well, anything except beep Mo's Chosen. She'd avoid ever hearing the woman's name, if she could.

"I promise." Mo sounded strained. "I didn't want to do this," she said as she drew back and wiped her eyes. "No more talk. Let's do something."

"I'm sorry about not telling you about the transfer sooner," Lesley murmured.

"Forget it, Les. No matter when you'd told me, I wouldn't have liked it. There's nothing you could have done to make this easier." Her face tightened. "I'm still angry, but not at you. I'm angry at how stupid this separation is and at how little everyone trusts us."

"They're trying to protect us."

Mo snorted. "Enough talk."

Lesley touched her forehead to Mo's and gently kissed her lips. "Lake?"

"No. Next time we go to the lake, we go as Chosens." She gave Lesley a defiant look, then relaxed when Lesley didn't challenge her. "How about the Dance Hall?"

"Are you sure? You couldn't dance at David's."

"I've calmed down since then." Mo paused. "But I can't act as if everything's wonderful. I may get a little teary-eyed now and then." She pressed the palm of her hand against Lesley's cheek. "Don't feel guilty because I'm blubbering on the dance floor and you're not. You'll fool everyone else, but not me. I'll know you feel as bad as I do."

Lesley covered Mo's hand with her own and struggled for control. Mo could see through her because they shared a level of trust and intimacy that Lesley would never share with anyone else.

"But let's try to forget, just for tonight," Mo said. "Let's go to the Dance Hall and pretend we're eighteen again." She smiled through her tears. "Remember the first time we went there after we turned eighteen?"

"It was during our first break from the Military Academy," Lesley said, nodding. "We couldn't go before then because someone," she tapped Mo's nose, "hadn't turned eighteen yet."

"Yeah, that's right. We had so much fun that night! Remember how grown-up we felt?"

Lesley chuckled.

"Twenty-five seemed so far off then, but here we are." Mo sighed, then slapped her hands against the table and pushed back her chair. "So let's go dance the night away. Let's close the place. It'll be a while before we dance together again. And we *will* dance together again, Les. We will."

Lesley almost believed her.

MO DROPPED HER bag into the cargo container and shut the container's lid. She closed her eyes, slowly inhaled, and exhaled through her mouth. Nope, that didn't help one bit—she still shook inside and felt as if her stomach were digesting lunch over and over. She took another deep breath anyway, then hopped off the aviacraft.

Only Les stood outside. At least she'd been standing when Mo had entered the craft—now she was pacing.

Mo had said good-bye to Papa and Nathan at the house. Papa had been uncharacteristically worried, insisting that she beep him when she reached the *Falcon*. Did he think she'd fail to report? That would be insane and counterproductive—the whole purpose of this charade was to protect her precious reputation and career. What a flaming farce— no! Anger would have to wait. When she got to the *Falcon*, she'd go to the simulators, load up a combat sim, and shoot everything that moved. Would anyone object if she asked Larry to modify the sim so that all the ships looked like Finney? Probably, since it would violate Article 117.

Les's cloak billowed as she spun around to pace in the opposite direction. Mo didn't understand why Les had worn a civilian cloak. Les wouldn't have upset her by wearing her Interior cloak, since she'd already worn it several times since receiving it. So why a civilian cloak today? Mo had asked, but Les had changed the subject. She hadn't pressed her—they didn't have time for arguments or in-depth discussions.

"I'm ready to go."

Les continued to pace, oblivious to her.

"Les!"

Les stopped mid-pace and looked at her.

"I'm ready to go." Her breath quickened. She clenched her hands and dug her fingernails into her palms. For both their sakes, she needed to hold herself together for the next few minutes. She could fall apart in the aviacraft, leave the flying to auto-navigation. She still didn't fully trust it, but this once, she'd make an exception.

Les stood in front of her. They stared at each other. Mo didn't know what to say. What could she possibly say that would mean anything? Everything she thought of sounded trite.

"Well." Les reached out to straighten Mo's collar. "Don't forget to do your laundry. Keep up your violin. And tidy your quarters every once in a while," she said, completing her work on the collar with a pat. "And . . . um . . ." Her mouth moved but nothing came out. Blood flooded her face; she blinked rapidly.

Mo swallowed. Watching Les struggle was unbearable, especially when she was on the verge of breaking down herself.

"Know that I'll be thinking of you every day." Tears rolled down Les's cheeks; she didn't seem to notice. "And know that I love you. I love you very much."

"I love you, too," Mo managed to say before collapsing into Les's arms and weeping. She held Les; Les held her; they cried until they were spent, and still clung to each other. "This is not good-bye," Mo said into Les's shoulder. "We'll see each other again. We'll see each other again." She grabbed Les's cloak, balled it in her hands. "You remember that, okay? We will see each other again." She thought she felt Les nod, but wasn't sure.

Les drew back, took Mo's face in her hands, and gazed at her.

"I know, I look like a wreck," Mo said, attempting a smile that probably made her look worse.

"You look beautiful." Les's eyes welled again. A tear escaped and ran down her cheek and onto her neck. She wiped it away. "I have to go now."

Mo pressed her lips together and started sniffling. She still had her arms around Les and didn't want to let her go.

Les reached behind her, unlaced Mo's fingers, and kissed Mo's hands. "I have to go."

"No. Not yet." She pulled her hands from Les's and reached for her. They locked lips and shared a tender, lingering kiss that might have to last them the rest of their lives. Mo felt dazed when Les kissed her forehead. "You'll let me know if your Papers come, like you promised, right?" she remembered to say.

Les nodded and started to open her mouth.

Mo shook her head. "Don't say anything. Just go."

They met each other's eyes. For a moment, only the two of them existed. Then Les squared her shoulders, whirled, and walked away.

Mo wanted to run after her; she wanted to lunge at her and pull her sleeve and beg her to stay for another minute or two; she wanted just one more hug, one more kiss. *Please!* She grabbed her head with both hands and watched as the distance between them lengthened. *Keep walking, Les, keep walking. Don't look back.* If she looked back, they'd both be lost. Over the coming months, Mo would believe for both of them. But right now, she was relying on Les's strength to resist the magnetic force pulling them together.

Les was growing smaller; Mo had to squint to see her. Then she was gone. Gone. Mo stayed for a minute, half expecting Les to suddenly reappear and run back to her. But she didn't. Les was gone, maybe forever. *No! Believe!* They hadn't said good-bye. This wasn't the end. They'd hold each other again—as Chosens.

APPENDIX - ABOUT RYMELLAN SOCIETY

·····

Lesley and Mo live according to the Rymellan Way, as all Rymellans do. The Way, as it's usually called, is an umbrella term for two sets of articles that govern Rymellan life: the Chosen Tradition and Rymellan Law.

When we meet Lesley and Mo in *The Dance*, they're on the cusp of adulthood, planning their futures. However, one decision they won't make for themselves is whether they'll have children. In accordance with the Chosen Tradition, the Chosen Council selects mates for Rymellans. Those with a match (a Chosen) are Joined and permitted to have children. Those without a match (Solitaries) can form relationships, but their relationships aren't recognized by the state and they're not permitted to reproduce. If a Rymellan is a Solitary, he or she receives a Solitary Notification from the Chosen Council on his or her eighteenth birthday.

Once Joined, Rymellans really do remain together until death do they part. Chosen Violations—violations of articles in the Chosen Tradition—are capital crimes. They generally involve acts that violate a Chosen bond. For Chosens, that would include what we call adultery, flirting with anyone other than one's Chosen, and abandoning one's Chosen. Solitaries must also respect Chosen bonds. Flirting with or sleeping with a Chosen would definitely land a Solitary at an execution site. Publicly doubting the Chosen Tradition, the Chosen Council, or a specific match are Chosen Violations that might be committed by any Rymellan.

On Rymel, homophobia doesn't exist. Also, Rymellan reproductive technology enables women to have biological children together. The Chosen Council Joins men with women, women with women, and men with men. However, male/male Chosens do not reproduce. The Chosen Tradition dictates that children must be carried in a biological parent's womb, and that wouldn't be possible if both parents were male.

 DISOBEDIENCE MEANS DEATH